THE UNDER DOGS
THE COMPLETE CASES OF
MADAME STOREY, VOLUME 3

THE UNDER DOGS
THE COMPLETE CASES OF
MADAME STOREY, VOLUME 3

HULBERT FOOTNER

INTRODUCTION BY
ROBERT SAMPSON

ILLUSTRATIONS BY
DOUGLAS HILLIKER
ROGER B. MORRISON
JEAN PASTORET

COVER BY
PAUL STAHR

POPULAR PUBLICATIONS · 2022

TABLE OF CONTENTS

A PRACTICAL PSYCHOLOGIST, SPECIALIZING IN THE FEMININE

by Robert Sampson

"I have yet to meet a man bold enough to face me down. How could I surrender myself to one whose soul was secretly afraid of mine? So here I sit. You know that the Madam I have hitched to my name is just to save my face. No one would believe that a woman as beautiful as I could be still unmarried and respectable. But I am both, worse luck."*

THAT IS THE authentic voice of Madame Rosika Storey, celebrated psychologist and consulting detective. As usual, she speaks with hard, good sense, tempered by a dry wit that flickers like imp light around her remarks. She has long since discovered that you may boldly speak personal truths if your voice is suitably ironic.

Unmarried, Madame Storey began her series in the 1922 *Argosy All-Story Weekly* and unmarried she left *Argosy* in 1935. She appears in about thirty novelettes and short stories, one short novel, and four serialized novels. Her adventures, written by Hulbert Footner, were collected into ten books that contain all the novels and most of the shorter material. During this professional activity, her heart was touched several times. But beautiful detectives who

---

* Hulbert Footner, "Madame Storey's Way," *Argosy All-Story Weekly*, March 11, 1922, p. 220.

carry series do not easily love and marry. Not if the series writer is alert. And Hulbert Footner was most alert.

Rosika Storey appeared about thirty-five years after Sherlock Holmes's initial case. Even across that distance in time, Holmes's shadow fell weightily on her. She practiced The Science of Deduction only casually, but there were other, greater similarities. Like Holmes, Madame Storey was steeped in idiosyncrasies, with a personal superiority that denied the possibility of error. They shared a similar penchant for disguise and a distinctive home base, and both guided the usual covy of bewildered police. Finally, both enjoyed that most necessary ingredient, a literary friend to record their adventures in the terrible authority of the first-person singular.

Madame Storey makes her first entrance as a smiling and enigmatic figure, dressed in high fashion.

> She was very tall and supremely graceful. It was impossible to think of legs in connection with her movements. She floated into the room like a shape wafted on the breeze. She was darkly beautiful in the insolent style that causes plainer women to prim up their lips.
>
> She wore an extraordinary gown, a taupe silk brocaded with a shadowy gold figure, made in long panels that exaggerated her height and slimness, unrelieved by any trimming whatsoever.... [S]nuggled in the hollow of her arm she carried a black monkey dressed in a coat of Paddy green and a fool's cap hung with tiny gold bells.*

---

* Ibid., p. 214.

She arrives like cultural shock. Let the women prim up their lips. Their reaction acknowledges her skill at displaying exqui-sitely calculated glimpses of a unique professional image. She has coolly planned the effect of her appearance, her offices, her eccentricities. For she is a busi-nesswoman, selling her intel-lectual skills to a society which prizes the unique and expensive. A society, also, where women are rarely granted more than second-ary partnerships. Her image is of serene competence, remote and imperturbable as the floor of Heaven. It "kept fools at arm's length," and it drew the wealthy clients in.

First part of "The Under Dogs" (Argosy All-Story Weekly, January 3, 1925). Madame Storey, not shown, is working the handle of the broom.

That image is enhanced by various theatrical devices. These range from her jewel-box office suite to her monkey and her cigarettes.

Cigarettes: She smokes constantly, and her ashtray overflows. This is suspect behavior in the 1920s. Women enjoyed such minor sins only vicariously ("Blow some my way"), since use of cigarettes implied inoperable turpitude. Not that smoking is her consuming vice. Two puffs and she is done. Her cigarette is less an artifact of Hell than a suggestion of strangeness and giddy depths.

As is her monkey, Giannino. He is a little black nuisance, trained to take off his hat and bow on command. He is customarily dressed in costumes that complement

Madame Storey's clothing. Part of his life is spent sitting on her shoulder, part sitting on top of that large picture in her office. From there, he descends discreetly to steal the cigarettes smouldering in her ashtray.

Giannino affords a touch of the bizarre. He is a sort of living accent, his presence emphasizing the beauty of her office, as a painter's single touch of red focuses a composition. And her office is very beautiful. It was, says Bella Brickley, the series narrator,

> more like a little gallery in a museum than a woman's office; an up-to-date museum where they realize the value of not showing too much at once. With all its richness there was a fine severity of arrangement, and every object was perfect of its kind.... It was only as I came to know it that I realized the taste with which every object had been selected and arranged.*

Taste, Discrimination, Perception, Control: Characteristics more appropriate for a Roman senator than a feminine detective in a pulp magazine. However, Madame Storey rises above her virtues. Within that darkly shining exterior prances a joyous girl, delighted with her own effects. Not that she is overwhelmed by her own image. If the essence of a French salon glows about her, it is not only for her private enjoyment but because it is indispensable to the conduct of her business.

Behind the gracious facade, she runs a tightly controlled establishment. She employs a permanent cadre of investi-

---

* Ibid., p. 215.

gators. She has direct ties in the District Attorney's office and police headquarters. She is constantly embedded in crime investigations of freshly murdered folk, underworld characters, and glitter-eyed geniuses gone bad.

For all this, she does not consider herself a detective. She is, she says, a "practical psychologist specializing in the feminine." As a psychologist, she is intensely sensitive to the small change of human interaction—the face's movement, the voice's hesitation and slur, the unconscious drives that shape dress and conduct.

She is extraordinary and unique. No other heroine in popular literature approaches her. Through the series she slips with self-possession and wit, exquisite and unapproachable. She attains a stature rivaled by no other female investigator until the rather different flowering of Jane Marple, six years later in 1928.*

In 1922 mystery fiction, a female detective was no longer a shattering wonder whose presence caused horses to shy. For sixty years, since about 1861, legions of policewomen, private inquiry agents, and amateur lady investigators had earned glory in popular fiction pages.** Of these clever women, some became secondary continuing characters in extended series—as did Ida Jones, who joined the Nick Carter works in 1892. Others starred briefly in their own series, although few lasted as long as Ida. Among these

---

* A series of short stories featuring Miss Marple began in the June 2, 1928 *Detective Story Magazine*. These were later collected as *The Tuesday Club Murders*. No information is available concerning the initial English publication.

** Michele B. Slung, "Introduction," *Crime On Her Mind* (New York: Pantheon, 1975), p. xvi. In this interesting essay, Slung discusses the first appearance of the female detective who seems to have stepped on stage in either 1861 or 1864. The exact date seems open to doubt. Slung remarks (p. xix) that between 1861 and 1901, "no fewer than twenty women detectives made their appearance."

detecting women were Loveday Brooke (1893), Dorcas
Dene (1897), and Lady Molly of Scotland Yard (1910),
English all and very capable. "The special qualifications
of these heroines lay in their vivacious energy and brisk
common sense, aided by their 'female instincts'." * Some
were aided by other special skills. Judith Lee's 1912 investigations were made possible because she was a lip reader.
When her cases were reprinted in *All-Story Weekly* (1915),
the letters column buzzed with controversy. Was lip reading possible? Were there to be no more secrets?

Before the Judith Lee agitation, several other feminine
detectives had occupied series in American magazines. In
1912, Arnold Fredericks (pseudonym of Frederic Arnold
Kummer) published the first of five novels featuring Grace
Duval, one half of The Honeymoon Detectives. The adventures ran in *The Cavalier, All-Story Cavalier Weekly*, and
All-Story Weekly into 1917. Grace was all female instincts
and also trouble prone. Customarily she worried one end
of the string, while her husband, a renowned investigator,
fussed at the other.

During 1913, Arthur B. Reeve introduced Constance
Dunlap to *Pearson's* magazine. Constance, a reformed
criminal, wandered through mystery-adventures densely
packed with semi-scientific apparatus. Her mystery solv-
ing was more a matter of luck and good sense than tech-
nical skill.

But the style of the period emphasized luck over almost

---

* Ibid., p. xx. Several current collections include examples of these early stories. In
addition to *Crime On Her Mind*, you may find Alan K. Russells's *Rivals of Sherlock
Holmes, Vols. 1* and *2* (New York: Castle, 1978 and 1979). Other stories are included
in the Hugh Greene collections *The Rivals of Sherlock Holmes* and *The Further Rivals
of Sherlock Holmes* (Penguin, 1970 and 1973). In spite of the title duplications, the
books' contents are all different.

everything else. The feminine detectives of the mid-teens were not professionals in the manner of Ida Jones and Loveday Brooke. Rather, they were highly decorative amateurs, like Anna Katherine Green's Violet Strange, turned detective by chance. Their successes depended largely on the generosity of their authors.

Both Nan Russell (1920) and Dr. Nancy Dayland (1923) were extreme examples of this type.

Nan Russell was cute and dear and delightful and adorable, and how she became a genius private investigator is beyond knowing. She appeared in a five-episode series in *Argosy All-Story Weekly* written by Raymond Lester during 1920. They all adored her at the detective agency. In her presence, those cynical tough detectives turned to sugar cakes. Her portrait in oils hung in the boss's office. Her own private office was furnished in exquisite taste, a flower here, a rare antique there. She was so pure, so clever, so lovely, the flower of the agency, wrapped in steamy adulation. Nothing physical; it was all high and spiritual.

Similar uncritical adoration is the leitmotif of Florence Mae Pettee's series about Dr. Nancy Dayland. Dr. Nancy was a practicing criminologist who worked the pages of *Argosy All-Story Weekly, Action Stories,* and *Flynn's*. She mixed Sherlock Holmes with Nancy Drew, and displayed all Nan Russell's characteristics in a jaunty, teen-aged way. Except that she stimulated awe and respect, rather than love, and so was condemned to a chronically sterile emotional life.

By the time Madame Storey arrived oh the scene, the feminine investigator was a solidly established figure in the world of detective fiction. But that should not imply that

*Detail from the heading of "It Never Got into the Papers," Part 1
(Argosy All-Story Weekly, March 24, 1928). Madame Storey and
Giannino receive a client in her office. The story says that it's an office.*

these women were realistically drawn. Few were as substan-
tial as a cloud of perfume. They adventured through a world
remote from the angular realities so familiar to those who
do not dwell in fiction. It was also a world distorted to
shield the female detective from reality's sharper edges.
A world quite purged of human emotions and human
complexity. This neglected area, Hulbert Footner noted
and attempted to fill.

Hulbert Footner (1879–1944) was another of those
Canadian-American writers who contributed so weightily
to the American pulp magazines. Born in Ontario, Footner attended high school in New York City and became
a journalist there in 1905. He moved to Calgary, Alberta
in 1906, to begin his professional writing in earnest. After
publishing a number of short stories, he sold a first novel
to *The Outing Magazine* in 1911. Thereafter his work—
short stories, novelettes, and serials—appeared steadily

in *Munsey's, Cavalier, All-Story Cavalier, All-Story, Argosy, All-Story Weekly,* and, later, *Mystery.*

His first five novels dealt with adventure in Canada and the North West. These were partially based on his experiences in the North Woods. He moved back to New York City about 1914 and, for a period, played parts in a road show of William Gillette's play Sherlock Holmes.* Footner later used this experience in writing and producing his own plays. By 1916, he had also written the first of his mysteries. A few years later, he bought a seventeenth-century house in Lusby, Maryland (the general scene for several later novels). There he lived until his death in 1944.

The Madame Storey series started in the middle of Footner's career and continued for almost fifteen years. The series shows considerable stylistic change. It begins with a strong emphasis on character and problem, featuring those usual 1920s elements, a detective of dazzling ability scoring off police who barely get along. As the 1930s are reached, the stories shorten, become increasingly active and violent. The character portrayal and complexity of character interaction also simplify, and the problem mystery is converted to brisk mystery adventure. It is not necessarily a defect. But it is a measurable change.

Technically, all the stories may be classified as mysteries, and it is true that most propose a mystery to be solved. This is not always the most important element. Frequently the identity of the criminal is known before the mid-chapters. The balance of the story then concentrates on that intricate

---

* Unsigned article, "The Fiction of Hulbert Footner," *Argosy All-Story Weekly,* March 31, 1923, pp. 321-23. Additional biographical material on Footner also appeared in *Argosy,* Septembers, 1931, p. 716.

duel between villain and Madame Storey as she seeks to complete her case before its fragile strands are destroyed by her opponent.

The initial tales depend heavily on character interaction. The people of the story constantly respond to each other, forming opinions and reacting as dictated by their personalities. The solution of the mystery is, first of all, a matter of psychology. Personal motives are of importance. Clues, as such, are distinctly secondary.

The continuing characters, themselves, are fully developed by 1924. They do not essentially change afterward and are treated warmly in stories rich and various.

The first of the series was "Madame Storey's Way" (March 11, 1922), published in *Argosy All-Story Weekly*. It is a surprising fiction to discover in that bastion of action adventure, for the story contains about the same amount of physical movement as an essay by Emerson.

"Madame Storey's Way" is presented in two distinct parts, like an apple sitting on an orange. In Part I, Bella Brickley, narrator of the series, answers a newspaper ad for a job, competes with other women for an unknown position, and is selected as Madame Storey's secretary and Watson.

In Part II, we are presented with the first mystery. Ashcomb Poor, a wealthy philanderer, is found shot dead in his home. His wife's secretary is arrested for the murder. The Assistant District Attorney permits Madame Storey to interview the girl in that glamorous office. (Like Nero Wolfe after her, Madame Storey recognizes the positional advantage in having police and suspects come to her.)

By this time, Rosika has privately visited the scene of the

crime and removed certain clues overlooked by the police. After a series of interviews with major witnesses, she calls all together in her office and the guilty party is revealed.

Most of the story occurs within five long scenes. Madame Storey is always before us. The dialogue is crisp, clear, glittering with sudden wit. Sequences of sentences fly past, terse as in a dime novel. Whole pages of dialogue are used. You have the feeling of strong movement. Yet the characters, peering intently at each other, barely twitch. They act and react upon each other. It is a remarkable *tour de force*.

— Madame Storey conducts a satisfyingly highhanded interview with a room filled by job applicants and speaks candidly with Bella.

— She fences astutely with Assistant District Attorney Walter Barron, who has illusions of matrimony.

— She serves tea and cakes to the secretary accused of murder.

— She consults with the murdered man's wife.

— She allows two lovers to explain to each other their bizarre behavior.

Talk scenes. But not static. It is like watching planes of colored smoke drifting one through the other, the immediate interplay of character. Each scene fulfills a triple function: to elaborate the characterization of Madame Storey, to provide necessary facts about a main character, and to clarify another scrap of the puzzle.

The second story of the series, "Miss Deely's Diamond" (May 26, 1923), differs radically from the first. This is filled with movement. A large diamond has been stolen; the gem has an intensely romantic history which reads as if

composed by Conan Doyle. Its
history aside, the diamond seems
to possess certain supernatural
attributes. It is said that, if you
look directly at it, your unreal-
ized self will fully develop, like a
photographic print in solution.
Whether that development is
for good or evil depends on the
hidden state of your psyche.

"Wolves of Monte Carlo"
was a short story, rather
than a novelette, filled
with non-stop movement,
violence, and menace in
the 1930s action style.
Argosy, *August 5, 1933.*

Superstition or not, that
personality alteration is the chief
means Madame Storey uses to
trace the diamond as it is carried
among the small towns and rural
houses of New York State, through a series of owners and
violent episodes. Finally, the diamond is traced back to
New York City, where it is recovered. Madame Storey does
look full upon it. She remains unaffected—except that she
spends every loose dollar of her fortune to purchase it, a
matter of $150,000. Practical psychology applied to the
feminine seems a rewarding profession.

Bella Brickley, however, positively refuses to look at the
diamond. She clasps hands over eyes and turns away. But
then, Bella is not all that secure in herself.

Secure or not, Bella is one of the most interesting narra-
tors in a popular fiction series. In person, she is freckled,
red-headed, and plain. These characteristics scald her, and
she has rigidly schooled herself to accept her lack of beauty.

"I am so plain," she writes.

Or she remarks, flat-voiced: "…[H]aving no pretensions to beauty, I don't have to be jealous of other women."

Those splendid men who step into the consultation room pass by her with only cursory glances. Their indifference is recorded in icy slivers of prose.

At their first interview, Madame Storey tells her:

> "… [Y]ou are suffering from mal-appreciation. Those two ugly lines between your brows were born of the belief that you were too plain and uninteresting ever to hope to win a niche of your own in the world….Think that cross look away and your face will show what is rarer than beauty, character, individuality."*

When it suits Rosika's purposes, she is nothing if not plain spoken. It is sour medicine, administered with the knowledge that Bella will not crumble under it.

That Bella eventually rids herself of that cross look and stops dragging her hair back from the roots may be inferred. Nature provides other compensations. She is remarkably perceptive, and her tart, good sense, crisp as fresh lettuce, makes her prose a constant joy. Her opinions sting. Even plain, even red-headed, she is appealing.

She is the key to the series. All events filter through Bella. Like other Watsons, she is easily puzzled. Unlike most Watsons, she has a deadly accurate eye:

On a chauffeur: "one of those exalted creatures with the self-possession of a cabinet minister."

On an elaborate mansion: "The richness of it all was

---

* Footner, "Madame Storey's Way," p. 216.

simply overpowering, but I could not conceive of anybody being at home in such a museum."

On a wealthy wife: "She looked as rare and precious as a bit of Venetian glass. This ethereal exterior covered very human feelings."

On hotel hangers-on: "They were divided mostly into two classes: philanderers and pan-handlers."

On a ball: "All the family jewels in Newport were given an airing it seemed—mostly decorating the bodies of dowagers that they could do very little for."

On meeting a fancy man: "He whirled around and bowed…. My hand was horribly self-conscious in the expectation that he might offer to kiss it. I wondered if it was quite clean."

On a foolish client: "in an overstuffed baby-blue armchair sat Mrs. Julian, overstuffed herself, and enveloped in God knows how many yards of lavender chiffon."

These terse assessments glint through the stories, leaving painless cuts, as if the prose were sprinkled with delicate crystals of glass. From the beginning to the end of the series, you see through Bella's eyes. And what you see, from the homes and habits of the wealthy to the homes and habits of the underworld, is rendered in clear little terse images, delicately polarized. Miss Brickley is artlessly candid in describing her reactions, and she responds to each person and event. But be cautioned. Although you read her remarks with pleasure, remember that they are part of her characterization. Behind them lurks the amiable intelligence of Hulbert Footner, and the story told by Miss Brickley has been filtered through her and colored by her understanding.

Those things that you most devoutly desire have a way of arriving spangled with things you don't ever remember wishing for. Bella wants an interesting job working for a supremely beautiful woman. That she gets. She also gets a continuous stream of adventures dangerous enough to gray that red hair.

Bella does not like adventures. Field work leaves her edgy. She does not think clearly under stress. At the moment of action, she functions in a numbed calm. But before that moment, she has the shakes and, afterward, the hysterics.

Madame Storey, on the other hand, relishes action and searches eagerly for excuses to leave her 1850 French drawing room suite to travel underworld ways, hip-swinging and shrill. Since women jaunt about most invisibly by twos, she carries Bella along—and into astonishing situations.

Madame Storey's predilection for adventure explains why Bella finds herself sitting in h hardcase speakeasy with her hair clipped short ("The Under Dogs"). Or fleeing through a deserted mansion with gunmen straining after them ("The Butler's Ball"). Or looking down Mafia pistols ("Taken for a Ride"). Or tied and gagged in an automobile being driven over a cliff ("The Richest Widow").

> I was trembling like an aspen leaf.... By a little catch of laughter in [Madame Storey's] breath, I knew that she was enjoying every moment. Well, that is her way.

At first, the adventures are less harrowing. "The Scrap of Lace" (August 4, 1923) and "In the Round Room" (March 1, 1924) are problem mysteries, not quite as formal as those of Agatha Christie. In both cases, the investigation is conducted at vast mansions, amid the odor of money and the flat stink of relationships gone wrong. "Lace" requires a murder method somewhat too elaborate to be practical and ends with Madame Storey revealing the killer before a group. "Round Room" contains a murdered woman, a secret door, and a lot of confusion about who did what. The murderer (who turns out to be insane) has a marvelous alibi. Madame Storey must lead the county prosecutor around by the ear, since, being congenitally defective, he can do nothing but bluster and blow.

The prosecutor is an early example of the species *officialus boobus* that swarms densely through the series. Most of these are political law enforcement hacks, otherwise depicted as mincing popinjays distended with conceit. They are blood relations to the officials who swaggered brainlessly through those awful low-budget mystery films of the late 1930s.

Not all law enforcement people are fools. Inspector Rumsey, New York Police, a solid, sharp professional, is Madame Storey's main link to police headquarters. The Crider brothers, both investigators employed by the Madame, never miss a lick and are competent, clever men.

Of the various sheriffs, coroners, police commissioners, and district attorneys, the less said the better. A more appalling aggregation of blowhards has rarely been assembled.

Footner uses these dolts to make Madame Storey's life less easy. But their presence also illustrates his unfortunate tendency to cast characters as representative types—unfortunate because he was a singularly persuasive writer who could almost make one of these hollow figures come alive. Almost.

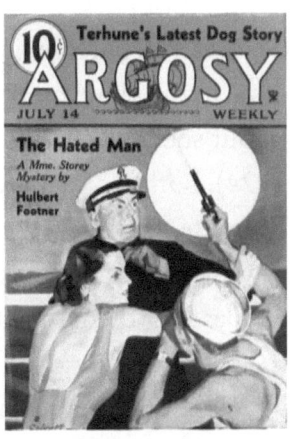

Besides the dreary catalog of law enforcement types, other standard characters pepper the series. These include the villain, whose intelligence is dangerously quick and, often as not, has an uncontrolled yen for Madame Storey.

And there are the low-echelon men and women of the underworld. Most are practicing criminals, crude, violent, and

First part of "The Hated Man," later published as Dangerous Cargo. *Madame Storey, looking about eighteen, saves a life—but not for long.* Argosy, *July 14, 1934.*

fundamentally decent. If the truth must be told, Rosika has a sneaking fondness for them. Since they are impossible socially, she can like them and, as in "The Black Ace," find her heart twinged by them.

Other standard characters include tainted society flowers; the arch-wealthy, decayed by possessions; and clever older men and women, like parental echoes, who support Rosika, no matter what the occasion.

"The Viper" (April 12, 1924) is one of the high points of the series. The story has great force. On the surface, it seems the investigation of a series of crimes committed by a thieving secretary who has murdered her boss. Under the surface, it is a leisurely exploration of a murderess's strange character. Footner's handling of interpersonal nuances is graceful and exact. The story's action is split between New York and Paris. Bella has the joy of going to France and is decidedly deflated when she is sent home, in a couple of days, to run the American end of the investigation.

But she gets over it. And, in "The Steerers" (August 2, 1924), both women are off to England on a cruise ship. En route, they meet a merry pair who spend all their days traveling the liners, making friends with susceptible marks and leading them to another set of friends, the fleecers of these sheep. This comfortable arrangement is shattered when they befriend Madame Storey.

"The Under Dogs," the first novel of the series, was published as a six-part serial in *Argosy*, January 3 through February 7, 1925. Much of the adventure occurs in an underworld only slightly modified from the Jimmie Dale model described by Frank Packard back in 1914. On the whole, the criminals are more believable than those appearing in Packard's work, and they are at least as vicious. The serial also considers the links between crime in the social deeps with crime in the city's high places.

Matters begin with violence. A girl, promising sensational revelations, is on her way to Madame Storey's office. Before she arrives there, she is clubbed down and kidnapped. Attempting to search out the girl, Rosika and Bella (who is horrified by the idea) move into the underworld. The cool, high-fashion Rosika suddenly shows a genius for disguise and an ability to shine in low company, down among the East Side gin mills.

Her investigation gradually narrows to a house on Varick Street, populated by very hard cases, male and female. There are dead men under the basement floor, a chained prisoner in the attic, and a reluctant gang of crooks being blackmailed to work the will of a mastermind, dimly seen.

Masterminds, rather. The pair of them get busted in a melodramatic finish, and off they go to Sing Sing. The Big Boss, an attorney, is understandably irritated at being foiled by that "tall, skinny woman." While glooming in his cell, he works up a magnificent

This drops upon our heroine in "Madame Storey in the Toils" (August 29, 1925). The frame-up is thorough. Rosika is accused of poisoning a woman with frosted cakes. The motive: to marry the woman's husband. Unfortunately for the plotters, Rosika slips gracefully from poor old Inspector Rumsey's clutch; she conducts her investigation, and routine office business, while a fugitive, and nails to the cross the entire batch who attempted to do her in.

Then back to England, on business, in "The Pot of Pansies" (April 30, 1927). This lightly science-fictional episode turns upon the development of a colorless, odorless, fast-acting gas by a scientist who wishes to end war. Instead, he gets murdered for the secret. It does the killer no good. Madame Storey is on him before he can draw an easy breath. Naturally he is upset:

> "That woman is a she devil!" he screamed. "She's not human. She kept at me and at me till I near went mad. She ought to have been in the Spanish Inquisition, she should! What's she doing over here anyway, plying her trade? Aren't there enough murders in America?" *

That odorless, colorless, quick-acting gas is one of the more durable devices of pulp fiction. Those with

---

* Footner, "The Pot of Pansies," *The Velvet Hand* (London: W. Collins, 1933), p. 84.

long memories will recall that the famous costumed mastermind, Black Star, used a similar gas to steal and rob through the pages of *Detective Story Magazine,* way back in 1916; that jolly fellow, the Crimson Clown (also featured in *Detective Story*) had been using a similar gas since 1926; and Doc Savage, the bronzed scientific adventurer, would use an identical gas throughout his career, 1933-49. Whether 1916 or 1949, this gas was a science-fictional device used to accomplish the impossible and speed the action. By the time Footner incorporated it into "The Pot of Pansies," the marvelous gas was a fictional convention, accepted if not believed, like egg-carrying rabbits and Yuletide spirits. Footner uses the invention as a reason for the action, not as a device to advance the action. In so doing, he enhances the probability of his story, although not by very much.

"The Black Ace," a six-part serial, January 12 through February 16, 1929, was later published as a book titled *The Doctor Who Held Hands.*

Of this novel, the *New York Times* remarked:

> ...[N]ot only is the plot utterly preposterous but it is so clumsily constructed that the saw marks are apparent to the most inexperienced eye.*

More moderately, "The Black Ace"/*The Doctor Who Held Hands* is not the very best of the series. The plot (which is apparently what stuck in the *Times's* craw) is one of those revenge things, requiring that the villain be insane.

---

* *New York Times,* July 28, 1929, p. 13.

There is, you see, this brilliant psychologist, Dr. Jacmer Touchon—Madame Storey's teacher and rejected suitor—who has simmered for years over the flame of her growing professional reputation. Touchon has made a nice thing out of blackmailing patients. Now, hankering for ever greater achievements, he plans to bring Rosika to her knees. To crush her pride. To dominate her soul. To whomp up on her spirit. After she is well tamed, he'll marry her and show her off.

To such plans—had she been consulted—Madame Storey would have responded by puffing out a cloud of smoke and remarking, in her driest tone: "Ah, Jacmer is a most incorrigible man."

Having thoroughly misjudged his prey, Dr. Touchon puts his dream into operation. First, he sends a minion to hire Rosika to investigate the great Dr. Touchon himself. Then he proceeds to discredit her by organizing a gun attack in her office. Two men are killed in this action.

Newspaper sensation.

Touchon's manipulations permit an extraordinarily bone-headed detective to solve the murders. Rosika doesn't believe the solution for a second. But she pretends to accept it, and, while being courted by Touchon in the evening, is slipping out late at night to scour the underworld, hauling poor, quaking Bella along.

They are hunting for a young man with a scarred face, the third member of Touchon's gang.

Scarface doesn't know this. His boss (Touchon) has kept well concealed, known only as a mysterious voice. Scarface would, in fact, like to kill the man (Touchon again) who shot down his best friend in Madame Storey's office.

Once more disguised as flowers of the night, Rosika and Bella go forth into a gay round of nightclubs and gambling joints. Eventually they locate Scarface and, after harsh adventures, maneuver him into Touchon's presence. Thereupon all the cookies fall off the tray, and Touchon, having been choked black, goes up the river to a quieter life.

The story really isn't full of sawmarks. But parts need a lot of lubrication to get down.

"The Butler's Ball" (June 28, 1930) is one of those Agatha Christie things in which one person, of a group sitting at a table, shot the victim. It doesn't help that all are in costume. Madame Storey and Bella are on the scene hunting for jewel thieves.

(During this story, Bella remarks that her legs look pretty nice in her costume; as, elsewhere, she has remarked that she has an attractive neck and arms, we may guess that her mordant self-image is beginning to change.)

The women find the jewel thieves, indeed they do. They end up fleeing for their lives through a deserted mansion, the gang all pistoled up and hot after them. They escape with the help of the fire department, and Bella has a fine case of hysterics when it is all over.

She really does not enjoy action.

But action is increasingly her lot, for the series has entered the 1930s.

In "Easy To Kill" (six parts, August 8 through September 12, 1931), Rosika is hired to deal with a Newport extortionist. He turns out to be a wealthy young genius. Gloves come off immediately. At various times, the women are (1) in jail; (2) tied hand and foot, waiting to be wrapped in sheet lead and dropped into the Atlantic; (3) locked into the upper story of an old wooden hotel set afire by fiends.

They escape and take refuge in the rat-hole of a room rented by two small-time street crooks. In a charming scene, Rosika and Bella, bedraggled in their ruined evening dresses, sit on an unmade bed and gobble ham and scrambled egg sandwiches, three inches thick. The stick-up boys eye them tentatively. But Rosika is too skillful a hand to let sex surface. How adroitly she converts their benefactors' half-awakened lust to friendship. How swiftly she dominates their minds and enrolls them in her cause.

Next day, helped by a rich old recluse, she sets a trap for the villain. And through the swirling mist he comes. Is trapped. But the local police fumble his capture. He flees to his yacht, on which he suicides, aided by half a ton of TNT.

So much violence, so many escapes, so many guns and gunmen, clear indication that the 1930s are well upon us.

No time, now, for formal mystery problems and psychological studies. The stories are bright red, rushing furiously forward amid a high metallic whine. Descriptions are pared to the quick. Bella's annoyances more rarely reach public print. Calculated suspense rises shimmering from the superheated narrative. Again physical danger threatens, antj still again. Once more they are captured, tied up, helpless in the power of…

NOW IT IS mid-1933, and Madame Storey makes a major sortie from *Argosy*. She bobs up in *Mystery* in a lightly inconsistent series of short stories.

Mystery was a fancy, over-sized, slick-paper publication which had begun life as *The Illustrated Detective Magazine*. It was distributed through Woolworth's 5 and 10¢ stores and was aimed, with great precision, at a female audience. The magazine was lavishly bedecked with photographs of consummately 1930ish models posing rigidly in re-enactment of story scenes. Madame Storey is not successfully impersonated.

The series' premise is that Rosika has been retained by the Washburn Legislative Committee to investigate the police department, city not really stated. In performing this ambitious assignment, she spends much of her time handling problems that the Chief of Detectives, Inspector Barron, has fallen flat on. As is the case with so many other males in the series, Barron takes one long look at Rosika and his voice drops two octaves. While he regards her presence as a professional insult, yet he is smitten. He babbles. He is all ham-handed gallantry, dismal to see.

In "The Sealed House" (July 1933), Rosika pries open the so-called suicide of a "bad woman." Within the woman's home, sealed by court order until legal machinery moves, there are traces of repeated break-ins and searches. Madame Storey deftly locates a blackmailing document, and the whole case suddenly pops apart.

It pops in a matter of paragraphs, with a speed characteristic of the series. The stories are compressed as dried fruit bars, and the endings seems breathlessly rushed.

"Which Man's Eyes?" (December 1933) begins with Rosika and Bella being warned to drop their investigations of the local drug ring. When they don't, four gunmen invade the Storey premises one night and machine-gun Rosika's bedroom. But she isn't in the bed and nabs the scoundrel responsible, right in the heart of police headquarters.

Through all this action, Inspector Barron is making over-ripe sounds at Rosika. She finds him intensely repulsive. Somewhat later, she finds that he is connected with the drug ring and that his soul is blotched black.

At this point in the series, the drug ring decides to discredit our heroine, since she has made such a nuisance of herself. In "The Last Adventure with Madame Storey" (May 1934), she is framed for murder—how these themes do repeat—and for narcotics distribution from her own home. Detained by the police, she demands an immediate preliminary hearing and whisks her usual dazzle from the air. Suddenly the evil are confounded. Suddenly all is wonderful. Barron is bounced from the force and the series, with a final breathless lurch, stops as abruptly as an airplane flying into a cliff face.

Slightly before the *Mystery* series ended, Rosika returned to *Argosy*, her one true love. The women go off to summer in France in "Wolves of Monte Carlo" (August 5, 1933). Immediately they are abducted, tied up, and nearly thrown from a cliff. And that's only a warning to keep their noses out of other people's business. They don't, with success.

Another month, another abduction. In "The Kidnapping of Madame Storey" (December 2, 1933), gangsters carry her off. And also Bella. As you may have anticipated, the crooks are suavely outwitted.

Another year, another vacation. "The Murders in the Hotel Cathay" (November 17, 1934) counterpoint a series of vast swindles. It all happens in China, in a twisting, fascinating story. Bella finds an interesting young man who gets murdered two hours after he meets her. Madame Storey deduced the circumstances from the evidence of a broken chair. Then she finds two bodies tucked into a flower bed within the hotel. From this point on, matters grow violent.

The final Madame Storey novel appeared in 1934. "The Hated Man" (six-part serial, July 14 through August 18, 1934) was later published under the title *Dangerous Cargo*. In this, Madame Storey is retained by a rich pain in the neck. He wants her to keep him from being killed during an extended cruise. She does not quite succeed. The murderer is caught after an extended game of thrust and counter-thrust. During these proceedings, Bella finds a body in the swimming pool; you can imagine what that does to her composure.

"The Cold Trail" (January 12, 1935) tells how a tricky lawyer decisively fools Rosika. His baleful touch leads her case wildly astray and only desperate measures retrieve the situation. It all comes back on the rascal, at last. But it is her worst setback of the

To cool her humiliation, she takes Bella on a cruise to France in "The Richest Widow" (August 31, 1935). Promptly up jumps a murderous young man who has found a swell way to vanish himself and wife from a ship in mid-ocean. Rosika finds him out. Whereupon he sets bloodthirsty French killers to catch both woman and murder them. After a motorboat chase, they escape back to the ship, if narrowly. And justice is, after all, done.

There the series ends, and there we leave them after stressful triumph. There, the darkly splendid Rosika, her mind shining, and Bella, plain, red-headed, aware. Around them lift the 1930s, a black and scarlet haze, no proper place for a practical psychologist specializing in the feminine. For this time, a coarser meat was carved.

Madame Storey had, however, made the transition to 1930s fiction more gracefully than you might imagine. She retained her intelligent audacity. And if her stories had thinned, they had remained literate and witty, generating pleasing excitement.

But Rosika's real place was in the 1920s, a less convulsed time. There, in a setting of her own choice, she performed her gilded miracles; there, she slipped casually between the social classes, welcomed by Newport wealth, accepted by the underworld. It is the same social flexibility shared by all great detectives, from Nick Carter to Lew Archer.

Perhaps Rosika Storey was flexible, perhaps ambivalent, in her role as a goddess of detection. Hers seemed the world of wealth and taste, where the golden apples glimmered, quietly rich and discreetly arranged. But she required more. Some turmoil in the blood teased her. Taste, discrimination, perception, control, those laudable virtues, lacked a nourishment vital to her mind. That nourishment she sought in the underworld, plunging into it like an otter into a pool, swimming down among the dreadful shapes there, refreshed by their rude simplicities.

She is more complex than Footner bothered to tell us. But writers do not tell everything. Even if they know.

And so we end as we began, not quite understanding her. Which is entirely proper.

No woman of any sense reveals every last thing about herself. There must always remain a final question.

—Robert Sampson

THE STEERERS

AFTER THE ARREST of the Princesse de Rochechouart, Mme. Storey prepared to resume her interrupted vacation. She raised me to the seventh heaven of delight by suggesting that I accompany her back to Paris "as a reward for good work." I had had but a three days' tantalizing taste of that delicious city before I had been obliged to hasten back to America in connection with the Rochechouart case.

At a week's notice we engaged accommodations on the *Gigantic,* the queen of all liners. The grand rush eastward across the Atlantic was now about over for the season, and we were able to obtain whatever we wanted. Two rooms *en suite* on D deck with a bathroom, at a price which took my prudent breath away. What a joy it was to study the plan of that amazing ship. I could almost say that I was familiar with every turn of her innumerable corridors before I ever went aboard.

I drove direct to the pier from my boarding house, and, as it happened, I arrived first. Once more I shared in the intoxicating confusion of sailing day. Before you mount the gangway a clerk looks at your ticket and checks you up on the passenger list. This person said to me:

"Miss Brickley? You are travelling with Madame Storey, are you not? Your rooms have been changed at the request

of Captain Sir Angus McMaster. You have been assigned
to C47, the Imperial suite."

The Imperial suite! I looked at him with my mouth
hanging open. Why, the cost of this suite is $6,000. A
mere thousand a day for the voyage! I was speechless—but
no comment was required from me. At the magic words
"Imperial suite" all the stewards standing about began to
bow, and I was wafted on board before I well knew what
was happening to me.

I knew the plan, but the ship itself was a revelation to
me. It was not like a ship at all, but a palace with soaring
pillars supporting the domed ceilings, and noble, sweeping stairways. As for our quarters; well, I could only look
around me with a sigh of half-incredulous pleasure. To
come from a boarding-house bedroom to this! It was like
a fairy tale. One entered first a delicious sitting room, set
about with easy chairs and sofas; this led through two pairs
of French windows to what they called the veranda, an
outdoors room with a whole row of big windows opening
to the sea. The sun streamed in, gilding the quantities of
flowers blooming in window boxes. The furniture here was
of wicker; it was like a garden.

The bedrooms opened from the veranda, right and left;
Mme. Storey's and mine. Each of these had its row of big
windows opening over the sea. They were just such luxurious nests as a woman might dream of, the walls cunningly
inlaid with rare woods, and the ingenious and beautiful
appointments a continual surprise. Back of the bedrooms
were bathrooms, wardrobe rooms, maids' rooms galore.

In a few minutes my beautiful young mistress arrived

attended by a retinue of stewards. When they had gone, she broke into a laugh at the sight of my awestruck face.

"We appear to be in luck, my Bella," she said.

"Do you know the captain?" I asked.

"I have crossed on his ship before," she said; "but captains are a race apart. I did not suppose he would remember *me!*"

"He evidently has," I remarked.

There was a tap at the door, and I admitted an imposing *maître d'hôtel*, who bowed low, and conveying the compliments of the Ritz-Carlton restaurant, begged that Mme. Storey and Miss Brickley would consider themselves the guests of the management during the voyage. He was followed by a boy bearing an armful of Radiance roses with more compliments. It appeared that this marvellous ship even had hothouses somewhere up above. The third tap on our door—we were out in the stream by this time— was given by an immaculate apprentice, who said in his charming English voice:

"The commander's compliments, and would it be agreeable to Madame Storey to receive him before lunch?"

"It would be highly agreeable," said my mistress.

To me she murmured with a lift of her eyebrows: "Verily, the mountain is coming to Mahomet!"

Captain Sir Angus McMaster, R.N.R., C.V.O., and goodness knows what else besides. Ah! there was a man for you! Every inch the commander of men, and a gallant and simple-hearted gentleman to boot. There was that in his stern gray face with its rather melancholy eyes which induced instant and complete confidence; something, too, to make you shiver, if your conscience was bad. In his blue and gold, with a string of orders across his breast, he was magnificent without being in the least foppish or at all conscious of his grandeur. The simplicity of the man was his most conspicuous quality.

His eyes paid instant tribute to my mistress's beauty. "How glad I was to discover that you were making this voyage with me," he said.

"You remembered me among so many thousands of passengers!" said Mme. Storey.

"That was not difficult," he said with a quiet smile.

"My secretary, Miss Brickley," said Mme. Storey, bringing me forward.

The bow he gave to plain me was just the same as if I had been the grandest of ladies.

We all went out into that charming veranda with the sun on the flowers and the breeze from the sea and seated ourselves. Sir Angus accepted one of Mme. Storey's cigarettes.

"I am not going to attempt to thank you for all this," said my mistress, waving her hand about. "You must know how we are enjoying it."

"It was all I could do," he said, "and little enough… It

would ill become a sailor to beat around the bush," he went on. "I come to you for help, my dear lady. I am in a quandary, and, of course, being the commander, I dare not confess it to anybody on board. I don't suppose it has ever occurred to you, but a captain leads rather a solitary life. It is not often that I may relax like this."

"You interest me extraordinarily," said Mme. Storey. "I should be so proud if I could help. Please go on."

"It's quite a long story," said Sir Angus, "but rather a curious one. I hope it will not bore you."

"I know it will not."

"It began early last season," he went on. "On a westward voyage. My attention was attracted by a certain good-looking young couple among the passengers; a Mr. and Mrs. Lionel Dartrey. I can't say what it was about them that aroused my suspicions, for their actions on board were irreproachable; I suppose I had what you Americans so expressively term a hunch. I was convinced from the first that there was something queer about them.

"As you no doubt know, we have detectives mixing with the passengers—unpleasant to think about, but unfortunately necessary on so large a ship—and I desired that these people report to me concerning the Dartreys. The reports were nil. The man did not gamble; the lady, while much sought after by other gentlemen, was entirely discreet in her behaviour. Mrs. Dartrey was not by any means the conventional 'charmer,' for I could see for myself that she was very popular among the women passengers. The two of them occupied an expensive room and had every appearance of being well-born people of ample means.

"Still I was not satisfied. That hunch continued to tease

me. So I proceeded to make friends with them myself as the opportunities offered. The man I found to be merely a handsome, aristocratic nonentity; it was impossible to talk to him; he merely made well-bred noises. But the lady was both sprightly and amusing. One of those impulsive women who are apparently all on the surface, and yet— and yet— To tell you the truth, neither of them gave me the slightest cause for suspicion, yet my suspicions grew.

"I had them followed when they left the ship. It was reported to me, to my surprise, that they simply went down West Street and boarded the *Allemania* of the Brevard Line, which was sailing that day. We were a day late. This gave me food for thought. This was in April. Six weeks later they again turned up on my ship, bound for New York. I overheard Mrs. Dartrey make a laughing remark to the effect that she only really lived on board ship, and her husband was obliged to humour her often. Again they took the *Allemania* back to Southampton on the following day.

"My curiosity was now thoroughly aroused. As opportunity offered, I communicated with the other captains of our line by wireless at sea; also with the captains of the Brevarders *Baratoria* and *Ruritania;* and I had no difficulty in establishing that the Dartreys had spent the entire season in flitting back and forth between New York and Southampton on the six big express ships of the two lines. Our schedules are so arranged that they were able practically to jump from one ship to another at each end. We leave New York on Wednesdays, you see, and land our passengers in Southampton on Tuesdays, or, at the latest, Wednesday morning. Whereas the Brevarders leave Southampton Wednesday at noon and arrive in New York on Tuesdays.

In six weeks, having made the rounds of all six ships, they were back on mine again, you see.

"I reported all this to my head office, and thereafter the Dartreys were followed by expert detectives. But nothing came of it. About the first of August they gave up their ferrying of the Atlantic and retired to a charming little flat in Sloane Street, London, where they entertained some of the smartest people of the fashionable world and otherwise proceeded to enjoy themselves. Dartrey, it appeared, was the younger son of an impeccable British family; his wife an American. It was shown that they enjoyed a highly respectable banking connection; their income, which amounted to no less than ten thousand pounds a year, came to them in the form of dividend checks from great American companies. It was all in the lady's name.

"As a result of this investigation, my company intimated to me that I had discovered a mare's nest, and indeed I began to think myself that I had. Eccentric people, no doubt, but there are plenty of those; nothing in the world to suggest that they were crooks. But early this season they turned up again on my ship—only travelling eastward this season, and presumably westward on the Brevard Line. I am convinced that they are swindlers of the most dangerous sort, and I feel that I owe it to my passengers to protect them from such. My company is not backing me in this; I am dependent on my own efforts. It seemed providential when I learned that you were making this voyage."

"The Dartreys are on board, then?" asked Mme. Storey.

"They are," he said with a dry smile. "In the pink of condition."

They were led away by the police.

Mme. Storey looked at me with a somewhat rueful twinkle.

"Why do you smile?" asked Sir Angus.

"This is the second time this summer that I have started
off for a vacation—"

"Ah, I should have thought of that."

"No, I meant it as a joke merely. I am not really worked
to death, you know. And you are a person who does not
often ask favours. One regards it as a privilege therefore…"

"You are too kind," he murmured.

"Besides, it appeals to me," said Mme. Storey. "As a

diversion on shipboard. A sort of deck game. But, I say, don't you think you have started off rather indiscreetly by displaying me so prominently in the Imperial suite?"

"Bless me! I never thought of that!" he said blankly.

She laughed at his simplicity. "Oh, well, I don't suppose it makes much difference. If these people are really experienced international crooks they probably know all about me, and I couldn't expect to accomplish much by direct methods. But there is Bella here. By a lucky chance we came on board separately; and none of the passengers can know as yet that she is my secretary. Bella, would it break your heart to divorce yourself from the Imperial suite?"

"Not if there was anything interesting going on," I said.

"Good. Then, Sir Angus, can you furnish her with another room and another name for the voyage? And supply me with a young woman to play her part?"

He rose. "I am sure that can be arranged. The purser will help us. I shall speak to him at once. And, my dear lady, I cannot sufficiently thank you. Of course, if my suspicions prove to be justified, the company will—"

"Ah, don't speak of that," said Mme. Storey. "You are the commander of us all now, and I am proud to be able to help, if ever so little."

2

IT TURNED OUT that there was a certain Miss Gaul down on the passenger list who had failed to come aboard; and I therefore took unto myself her name and her cabin. The latter was B3, a large and pleasant room up in the bow; with one window looking forward and another to starboard. Within an hour that marvellous man, the captain, had a telephone installed, so that I was able to communicate freely and secretly with Mme. Storey.

Only a step from my door were the great public rooms of the vessel, which were all on B deck: lounge, grand entrance, palm court, etc. These noble apartments were really two stories high, with domed ceilings that made them look even higher. The designer had had the ingenious idea of dividing the great funnels of the vessel and running them down at the sides, so as not to obstruct the view. One could therefore look through the whole magnificent suite. Flooded with sunlight, it was an unforgettable picture. The most ordinary-looking men and women moved in this vista with the dignity of eminences.

Meanwhile the niece of one of the engineer officers who was travelling in the second cabin was brought forward to play my part. She was a pleasant girl who looked both intelligent and ladylike. I confess it caused me a good many twinges of jealousy to see her privileged to associate with

Mme. Storey at all hours, eating with her in the restaurant, and so on; but I consoled myself with the reflection that I had the responsible job.

Mme. Storey had said: "I am convinced that the captain's suspicions of the Dartreys are well founded. An honest man's instinct is not to be despised. The fact that he has never been able to get anything on them suggests to me that they are only agents or steerers in the game. They operate only in the early part of the season, when rich Americans are flocking to Europe; consequently, the real trick, if I am right, must be turned in London or Paris. We are lucky to catch them on an eastward voyage."

Later she telephoned me that she had learned from the second steward that the Dartreys were to eat in the regular dining saloon instead of the Ritz-Carlton restaurant, and that they had been assigned to table number 120. I was to be allotted a seat at 123 not close enough to attract their attention, but sufficiently near to afford me ample opportunities for observation. I was not to pay any particular attention to them, and above all must not appear anxious to make friends. Let the first overtures come from them, if possible.

If they did make up to me, I was to represent myself as the daughter of a wealthy, undistinguished couple in some large western city, say Cleveland. Let my father be a manufacturer of oil stoves who had sold out to the Standard Oil. I had lately been released by death from a long, dull term of servitude to my aged parents, and I was now making my first timid essay in the direction of Europe and culture. Further details Mme. Storey left to my imagination. I objected that I had no black clothes, but she said that made no difference; many people nowadays did not believe in wearing mourning.

Full of the liveliest curiosity, I went down in the lift to the grand saloon on F deck. I had picked out my table, on the plan. But when I took my place I saw that table 120 was as yet unoccupied, and for a few minutes I was able to apply myself to my luncheon undistracted. Comical it is, during the first meal aboard ship, to see everybody taking stock of everybody else.

While they were still fifty feet away from their table, I recognized my couple by intuition. Among that ship-load of distinguished and expensive-looking people, nearly all heads turned to follow them as they passed through the saloon. What is the mysterious quality in people that causes all heads to turn? Personality, of course. Yet I have noticed that a determination not to be overlooked serves almost as well.

The lady walked first. My rapid first impressions ran: an ugly, attractive woman with a good-humoured smile; some years older than her husband, but sure of her power over him; frankly made up; hard to tell where nature ends and art begins; but made up with the view of accentuating her own personality; beautifully dressed in the extreme of the mode, but without overstepping the bounds of good taste. The sort of woman who has raised dress to the dignity of a fine art. In short, a highly interesting subject.

The man was more ordinary. He was of the type that used to be called the haw-haw Englishman. Very good-looking, to be sure, with curly dark hair, bright blue eyes, and a lazy, athletic frame. But rather sullen-looking. This I realized on closer examination was merely the result of stupidity. He

was thick. But an uncommonly handsome animal. Some
women ask no more of a man, of course. He was turned
out in a masculine style as finished as his wife's in hers.
The English have without doubt the best-dressed men in
the world.

Their manners were better than those of most of the
people in our vicinity. They looked at nobody but took
their places without the least self-consciousness, and talked
to each other in low tones with light smiles. You cannot
be sure about married people on parade, of course; they
might have been quarrelling fiercely. Still I gathered that
the young man with his expression of haughty disdain
(nothing in the world but stupidity) still looked on his
wife as rather a wonderful person, and was like putty in
her quick, pretty hands. And well he might; I thought her
rather wonderful myself.

I was too far away to hear anything of their conversation; so my impressions were confined to the visual. I said
she was an ugly woman; I mean her mouth was too wide
and her nose too flat. I began to recognize her type, which
is a rare one, and monstrously effective. She had the air of
flaunting her ugliness; as much as to say: my ugliness is
more charming than the insipid beauty of other women.
Ah, how clever that is! Such a woman is like a breath of
fresh air in a hothouse. Mere beauty is a bit overdone.
Indeed, I was so strongly attracted by her, I was finally
obliged to pull myself up roundly. Look here, I reminded
myself, she's a crook, and this charm of hers is her stock
in trade.

The only thing that might possibly have suggested that
Mrs. Dartrey was otherwise than as she seemed, was her

continual alertness. She was always on the qui vive. But then many perfectly respectable people are like that. In fact, never to be caught napping is the essence of a smart, worldly manner.

When I had learned all that my eyes would tell me, I finished my luncheon and made ready to leave the dining saloon. My way out lay behind Mrs. Dartrey's chair. In the instant of passing I caught these murmured words:

"…cut up rough at this late date…"

Which was piquant, but not very informative.

I telephoned my impressions to Mme. Storey when she returned to her cabin. "If you want to look her over you may know her by her costume," I added. "She is wearing a very smart sports dress of Paddy-green silk, with pleated bishop's sleeves caught tightly at the wrists, and a pleated skirt. A rakish little white hat with a tiny green feather stuck in the band."

"The deck steward has placed her chair next to yours on Deck B," said Mme. Storey. "I shall have plenty of chances to size her up as I stroll by."

I sought my deck chair. Sure enough, the chair along-side was marked "Mrs. Dartrey" on its little ticket. I sat down prepared to await developments, with a book for camouflage.

But the passing throng was more interesting than the book. After the sultry pavements of the city, the sea air was delightfully invigorating; and it appeared as if nearly everybody on board had the impulse to promenade after lunch. What a throng! Soldier, sailor, tinker, tailor, rich man—and, no doubt, if the truth were known, poor man, beggarman, thief. Not to speak of their ladies. After all, the crowd on board the queen of liners was much the same as the crowd on any liner, only there were more of them. There is a tradition that really distinguished people must keep to the seclusion of their cabins. I suppose it helps keep up the fiction of their exclusiveness, but it must be very dull for them.

After a while I saw my lady coming, her billowing green dress visible from afar. But she had no intention of stopping at her chair. Although we had been but three hours at sea, she already had three admirers: an elegant youth, a very solid business man, and a rather distinguished-looking foreigner. She was walking so fast as to make them all appear slightly ridiculous in their efforts to keep pace with her, and avoid colliding with slower promenaders.

I noticed that she was a little too broad for the pure line of beauty; the pleated dress was subtly designed to minimize it. Not that she seemed to care. She hastened along regardless, her long eyes sparkling, and her carmined mouth at its widest as she flung back a vivacious word now to one, now another of her followers. Every time they passed, I caught a snatch; but this time I did not feel that I was missing much. This sort of rattle is always the same.

After about half a dozen tours of the promenade deck she stopped in front of me and in her downright way plumped into her chair.

"Run along now," she said coolly to the men. "I'm going to invite my soul. And perhaps I shall take forty winks. You may wake me up at tea time."

It was odd to see how, the moment they left her, the three men flew apart from each other with indifferent looks. Mrs. Dartrey instantly turned to me with her attractively and disarming grin.

"I adore men," she said; "but suddenly you tire of them, don't you?"

The suddenness of her approach disconcerted me rather, but of course it was quite proper for me to betray a little diffidence. "Well, I don't know," I said.

"Don't you like men?" she asked.

"Yes, but—"

Without waiting for me to finish she rattled on:

"I'm so glad the deck steward didn't put a man next to me, or I shouldn't have been able to escape the creature. Women are much more comfortable as a steady diet."

"Do you think so?"

"Yes. The reason men tire you is because you cannot be honest with them."

"I should have said from what I overheard that you—"

"Oh, I only make believe to be honest with them. They like that. It flatters them. But if you were *really* honest, heavens! they would fly in terror!"

We laughed together.

"But the dear things!" Mrs. Dartrey resumed. "They lend a spice to life, don't they?"

"I have known very few men," I observed.

"Really!" she said. "I suppose you're a sensible woman."

"Ah, don't say that! No woman wants to be thought that."

"I wish I had more sense," she said with a sigh. "It's high time. There's nothing in this game, really. But somehow, without a lot of men running in and out, the world would seem very empty to me. Do you remember the old song:

"Reuben, Reuben, I've been thinking,
    What a queer wurruld this would be,
If the men were all transported
    Far beyond the Northern sea."

"I have heard it," I said.

"You're too young to remember when it was all the rage," said Mrs. Dartrey.

"Too young!" I exclaimed. "I am certainly as old as you."

"Ah, my dear lady, if you knew!" she cried. "But I shan't tell you. Not that I care much, either. For youth and beauty are not nearly so important as women suppose. I have neither, and I still attract men. I am much more popular than I was as a debutante. What is important is zest. To be in love with life, to be in love with love—that is the thing! Apparently, when a person is really crazy about living, he or she gives off certain rays—I am no metaphysician and I can't explain it, but apparently it's irresistible. So, although my hair is growing gray under the dye, and my hips are elephantine, I am not worrying, because I cannot feel the slightest falling off in my zest. When I become absolutely raddled with age I shall live in Paris, because Frenchmen do not mind how old a woman is if she still has verve. Do I shock you?"

"Ah, no! no!" I said quickly. "Please don't say that. One becomes so tired of small talk."

"Yes, and on shipboard it is particularly small," said Mrs. Dartrey. "Effect of the sea air, I suppose. I simply won't stand for it—except perhaps from a handsome man. They rarely have any sense. But not from women. I insist on saying whatever comes into my head, and if it's too strong for the dears, I move on."

"Well, please don't move on from me," I begged. Mindful of the character I was playing, I added: "I have had scarcely any experience of life, and such talk is like an invigorating breath from the great world."

"You have not the look of an inexperienced woman," she ventured.

"I've had a long struggle with myself," I said, "I suppose that makes me look like a veteran."

"Not a veteran, my dear, but a gallant young captain."

This provided me with opportunity to tell my simple tale. How I had been immured in a tiresome Middle West village for years and years, tending my father and mother and watching life slip by. How at length Death had released me, and I was venturing forth to seek experience, too late, I feared.

"Not too late if you have the wherewithal," she said, with rather a vulgar little gesture of counting money. She had many little vulgarities which, somehow, were not offensive in her.

"Oh, I have plenty of money," I said with a grand carelessness. "But I don't know how to—how to get on with—with people."

She did not rise to my little lure. If she had any scheme for helping me to get rid of my money, she kept it to herself. She merely made sympathetic sounds, and that kitten mind of hers darted off at a tangent.

"I can scarcely wait for evening! I have a duck of a frock to sport to-night. Picked it up yesterday in New York. Little shop on Forty-fifth Street. I prophesy that Euro-

pean women will soon be coming to New York to buy their
clothes. It's wonderful. Oh, how I adore pretty clothes!
Black net, my dear, over strange bright shades of green
and blue. Under the net there is black malines cut in panels
which separate when you walk showing the vivid colours,"
et cetera, et cetera.

WHEN I COULD get a word in, I cast another fly. "Would
you advise Paris or London for me?"

"Do you speak French?" she asked.

"Oh, a little book French."

"Then I'd say London. Book French will order you what
you want, but you cannot make friends on it. Except, of
course, with Americans in Paris. Somehow, I always detest
my own countrymen abroad. They're neither fish, flesh, nor
good red herring."

In turn she told me a good deal about herself, but noth-
ing very confidential. Much of it I had already heard from
Sir Angus. I noticed one discrepancy. Mrs. Dartrey said
that she and her husband were obliged to make frequent
trips to and fro across the Atlantic, because they lived in
England and all her husband's money was invested in
America. I knew from Sir Angus that the money was hers.
This seemed like unusual delicacy on her part.

We had a long talk. I liked the woman amazingly.

Promptly at four o'clock two of her swains were to be
seen approaching from opposite directions. Mrs. Dartrey's
eyes sparkled.

"Ah, the dears!" she cried. "Having put them out of my
mind for an hour, I am prepared to adore them again. You
and I have had a good time, too, haven't we? It is so stim-

ulating to meet an intelligent woman. We shall see more of each other. Adieu, for the present."

She sprang out of the chair like a girl, and with a swing linked arms with the two men as they came up. They paused for a moment, discussing what they should do. Mrs. Dartrey turned up her ugly nose at the suggestion of tea. The third admirer being seen to approach at that moment, it was decided to go up to the smoking room for a man's drink and a couple of rubbers of bridge.

I gave them ten minutes and then proceeded to make a tour of A deck myself. Through the windows of the smoking room I perceived that they were indeed absorbed in their game. Dartrey was there too, in another game. I decided that they were good for at least an hour and that I might safely venture to visit Mme. Storey, who had told me that she would be taking tea in her own suite.

I found her on the enchanting veranda of the Imperial suite, clad in a lovely négligé, and reclining in a *chaise longue*, looking over the sea. The pleasant-faced girl was reading to her from "Le Mort d'Arthur," but my mistress was almost asleep.

"Ah, Bella, what heavenly comfort!" she murmured. "The sense of the book is lost on me, but the music of the old English charms my soul!"

The girl vanished. Mme. Storey raised herself and lighted a cigarette. "What luck?" she asked.

I reported my conversation with Mrs. Dartrey word for word, as nearly as I could remember it. Mme. Storey, listening with a half smile, made no comment except to murmur occasionally:

"She is cleverer than I thought!"

When I had done she asked: "What do you think of her?"

"I like her," I said at once. "Who could help doing so? An impulsive, scatter-brained, fascinating woman, full of vim and go. Such a person is like a stove in a cold room. I think Sir Angus must be mistaken. To me she seems perfectly transparent. To imitate that sort of thing would require a cleverness too infernal."

"Nevertheless, I believe she is just as clever as that," said Mme. Storey. "She doesn't exactly imitate that honest air. She plays up her own natural self to gain her ends. The honest dishonest people, my dear, are the most subtle deceivers of all. And she's really attractive, of course, or she wouldn't have a soft job on the *Gigantic*."

I felt a little abashed. "I cannot doubt your insight," I said.

"This is not insight but outsight, my Bella," she said, laughing. "You see I happen to know that lady."

I looked at her in astonishment.

"I passed her on deck," she went on, "and I discovered that I had seen her once before. It must be all of eight years ago, but one would not forget that vivacious countenance. It was in Rector's of giddy memory. Inspector Rumsey pointed her out to me. She was then the companion of the famous 'Smoke' Lassen, the most brilliant confidence man that America ever produced. He has disappeared; dead, perhaps; he was an old man even then. The girl's name was Beatrice Breese; better known as Trixy Breese; and still more widely known throughout the underworld as Breezy Tricks."

"What can her game be?" I exclaimed.

"We shall find out."

"I gave her every opportunity and she didn't—"

"She wouldn't, the first day out."

"It must have to do with men."

Mme. Storey shook her head. "No, she uses men as a cover for her real operations. Every word of hers to you suggests that women are her mark. I fancy that the seat of operations must be in Paris, since she refused to name Paris to you too precipitately. Ah, Paris is the home of the most subtle swindles ever evolved by the wits of man—as well as everything else that is ingenious and amusing. It is fortunate for us if it is so, since we are bound to Paris."

"What part do you suppose her husband plays?" I asked.

"No part—except the part of her husband. He is essential to her. Under the ægis of his respectable name and family connections she feels perfectly safe. I've been observing him. He's an easily recognizable type: a young aristocrat vitiated by every expensive appetite, and thrown on the world without the means of satisfying them. She provides everything he wants, and he is content."

"But they seem to be genuinely attached to each other," I objected.

"Why shouldn't they be?" said Mme. Storey, smiling. "Love is not necessarily respectable, my Bella."

3

AFTER DINNER THE magnificent lounge of the *Gigantic*
was cleared for dancing. I watched from the side lines. All
dances are called "brilliant," but this one really had a sparkling appearance, the great hall was so beautiful and all the
women so well dressed. No self-respecting woman would
have allowed herself to walk out on that floor had she not
full assurance of looking her best.

Mrs. Dartrey made a late and effective entrance in the
"duck of a frock," which fully justified her encomiums. The
three admirers were now increased to half a score. Funny,
isn't it, how a man likes to make one of a crowd about a
popular woman. If I was a man, I'd be hanged if I would.
And from the woman's point of view I should think the
crowd would cut her off from anything real. Other women
didn't think of this, and you could see them watching Mrs.
Dartrey with a sickly envy out of the corners of their eyes.

I observed that the handsome, sulky-looking young
husband crossed the floor when she entered, and it was
to him that she gave the first dance. He was crazy about
her. She danced ecstatically; dance after dance. I remained
watching until after midnight, and she was still keeping it
up unflaggingly. What astonishing energy! I wondered if,
when her cabin door closed behind her, a reaction set in.

Next morning, at the women's hour, I met her in the

Pompeian swimming pool down on G deck, deep in the
hold of the vast ship. She was swimming tirelessly back
and forth as if she still had superfluous energy to get rid
of, and the other women were standing about looking at
her. She gave me a gay wave of the hand as she went to her
dressing room.

I did not have a chance to speak to her during the morning, but I saw her often: playing tennis up on the sun deck;
promenading briskly; talking animatedly to this person
and that. Her method was the same with all; she would
march up to anybody she fancied and plunge into the very
middle of a conversation. Most people were charmed by it;
and if they were not, the insouciant Trixy simply went on
to somebody else. There was plenty of material on board
to choose from. She and her husband did not come down
to lunch, and later I saw them the centre of a gay party in
the Ritz-Carlton restaurant on B deck. The champagne
was flowing copiously.

Later, she flung herself into the chair alongside me on
deck. "I'm drunk, my dear," she announced merrily. "I do
wish people wouldn't give me champagne. I am rattling
with it."

I laughed encouragingly.

"Ah, this is good!" she said, stretching herself. "The one
quiet hour of the day. Let's talk about men."

"Don't you want to sleep?" I asked.

"No! I grudge the hours given to sleep. Life is too short.
I've been looking forward to a rational conversation with
you." She glanced down the deck. "If only my husband does
not interrupt us. The poor fellow complains that I neglect
him on shipboard."

"He seems very devoted," I remarked.

She favoured me with an indescribably wicked, merry smile. "Oh, my dear, if you only knew! You would never imagine, seeing him so perfectly dressed, so indifferent looking—it is really quite terrible!"

"What is?" I asked.

"His ardour," she said, with eyes momentarily downcast.

"Oh!" I said.

"He is really too sweet!" she rattled on. "And I adore him. But it's just a leetle wearying sometimes to inspire a greater devotion than you feel yourself... Funny, isn't it, and me years older than he."

"How do you manage it?" I asked.

"I wish you were married," she said. "Then we could talk about things."

"Why can't we anyway?" I asked. "I'm grown-up."

She shook her head. "If you were married you would understand things—without explanations. To explain would be—horrible, you know."

"How long have you been married?" I asked.

"Two years. He is my third husband. One died; one I was obliged to divorce. Divorce is wonderful, isn't it? The greatest aid to marriage that was ever invented!"

This was a novel idea to me, and I suppose I looked my astonishment.

"I mean," she went on, "with the possibility of a divorce always present, married people cannot afford to get careless with each other. They must play up or expect to get the razz."

"I wish I had your art," I said with a sigh.

"I have no art," she quickly returned. "I am just myself.

Heavens, my dear, I'm the laziest-minded woman alive. If I had to think and contrive how to attract men, I should still be *une vierge*. No, men just seem to fall my way. I can't help it."

To-day, with Mme. Storey's hints to guide me, I was able to perceive that my irrepressible friend was *not* so spontaneous as she had seemed at first. Behind the merry, careless glances, there was the hint of something watchful. I became aware, gradually, that I was being subjected to a sharp scrutiny. We went on to talk of my supposed situation, and I felt as if a delicate, searching probe was being used on me. I was put to it to maintain my assumed character.

Somewhere during the course of our talk, Mrs. Dartrey made up her mind about me, and her manner began to change. She did not become rude or indifferent, but only cooled off. I anxiously cast back in my mind to discover what I could have said to put her off, but could not think of anything. It was impossible, I thought, that she could suspect me. Mme. Storey had said, with a woman as clever as that, it would be dangerous to make overtures of any kind and that I had better hold myself perfectly passive and let come what would come. This I had faithfully observed, yet it seemed as if the skittish lady had taken alarm, somehow. She finally fell asleep in the chair beside me—or made believe to do so.

On the following afternoon, when I came to my chair, I was greatly chagrined to discover that she had had the deck steward move her chair away.

I had been looking forward to dining *tête-à-tête* with Mme. Storey in her suite that night, but now my pleasure was all spoiled. Having made sure that the Dartreys had descended to the dining saloon, I went to keep the appointment, heavy with a sense of failure.

The little table was set out on the veranda of the suite, close beside the ship's rail. There was no light except one tiny bulb on the table under a rosy shade. Sitting there, we could look over the rail at the moon shining on the heaving sea. The delicious food was served piping hot from Mme. Storey's own pantry. It was all perfectly enchanting—or would have been had not my spirits been so low.

"What's the matter?" asked my kind mistress.

"I have failed," I said bitterly. "Mrs. Dartrey has become suspicious of me. She has shaken me."

"There is no reason for you to feel cast down," said Mme. Storey. "This was inevitable. She has not become suspicious of you. She has simply made up her mind that you are not timber suitable for her cutting, and, being a busy woman, she does not intend to waste any more time on you."

"I cannot think what I could have done," I said.

"You didn't do anything. Remember, she is looking for a gull. You are obviously not a gull, nor could you create the effect of a gull. She's a psychologist, too."

I began to feel a little better. "Still, I have failed," I said. "As far as she's concerned, my work is ended."

"I should say it was just beginning," said Mme. Storey. "Your job now is to find the gull and attach yourself to *her*."

Well, my appetite came back, and I suddenly found the moonlight on the sea glorious. My chief fear had been that Mme. Storey would be disappointed in me.

"I should say take plenty of time to it," she went on. "You still have three days and a bit before Cherbourg. Under the circumstances it would be quite proper for you to sue for Mrs. Dartrey's favour a little. She will no doubt snub you, but you can be the least bit persistent, as if regretful at losing your vivacious friend. Find out if you can whom she has chosen for the slaughter, and approach them when they are together. If you can contrive to have Mrs. Dartrey introduce you to the other woman, the rest will follow quite naturally."

All of which was done as Mme. Storey enjoined. I observed next morning that Mrs. Dartrey had had her chair carried around to the starboard side of B deck, where it was now placed beside that of a sallow, discontented-looking woman, very richly dressed. I wondered if this could be the prospective victim. On the other side of the woman sat a rather attractive man, her husband, apparently.

I let the whole day pass without making any move, closely observing Mrs. Dartrey whenever the opportunity offered. By this time she had a hundred intimate friends of both sexes. She was always in confidential chat with somebody, leaning over the ship's rail or perched on the edge of a chair, and it was not easy to decide which might be the chosen ones. She greeted me brightly but gave me no opportunity for conversation. However, when I saw her after tea in close confabulation with the sallow woman, I doubted no longer. Mrs. Dartrey's careless manner was exactly the same to this one as to any other, but her companion betrayed a secret, strained eagerness as she listened, which gave everything away. The husband's chair was empty.

I continued to promenade the deck until I happened by

during a lull in their confidences. Whereupon I stopped in front of Mrs. Dartrey and said: "I miss you."

She looked up at me with a little start of recognition, subtly insulting. "Oh," she said, "I'm sorry I had to move my chair. But there isn't a breath of air around on the port side in the afternoons."

"That's so," I said, still hanging about.

"Why don't you move over here?" she asked with a glance down the line, knowing very well that the rank was filled.

"There isn't any room."

I purposely prolonged the awkward pause and glanced suggestively at the other woman. Mrs. Dartrey evidently thought, as I wished her to, that the easiest way out was to introduce us, and she said:

"Mrs. Ellis, Miss Gaul. Silly to introduce people, isn't it, when we all talk to each other anyway."

We laughed inanely. I was satisfied. I made some inconsequential remark and walked on. Nor did I make any further move that day to improve my acquaintance with Mrs. Ellis.

From the passenger list I learned that she was Mrs. John W. Ellis and that she and her husband occupied one of the best rooms on D deck, which suggested that they were people of wealth. The purser told me that they had booked from Minneapolis and that they were apparently inexperienced voyagers. I suppose he made further inquiries of the room steward or stewardess, for he later volunteered the information that the couple quarrelled a good deal in their cabin. I regarded the husband with interest. He seemed superior to his wife; a man of some distinction;

but looked nervous and perhaps ill-tempered. They were going to Paris.

Next morning, when I started my promenade, I found Mrs. Ellis sitting between two empty chairs. So I dropped into one with an ingratiating smile at the sallow woman. She gave me a look none too friendly, but I made believe not to see it.

"Have you seen Mrs. Dartrey?" I asked.

"No," she said.

"Isn't she a wonderful woman?" I said. "So full of energy and spirits."

"Yes," said Mrs. Ellis in her graceless way.

She was clearly reluctant to talk about her friend, and it would have been highly foolish for me to pursue the subject. So I made up talk about anything and nothing. It was uphill work, for Mrs. Ellis was both suspicious and touchy. She hadn't anything against me personally; that was just her ordinary attitude. She was a woman of about forty, and would have been very good-looking, with her raven hair and good eyes, had it not been for her sallowness and her intensely disagreeable expression. I couldn't make up my mind whether biliousness had ruined her disposition or her bad disposition had soured her digestive juices. Either might have been true.

Finally I discovered that the key to unlock her nature was—flattery! I said: "I'm so glad Mrs. Dartrey introduced us. I should never have dared to speak to you without. One should on shipboard, I suppose, but I simply haven't the assurance. And I did so want to know you. You attracted me from the first."

A tinge of pink appeared in Mrs. Ellis's sallow skin, and

her whole expression softened in fatuous gratification. I perceived that there was no danger of feeding it to her too strong. "What was it about me that attracted you?" she asked, keenly interested.

"These things are hard to explain," I said, "I suppose it was because you looked so superior to the other passengers."

"Oh, the others," she said with a sneering look down the line; "dreadful people, aren't they?"

"They look it," I said. "I haven't felt like talking to any of them."

"I never talk to people when travelling," said Mrs. Ellis. "One must maintain a certain reserve. One owes it to one's self."

"That was it," I said. "It was your air of reserve which attracted me."

I devoutly hoped that she wouldn't report my words to Mrs. Dartrey. The latter would have instantly comprehended that I was after something. However, there was little danger of such a thing happening: Mrs. Ellis was too much of a fool.

"I'm a queer sort of person," Mrs. Ellis went on, delighted with her subject. "Very few understand me. When I give my friendship, a warmer and more disinterested friend does not exist on earth. But I am slow to give it. I insist upon worth in the object. And I am implacable. I never forgive a wrong in friendship."

"You must have many devoted friends," I murmured.

"No," she said, "not many. My standards are too high. I scarcely know what women are coming to nowadays. Even the so-called best women I find to be unscrupulous liars and scandalmongers—if not worse. I will have nothing to do with such, whatever their position may be."

"It does you credit," I said.

"My husband is the most prominent attorney in Minneapolis," she went on: "counsel to the biggest corporations in the Northwest. As a leader, I am an especial object of calumny. It cannot touch me, of course, but as I will not compromise with such people the result is that I lead rather a lonely life."

"I suppose it is inevitable," I said sympathetically.

"You would not believe some of the stories I could tell you about the so-called best people of Minneapolis," she said viciously, and forthwith launched into an involved and excessively tiresome tale of country club machinations. I will not bore you with it. Suffice it to say that the teller appeared as the high-minded heroine, while all the other women were hussies. Another tale followed, and another. Mrs. Ellis looked upon herself as the most beautiful, the cleverest and the noblest of women, and was enraged because nobody else would accept her at her own valuation. Evidently in her home town, she was avoided like the plague.

She was particularly bitter on the subject of philandering. Evidently all the other women of her set were engaged in more or less innocent flirtations, whereas no man ever looked at Mrs. Ellis. Consequently, she had rationalized herself into a very snowdrop of purity and was scathing in her animadversions upon sex. But, ah, what a tormented envy spoke in her words!

So much for my success with Mrs. Ellis. She always welcomed me after that, though of course I was no more to the egotistical woman than a sort of mirror in which she saw herself reflected as she wished. She never cared to hear me talk about myself. In order that I might not appear to be cultivating her acquaintance secretly, I used to stop sometimes when she and Mrs. Dartrey were together. At such moments neither lady betrayed overmuch friendliness, but I persisted until I had established my point. I would then pass on as if a little saddened by their lack of cordiality.

I must emphasize the fact that there was never the slightest suggestion of secrecy in Mrs. Dartrey's communications to her friend. She did not whisper, nor cast meaning looks, *et cetera,* but was always her impetuous and rather noisy self; and as far as I could judge the style of her talk was exactly the same as she had used toward me in the beginning.

I discovered another significant fact about Mrs. Ellis. Later that same day, as I passed along the deck, her husband was in the next chair, and I judged from their expressions that they were quarrelling in bitter whispers. Mrs. Ellis did not see me at all; her face was yellow and hateful; there was something unspeakably piteous in it, too; and in a flash the domestic situation became clear to me. She was passionately in love with her husband, whereas he was tired of her and exasperated beyond endurance by her foolishness. I was sorry for them both.

I made my next reports to Mme. Storey with more confidence, and she was good enough to commend me unreservedly. I went on to describe Mrs. Ellis's wonderful jewels, her rope of pearls, her emeralds, her beautiful diamond ornaments.

"Those, I suppose, constitute the stakes of the game," I said.

Mme. Storey shook her head. "Indirectly, perhaps," she said. "But we have nothing so simple to deal with as straight robbery. They could never have got away with robbery for two seasons without having a hue and cry raised against them."

4

ON THE NIGHT before we were to disembark at Cherbourg, that immemorial function, the captain's dinner, was held in the grand saloon. This event was supposed to mark the culmination of the social activities aboard ship, and every woman saved her prettiest dress for it. All the dinners were so extraordinarily elaborate there was not much more that the steward could do; but what he could do he did; and upon glancing down the menu one realized that the four corners of the globe had been ransacked for delectable dainties. All the toys and favours were distributed that are considered to add to the gaiety of the feast.

Sir Angus, in dress uniform, was the most dignified figure present. One could worship such a man, with his urbanity, his sorrowful, stern face, and his cool habit of command. He very rarely appeared among the passengers. None but a fool would dare to approach so noble a figure with impertinent questions; but unfortunately the fools on shipboard seem to be even more in evidence than elsewhere. Sir Angus masked with polite smiles the tedium that the interminable dinner must have caused him.

There was a great treat saving for me afterward, because Sir Angus had asked Mme. Storey and me to take coffee with him in his own quarters up on the bridge. What a delightful spot that cabin was, so cool and remote above the bustle of the ship. One could hear the steady rush of the wind outside, and the sighing voice of the sea. Here one was really aware of being at sea. The furnishings were unexpectedly simple, and Sir Angus's private knick-knacks, scattered about, gave it a homely aspect. The dear man's artistic taste was not very highly developed, but one could not think the less of a sailor for that.

My mistress looked positively regal in a plain evening gown of a cool red brocade that the famous Craqui had designed for her earlier in the season. Sir Angus's face became soft and beautiful with a chivalrous admiration as he looked at her. It was a very fine tribute.

But Mme. Storey insisted on bringing me forward. She suggested that I tell Sir Angus the story of the drama which was developing on board. I did so.

"I knew I would not be appealing to you in vain!" he cried. "I am sure this ugly business will be cleared up now. How do you suppose it will work out?"

"Unless I am very much deceived," said Mme. Storey, "Mrs. Dartrey will furnish Mrs. Ellis with an address in Paris. That will finish Mrs. Dartrey's work. She goes on to Southampton, and, as the rush of rich Americans is slackening now, she will no doubt be free until next season, to amuse herself with her fashionable English friends. As to what is to take place at that address in Paris I cannot, of course, tell you yet. But Bella and I will make it our business to find out."

"You are wonderful women!" said Sir Angus solemnly.

Fancy my pride at hearing myself coupled with Mme. Storey like that.

Sir Angus presented me, as a souvenir, with an ink-well

in the form of a model of the *Gigantic's* bridge, with all the telegraphs reproduced in silver gilt. I believe it was among his most cherished possessions, and certainly it has become one of mine.

Next morning we dropped anchor in the harbour of Cherbourg, and as the tender came alongside there was a great business of good-byes among the company of passengers which divided here. Mrs. Dartrey, who looked very piquant in a white sports costume with Chinese embroidery, was most affable to me.

"When you come to London, do drop in on me," said she.

But she did not intend it to be taken seriously. I thought: "If I do come perhaps it will be on an errand that will astonish you."

Out of the tail of my eye I observed her parting with Mrs. Ellis. She was too clever to give anything away; all gaiety and carelessness; but the other woman was visibly moved. She whispered something to Mrs. Dartrey that I could not catch, but I read its purport on her lips. It was a murmur of thanks for some benefit conferred.

Mme. Storey and I were to travel separately to Paris, of course. I had purposely omitted reserving a seat on the train, as I wanted, if possible, to get into the same compartment with Mr. and Mrs. Ellis. I succeeded in doing so, but obtained little benefit from it, for Mrs. Ellis, ill at ease in the presence of her husband, scarcely opened her lips to me the whole way. Moreover, I do not think she ever looked out of the window, though this was her first visit to France. She sat staring straight ahead of her, her twitching hands and tapping foot betraying a curious inner excitement.

Her husband studied a copy of the Paris edition of the New York *Herald* that he had purchased on the *quai*. One wondered why such a couple had come abroad.

In the bustle of collecting our belongings as we drew into the Gare St. Lazare I forced Mrs. Ellis to take some notice of me.

"There are never enough porters, of course," I said with a laugh. "They run alongside the train as it comes to a stop, and the way to make sure of one is to pass your bags out of the window."

Mr. Ellis thanked me for the tip.

"It has been so nice to know you," I said to his wife in a lower tone. "I hope I may see something of you in Paris."

"Surely," she said. She did not mean it either. It was clear that even my flattery had no weight against the secret new excitement that filled her.

"Where are you going to stop?" I asked.

"Er—the Continental," she said, with an uneasy glance at her husband.

When I got myself and my bags into a taxi, I put the Ellises out of my mind. I thanked my stars that my own heart was unclouded and I might freely give myself up to the delight of sniffing that rare atmosphere and feasting my eyes on the blithesome spectacle of the boulevards. Why is it—why is it that the mere thought of Paris moves one's heart to a gaiety that is almost painful? I can't explain it. I only know that I would rather go to Paris when I die than to heaven.

Although I had only known Paris for three brief days before, I felt as if I were coming home. I murmured over the names of the streets, finding the syllables sweet in my

ears: Rue du Havre; Rue Tronchet; around the frowning
Madeleine, and down the sparkling Rue Royale to the
glorous panorama of the river.

Mme. Storey and I were joyfully reunited in the same
charming salon at the Crillon that we had had before. Its
windows, which looked out over the Place de la Concorde,
commanded the finest view in Paris, with the Jardins des
Tuileries on one side, the Champs-Elysées on the other,
and the river in front. We did not stop to unpack, but
rushed out into the streets again. Mme. Storey, not telephoning to any of her friends, gave up the rest of that day
to me. We dined at an enchanting out-of-doors restaurant
up on Montmartre and went to see the Ballet Russe.

Next morning I had to get into harness again. About
eleven I set off down the Rue de Rivoli to call on Mrs. Ellis
at the Hôtel Continental. I had a disappointment. They
were not there. They had reserved rooms, I was told, but
had not come, nor had any word been received from them. I
went to the New York *Herald* office, but they had not regis-
tered there, as all good Americans do; neither was there any
information forthcoming at the American Express. I was
forced to the conclusion that Mrs. Ellis had persuaded her
husband to change hotels expressly to avoid me.

Mme. Storey took it with a shrug. "It's not fatal," she
said. "Such a green pair, and so rich, could not lose themselves in Paris. I know a woman who will find them for us
within an hour or so."

She telephoned to a certain Mlle Monge, who, it
appeared, had served her before.

In less than an hour word came over the wire that the
Ellises were at the Majestic on the Avenue Kleber, near

the Etoile. Mme. Storey instructed Mlle Monge to await me there in the foyer. She would know me by my red hair and chapeau vert.

To me Mme. Storey said: "Point out Mrs. Ellis to her, and let her follow the American about Paris. I shall have to leave this case pretty much to you two, as I am obliged to let my friends know I am here. In Paris I am not supposed to have any serious occupation."

In the magnificent Hôtel Majestic I was approached by a charming brown-eyed person very modishly dressed in black, who introduced herself as Mlle Monge. She was not at all one's idea of the typical Frenchwoman, she had such a modest and reticent manner; but I was beginning to learn that, as of other peoples, there are all kinds of French. Her English was as good as my own, and I felt from the first that we should be friends.

It was now the hour for *déjeuner,* and the restaurant was thronged. All I had to do was to point out the Ellises where they sat by a window and leave the rest to Mlle Monge. It was arranged that she should call me up at the Crillon at three, or as soon thereafter as possible. I was then free to kick up my heels on the Champs-Elysées.

In due course I got my call. The Ellises had left their hotel together, Mlle Monge reported, and had driven to the Galeries Lafayette, where Mrs. Ellis had gone in. But she had only waited inside the door long enough for her husband to drive away. She had then hailed another taxi and had herself driven to a house in the Rue des Tournelles in the Marais, a quarter of old Paris. She had remained in this house nearly an hour. Upon inquiring of the concierge, Mlle Monge learned that she had asked for a M. Guimet, who had the best apartment in the house. M. Guimet was a savant (scientist) and much respected in the neighbourhood, it appeared. Mrs. Ellis had then returned to the Majestic, where she now was. Mlle Monge was telephoning from there.

Mme. Storey was not available at the moment. I felt that the first thing to do was to obtain further information about this M. Guimet. I so told Mlle Monge, and said I would immediately come to the Majestic to relieve her.

When I entered the Majestic for the second time, the first person I beheld was Mrs. Ellis, who was walking back and forth in the foyer in an uncertain way. She saw me at the same moment and came hastening toward me.

"What a surprise!" she cried. "How are you! It's so nice to see a friendly face!"

This was rather disconcerting. I was still more astonished by the change in her appearance. She was openly and feverishly excited now; a bright red spot burned in either of her sallow cheeks, and the pupils of her eyes were as much distended as if she had atropine in them. A dangerous excitement.

"Are you very busy?" she went on breathlessly. "I'm dying to go shopping and I don't know where to go or what to ask for."

I saw that I need have no anxiety about explaining my presence in the Majestic. "Just a minute until I make an inquiry at the bureau," I said. "Then I'll be happy to go with you."

In a shadowy corner of the foyer I saw Mlle Monge taking us in. It was not necessary for me to communicate with her then, as she had her instructions. I inquired for a mythical person at the bureau and then returned to Mrs. Ellis.

"My friend has not arrived," I said.

She was not in the least interested. As we stood on the sidewalk waiting for a taxi, her head kept turning from side to side.

"That man stared at me," she said with a simper. "I mean the young man in the shepherd's plaid suit who just went in. Oh, Paris! Paris! Paris!"

"You are happier than you were yesterday," I ventured.

With a lunatic change of mood she whispered dully: "Is it happiness?… I don't know… I'm terrified."

I wondered if she were a secret drinker. I had seen no signs of it on shipboard.

A taxi came up. I told the driver to take us to the Place de l'Opéra as a good point to radiate from. We hustled down the Champs-Élysées. Mrs. Ellis stared with an unwholesome eagerness into the faces of the people in the passing motors.

"It's more fun walking," she said. "More chance of an adventure. And yet, not an hour ago, when I was coming home in a taxi, a man in another cab raised his hat to me and smiled. Such a gentlemanly looking fellow with a gray Fedora and a monocle. I was quite flustered. And, my dear, he ordered his chauffeur to turn around and follow. But I lost him in the traffic… I must tell you, I had taken the taxi in order to escape a young fellow in the street who brushed against me and smiled… Isn't this a dreadful city? How it makes one's heart beat!… It will seem very dull in Minneapolis. Our men are such stick-in-the-muds. No verve, no romance, no abandon."

"What is it particularly that you want to buy?" I asked.

"An evening gown. Something I can wear at dinner to-night. I want to charm my husband. My dear, I've gradually allowed myself to dress in as dull a style as if I were over forty!"

Which of course she was!

It is not so easy to buy good ready-made dresses in Paris, but Mme. Storey had told me of a little shop in the Rue du Faubourg St. Honoré to which the great dressmakers sent their model dresses to be sold, and thither we had ourselves carried. I soon perceived that Mrs. Ellis had no intention of listening to any advice from me and ceased to offer it. She chose a snaky sheath gown covered with green sequins. It was a gorgeous affair, but most unsuitable for her; made her skin look as yellow as saffron.

Nevertheless, she stood clad in it before a long mirror, and raising her arms above her head, like a girl, murmured dreamily: "I am charming!"

She refused to leave the shop until she had seen the dress dispatched to the Hôtel Majestic by a midinette.

Out in the street again, she said with a sidelong look: "Let us go to a café. One of those places where we can sit out on the street and watch everybody. Which is the most famous rendezvous of them all?"

"The Café de la Paix, undoubtedly," I said. "They call it the centre of civilization. If you sit there long enough, everybody in the world will pass by, they say."

"In such a place we are sure to be spoken to," she said with a secret smile. "Would you be afraid?"

"Not at all," I said.

"What would you do?"

"Speak back again—if I liked the looks of the speaker."

"Oh, you're so matter-of-fact," she said impatiently. "That will never get you anywhere."

"Where do you want to get to?" I asked, smiling.

Her strained face showed no answering smile. "I want—I want—" she said incoherently—"I want everything life has to offer. After this I mean to take it as my right. I am no common woman. Colour! perfume! happiness! I will lavish my treasures!... Will you agree this afternoon to follow wherever adventure may lead us?" she demanded breathlessly.

"Yes," I said. I felt safe in promising.

"I am utterly reckless!" she cried. "The spirit of a bacchante has entered into me. I mean to drain the cup of life to the dregs!"

You would have had to see the aging, sallow woman to appreciate how tragi-comic this sounded.

It suddenly occurred to her that it was hardly in line with her moral protestations on shipboard. "I expect you disapprove," she said with another sidelong look. "But I can't help it. Something within me is released. I don't care what happens."

"I am no moralist," I said. "I would like to cut loose myself."

"Then stick to me," she said with an insane archness. "Wherever I go, things are bound to happen!"

In a few minutes we were seated at the famous corner where all the streams of Paris converge. It was crowded, as it always is, by night or day, and we had to hang about until one of the little tables in the front rank was vacated and we could pounce on it. The passing throng all but trod on our feet. I could have been perfectly happy just watching. I suggested coffee, tea, or an ice to Mrs. Ellis, but she would have none of it.

"What are those people drinking?" she asked, indicating a particularly rakish-looking couple at the next table.

"Fine à l'eau," I said. "That is Parisian for brandy and soda."

"I'll have one of those," she said.

I did not expect to obtain any information from her by direct questioning; still, I thought it was worth trying. "What have you been doing since we got here?" I asked.

"Oh, nothing in particular," she said inattentively. "Just looking around."

"What did you do this morning?"

The secret look on her face intensified. "My husband and I drove around town in a taxicab," she said with a calculated vagueness.

"What I would like to see is a bit of old Paris," I hazarded. "If I only had somebody to take me."

"I am not interested in anything old," she said. "...The Englishman with the blue collar is staring at me."

I saw that it was useless to pursue my questions.

The woman beside me was obsessed. Her head kept turning restlessly this way and that, her distended eyes searching in the faces of the men who sat near. Fattish, complacent creatures, most of them; settled in their chairs as if somebody had squashed them down on the seats rather hard. I got no suggestion of the rampant male that Mrs. Ellis affected to perceive everywhere. A good many of them were staring at her naturally, her actions were so peculiar; but it was not at all in the manner that she fondly supposed. It made me rather uncomfortable, but it was all in the way of my job. Of course, nobody spoke to us.

For more than an hour she kept up the pretence that she was the cynosure of every eye. "I hope you'll forgive me for making you so conspicuous," she said archly. "I suppose you are not accustomed to it."

I assured her that was all right.

She ordered cigarettes and attempted to smoke one with airy grace, but choked over it. One noticed, notwithstanding her confidence, that she was excessively bitter in her censures upon such women who passed as had annexed a man.

And then, suddenly, the game seemed to be up. She rose abruptly. She had had several ponies of cognac and was slightly affected by it.

"I congratulate you on your success as a chaperon," she said, crassly ill-natured. "I will have to give you a testimonial: Warranted to keep men at arm's length! I don't know why I came out with you, I'm sure. I wish Mrs. Dartrey was here."

I consoled myself for her rudeness by thinking: "If she were here, my lady, no man would look at you!"

I put her in a cab and sent her to the Majestic. I knew she was expecting to meet her husband there and would be safe with him during the evening. And that liberated me. I returned to the Crillon with a light heart.

Mlle Monge reported that she had made further inquiries in the Rue des Tournelles but with small results. It appeared that none of his neighbours had a speaking acquaintance with M. Guimet, who was described as a studious and absent-minded scientist. He had been living in his present quarters for two years. Nothing was known of his antecedents. An elderly *femme de ménage* cared for his wants. She was well liked by the tradespeople chiefly because she was a liberal spender. A certain éclat attached to M. Guimet's establishment because of the handsomely dressed ladies who occasionally called upon him. Mlle Monge had then inquired at the Institut de France, and of the other learned societies, but had been unable to learn anything whatever concerning a scientific man by the name of Aristide Guimet. He was not known to the police.

5

LATE IN THE afternoon of the following day I ran into Mrs. Ellis by accident as I crossed the Place Vendôme. That dependable Mlle Monge had her under observation. Mrs. Ellis looked at me point-blank without a sign of recognition. In order to get her attention I had to run after her and take her arm. A further extraordinary change had taken place in the woman. She seemed to have broken up overnight. Her hair was untidy and her eyes had the dulled look of one suffering from shock; her colour was ghastly.

At first I made believe not to notice anything amiss. "Fancy!" I cried, "of all the millions in Paris, you and I to meet here!"

"Let me alone," she muttered thickly. "I don't want to talk to you."

"Shall we go to Rumpelmayer's to tea?" I said.

She attempted pettishly to free her arm, but I clung to it. "You are ill," I said. "Let me help you."

"I'm all right," she muttered. "Let me go."

She was hardly a sympathetic figure; nevertheless, I was strongly affected on her behalf. After all, she was my countrywoman, and I had reason to believe her the victim of some devilish plot. I summoned the first passing taxi and put her into it. She was too apathetic to resist me. I told the man to drive to the Crillon. Mrs. Ellis's witless aspect scared me. I began to feel that this case was getting beyond me, and I determined to send Mlle Monge after Mme. Storey, who was having tea with friends at the Ritz. I saw the Frenchwoman discreetly following in another cab.

I seated Mrs. Ellis in the little salon of our suite while I talked to Mlle Monge out in the corridor. She said:

"Mrs. Ellis made a round of the fashionable jewellery shops on the Rue de la Paix this morning. It was so early the shops were empty, and I couldn't follow her in without attracting attention, so I cannot state what her errand was. As far as I could see from the street, whenever she stated her errand, she was taken into a private room.

"She had *déjeuner* alone at the Majestic. Immediately afterward she had herself driven to the Rue des Tournelles again. She remained in that house about the same length of time as before. Neither before nor after that visit could I see any change from her usual look. She was always a little wild. She returned to the Majestic and had herself carried up in the lift. In a few minutes her husband descended, his face distorted with anger. I assumed that they had quarrelled. He left the hotel. Mrs. Ellis came down, and she then looked as you see her now. She left the hotel like one walking in her sleep. She walked the entire distance to the spot where you met her, seeing nothing."

I told Mlle Monge to ask Mme. Storey to come at once, if she could, and to proceed directly to her bedroom, where I could speak to her before Mrs. Ellis saw her. I then returned to Mrs. Ellis.

"I am your friend," I said frankly. "Can't you tell me what is the matter?"

She struggled for some semblance of self-control. She

wished to deceive me. "It is nothing," she said. "I feel a little ill. I am subject to it. I will just rest a little and then go home."

I appeared to be satisfied. "Is there anything I can get you?" I asked.

"Smelling salts," she suggested.

I fetched her the bottle. She sniffed of it gratefully and made out that she felt better. She kept her lids lowered to hide the look of blank agony in her eyes. It was very affecting.

"Shall I have tea brought up here?" I asked.

A nauseated look crossed her face. "No, please," she murmured. "I could not eat. I will go now."

By one expedient and another, I detained her for five minutes. At the end of that time I heard the door of Mme. Storey's room close. I went to her and swiftly explained the situation. She returned with me to the salon.

"This is Mme. Storey, Mrs. Ellis," I said.

It was too much for the nerves of the shaken woman. She lost her grip again. "What does she want of me?" she said hysterically. "Why was I brought here, anyway? I wish to go!"

There was a comfortable, sunny-tempered quality in Mme. Storey's smile. "Let me explain myself first," she said. In a difficult situation, she always deals frankly. She described the nature of her profession and told how, upon boarding the *Gigantic,* Captain Sir Angus McMaster had asked her to do a favour for him.

"He believed that Mr. and Mrs. Dartrey were dangerous swindlers," she said.

Mrs. Ellis's jaw dropped.

"The Dartreys, *swindlers!*" she gasped. "That can't be!… At least they got nothing out of me!"

"Not directly," said Mme. Storey. "But we believe they are working with somebody in Paris. Did they not send you to a man in Paris?"

The effect of this on Mrs. Ellis was startling. Her arms went up to her head in an utterly distracted gesture. "Oh, my God!.. Oh, my God!" she stuttered. "A swindle! It can't be so!"

"Was it M. Aristide Guimet in the Rue des Tournelles?" asked Mme. Storey softly.

"I don't know what you're talking about!" cried Mrs. Ellis. "I never heard of that name or of that street!"

"We had you followed," said Mme. Storey deprecatingly. "You were there yesterday and again to-day."

Mrs. Ellis, wild with terror, endeavoured to save her face by flying into a passion. "You had me followed!" she cried. "As if I were a criminal! How dare you! How dare you! My husband shall know of this! Have I not the right to go where I please?"

"Oh, assuredly," said Mme. Storey. "I only wished to save you, you see. If I have failed to do so, I blame myself very much. But I had no idea it would happen so quickly."

"I have not the least idea what you are talking about," said Mrs. Ellis. "It sounds to me as if you were out of your mind."

"*Please,* Mrs. Ellis," said Mme. Storey, with her most winning manner. "Let us talk this over reasonably. Suppose you have been fooled: that is no disgrace. It happens to all of us. If you have lost your money, don't you want me to get it back for you?"

"I don't know you," cried Mrs. Ellis. "How am I to know but that you are a swindler?"

Mme. Storey smiled. "I have not asked you for anything but a little information," she said. "You can easily satisfy yourself about me by cabling to anyone you may know in New York, or, better, by sending a wireless to Sir Angus."

Mrs. Ellis abandoned that line. "I have lost no money," she said. "Where would I get any money to lose? Our funds are all in my husband's hands."

"Where are your jewels, Mrs. Ellis?"

The woman caught her breath sharply. A moment passed before she could command herself sufficiently to speak. "In my jewel case," she said tremulously. "Where else should they be?"

"What were you doing in the Rue de la Paix this morning?"

"Buying some new ones," she said with a laugh that was meant to be careless and offhand but only had a lunatic sound.

Mme. Storey approached from another angle. "Sir Angus and I believe that this game has been going on for two years," she said. "Within that time many American women must have been deceived and robbed. And it appears to be such a devilishly clever game there's no reason why it should not go on indefinitely unless we break it up. Won't you help me to do that, Mrs. Ellis, for the sake of saving other women?"

An unnatural calmness descended on Mrs. Ellis. Her eyes were perfectly daft, but her voice was under fair control. "I would be glad to help you if I knew what you

were talking about," she said. "But it sounds like rank melo-
drama to me."

"Prove your good faith by telling us why you went to see
M. Guimet," challenged Mme. Storey.

Mrs. Ellis hesitated blankly—then, evidently, a word of
mine recurred to her. "I merely wanted to see a bit of old
Paris," she said.

"Who told you about M. Guimet?"

"Somebody in America—I scarcely remember who. I
am not in the least interested in M. Guimet but only in
his old house. And now I hope I may be permitted to go.
Unless I am being detained here by force."

"The door is unlocked," said Mme. Storey. "But let me
make a last appeal. Here we are, three American women
in a foreign city. Surely we ought to stand together. There
is evidently a devilish trap set for our women in this city.
Won't you help me to destroy it?"

"Really, my dear lady, you are too dramatic!" said Mrs.
Ellis. "You ought to go on the stage."

And with an affected laugh she passed out of the room
with that corpselike face, and those eyes mad with pain or
terror—or both. It was too dreadful to see. But we had to
let her go, of course.

When the door closed behind her, Mme. Storey sighed.
"God save us from fools!" she said.

I said: "The woman must be criminally involved in some
way, to be in such terror of having the facts known."

Mme. Storey shook her head. "Most likely it is only
folly," she said. "A woman would far rather be shown up as
a crook than a fool."

"There was a threat you might have used," I suggested.

"I know," said Mme. Storey, "to tell her husband if she didn't come across. I thought of it. But I was afraid of driving her to some desperate act. She is completely unbalanced."

The faithful Mlle Monge followed Mrs. Ellis out of the Crillon, and later she reported that Mrs. Ellis had returned to the Majestic, where she had later dined with her husband in at least apparent amity. We were somewhat reassured in mind by this news.

But early next morning Mr. Ellis went to the Préfecture de Police to report that his wife was missing. We were immediately informed of it by Mlle Monge, who was on duty at the Majestic at an early hour. Mr. Ellis told the police he feared his wife might have taken her own life. She had threatened to do so the day before. A neurotic and highly emotional woman, she had frequently threatened to kill herself, and he had not supposed that she meant it. She had retired for the night apparently in a better frame of mind. But sometime during the night she had arisen while he slept, and had stolen from the room.

A watchman in the Majestic reported that a guest who answered to the description of Mrs. Ellis had come downstairs fully dressed just as day was breaking. Upon his asking her how he could serve her (he spoke English), she had said that she wanted to go to the Orleans station to meet a friend who was arriving by a night train, and would he get her a taxicab. She departed in it. The driver testified that he had indeed taken her to the Orleans station, which as everybody knows is on the *quai*. She was not seen after that.

A few hours later the unfortunate woman's body was

recovered from the river at St. Cloud, having evidently drifted to that point from one of the city bridges.

Mme. Storey, Mlle Monge, and I immediately went to the Préfecture to tell what we knew of the case. This building was on the Île de la Cité, opposite the huge Palais de Justice where I had once been to see the Sainte Chappelle and Marie Antoinette's cell. The Préfecture was not an ancient building, but, like all French public buildings, very imposing with its statuary, paintings, *et cetera*. How different from 300 Mulberry Street, New York!

The officers were admirably sensible and businesslike. You will find the high officers of the police everywhere much the same, only the French are more formal and polite than others. M. le Préfet himself, to whom we were finally shown, was a perfect little Chesterfield of deportment, but with a face as cool and keen as polished steel. It would have been *infra dig.* for such a personage to have betrayed any astonishment at Mme. Storey's account, but he was astonished. One could feel it.

"Should you not have conferred with me before?" he asked reproachfully.

"I intended to do so as soon as I had any evidence," said Mme. Storey. "So far it has been only guesswork."

M. le Préfet wished to give orders to have the man Guimet taken into custody at once. Mme. Storey earnestly remonstrated with him.

"If you do so, I fear that he will escape us. We have no evidence against him. The woman is dead, and there can be no witness to the act of his receiving money from her. He is, or I miss my guess, one of the most plausible rascals in Christendom, and you will be forced to let him go. He will disappear for a while, only to resume his game later on, or another game just as devilish. I beg of you to allow me to pursue my investigation in secret—in coöperation with you, of course—until we have him. I ask you even to keep the fact of Mrs. Ellis's suicide out of the papers, that he may not take alarm."

Up to this time Mme. Storey had not mentioned her name, and his next question was the natural one: "Who are you, *madame?*"

"Rosika Storey," she said.

He knew. He leaped to his feet and made her a profound bow. Then he kissed her hand. Frenchmen can do that sort of thing without any sacrifice of dignity. Compliments flowed from him in a stream.

Mme. Storey insisted on identifying herself by her passport. "We have never met," she said, "because it is my fancy to allow it to be supposed in Paris that I am merely a person of leisure. If you will be good enough to communicate with Captain Sir Angus McMaster of the *Gigantic,* he will confirm what I have told you about the events on shipboard."

M. le Préfet would not hear of such a thing, but I have no doubt he did communicate with Sir Angus.

The upshot was that he agreed to let Mme. Storey proceed in her own way. He told us for our information that it had been established that Mrs. Ellis had disposed of the greater part of her jewels to various jewellers in the Rue de la Paix. The money she had received for them had disappeared, of course.

Mme. Storey asked him to convey the substance of her communication to the bereaved husband in order to save her the painful task of telling Mr. Ellis herself. "He is sure to think I ought to have told him in the beginning," she said. "But I couldn't do that on a mere suspicion. It wouldn't have made any difference, anyway—except, perhaps, to hasten the poor woman's suicide by a day or two."

From that time forward we worked in close coöperation with the Paris police. They must have a tighter rein on the newspapers than we have; for no word of Mrs. Ellis's suicide appeared.

6

THE THREE OF us returned to the Crillon to confer. A certain jealousy developed between the excellent Mlle Monge and myself. Each of us was keen to obtain the assignment of calling upon M. Guimet.

"I know Paris and Paris ways," said Mlle Monge.

"But he looks for Americans," said I.

Mme. Storey vetoed both suggestions. "Their whole business is conducted with absolute circumspection," she said. "They are not taking any chances. We may be certain that the Dartreys have some means of notifying M. Guimet whom to expect. The essence of a clever confidence game lies in that. An outsider would never gain admission to M. Guimet's apartment, and a false move on our part would ruin everything… Let me think a moment."

The result was that she announced I must go to London.

I set off that same evening via the night boat between Le Havre and Southampton, armed with letters to Scotland Yard both from Mme. Storey and from M. le Préfet. The journey was a great pleasure to me, but I do not mean to hold up my tale while I relate my first impressions of misty London, which has a beauty of its own, oh, so different from Paris! London did not amaze me so much, but was perhaps dearer, more like home.

In the great red brick building on the Embankment I

presented my letters and was very courteously received. Steps were instantly taken to have the Dartreys placed under surveillance. What we were after was to discover how they communicated with M. Guimet and to intercept any messages they might send him.

There was nothing I could do to help in this, and I spent the next two days in seeing London. I was in frequent communication with Mme. Storey by telegraph, but I may say that nothing of importance happened in Paris while I was away. The police were keeping a quiet watch on M. Guimet to make sure that he did not slip through our fingers.

On the morning of the third day I was summoned back to the office of the Chief Inspector of Scotland Yard. This was a burly sober Saxon, the exact antithesis of the dapper M. le Préfet, but in his own style no less keen. He said:

"I think I have what you want. As you may know, my men had instructions once before to watch Mr. and Mrs. Dartrey and were familiar with their habits. Now, as then, we found that everybody who visited them was above suspicion. Neither did it yield any results to listen in to their telephone conversations, or to examine the letters they received and sent. This time I put the cleverest female agent I have to watch Mrs. Dartrey, and she has laid bare the lady's simple and ingenious scheme for communicating with her principal in Paris.

"At nine o'clock last night Mrs. Dartrey (my agent close at her heels) dropped in at the Underground station at Sloane Square and used one of the public telephones there. My agent went into the adjoining booth to listen. But she had a difficult task to take down what she heard, for Mrs.

Dartrey spoke a strange sort of gibberish unlike any known language. My agent was able to get it phonetically, chiefly because the person at the other end of Mrs. Dartrey's wire also had trouble, and Mrs. Dartrey was obliged to repeat a good deal.

"The number that Mrs. Dartrey called up proved to be a public house in the East End. A man was waiting there, evidently by prearrangement, to receive her call. He was not known in that public house. The name he gave was Thompson, but of course that signifies nothing. I will furnish you with a description of him. Long before we got there he had his message and was gone, of course; and the message is now undoubtedly on its way to Paris. I judge that he carried it himself, since these people have a wholesome distrust of the post office.

"Now for the message itself. When it was laid before me I judged that it was written in cryptogram, and I handed it over to an expert that we have in such matters. It gave him no great difficulty to decipher it. One of the simplest forms of a cryptogram, it was nevertheless very effective when spoken over the telephone, and none but a person of uncommonly acute hearing could have taken it down. I did not rouse you out of bed when we had succeeded in translating it, because, as you will see from the context, you have plenty of time in which to act.

"Here it is. Some of the words are missing, but the sense is clear. A very simple cryptogram, but there are several arbitrary rules to confuse you. Generally only the initial consonant is transposed, but, in long words, the consonant beginning the middle syllable will be changed also. The letter J is placed before all words beginning with a vowel. Th stands for Sh and vice-versa. Sometimes there are intentional mistakes in grammar. Sometimes, when the jargon was awkward, a word would be spoken straight. And so on.

"Just as a curiosity I will set down a few sentences of the original. When I spoke it over to myself I was astonished that anybody could have taken it down by ear.

Conversation in Sloane Square Station, 9 p.m. August 11. (Taken down by No. 134.)

"Jar voo share?...
"Han voo keer de glain?...
"Rake shis mown...
"Nis deery hopley jis humming ro garris dunmay lext feek. De hame jover fith ker jon pyganric bix feeks jaggo. Sin jin jingnand bince. Thee sit tight jaway sut rimid laycher pot hold weet nater. De det ker jon breet wour mays jago. Rooker (several words missing here) Kadker minner dy glace nast light. Pave jit rooker strong. Pot ker jail jecksited. Font wail jus low." *Et cetera., et cetera.*

The translation follows:

"Are you there?...
"Can you hear me plain?...
"Take this down...
"Miss Mary Copley is coming to Paris on Monday next week. We came over with her on *Gigantic* six weeks ago. Been in England since. She bit right away, but timid nature, got cold feet later." "I" (for the pronoun "I" Mrs. Dartrey

always said "Be" meaning "Me," but I will not so write it every time) "met her on street four days ago. Took her (words missing here) Had her dinner my place last night. Gave it to her strong. Got her all excited. Won't fail us now.

"She is travelling with her parents. Has obtained from them permission to make five days' trip to Paris with supposed woman friend. So she comes alone. No difficulty with money question in this case. She is well off in her own right. Has cabled to her banker to sell certain securities and remit by cable. Carries with her about twenty-five hundred pounds Bank of England notes. We can get more later. Suggest you urge her to return. They are not sailing for America until October.

"This woman does not quite fill your specifications, since she comes of a long-established New England family and looks fairly intelligent. But I assure you she's another fool. I have got her going strong. She is ripe for your dope. Her father inherited money. He's a sort of dilettante scholar; they spend half of every year in Europe. He's a downy bird. Not the sort to make trouble if he got on to anything.

"The girl is thirty-three years old and has already lost whatever looks she may have had. She realizes that she's on the shelf and is desperate. I know her inside out, because I've had to listen to her confidence *ad nauseam.* She has led a society life and was fairly popular during her first season or two, but has seen younger girls supplant her. She's not of an especially amorous disposition, and you can't work that line. But she has a lust of power; it enrages her that her girlhood friends are all able to put it over her with their husbands, their houses, their children, while she is still 'a daughter at home.'

"She had her only serious love affair about five years ago. At that time she became engaged to a young engineer who was building a state road near her home at Pride's Crossing, Mass. But her dearest girl friend took him away from her and married him. This wound has been festering in Miss C's breast ever since. The two have been married long enough now to begin to tire of each other, and Miss C's secret dream is to bring the man to her feet and spurn him. She dreams of breaking up her friend's home and establishing a home of her own. There's your material for you.

"This is probably the last I'll send you this season. Can we meet in the fall? How did the Ellis woman pan out? On the last trip of the *Gigantic* Rosika Storey was aboard, but she never noticed me. The captain has it in for me, though. Next season I think I'd better give the *Gigantic* the go-by. How about the big ships of the French line and the Dutch line? We've never tried to work them. We've had a first-rate season. Can't you raise the ante a little? The expenses are terrific, and L. is restive. Another thousand or two would soothe him. Come across, like a good fellow.

"Miss Copley is booked by the Folkestone-Boulogue route, Monday morning. I have recommended her to the Hôtel Wagram, Paris. I don't doubt but you will see her within an hour of her arrival."

I PINNED THIS precious document to my underclothing and contrived to catch the eleven o'clock express from Victoria via the fashionable Dover-Calais route. I reached Paris in time to have dinner with my dear mistress at Voisin's, a delightful old-fashioned restaurant that she affected.

Between courses she smoked and regarded the paper

with a half-smile. "We did well to wait for this," she said. "They can hardly escape us now."

"How will you proceed?" I asked.

"Well, on Monday afternoon, with the assistance of M. le Préfet, we must kidnap this Miss Copley upon her arrival at the Hôtel Wagram and detain her long enough for you to go call on M. Guimet in her name."

This was the most important task I had ever been given, and my heart was proud.

"Our principal difficulty," she went on teasingly, "is that you have not lost your looks, my Bella."

I blushed.

"However, M. le Préfet must certainly have artists in make-up on his staff. It ought not to be hard to endow you with a bad complexion and a wig of lifeless hair. Your clothes I will see to myself. Fortunately Mrs. Dartrey does not describe her appearance, so we have a free hand... Mrs. Dartrey says she looks intelligent but is a fool. That's all right. Between now and Monday I must drill you in acting the fool. Which sort will you choose to be, a dumb fool or a talkative fool?"

"Oh, a dumb fool," I said. "I might run out of talk at the critical moment."

"Very good. A dumb fool very often has a suspicious and pathetic expression—like this."

She exaggerated, of course, and it set me off on a peal of laughter. But I was obliged to practise the look until she expressed herself as satisfied.

"The way to be sure of holding that all the time you are in his place," Mme. Storey continued, "is for you to keep repeating to yourself: 'I am a fool; I am a fool; I am a poor dumb fool!'… Look around the restaurant and repeat that to yourself… Excellent!

"Let your body slump a little and practise shambling in your walk," she went on. "Infallible indications of a fool. And make out that you do not understand what he says to you. Frequently ask him with a dense look to repeat his words. All this will come to you naturally if you keep assuring yourself that you are a fool… Another thing that I've noticed about a fool is she nearly always has some senseless tags of speech that she works in and out of season. I used to know a girl who was perfectly unable to say plain yes or no. It was always, 'Yes, my soul,' and 'No, my father.'… This *riz de veau béchamel* is good, isn't it?"

"Yes, my soul," I murmured.

"Splendid!"

7

MME. STOREY STILL insisted that this was my case, and I was assigned to go to the Wagram on Monday afternoon to apprehend Miss Copley. My mistress had become involved in a whirl of gaieties and had engagements at all hours, but she expected to be at the Préfecture later, to assist in questioning the woman. The boat train was due in Paris about four, and I was in the foyer of the hotel at that hour. The Wagram is one of the several elegant places on the Rue de Rivoli that cater almost exclusively to Americans. I identified myself to the management, so that I was allowed to stand by the desk of the bureau without question. I had the assistance of an *agent de police* in plain clothes, but I left him out on the pavement.

Several guests arrived at once from the Gare du Nord. I watched their hands as they wrote their names in the book. When I saw "Miss Mary Copley" in a cultivated hand, I looked eagerly in the face of the writer. She was the sort of person that one hesitates whether to call a girl or a woman. She no doubt thought of herself as a girl and dressed the part, but Time had already unkindly marked her face with lines and hollows. She was well enough dressed, but clothes couldn't do much for her, and evidently, in her respectable Boston set, make-up was still considered bad form. In all she was a most ordinary-looking person, dull-coloured and repressed. One would never have picked her out as a likely victim of an International swindle.

She was assigned to a room. As she proceeded toward the lift I intercepted her. "May I speak with you a moment?" I asked.

She looked at me in great astonishment; but there was nothing in my appearance to cause her any especial alarm. "Why—what is it?" she asked.

I drew her out of hearing of the boy who had her valise. "I have to ask you to come with me to the Préfecture de Police for a little while," I said.

Naturally the poor woman was shocked. "But what—but why—" she stammered. "What does this mean?"

"Do not distress yourself," I said soothingly. "You are not under arrest, of course. M. le Préfet wishes to ask you a few questions concerning the reason for your visit to Paris."

She had turned as white as paper and was shaking uncontrollably. Heaven knows I would have reassured her if I could. "I have no reason for coming," she said, "except to look about and—and make a few purchases."

"Then come and explain that to him," I said soothingly. I didn't want to become involved in an argument with her there in the foyer.

"I haven't a friend in Paris!" she murmured wildly. "What am I to do? What am I to do?"

"I am an American woman, like yourself," I said. "I will see that your interests are safeguarded. No one will harm you; we wish to save you from harm."

"I won't go with you," she said hysterically. "Although I am in a foreign city, I suppose I have some rights. I have done nothing. I will send to the American Embassy for help. My people are known there. I won't go."

"You wouldn't like your people to know why you came to Paris, would you?" I said at a venture.

It was cruel, I suppose. She looked at me white and horror-stricken. "I—I don't understand you," she faltered.

"Come," I said soothingly. "I have an agent of the police outside. Don't force me to call him in and make a scene here. Come quietly, and you'll be back here in an hour, and nobody the wiser."

"I don't know you," she said. "You may be—"

"Ask at the desk," I said.

She did so. By this time all the other arriving guests had gone to their rooms.

The manager said with apologetic shrugs and bows: "This lady bears a letter from M. le Préfet de Police. She has the power to exact what she wishes."

Miss Copley gave in. I made her put her money in the hotel safe. She followed me out on the sidewalk with hanging head. I hailed the first passing cab, and we got in. When the *agent de police* climbed after us, she shuddered.

We turned around in the street and, darting under the archway of the Louvre, whirled across the Place du Carrousel at the usual breakneck speed of Paris taxis.

"Can't you tell me what this means?" said Miss Copley.

"I have told you," I said.

"Do you know yourself what is behind it?"

"Yes," I said, "but I am not the person to question you."

"You must see how you are tormenting me."

"Well, I can tell you this," I said. "You appear to have

fallen into the hands of dangerous sharpers. I refer to Mrs. Dartrey and the man Guimet you were on your way to see."

She looked at me in extreme horror. "Sharpers!" she gasped. "Oh!... *Oh-h!*" Then she quickly averted her face from me. Presently she said in a muffled voice: "There must be some mistake. I don't know any such people."

I let it go at that. "You ought to be thankful to us for saving you your money," I said. "Ten thousand dollars is a lot to lose."

She asked one more question as we crossed the bridge. "If you are an American, how do you come to be working for the Paris police?"

"I do not," I said. "My employer is Madame Rosika Storey of New York. Have you ever heard of her?"

She hesitated, and I saw that my mistress's name *was* familiar to her. "You will see her directly," I said. "She is working with M. le Préfet on this case."

Three minutes later we were in the office of M. le Préfet. Mme. Storey was already there. Miss Copley was in a pitiable state of nerves; shaking incontrollably; biting her lips.

"Cheer up!" said Mme. Storey kindly. "No danger threatens you now. You are in the hands of your friends." In order to give the girl time to collect herself, she related to M. le Préfet an amusing passage that she had had with a taxi driver on the way to his office.

Finally she said to me, "You have explained the situation to Miss Copley?"

I nodded.

"I don't understand what it is all about," cried Miss Copley. "I don't know what you want of me. There must be some mistake."

"We want you to help us bring these sharpers to book," said Mme. Storey.

"*I* help you!" cried the girl hysterically. "*I* testify against them! It will all be in the newspapers. I should be disgraced. My parents—my parents—"

"Not at all," said Mme. Storey. "I think I may promise you that you will be exhibited in an entirely favourable light. It will be shown that you acted as you did simply to save other women. Is it not so, M. le Préfet?"

"Assuredly, *madame*."

But terror turned the girl absolutely stubborn. "I know nothing! I know nothing!" she repeated. "There is some mistake. You have got hold of the wrong person!"

".Listen," said Mme. Storey. She began to read Mrs. Dartrey's communication to M. Guimet.

Midway, the girl stiffened out in her chair, her eyeballs rolled up, and she began to shriek in pure hysterics. One hardly looked for that in the New England type. But under that thin veneer she was no different from another foolish woman.

M. le Préfet shrugged expressively and pressed a button on his desk. He said something in French which one might translate as:

"Hysterics is a cornered woman's last resort."

What we would call a police matron entered the room. At a nod from M. le Préfet she took hold of Miss Copley's arm and led her away.

"We will proceed without her," said Mme. Storey.

HALF AN HOUR later, in a sort of dressing room at the Préfecture, I surveyed myself in a long mirror with some astonishment. There was a retired actor attached to the police in the capacity of make-up man, a jolly old man, and he, in consultation with Mme. Storey, had transformed me beyond recognition. I did not of course resemble Miss Copley, but I exactly reproduced her type. I was the slightly faded girl; the woman who was not quite a woman.

"Turn around and let me look at you," said Mme. Storey.

I whispered to myself: I have been taught to carry myself with a certain assurance, but at heart I am a fool; a hysterical fool. I turned around.

"Admirable!" said Mme. Storey with a smile. "Hold that look!"

We proceeded down to the entrance together, and she whispered my final instructions to me.

"You have ten thousand dollars in marked bills. Your grand object is to get Guimet to take it from you. You will find an *agent de police* in the dress of a street idler loafing at the entrance to the courtyard of the house. There are other agents in the neighbourhood. Once Guimet has taken the money, you may come out and order his arrest. Should any accident happen, should you be in any sort of danger, you may summon the police by blowing upon the whistle which has been furnished you."

"My greatest difficulty will be to open the conversation with Guimet," I said. "I shall have to find out exactly what Miss Copley was to come to him for."

"Well—let us say that *monsieur* possesses the secret of the charm of women," said Mme. Storey with a subtle smile. "That is what you are willing to pay ten thousand dollars for."

"So that's it!" I said.

"How could it be anything else?" said Mme. Storey.

"Consider the style of the talk of the decoy—that is to say Mrs. Dartrey. Consider the actions of Mrs. Ellis, who thought, poor soul, that she had purchased the secret, until her husband turned from her in disgust. Consider what Mrs. Dartrey said to Guimet concerning this last victim."

We had arrived at the door.

"*Au revoir,* and good luck!" said Mme. Storey.

8

MY ROUTE LAY eastward along the unfashionable part
of the Rue de Rivoli and its continuation, the Rue St.
Antoine, which is like Fourteenth Street, New York. The
Rue des Tournelles was the last turning to the left before
you reached the Place de la Bastille. Here you plunged at
once into the Seventeenth Century. It was the fashionable quarter in those days; now it is somewhat miscellaneous. The houses were so plain and well built they scarcely
looked ancient, but only solid and deadly respectable. Each
one of the old mansions was entered through an archway
leading to a courtyard, in which you caught glimpses of
beautiful fountains. My destination, number —, seemed
to be one of the finest houses in the street. The courtyard
was still paved with the original cobblestones in which the
iron-shod wheels of the old coaches had left deep ruts. I
saw my supposed idler lounging outside the archway.

As in all Paris houses, you rang a bell, and the concierge
poked her head out of the window in the entry and inquired
your business. "Monsieur Guimet," said I. *"Premier étage,"*
said she, with an inquisitive and comprehensive survey of
my person, and pulled a wire which was connected with
the latch of the door.

I mounted the noble old stairway with a fast-beating
heart. There were several doors opening on the first land-

ing, and I knocked on one at random. It was the wrong one; another door was opened by a very neat old woman who looked like a peasant. She looked me over in no friendly fashion and asked me curtly what I wanted.

"Monsieur Guimet," I said. I could not conceal my breathlessness, but that, of course, was quite in character.

"You can't see him," she said bluntly. "He's busy."

"Can't I wait?" I asked.

"That won't do you any good. He is always busy."

I was dismayed. Could there have been any slip-up in our plans? I wondered. Had he been warned against me? "But—but—" I faltered—"I have come such a long way to see *monsieur*. All the way from England."

"He didn't ask you to come, did he?" she said rudely.

It occurred to me that the best way to find out if they suspected me would be to make believe to be discouraged, so I half turned from the door with a crushed air.

The woman immediately said: "Well, I'll take your name to him, but he never sees ladies when he's busy."

I gave her my supposed name, and she left me standing out on the landing. My heart was light again, for I was sure that this blunt reception was merely part of a clever bluff.

The old woman presently returned with a slightly less forbidding expression. "*Monsieur* says he will see you since you have come so far," she said.

I stepped into a beautiful octagonal foyer panelled with velvety walnut which had never been desecrated by varnish. The little room was quite bare. Crossing it, we entered a noble salon which occupied the whole of that side of the building and looked down into the courtyard. This room had been designed for splendid entertainments, but was now filled from end to end with scientific instruments and chemical apparatus, all very bare and workmanlike. Three or four linen-coated students bent over the tables in deep concentration or manipulated the instruments. The lovely old painted ceiling of Venuses and cupids looked down very strangely on this scene.

My guide, turning to the right, led me through half this room, then, with another turn to the right, through a small library, or a storehouse of scientific books. Finally, with still another half turn, she opened a door and allowed me to pass her into another beautiful little panelled room. Now, my sense of direction is excellent, and I immediately realized that this little room had its own door on the foyer, and I had been led all the way around merely for the purpose of impressing me.

This was the cabinet of the master. My first impression was of a withered little man in a black skullcap. He was seated at a table with a pair of calipers in his hand, tracing a mysterious design on a large sheet of Whatman paper. He did not look up at my entrance, and I had ample opportunity to look about me. The single window in the room looked toward a narrower courtyard in the rear. This room, too, was filled with scientific apparatus whose uses I could only guess at; mere stage settings, I judged, since he already had a fully equipped laboratory outside.

He raised his head, and I saw a handsome, hawklike old face with a pair of dark, still youthful eyes. He burst out at me surprisingly in French; very good French too; good enough to have deceived my ears.

"*Madame*, I am a serious man, a scientist! I am engaged in deep researches for the good of humanity. Must my work be interrupted by the knocking of light-minded women at my door?"

Behind the assumed anger there was the hint of a twinkle in his eyes, which suggested that he appreciated the joke of the situation. Evidently this man was a rogue out of the sheer love of roguery. It rendered him insidiously attractive. But of course I had to suppress the answering grin that pulled at my lips. A foolish woman like Miss Copley would have been terrified by his outburst. I tried to make myself look senseless with terror.

"I didn't know," I stammered. "Excuse me—I was led to suppose—I thought—"

"Speak English," he said. "I understand it."

The instant he said it, I knew he was my own countryman. There was an overtone that suggested the streets of New York; the merest hint of what used to be called a Bowery accent but is now universal from Coney Island to Clason's Point.

"I am very sorry to have disturbed you," I said, "but—"

"What do you want of me?" he demanded.

I supposed that Miss Copley and the others would have been a good deal confused here. "I understand," I stammered, "that is I have been told by a lady—that you have something—a secret—"

"Please speak out, *madame*. My time is valuable."

"The charm of women," I mumbled.

He shrugged magnificently; hands, arms, shoulders, head, eyebrows, all had a part in it. "What folly! There is no panacea for that!" He made believe to return to his work.

I suspected that a stupid woman such as I was portraying

would be dogged enough in the pursuit of her own ends, so I sat tight.

"Well, why don't you go?" he said, looking up.

"I am sure there is no mistake," I said. "Mrs. Dartrey told me—"

"I know no such person."

"Oh, I suppose you have forgotten her. But she has been to you. You gave her something—"

"My dear *madame,*" he said impatiently, "this is unworthy of the attention of a scientific man. What is this charm of women that you set such a store by? Merely a disturbing element in life. It distracts men from their serious work and sets them flying at each other's throats. It is responsible for all the follies and crimes and misfortunes of humanity! Why should I spread that which had much better be wiped out and destroyed?"

Ah, the clever rascal! While he was apparently disparaging what I wanted, he was really rendering it twice as desirable.

I sat on in dumb obstinacy.

"It is useless for you to remain," he said, fussing among the objects on his desk.

"I am prepared to pay well for it," I murmured.

"What, *madame!*" he cried, furiously indignant "Do you take me for a marketman? Or a peddler of love philtres? Please leave me!"

Somewhere about this point Miss Copley, I fancied, would have begun to cry. I couldn't actually make the tears come, but I wrinkled up my face as if they were near.

M. Guimet jumped up with a distracted gesture. I saw that he was a short man who had been powerful in youth.

"Ah, *mon Dieu!*" he cried. "Am I to be treated to a display of emotion now? You have destroyed my whole day for me! I wish to Heaven there were no such thing as the charm of women!"

This was a subtle admission, you see. I pressed my handkerchief to my eyes and made my shoulders shake. "I wanted it so badly!" I murmured with a piteous catch in my breath. "I have come so far—"

M. Guimet walked to and fro, snorting.

Finally he came to a stand. "Well, since you have ruined my day anyhow, I may as well tell you," he said. "I do possess such a secret, but I am obliged to deny it like an infection of leprosy or I should be swamped, *swamped* by your scatter-brained sex."

I let the sun break through my grief. "And you will give it to me!" I said, clasping my hands.

"Wait a minute!" he said, holding up his hand. "I should have destroyed the recipe long ago and forgotten it were it not that my serious experiments are so frightfully expensive. Of course, I enjoy grants from the government, but it is not enough. And once or twice in the past I have sold my secret to a rich woman in order to enable me to carry on my great work for La France!"

I wish you could have seen the noble attitude he struck for La France—this denizen of the Tenderloin district, or I missed my guess.

"Is the hint sufficient for you, *madame?* If you are not a rich woman, go away, for the love of God, and leave me to my work."

"I'm not exactly rich," I said, "but I can pay well. How much will it be?"

He waved his hands violently. "Don't talk to me of money!" he cried with tears in his voice. "I am no chafferer, I am a scientist. If you are rich, give largely to my work. I assure you I won't count it."

This was magnificent but vague. "I have the money with me," I said, raising my handbag.

"I won't take it! I won't take it!" he said. "I am an honest man. I insist that you sample my recipe first. The effect, I may say, is instantaneous. If you are satisfied, you may come back to-morrow for a supply."

He opened a wall cupboard, and I beheld rows of bottles containing diverse coloured liquors and powders with Latin labels. I have no Latin, but if I had, I doubt if I could have made much of those labels. He impressively set out a number of these bottles on his desk and brought a graduated glass and a chemist's scales contained in a glass case, that not even a grain of dust might disturb its delicate balance. Then he sat down and proceeded to measure and weigh with the nicest care; holding up the graduated glass to the light, and squinting at it exactly as you see in the pictures of the old alchemists.

An ounce of this liquid; a few drops of that; a gramme of an odd-coloured red powder. As the various bottles were uncorked, different pungent and delicious perfumes filled the room. Mme. Storey, with her marvellous sense of smell, would probably have recognized them all; but I only got a generally alcoholic effect and one particular perfume that I guessed to be nothing but *sirop de grenadine.* All this he put in a curious antique bottle, holding something less than a pint.

While he mixed, he conversed with the greatest affability. His bearlike reception of me in the beginning had evidently been designed only to show up his present charming manners by force of contrast. It is an old trick. In this he overreached himself a little; for there was more than a trace of oiliness in him now that betrayed the sharper. But, of course, since he designed to deal with fools only, he felt that he did not have to be too particular.

"Do you know whose house this was?" he asked me. "It is quite famous."

"No," said I.

"The marvellous Ninon de l'Enclos lived here during the late Seventeenth Century. These very rooms, in fact, were hers."

"I've heard of her," said I.

"Who has not heard of her? She was not, perhaps, a paragon of virtue" (an expressive shrug here), "but we must not be censorious. A matchless woman! At ninety years old men fell at her feet. In the history of the world there was never another like her. What is still more remarkable, they say she was not beautiful. She had wit; she had learning; above all, she had charm. Think of a woman who had for lovers in succession such men as de Coligny, D'Estrées, La Rochefoucauld, Condé, St. Evremond. They speak of Voltaire too, though he was but a lad when she was old. Anne of Austria, the great queen herself, was no match for Ninon de l'Enclos, and strove to combat her influence in vain. They say that this little room was her own private cabinet. If you close your eyes perhaps you can feel that exquisite presence here still.

"Of course, I did not engage these rooms for that reason, but because the salon outside, with its good light, made such an admirable laboratory, and this little room a quiet study for myself. When I came here, the panelling of this room was somewhat in disrepair, and in examining it with a view to its restoration I discovered a little iron box hidden in the wall. I forced its lock myself, and inside I found a single scrap of parchment, upon which was engrossed in a crabbed Seventeenth Century hand a formula. With my knowledge of chemistry I instantly recognized the purport of this formula. It was thus, *madame,* that I stumbled on the secret of the great Ninon de l'Enclos's imperishable charm!"

I gazed at the man in sheer admiration of his cleverness. It was no wonder that poor silly women fell into his toils. The contest was too unequal.

"Not altogether a secret," he went on. "Certain elements of the preparation are known to all Frenchwomen, and that is why they are more charming than the women of other races. They are not more beautiful, as you can see for yourself. The women of your glorious young country far surpass them in looks. But they have charm.

"And they know but one element, perhaps; two at the most. The great Ninon combined them all. Where she got her knowledge from I cannot tell you. She was a learned woman for that day, but I think it more likely that some unknown chemist who loved her devoted his whole life to the search. What a gift that was to lay at the feet of one's beloved!

"In the Seventeenth Century the science of chemistry was in its infancy. When I read the recipe with my knowledge of the great discoveries that have been made since, I instantly saw how it might be made a hundred times more potent. We have marvellous essences at our command that they never dreamed of. This tincture, for instance…"

He held up a bottle containing a fluid of a strange bright orange colour.

"This bottle contains the wherewithal to drive all Paris mad. But the single drop that, as you may have observed, I allowed to fall into the mixture is sufficient to change the colour of your whole existence, Madame. I confess I was startled by the results of my experiments. To be in the possession of so dangerous a power may well frighten an honest man and render him humble. I have kept it a secret so far as I have been able, and when I die it will die with me."

He played his part to perfection. A little too perfectly, if anything. A sincere man would not have been so obviously pleased with himself.

"Charm is really no more than health," he went on. "By that I mean *perfect* health. There is not one person in ten thousand who knows the feeling of perfect health: the ability to realize and enjoy one's faculties to the full! Ah! the unreasoning joy of the light heart; the sparkling eye, the springing step; the power to command all hearts!"

By this time the elixir was ready. He filled a tiny liqueur glass with the dark liquid and signified that I was to drink it. I hesitated for the fraction of a second; the ugly little thought like a snake darted through my mind: Suppose this gentleman adds murder to his other accomplishments? Observing my hesitation, he picked up the glass and tossed off the contents.

"I like the taste," he said, "but it has no effect on me. It acts only on the more delicate feminine organization… It is just as well," he added with a roguish smile; "I could not afford to be charming. I am too busy."

He filled another tiny glass, and I drank it. It *was* pleasant, and one's gullet tingled as it went down. I was reminded of drinking *fine à l'eau* with poor Mrs. Ellis a few days before. In short, the elixir was nothing more nor less than fine brandy with various flavouring extracts added. A lovely glow spread through my veins. I could very easily imagine that I was becoming charming.

We parted in the greatest friendliness.

"Until to-morrow," said M. Guimet.

"I shall be here early," I warned him.

"It is all one to me," he said with a shrug. "I am at work early and late."

"And the money?" I said. I felt sure Miss Copley would have said something about it.

"Oh, bring all you have," he said with a superb carelessness.

On my way out of the building the disguised police agent was still lounging in the archway. As I passed him without making any sign, he understood there was nothing doing that day. I did not see what became of him. There were no cabs in that quiet street, and I made my way toward the Rue St. Antoine.

I had not gone far when I met a good-looking young Frenchman with an adventurous eye—rather a flash type. He smiled at me in a certain way; half insinuating, half insolent, and raised his hat. Now this sort of thing never happens to me, and I got a great start. The wild thought came to me that perhaps there *was* something in the elixir; maybe I was turning into a charmer!

But sober sense instantly corrected it. That was what that poor foolish Mrs. Ellis had thought, of course. It explained her half-insane actions during the afternoon we had spent together. The flash young man was only a plant—the cleverest bit of business of all in this elaborate tragi-comedy. I hurried on, looking scared and pleased, as I fancied Miss Copley might have looked.

At the corner I had to wait for a moment. He came up close and whispered some inanity in my ear: "Don't be in such a hurry."

I stared straight ahead. It was fearfully exciting and not exactly unpleasant. I still had a merry jingle in my veins from the brandy.

"May I come with you?" he asked. "You are so nice."

A taxi drew up at the curb and I sprang in, pulling the door after me without letting it out of my hand. "Drive on," I said breathlessly to the driver. "Anywhere."

And this was not all. I had not driven but a block or two when I saw a man in a cab going the other way making signals to me. This was quite a distinguished-looking person with a flower in his buttonhole. He leaned out of his cab smiling and bowing repeatedly. I looked at him stonily. Glancing back, I saw that he had ordered his driver to turn around. My chauffeur saw it too, and asked me with a grin if he should stop.

"Certainly not!" I said. "Drive me to the Hôtel Wagram."

This coincided with an incident that Mrs. Ellis had told me of.

From the hotel I telephoned a brief account of what had occurred to M. le Préfet, also to Mme. Storey, who had told me that I would find her at the house of a certain friend at that hour.

9

THE NECESSARY DELAY in arresting M. Guimet put M. le Préfet in somewhat of a quandary concerning Miss Copley. He had no legal right to lock her up overnight, and he had every official person's dread of international complications. On the other hand, if he let her go, such was her terror of any exposure, he was sure she would attempt to put the man on his guard.

M. le Préfet solved the problem by having Miss Copley put on the boat train for England. Even so, she might telegraph to M. Guimet, but it was easy for the police to intercept telegrams. As a matter of fact, she did telegraph. She must also have telegraphed to Mrs. Dartrey, for later in the night a wire was intercepted from England in their peculiar code, which we had no difficulty in translating as:

"Beat it quick."

All this made us anxious. I returned to M. Guimet's at nine-thirty next morning, which was as early as I dared risk it. To have called earlier would, in itself, have made that canny gentleman suspicious, I feared. I had my police whistle; and I was now furnished in addition with an automatic pistol in case of an emergency. I devoutly prayed that I might not have to use it.

This morning I was shown into M. Guimet's cabinet without any parley. The white-coated students were already at work in the big laboratory. What pains they all took to give verisimilitude to their game. In a way of speaking, it deserved to succeed.

M. Guimet appeared to rouse himself from his computations with difficulty. This bit of comedy reassured me. Evidently he had not as yet taken any alarm. Our interview was brief, for all he wanted now was the money, and all I wanted was for him to take it.

I handed over the fat packet of crisp white English notes. Notwithstanding his pretended indifference to money, he counted it with care.

"This will not carry my work very far," he said with a disappointed air.

For an instant I was genuinely terrified lest he might be going to hand it back. "It is all I have," I faltered.

"Oh, well," he said with a shrug; and I breathed more freely.

He threw back a panel in the wall revealing a little safe behind it. While he manipulated the combination he said:

"This is where I found the formula. I had the modern safe put in."

He stood in front of the safe while it was open, and I could not see what the contents might be. He put in the money I had given him, closed the door, and twirled the combination. Meanwhile, I took possession of the bottle.

This concluded our business, but such was my gentleman's love of histrionics that he threw in a little extra for good measure. Do you get the picture? The old man, but still handsome and dangerous-looking—except for his snuffy clothes, he did not at all resemble the scientist he was supposed to be—standing on the other side of his table, declaiming with graceful gestures.

"I need not ask you if you are satisfied with my cordial, since you are here. Never exceed the dose that I gave you yesterday, and do not take it more than once a day. I feel a change in you this morning, but that is not for me to say. I would rather have others tell you. I hope that I may be the means of bringing a great happiness into your life. One can see that you have found life disappointing hitherto— owing to the meanness and falsity of others. Well, hereafter you will not be dependent on others. You will be the sun from which they receive their rays.

"Ah, my dear *madame!* the possession of such a secret entails a heavy responsibility upon me. I would like to publish it broadcast for the benefit of womankind. But it does not seem fair to do so unless I could at the same time furnish a corresponding stimulus to men. I am a man. I cannot betray my own sex. Our ascendency is already seriously threatened. Where would men be if I put such a weapon into the hands of women?"

It was deliciously comic. I stored up every word, with a view to recounting it to my mistress later. I wondered what this man's life history must have been. A magnificent physical specimen in his youth, women must have been mad about him. Even in his old age he enjoyed life and was still not unattractive. What cleverness and humour! It was rather sad to see it devoted to crooked ends.

He was interrupted by the sound of voices somewhere near. Suddenly a door which had not been opened before banged in and a woman entered. It was the door I had marked which opened direct on the foyer. The woman was a middle-aged *bourgeoise* of whom one sees millions in Paris, making their thrifty purchases in the small shops. She wore a preposterous hat, a black "fringe," and a sober black dress over an old-fashioned corset which featured the bust. For the moment M. Guimet was as much astonished by her entrance as I was; but when she spoke we both recognized her.

"That woman is a bull!" she said, not loud, in English.

It was Mrs. Dartrey, marvellously disguised.

Things happened very swiftly after that. I whipped out my whistle and put it to my lips, but the two of them leaped on me, and I never got a sound out. The sturdy old servant, too, was there to help them. I was no match against the three of them. In not very many seconds my wrists and ankles were immovably bound with thongs of rag and my mouth gagged. One of the women must have torn off part of her clothing to furnish my bonds. They were very quiet about it. Evidently the students in the front room were not to be alarmed.

They flung me into a chair. The tears of bitter mortification sprang to my eyes, seeing all my work about to go for nothing. The biggest job I had ever undertaken. But how did they expect to get out of the house, I wondered. I was not entirely without hope.

How cool and swift they were in all their movements! Not much time wasted in recriminations. Guimet flung open the door of the wall cupboard as if to make a clean sweep of its contents.

"Let be," said Mrs. Dartrey. "The courtyard is full of police. If this woman does not come out directly, they'll come after her. How could you be so careless?"

"I had no reason to suspect danger," said Gilbert. "Who gave you the tip?"

"The real Miss Copley. The police sent her back to England last evening. She telegraphed me from Pontoise. I wired you."

"I didn't get it."

"Of course you didn't… Be quick."

"I will only wait for the money. We must have that."

"Be careful of the money she gave you. It is certainly marked."

"It would be still more incriminating to leave it behind, then. We'll throw it down a sewer."

"Is the way out clear?"

"You may be damn sure it's clear, my dear. There are not six men in Paris know of that passage, and they are archaeologists!"

My heart went down.

While they threw their swift sentences back and forth, the man was busy fetching a valise and opening the safe. The woman stood beside him while he worked at it. Apparently they forgot that I could hear—or else they didn't care.

"I went right out to Croydon to the aviation field," said Mrs. Dartrey. "But of course I couldn't persuade anybody to take the air until daybreak. Cost me two hundred pounds. I was in Paris by seven o'clock, but when I got here I found the police watching. I had to go away again and get this disguise."

"You are as wonderful as ever, my dear… Do you know this woman?"

"Hell, yes! She crossed on the *Gigantic.*"

"Why didn't you tip me off?"

"I didn't know she was after us… But at least I could see she wasn't a prospect, if you couldn't. She got nothing out of me."

"Don't rub it in, my angel… Who is she working for?"

"I don't know. The captain, maybe. I told you he had it in for me."

There was heard a loud, official knock-knock-knock on the entrance door.

"Come on!" said Mrs. Dartrey.

Guimet flung the safe door shut, and shot the panel across. To the old servant he said:

"Marthe, you remain. You know nothing. You are safe."

She nodded stolidly.

There was a third door in the little room. Guimet ran to it and flung it open. I had a glimpse of a plainly furnished bedroom on the other side. Mrs. Dartrey passed through the door first. Guimet lingered long enough to say to me with a devil-may-care grin:

"Au revoir, Red-hair! At any rate, there's one good jag in that bottle!"

They disappeared. I could not see what became of them in the little bedroom. My heart was full of a bitter, bitter chagrin thus to see him get away with a jest on his lips.

But presently the two of them came tumbling back across the bedroom, and into the room where I was. Gone was her cool, assured air, and the grin wiped off his lips. They were no more then than any two white-faced, hunted creatures. At the same moment we heard the entrance door smash in, and they hung in the middle of the room, their eyes darting wildly this way and that, like those of trapped animals. There were the sounds of many people in the foyer, and they ran out in the other direction through the book room. The old servant continued to stand stolidly by the window.

Then, sauntering through the bedroom with her most elegant air and into the cabinet came Mme. Storey; smiling and beautifully dressed; taking everything in with her amused eyes. A *gendarme* followed at her heels. She seemed like a beautiful apparition to me. I simply could not believe my eyes. It was the greatest surprise she has ever given me; and she has given me many.

At the sight of my plight, her face filled with concern. "Ah, my poor Bella!" she murmured, and motioned quickly to the *gendarme*.

He made haste to cut me free.

It seemed by this time as if the house was filled with police. They came in by every door. Guimet and Mrs. Dartrey were thrust back into the room from the book room.

"Ah!" cried Mme. Storey gaily: "Mr. Smoke Lassen, after all these years! What an unexpected pleasure!… And Miss Breese, I believe. We have never met, but I have often heard of you. I hardly expected to have the luck of finding you in Paris!"

The man looked at Mme. Storey with a face of unspeakable disgust. "Damn it all!" he cried fervently. "Is there no place on earth where I can escape the woman!"

Mrs. Dartrey said never a word.

They were led away by the police, and that about finishes my story.

I was keen to hear the explanation of Mme. Storey's magical appearance on the scene.

"No magic in it, my Bella," said she. "I dined last night with some French friends. Among the guests was a famous archaeologist, whose hobby is old Paris. I asked him about Mademoiselle Ninon de l'Enclos, and I immediately got what we would call at home an earful. In France the memory of the fair, frail Ninon is still cherished by every *homme d'esprit.* It appeared that among the treasures of my friend's collection were the memoirs in manuscript of a certain gallant of that day, who signed himself merely: Le Chevalier Sansregret. There's a pseudonym for you!

"My friend insisted, seeing how interested I was, upon driving around by his rooms on my way home. There he got the precious manuscript, which has never been published, and gave it to me to read. I read it in bed this morning while I was having coffee. A highly diverting tale. It appeared that Monsieur Sansregret was a very dear friend of Mademoiselle Ninon's, but for some reason or another he could not be acknowledged by her. Perhaps he was poor but charming. So he visited her by means of a secret passage which opened on a tiny street behind her house, called the Rue de Beausire. It is still there, and it is still called the street of the Fine Gentleman, though it is only a few hundred feet long.

"It instantly occurred to me that the passage might be there too, and that indeed it might have had something to do with the so-called M. Guimet's taking this house. It was then just about the time that you were due to arrive here. So I jumped out of bed, flung on a few clothes, telephoned to M. le Préfet for a *gendarme,* and hustled across Paris in a taxi.

"The passage had been particularly described in the

manuscript, and after a bit of a search we found it. And indeed we met Smoke Lassen and Breezy Tricks coming out of it. So there you are."

The man and the woman were subsequently tried and convicted under the French laws and sentenced to prison for long terms. I understand that in France there is less chance than with us of their being released before the expiration of their sentences. Well, I was genuinely sorry to see them go. They were a clever and amusing pair, and those qualities are not so abundant in a dull world that we can afford to lock them up. But as Mme. Storey said, what is one to do when we have such a plenitude of fools?

Lionel Dartrey was arrested in England; but nothing could be proved against him. However, he was punished too, even more severely perhaps than the others, for he was immediately cast out of the fashionable world which was everything to him.

The source of the Dartreys' munificent income was revealed. Lassen purchased the American securities in Mrs. Dartrey's name and forced her to endorse the certificates in blank. As long as she played the game he allowed the dividends to be paid to her, but he held the endorsed certificate, and if she had ever kicked over the traces, all he had to do was to have the stock transferred.

In the fall Mme. Storey and I returned to America on the *Gigantic,* and I may say the ship was ours!

THE UNDER DOGS

1

THE ANONYMOUS LETTER

THE TERESA DE GUION case, owing to the extraordinary prominence of the persons concerned, raised Mme. Storey to the very pinnacle of her fame; and she (as well as myself in my humbler capacity) had to pay the penalty of the attendant publicity. All day long our offices were thronged by the most diverse collection of human beings, ranging from bank presidents and society leaders all the way down to the cranks and semi-lunatics that make themselves known at such a time.

These people made the oddest demands upon my mistress; or requests for her aid; or appeals to her sympathy. Some wanted to divorce their mates; others to win back an erring husband or wife. Many persons, otherwise sane, firmly believed that they were being persecuted by an unknown enemy; others seemed to fancy that my mistress was a sort of soothsayer with magical powers. Still others, and this was the most numerous class of all, had not the shadow of an excuse for troubling us, except the desire to edge into the limelight that was beating so fiercely on Mme. Storey. Such were the hostesses who wished to ask her to dinner; and the gentlemen who, roused by the

extraordinary beauty of her published photographs, desired to ask her to dinners of another sort.

In order to protect my mistress, I was obliged to lock the door between my office and hers, and communicate with her over the extension 'phone. When I had to see her, I went around through the hall and the middle room. It was all very exciting, but it was wearing too. Amongst all this mob of suitors there was scarcely one who was entitled to serious consideration.

Those who were unable to come to our offices, wrote. Every day I had a stack of letters a foot high to open. It was a rule of the office that all letters must be read and answered—once. Of course, when silly people continued to write after they had received a proper answer, their letters went into the waste paper basket. The matter of these letters, I need hardly say, was even wilder than the preferred requests of those who called.

One morning there was an anonymous letter in the mail, which was rather curiously worded. I paid little attention to it at first, because I have a constitutional prejudice against anonymous letters. However, I laid it on Mme. Storey's desk amongst the others.

You can never forecast what she is going to do. Of all the scores of letters that day, it was the anonymous letter which attracted her attention.

We had a fairly quiet hour between twelve and one, and I was seated at her desk taking dictation. She picked up the letter in question, and studied it with narrowed eyes. In the other hand she had the inevitable cigarette.

"There's something about this…" she murmured.

"It's anonymous!" I said scornfully.

"Even so… An anonymous letter is only contemptible when it seeks to administer a stab in the back. This doesn't… Listen…"

When she read it, her warm, slow voice made me feel what there was in it.

DEAR MME STOREY:

Teresa de Guion deserved all she got. It did my heart good to see that high society dame yanked down from her perch. She deserves to get it harder than poor devils who have to go crooked to live. Say, it was fine the way you brought it home to her. Any other bull that I ever heard of would have shut right up as soon as he found who it was that had croaked the girl. He wouldn't have dared go any further. None of those high-up folks wanted you to show up one of their number. But although they were paying you, you saw it through. That was all right. Although you're a bull you seem human to me. I never expected to find myself writing to one.

"I suppose, when you read this letter, you'll laugh and chuck it in the waste basket. Oh well, I should worry. I ain't got nothing better to do. Do you ever take a job without pay? I guess not. You're not in business for your health. There's a girl called Melanie Soupert about to come up for trial in General Sessions for grand larceny. She's guilty, too. What is there about it then, you may ask. Well, if you wanted to make a quiet investigation of all the circumstances behind that case, you might turn up something startling. But you'd have to dig deep for it.

"There's nothing in this for you except the chance of helping a lot of poor damned souls without hope. Maybe that isn't much of an inducement. Don't get the idea that this letter is from Melanie. There's no use trying to get anything out of her. She's a hard case. Besides, she's being well taken care of. But there are others in it.

"If you are fool enough to take any notice of this letter, don't show your hand if you value your own life. At the first move you made against the interested parties your light would be put out just like pressing a button in the wall. If you are going to do anything, you might put a little personal ad. in the *Sphere*, just saying: "X: I'm on the job; Y." That would give me something to hope for. But, of course, you won't. After this, I'll have no way of communicating with you.

"Well, anyhow, you're a bit of all right, Mme. Storey. I like to think there are women like you going about outside. Life is a rotten mess, and it's us poor boobs that make it so.

                                          AN ADMIRER.

"What do you think of it, Bella?" asked my mistress with a thoughtful smile.

"It's from a crook," I said.

"Of course. One thoroughly familiar with the seamy side of life, and with 'bulls,' poor soul. That's what appeals to me. We have never had a crook for a client."

"You don't mean to take it seriously?" I said.

"It moves me," she said simply. "It rings like a genuine cry from the heart."

It had moved me too, when she read it, but I was filled with anxiety for my generous mistress, who offered such a shining mark for envy and hatred to shoot at. "It may be a trap," I said.

"Who would ever bait a trap with words like these: 'If you are fool enough to take any notice of this letter?'" asked Mme. Storey, smiling.

"Any one who knew you would know that that was the very way to catch you," I said.

She laughed outright. "But there are few who know me as well as you do, my Bella. You are supposing a superhuman cleverness in the writer."

"You cannot afford to go into anything with your eyes shut," I said earnestly. "Depend upon it, it's a rotten mess of some sort. He as good as admits it in the letter."

"He?" said Mme. Storey.

"Well, he or she," said I.

"But there can be no doubt as to the sex of the writer," said Mme. Storey. "Every sentence reveals the feminine. Who but a woman would beg for my help, and in the next sentence tell me I was a fool if I listened to her? Moreover, observe that though this is the letter of one utterly reckless, and though the anonymity releases all inhibitions, it is neither profane nor blasphemous. A reckless man couldn't help but curse."

"I heard a damn in it somewhere," I grumbled.

" 'Poor damned souls,'" quoted Mme. Storey. "It is not used in the sense of profanity there, but as a simple adjective… No; a woman wrote this. Her whole attitude towards me is that of a fellow-woman… Moreover," she went on in a lower tone, "it is from a woman whose nature is similar to my own."

I stared hard at that.

"If I was hard up against it," Mme. Storey went on, "that is just such a letter as I might write myself. That feeling of despair which makes the breast tight; that utter recklessness which makes one mock at that which one most desires—how well I know it! And so you see, my Bella, I could not possibly disregard this cry of pain."

"Just the same," I said, "it seems to me both dangerous and unwise to pay heed to an anonymous letter."

"But I know who wrote it," said Mme. Storey, smiling.

I stared at her, awaiting the explanation.

"It is from Melanie Soupert—whoever she may be."

"How do you know?"

"Because she says it isn't," said Mme. Storey, with her most provoking smile. "If this letter had been written by somebody else, it wouldn't be necessary for the writer to state that it wasn't from Melanie Soupert. Two sentences suggest that it was written in jail. She says first: 'I haven't anything else to do;' towards the end she says: 'It's nice to think of women like you going about outside;' *i.e.*, she was locked up."

"If she's got a good case, why doesn't she state it in her letter?" I asked.

"But she's got a rotten case," said Mme. Storey. "She says she's guilty. Can't you conceive of a woman who was in bad, and yet worthy of help? Indeed, that's the sort that appeals to me most. Her lawyer, presumably, has her case in charge. She says this is something *behind* the case. She begs me to save her, and serves notice that I can expect no help from her. How like a woman, my Bella!"

"I don't like it! I don't like it!" I cried unhappily. "Suppose the letter is genuine; why should you put yourself in danger? You could not protect yourself, because you wouldn't know from what quarter to expect it."

Mme. Storey laid her hand briefly on mine. "Your feelings do you credit, my dear," she said. "But I can't help myself. This letter has got me where I live. I must see the matter through. As for danger—well, you know that the danger of a situation is always grossly exaggerated in the prospect. Anyhow, a little danger will brisken us up. Our lives are too soft."

"Well—are you going to see her?" I said, giving in very unwillingly.

"No," said Mme. Storey, "she would repudiate her letter, I am sure. But when she comes up for trial, I'll have a look at her in the dock. Ask Crider to find out the date."

"If you're going by the letter," I said, "she warns you not to show your hand."

"You have me there!" said my mistress with a quick smile. "Well, I'll send you instead to report on the trial... Meanwhile, telephone the personal ad. to the *Sphere*, will you? 'X: I'm on the job; Y.'"

I obeyed with many misgivings.

2

THE GIRL ON TRIAL

FOR THE PURPOSE of attending the trial, Mme. Storey
furnished me with a bobbed brown wig, and an artistic-Bo-
hemian outfit that suggested Greenwich village. It was not
that we expected anybody in the court-room to recognise
me, but we thought, seeing that I would be working on the
case later, it would be just as well not to give any interested
person the chance to remember having seen my conspicuous red hair at the trial.

General Sessions, part three, was sitting in one of the
corner court-rooms in the Criminal Courts Building. I had
had previous acquaintance with those big, ugly, ill-ven-
tilated rooms which are equally stifling in summer or in
winter. Justice is always associated in my mind with the
smell of hot varnish and perspiring humanity. The case was
not of the slightest public interest; and so far as I had seen
was not even mentioned in the newspapers; nevertheless,
the benches were well filled, which suited me very well.

Recorder Teague was on the bench. He enjoys a wide
reputation for no reason that I can see, except that he *looks*
the perfect justice, with his lovely white hair and mild gaze.
I have seen him hand down some pretty raw decisions
when his temper was exacerbated by the warring lawyers.

But justices are only human. My case was not in progress when I entered the room. Various motions were being made in other cases, and the indifferent jury lolled in the box with their tongues out, one might say.

I saw several well-known persons in the court-room. Jim Shryock was sitting at the counsel table. The sight of that man always makes my bristles rise. I cannot understand how an honest community can tolerate such a parasite— much less heap honours and emoluments upon him. But there, I am one of the community myself, and I have never denounced him. He is a little, bald, fat man, with a sharp nose, and he seems to exude oily cunning at every pore. He is known as one of our leading criminal lawyers, and his services are in great demand, yet he can scarcely speak grammatical English. His success is not due to his powers of oratory, but to his command of deep and devious under-ground methods of political influence and graft. Every-body knows he's crookeder than the crooks he defends, but he continues to flourish like the green bay tree.

I also saw John McDaniels, the head of the well-known detective bureau. He was a burly Hercules, with a hard, closed face. Nobody could have mistaken him for other than a "bull." He prides himself on his taciturnity, and is supposed to be able to overawe criminals by his glare, and the turning of his cigar between his thick lips. We have been associated with him in several cases; opposed to him at other times; our general relations are friendly. Mme. Storey has no great opinion of his mental capacity; but he has achieved a considerable measure of success by dogged determination. His agency does a wide business.

When Melanie Soupert was called, I looked towards the

prisoners' door with the keenest curiosity. I saw a handsome, dark-eyed girl enter the court-room with a toss of
her black mane, and a defiant hand on her hip. That hand
had been placed just so to display a showy bracelet with
rhinestones. She stared at the spectators with insolent
contempt. It was obvious that every detail of this entrance
had been rehearsed. Poor little things! it is well that they
are able to obtain some satisfaction out of their appear-
ances in court!

A handsome girl, with regular features and a beautiful
strong body. She was clad in a smartly tailored blue suit
with a piquant little jacket. A true daughter of New York,
her feet were expensively and unserviceably shod in brown
suede slippers, daintily strapped and slashed. I knew that
the price of such slippers would keep a poor family in food
for a week. She wore no hat. Her hands were beautifully
kept, and she displayed them.

I sought to pierce through her hard, defiant stare to
what lay behind; but in vain, I could see nothing but a sort
of childish vanity and braggadocio. Yet I knew there was
something behind it, for I had had a peep into her heart
through the medium of her letter. It was a disconcerting
thought; I mean, that all the childish people we contemptuously put out of mind may have hearts. Melanie sat at
the counsel table in the chair that was pointed out to her,
and proceeded to powder her nose—though she had surely
done it just before entering.

All through the tedious preliminaries I watched and
weighed her, trying to solve the insoluble enigma of a
human being. I received many impressions; some of them
flatly contradictory. I had come there in no friendly state

of feeling towards the girl, and she was deliberately trying to antagonise everybody who looked at her; nevertheless, little by little, she won me. Watching her, I was reminded of certain blind and painful periods in my childhood when I knew I was acting like a devil, and my heart was breaking.

I saw that she was not as young as I had at first thought. Fully twenty-six or twenty-seven. I saw that her hardness lay wholly in the deliberately assumed expression of her eyes. Her features were rather softly and sweetly formed. One could see, under different circumstances, that same face turning gentle and girlish. Her eyes were large, and very expressive; such eyes are accustomed to tenderness.

It struck me that there was something quite splendid in her spirit. Certainly her defiant attitude was nobler than the attitude of the usual accused woman, who looks poor and put upon, and ogles the jury with woe-begone eyes. I had the uncomfortable feeling—which has visited me before—that our life is only too prone to crush and destroy the really fine spirits among us, while it exalts the smug and the petty. In short, this girl, who wished to persuade everybody that she didn't give a damn, caused a good-sized lump to rise in my throat.

The preliminaries over, she pleaded not guilty, and the trial commenced in earnest. It made me thoughtful to observe that Jim Shryock was defending her. Shryock was a big figure in criminal practice, and it was well known that only such of the accused as had plenty of money, or were of political importance, might hope to secure his services. Melanie and Shryock stood side by side at the counsel table, but none of the usual communications passed between them. Apparently the girl's own lawyer was included in her general scorn.

Every trial is interesting. The very structure of a trial corresponds to that of a play on the stage, with the bringing in of the verdict for the grand climax. And a trial—even such an unimportant trial as this one—brings together such a curious *dramatis personæ*. There was that fascinating problem of a girl; there was Shryock, the sublimated shyster; there was McDaniels, the honest, dogged bully; there was Mrs. Cranstoun, whose pearl necklace had been stolen, an exquisite, artificial, inane little person; there was Recorder Teague with his ascetic, beautiful face, probably calculating how he could meet the monthly household accounts, while he made believe to be listening to the evidence; and finally, there was me, taking it all in, and trying to strike through to the mystery that I was assured lay behind this very ordinary case.

Mrs. Cranstoun was the first witness. Mrs. Cranstoun was one of those egregiously expensive little matrons who pose as "leaders." Leaders of what, God knows! There are so many of these leaders scattered up and down Park Avenue, one wonders where they can collect enough followers to go around. Mrs. Cranstoun stated that she was the owner of a necklace of seventy-eight matched pearls that was valued, roughly, at thirty thousand dollars. She was very careful of her things, she informed the court; never left them lying about; never trusted servants foolishly; and had never before had a loss.

She had had a replica of the necklace made, she said, and kept the real pearls in a safe deposit box. Since all her friends knew that she possessed a necklace of that value, she naively explained, it did just as much good to wear the artificial pearls around. But occasionally she had to get the real pearls out, because if they were not worn sometimes she had been told they would lose their lustre. On such occasions, she said, she visited the safe deposit vault without telling anybody of her intention, changed the artificial pearls for the real, wore the latter for a couple of days, then returned them to safe-keeping. She did not even tell her husband when she was wearing the real pearls. Nobody could have told except an expert in gems.

She went on to tell how she had engaged Melanie Soupert—but under the name of Rose Dawson, as a parlour-maid. She had advertised in the newspapers for a parlour-maid. No, that was not her usual custom. She obtained her servants through a high-class agency. But there was a shortage at this time; they sent her nobody, and she was forced to advertise. She liked the looks of the girl, who was very neat and polite. She could see from her hands, of course, that she was not accustomed to domestic service, but all kinds of people drift in and out of service, and she was thankful to get anybody. The girl offered her references, which she did not investigate as closely as she ought.

The prisoner had been working for her a few days—a week, perhaps—when she, Mrs. Cranstoun, had occasion to get her pearls out of the vault. No, she was perfectly sure she had told nobody of her intention. The chauffeur drove her to the bank, of course, but she went there often, and for many other reasons besides getting out the pearls. During the rest of that day she wore the real pearls. That night she and Mr. Cranstoun attended the Follies. Upon retiring for the night, she dropped the necklace in a jewel-box, on her dressing-table, which had no lock. It was part of her system to treat the real pearls, when she was wearing them, exactly the same as the artificial ones.

In the morning, when she went for them, she found them gone. Mrs. Cranstoun gave the jury a moving account of her emotions upon discovering her loss, while Recorder Teague's Adam's apple moved up and down with swallowed yawns. Mrs. Cranstoun telephoned to the police, and within half an hour a detective officer was sitting in her living-room. All the servants were rigorously quizzed—Melanie amongst the others—and their rooms searched, but nothing came of it. The parlour-maid answered up as cool as you please, and the officer did not suspect her. He said it was an outside job, and affected to discover finger-prints on the window-sill.

The prisoner remained on for five days after the theft. Then she dropped a valuable *sang de boeuf* vase, and smashed it. When Mrs. Cranstoun reprimanded her, she answered back pertly, and Mrs. Cranstoun discharged her on the spot. Looking back, she could see, of course, that the girl had smashed the vase on purpose to pave the way for her escape from the house.

Meanwhile, there was no word of the missing pearls, and despairing of getting any results from the police, Mrs. Cranstoun consulted Mr. McDaniels, who had been recommended to her by a friend whose jewels he had recovered. Several of her friends had consulted Mr. McDaniels upon one occasion or another, with entire satisfaction. And, indeed, when she described the discharged parlour-maid to him, he had immediately said: "Melanie

Soupert." Within ten days Mr. McDaniels had recovered all her pearls from the various pawnshops where they had been pledged, and had secured the arrest of the girl.

While Mrs. Cranstoun was testifying, it was curious to see how she and Melanie sought to insult each other with exactly the same sort of glances of animal indifference. You know how women look at each other. In other words, the moral natures of accused and accuser were about the same; the difference between them was merely a matter of money. I never can understand this indifference of humans to humans. If a woman stole a pearl necklace from me I should be extraordinarily interested in her.

When Mrs. Cranstoun concluded her testimony, Jim Shryock arose and said: "No cross-examination." From the oily smile he bent upon the witness, one would have supposed that he was *her* lawyer.

This attitude of Shryock's was my first proof that this was not just an ordinary case. As the trial proceeded, he made it clear that he had no intention of exerting himself to get the girl off. From his cynical expression the jury might gather that the girl's guilt could be taken for granted. This made me very indignant. She was guilty, no doubt, but just the same she was not getting a fair trial. And the nerve of the super-shyster! He intended that everybody should see that he had abandoned the girl. It was absolutely unethical, of course, but such was the evil prestige of the man that nobody had the courage to call him.

The only other important witness was John McDaniels. An experienced witness, the big man was entirely matter-of-fact upon the stand. This was all in the day's work for him. He described the various steps he had taken to recover the pearls, and apprehend the girl, which I need not go into here. As soon as he heard Mrs. Cranstoun's tale, he suspected Melanie Soupert was the thief, because it was her speciality to engage herself as a parlour-maid and steal her mistress's jewels when the opportunity offered. One of the cleverest jewel thiefs in the business. Always worked single-handed. She possessed several genuine letters of recommendation from well-known women, which she had stolen or purchased from the real Rose Dawson.

McDaniels recited Melanie's criminal record with deadly particularity. She had first been arrested for stealing her mistress's jewels, when only seventeen years old. Had been sentenced to a reformatory, but being a first offender, and on account of her youth, had soon been parolled. Shortly afterwards she was back in the dock, charged with a similar crime; and this time she had received a prison sentence, which she had served, with the customary allowance off. Two years before, she had once more been arrested, and convicted of robbery, and had been sentenced to Woburn Prison for five years. After serving but a month or two, she had broken out of prison, and the unexpired sentence was still awaiting her at Woburn.

McDaniels had finally come up with her, he said, in a flat on Avenue A, where she was living with a young man called George Mullen, whom she had recently married. The proceeds of the robbery had partly gone to furnish the flat. This Mullen was a hard-working young fellow, unknown to the police. Apparently he was unaware of his wife's criminal activities. When he had learned of it, he had repudiated her. Upon being arrested, Melanie had admitted her guilt, but subsequently denied it.

These dry statements of McDaniels caused me to look at the girl with a new and extraordinary interest. I am a spinster, and no less sentimental, I suppose, than others. A bride! Ah, the poor young thing! The fact that she was a thief was not to say she was not capable of feeling all the tremulous happiness of a bride. And her honeymoon had been broken up by the brutal intrusion of McDaniels! And her young husband had turned from her! What a poor stick he must have been. Yet you couldn't blame him, either, if he had supposed her virtuous. It was a pitiful situation all round. Melanie sat listening with half a sneer on her comely face. God knows what pain that sneer conceals, I thought.

Shryock's cross-examination of McDaniels was merely perfunctory. No facts favourable to the girl were brought out.

To make a long story short, the jury returned a verdict of guilty without leaving their seats. Only one of the twelve betrayed any concern for the girl; an insignificant little man in the upper corner of the jury box, who looked at Melanie with compassionate eyes. But he had not force of character enough to make a stand against the other eleven. Mrs. Cranstoun, in her expensive clothes, with the pearls—real or phony—around her neck, openly exulted. Melanie herself gave no sign, except that the painful curl in her lip became emphasised.

Before sentencing her Recorder Teague hesitated. I had seen that Shryock's cynical attitude towards his client had made the worthy man uneasy during the trial. He was a political judge, and had to consider his reëlection; he dared not openly rebuke the powerful lawyer, but I am sure he would have liked to do something for the girl. He began to question her with a view to bringing out something favourable to her.

"Have you anything to say?"

"What's the use?" said Melanie, sneering.

"Is your husband in the court-room?"

"No."

"If you went straight, would not your husband return to you?"

Melanie's dark eyes flashed at him. "I wouldn't go back to him," she said. "He's yellow."

The judge bit his lip, and tried again. "Are your parents living?"

"That's neither here nor there," said Melanie. "They have nothing to do with this."

"Have you no desire to lead a respectable life?"

"Aah! sentence me! sentence me!" cried Melanie with harsh effrontery. "It's bad enough to be tried without having to listen to a moral lecture!"

What could anybody do for a girl like that?

The Recorder flushed, and took her at her word. Not less than five years, and not more than ten at Woburn Prison. This sentence to begin when she had finished serving her unexpired term there.

She was guilty and unrepentant; nevertheless, it caused my breast the sharpest twinge of pain. It was the thought of youth and beauty locked up useless in a narrow cell. All too clearly I could picture her as she would come out in ten years, or whenever it might be, faded, hard and desperate; quite spoiled.

Melanie stood up with a hard smile. Evidently she

intended to carry the thing through with the same reckless bravado. "Thanks, Judge," she drawled, hand on hip. And to the jury: "Much obliged for your consideration, gentlemen. Come and see me some time. You know my address."

One could hear the spectators catch their breaths in horrified delight at the girl's impudence.

But her feelings were getting the best of her. Her sneering assurance broke up. I saw her press her teeth into her lower lip, while her breast heaved irregularly. I felt it in my own breast. Hysteria. Suddenly she cried out in a high unnatural voice.

"You all think pretty well of yourselves, don't you? You, who come here to try me; and you who come to see me tried..."This, with a violent sweeping gesture. "Well, here I am! Look! Look! And to hell with you! Now you can go home and gorge yourselves, and snore in your beds. It's a grand thing not to be found out, isn't it? I'm thankful I'm not respectable. I'm a crook, and I'm proud of it. In my cell there'll be no strings on me. I don't have to lie to butter my bread. But you... but you! You're rotten, all of you. You respectable people work together to make the world a mean and dirty place. I despise you...!"

The rest was incoherent. It was curious to see how the hearers in the court-room revealed their natures. Either like Jim Shryock or Mrs. Cranstoun, they grinned with a hideous pleasure; or, like John McDaniels, they were stolidly indifferent. Recorder Teague flushed deeply with anger, and rapped smartly with his gavel.

"Remove that woman!" he commanded.

Melanie was hustled out, shrieking insensately.

I made my way out of the court-room along with the

other spectators. Most of them seemed to be curiously elated by the sensational conclusion of the trial, and even strangers discussed it with each other animatedly. But I felt a little sick at heart.

3

MME. STOREY

I WOULD LIKE to draw a complete, full-length portrait of my mistress, Mme. Storey, but it is beyond my powers. The best I can do is to portray her in action, and leave it to my readers to form their own conclusions. At this time I had been with her as her secretary for over two years; and it was true, as she said, that there were few people who knew her as well as I did. But that is not to say that I knew her completely; there was a high quality in her nature that escaped my comprehension. She was the only disinterested woman I ever knew. Imagine a woman whose judgment was never swayed by her feelings! In this respect I am no more than an average woman myself, consequently the manifestation of her disinterestedness always astonished me.

Like other great-souled people, she found but few souls to commune with on this dusty sphere. On the other hand, living in the full glare of publicity, she was much at the mercy of fools. In order to protect herself, she had gradually built up the Mme. Storey of the popular imagination; the tall, exotic, unmoved beauty, to whom, without any necessity of exerting herself, everything was revealed. She seemed to exist in an atmosphere miles above that of

ordinary people. Mme. Storey was she who could not be
deceived. A thousand stories were told of her extraordinary
insight as well as her personal foibles; her amazing clothes;
her cigarettes; the objects of art with which she surrounded
herself; her array of rare perfumes; the fantastically dressed
black ape who sat upon her arm. She had become almost
a legendary figure.

She had deliberately cultivated this faculty of inspiring
people with awe of her. It was good for business, and it kept
fools at arm's length. Well do I remember how terrified I
was when she first swam into my ken. But it was not the
real Mme. Storey. From very old people, or from children,
or from any soul in trouble, she made no pretence of hiding
her kind heart. After two years daily association I knew
her better than anybody. When we were alone together,
she threw off her public manner with relief; and emerged
keen, human, lovable and full of laughter. But there was
always a suggestion of that awe-inspiring quality behind;
something about her one could not quite reach.

She was one of the most beautiful women in New York,
but the fame of her beauty was far overshadowed by that
of her mind. Men marvelled at the *sangfroid* with which
she pointed to the solution of the most baffling problems.
At a single phrase of Mme. Storey's, whole vast structures
of evasions and circumlocutions and false reasoning would
collapse like a house of cards, revealing the simple truth.
Somebody said, after the famous smoke-bandit case: "The
cleverest man in town is a woman;" but that conveys a false
idea. Mme. Storey's wonderful mind was wholly feminine;
her success was due to the fact that she refused to force it
into masculine channels of thought. She worked by intu-

ition, that swifter and surer process of reasoning. Unfortunately, in a man-ruled world, intuition is at a discount, and
Mme. Storey was obliged to spend a good three-fourths of
her time proving to judges, juries, and other men, that her
unerring intuitions were true according to their cumbrous
rules of logic and reason.

Our offices are on the parlour floor of a splendid old
dwelling on Gramercy Park, which has been sub-divided.
We do not hang out a shingle, for the whole town knows
its way there. Mme. Storey describes herself as a "practical
psychologist," to which she sometimes adds, with a twinkle in her eye, "specialising in the feminine." The style and
the location of the rooms makes them equally well adapted
for either business or social activities. Sometimes Mme.
Storey gives parties in the beautiful long room, where the
famous treasures of the Italian renaissance are displayed.
Only her ultimate friends know the inside of the delightful
little house on East Sixty-third street, that she shares with
Mrs. Lysaght. Those rooms are decorated in a very different
style; less glorious, but more inviting.

On the day that I spent in attendance at the Soupert
trial, we left a boy in charge of the office, and Mme.
Storey remained working at home. She was busy with
the well-remembered case of Admiral Van der Venter,
who was subject to such curious lapses of personality. I
went to her there, and was shown into that enchanting
living-room, so quaintly furnished in the style of 1850. The
windows faced south, and overlooked a tiny formal garden
in the rear of the house. The invaluable Grace served us tea
and little chocolate cakes, and any one who had seen my

mistress *en négligée,* munching chocolate cakes, could not have thought her otherwise than purely feminine.

She listened with close attention to my account of the trial.

"What do you make of it?" she asked, when I had done.

"I was sorry for the girl," I said. "But I think we ought to keep in mind the possibility that there may be nothing in it, beyond what appears on the surface. She's a thorough egoist, and it may be she thinks there is something deep, dark, and mysterious about her case, just because it is her case. When she lost control of herself, and became hysterical, surely if there was anything behind it all, it must have come out then."

Mme. Storey shook her head. "Not badly argued," she said, "but I feel you are wrong. There is one false assumption in your reasoning. I have not found that women tell the truth in their hysterical outbursts, or that they give away anything they don't want to have known. Hysteria is largely a self-induced state, and a woman who can bring it on can make it work for her."

"But if she wanted help—"

Mme. Storey lit a cigarette, and thoughtfully puffed at it. "Bella," she said, "most of us only face the truth about our situation once or twice in a lifetime—some of us never. Suppose it came to this poor girl in the night, lying sleepless on the hard bunk of her cell, and she got up and wrote that letter to me on the spur of the moment. As soon as she sent it out, she would regret it. She'd rather die now than confess she was the girl who had written it."

"But how can we do anything for her without her coöperation?"

"I admit it will be difficult. But, perhaps, we can bring her back to a more amenable frame of mind... The case interests me. It smells of mystery. The inwardness of it was not revealed at the trial. The suggestion that she committed all these thefts single-handed will not hold water. Of course she did the actual lifting of the jewels, but she could not dispose of them without assistance. That business is too highly organised.

"Then there is this young man she was married to, who shook her so precipitately. That is unusual. Young people generally cleave to each other at such a time. An accusation of theft is nothing to a lover. It seems incredible that the young man should not even feel concern enough to attend her trial. We will have this George Mullen looked for.

"Finally, there is Shryock's extraordinary attitude," Mme. Storey went on, more like one thinking aloud. "There's a subtle, astute scoundrel! His connection with the case interests me more than anything else. He was the real prosecutor of the girl. He turned his thumbs down, and she was railroaded. I've long had my eye on Shryock. I consider him the most sinister and hateful figure on the local scene. I have longed to be able to open up the underground ramifications of his power. It would be odd, wouldn't it, if I was able to get him at last, through the means of an anonymous letter from one of his humblest victims? We've made a good bit of money the last year or two, Bella. We can afford to do a piece of work gratis for the good of the community. Oh, decidedly, as long as Shryock is mixed up in this case, I shall not drop it."

"What is the next move?" I asked.

"Katherine Couteau Cloke, the well-known prison

reformer, is a friend of mine," said Mme. Storey. "She's a sort of unofficial inspector of all the prisons, and makes frequent trips to Woburn. I'll get her to arrange an interview for me with the girl."

"But if you visited Woburn Prison it would immediately become known," I said. "Even if you went in disguise. Those places are full of spies, Shryock would certainly be informed of your interest in the girl."

"Oh, Bella, you're so confoundedly prudent!" said Mme. Storey, with pretended impatience. "However, I suppose you're right. You'll have to see the girl, then, and persuade her that we are her friends." She reached for the telephone. "Let us see if we can get hold of Miss Cloke now."

By great good fortune we caught that busy woman at a loose end, and a few minutes later she was seated beside us in the mellow, inviting living-room; a middle-aged woman, with a plain, strong, good, harassed face. Grace brought her fresh tea, but she refused the chocolate cakes.

"Ah, what a haven of rest!" she murmured, glancing around the room, and visibly relaxing.

"You should not wait until you are sent for," said Mme. Storey, smiling.

Evidently they were tried friends; they looked at each other with eyes of affection. No two women could have been more dissimilar. Miss Cloke was one of the dowdy, plain-spoken sort, that men affect to sneer at, but who accomplish a deal of good in the world. Certainly the prisoners of this state have a lot to thank her for.

"Did you ever hear of a jewel thief called Melanie Soupert?" asked Mme. Storey. "An old offender."

"Why, yes," said Miss Cloke at once. "One would not

forget that name. Let me see… she escaped from Woburn Prison two years ago, and was never apprehended. She had influential friends, one supposes."

"Indeed!" said Mme. Storey; "that's interesting."

"They can generally catch an escaped prisoner if they really wish to," said Miss Cloke, with the shrug of one who was disillusioned without being embittered.

"Her influential friends must have abandoned her," said I. "She's been sent up again, on another charge."

"Oh, I don't know," drawled Mme. Storey; "she may escape again."

I glanced at my mistress, wondering what theory she was evolving. Her face gave away nothing.

"Do you remember the circumstances of her escape?" she asked Miss Cloke.

That lady shook her head. "There is seldom anything spectacular in the cases where there is collusion. A prisoner turns up missing, and it's often hard to establish just how she did get away. Say a party of prisoners is taken for some special purpose to the outer yard of the prison; an entertainment, or welfare work of some sort. A complaisant keeper turns his back, and a prisoner strolls away, presently to be picked up by a waiting car—sometimes in the outer yard of the prison itself. Under modern, humane methods, escapes are more numerous than they used to be; but we contend that the loss is far outbalanced by the gain in other ways."

"Can you remember the girl herself?" asked Mme. Storey.

"Yes," said Miss Cloke slowly, "a handsome, dark girl, with a bold glance… An incorrigible!" she went on with a sigh. "One of the sort who sets all my work at naught. It's hard to be patient with such a one."

"Just how do you mean, incorrigible?"

"You cannot reach her better feelings. With such a prisoner any softening of the iron hand will immediately be taken advantage of; any trust you put in her will be betrayed. Such a one, vain, wilful, and defiant, always becomes a rallying-point for all the rebels in the prison; they make a hero of her."

"But the better feelings may be there," said Mme. Storey.

"Oh, certainly! That's what makes it so discouraging. Melanie Soupert is the sort of prisoner that my adversaries throw in my face as proof that my methods are not only mistaken, but positively harmful."

Mme. Storey told Miss Cloke the circumstances of the trial that day. In conclusion she said: "I suspect that this girl is a cog in some great evil machine. What you say about her having powerful friends confirms it. If I can catch her at the right moment, I hope to be able to save her from the machine, of which she is a victim as well as a part; and through her, to destroy the whole foul business."

"What is the nature of this machine?" asked Miss Cloke.

"I don't know," said Mme. Storey frankly. "All I can say so far is that Jim Shryock is in it."

"Shryock!" cried Miss Cloke with an indignant flash of her honest eyes. "If you could destroy him, you would be conferring a boon on us all! It is Shryock and all he stands for that I am fighting night and day, blindfolded! They strike me in the back!... I wish you luck with the girl," she went on with a rueful smile, "but...!" She ended with a shake of the head.

"I'd like Bella to talk to her," said Mme. Storey. "How can it be managed?"

"I go to Woburn next week on my regular visit," said Miss Cloke. "I am often accompanied by students, investigators and what not. Miss Brickley could make one of my party without exciting any remark. We could interview the girl, and I could leave Miss Brickley with her."

Mme. Storey shook her head. "Too obvious," she said. "If you sought the girl out like that it would excite remark. Woburn is full of spies, I suppose."

"Oh, my dear, yes!" said Miss Cloke, with her air of philosophic disillusionment.

"Besides," said Mme. Storey, "if you will forgive me for saying so, I suspect that you, that anything associated with the name of reformer, is like a red rag to this girl."

"That's true," said Miss Cloke, smiling.

"Then it would be better not to have Bella introduced to her under your auspices. Tell me, just what do you do on your visits to Woburn?"

"I have an assistant there in charge of welfare work. She makes her reports to me, and together we lay out the work for the subsequent month. She recommends individual cases to my attention—generally the incorrigibles; and, as far as time permits, I talk to these prisoners. I also have to consult with the Warden, and make my recommendations to him, which he takes under advisement."

"Well, let us not be in too great haste to act," said Mme. Storey. "Make your visit to Woburn next week without Bella. Find out exactly what is Melanie's situation in the prison, and on the basis of that we will make a plan for bringing Bella and her together naturally."

"Very well," said Miss Cloke; "and shall I drop a hint to the Warden that another rescue of the girl is possible?"

"Oh, no! no!" said Mme. Storey quickly. "As an escaped prisoner they will already be watching her closely enough. For goodness' sake let her friends get her out, if they are able!"

Miss Cloke stared at my mistress rather scandalised.

"You think I am very immoral," said Mme. Storey, laughing. "And so I am. But through this girl I could much better reach her masters, couldn't I, if she were free, and in close touch with her? What you ought to do is to drop a hint to the Warden that in this case the ends of justice would best be served by letting the girl escape. But that would be too unmoral, wouldn't it? So we'll just let matters take their course."

4

IN WOBURN PRISON

BEHOLD ME, TEN days later, established as a probation-ary nurse in the infirmary attached to the Woburn prison for females. The direction of the infirmary was so largely independent of that of the prison proper, we felt that I could take this job without exciting suspicion. My general ineptitude as a nurse would furnish a perfectly reasonable excuse for discharging me after I had got what I wanted.

The plan suggested itself upon our receiving Miss Cloke's report of Melanie's situation in the prison. She had been put in solitary confinement upon her arrival. After wild fits of hysteria, she had fallen into an apathetic state in which she could neither eat nor sleep, and her health had really begun to suffer. It was a simple matter to arrange for her transfer to the infirmary, where she would probably have been sent anyway. As a precautionary measure, the transfer was delayed until after I was already on the job. Nobody was taken into the secret except the Warden, the doctor, and the head nurse.

At the last moment, the plan was almost upset by the fact that, for some reason or other, Melanie suddenly recov-ered her interest in life. However, she was sent to the infirmary "for observation." She made no objection, of course, since it was much more comfortable there than in her cell.

The infirmary was contained in a separate building, in the outer prison yard, and had no connection with the cell block. The outer yard, with the handsome residences of the officials, the grass, flower beds, etc., did not suggest a prison, except for the encircling wall. The ground floor of the infirmary building was given up to an assembly room, and the two wards were on the second floor. There were two nurses on duty in each ward, and a male orderly out on the landing. At the foot of the stairs there was a steel gate, with two keepers on guard. The windows were all barred. So it was safe enough. I felt like a prisoner myself, once I was inside.

I was just a supernumerary to the two regular nurses in my ward. They were not in the secret, and they treated me like a real probationer. Hardest job on earth. Heavens! how I had to work. All the laborious and menial tasks in connection with sickness fell to my share. I prayed that this might not last long. It was understood that I must find my own opportunities of talking with Melanie; but in order to facilitate it, she was to be put in a sort of cubicle at the end of the ward. She was still technically, "in solitary."

Melanie was brought to the infirmary on the morning of the day after I had entered on my duties there. She was able to walk, of course. The head nurse delivered her to the ward nurse at the door of our ward. In the gray prison dress she made a much less brilliant figure than in the court-room; she looked thinner and her colour was bad. Nevertheless, she was in the highest spirits. When the door closed after the head nurse, she made an impudent face in her direction that caused such of the patients as were well enough, to giggle with laughter.

Melanie swaggered down the ward, chin up and hand on hip. "Hallo, girls!" she cried to the patients. "What's the good word? Looks to me as if you wanted a bit of cheering in here. Well, I'm the baby that can supply it. There's always somepin doin' where I am. I'm Melanie Soupert. (She pronounced it Soupairr). Guess you heard of me, eh? the warden's plague, the keeper's pest, the worst girl in Woburn! Down with the reformers!"

The patients received this with hilarity, of course. The ward nurse looked sour, but said nothing. One of the first rules of the infirmary was, that the quickest way to subdue an obstreperous patient was to ignore her.

I was told off to see that Melanie undressed and got into bed. She did not require any actual assistance. In the cubicle she continued to shout pleasantries over the top of the partition to the girls outside.

"Hey, there! you with the pink boojewar cap at the end of the row! You look like a live one when you're up. What's your name?"

The answer came back: "Sarah Mitchell from Syracuse."

Said Melanie: "Well, Syracuse Sarah, you and me'll be pals, eh? We'll liven things up around this dump. Who's askeared of a lot of nurses? What are you in for, Sarah?"

"Stickin' up a cigar-stand."

"Small stuff! Small stuff!" said Melanie scornfully. "I lifted a pearl necklace worth thirty thou. I wouldn't bother with nothing smaller."

And so on. And so on. Melanie paid not the slightest attention to me. It was a little too soon for me to make

myself known to her. So I just stood there, and when the
ward nurse had gone, smiled in a way to suggest to her that
she could count on my secret sympathy in her defiance of
the authorities.

She broke off her repartee to say to me: "Say, Sis, can
you wangle me a butt?"

For a moment I felt blank—then I got it. Could I get
her a cigarette. "I'm new here," I murmured. "I don't know
the ropes."

"Oh, we'll soon break you in. We'll soon break you in,"
she said cheerfully.

This loud, impudent cheerfulness was merely her prison
pose, of course. It had nothing to do with the real girl. One
would have to dig deep for that. Those flashing dark eyes of
hers suggested infinite possibilities. Just as on the former
occasion, I felt myself strongly drawn to her. She was dead
game, and that quality in man or woman is hard to resist.
Moreover, she was a beautiful young creature. The coarse
nightgown, and hideous gray jacket could not hide it.

ONE OF THE night nurses wanted to go to a picture show
in the prison, and I volunteered to remain on duty until
ten o'clock. The ill patients fell asleep early, and Melanie,
who was not at all ill, and extremely lively and wideawake,
was dependent on me for her amusement. The ward nurse
encouraged me to remain with her, as otherwise she would
sing in a loud voice, or shout over the wall of the cubicle.
Thus everything worked out to my advantage.

I sat on the foot of the high hospital cot, swinging my
feet; and while she joshed me, I debated how best to open
my business with her. My heart was beating fast; it is always
breathlessly exciting to give the handle of life a turn, not

knowing what sort of a tune is coming out of the box. With too much thinking of what I ought to say, I could say nothing. Meanwhile, the precious moments were flying. Finally I approached it this way:

"You're not sick. How did you come to get in the infirmary?"

"Oh, I was sick two days ago," said Melanie. "These officials always get round to a thing after it's over."

"What was the matter with you?"

"Melancholia," she said, grinning.

"Not much sign of it now?"

"Oh, I had a bit of good news, kid," she said, with her eyes shining, and her voice scaling up joyfully.

"What was that?" I asked.

But she instantly repented of the peep she had given me into her heart. "Oh, me mother-in-law went into a coma, and has lost the use of her tongue," she drawled mockingly.

"I'll tell you how you happened to get here," I said boldly. "I arranged it."

She stared at me in the purest amazement.

"I'm no nurse," I said.

"What the hell are you, then?"

"Private secretary to Madame Storey."

Melanie became very still. She had dropped all pose. She paled a little, and searched my face with deep, grave eyes. She said nothing at all.

"It was arranged to have you sent to the infirmary, so you and I could talk without exciting any suspicion, Mme. Storey sent me to see you about the letter you wrote her."

Still that silence. Her dark eyes, a little widened, remained fixed on my face with an inscrutable expression.

Stilled like that, her face was wonderfully soft and touching. A long, long silence. Finally her eyes fell, and she elaborately smoothed the bedspread with one hand. Evidently some sort of struggle was going on within her. The silence made me extremely uneasy; but it seemed best to me to let her work out the problem without interruption.

At last she said in low tones without looking at me: "You get me wrong, kid. I'm no fist with the pen."

"Perhaps not," I said. "But you wrote this letter."

"Was it signed with my name?" she asked cunningly.

"No," I said.

"Then how did she know it was from me?"

"Nobody can deceive her," I said. "She sees to the bottom of a thing."

"Oh, yes, I've heard of those know-it-all people," she said with a painful sneer.

I waited again, hoping to see her better nature assert itself.

"What was in the letter?" she asked with pretended innocence.

"What's the use?" I said. "You know."

Another silence while her lashes lay on her cheeks. Then, apparently, she made up her mind. With a toss of her bobbed head she said in a louder, harsher tone. "I don't get it, kid. I don't get it at all. I don't know why the hell anybody should write to Mme. Storey about me. I've got nothing to complain of."

I was deeply disappointed. When Melanie became profane, you felt that you had lost her. But I wasn't going to give up yet. "You asked her to help you," I said. "She wishes to help you. Are you going to turn it down."

"You will have it that I wrote to her. Excuse me, but you seem bugs to me on the subject, sister," said Melanie.

"Well, say that you didn't write to her then," said I. "She has interested herself in you for any reason that you like. She had me watch your trial for her, and she sent me here to talk to you."

"And after you told her the way I carried on at the trial was she still interested?" demanded Melanie.

"More than ever," I said.

An extraordinary expression passed over the girl's face. You could actually see the two elements of her nature struggling there. She sneered—and her eyes seemed to be about to fill with tears. "Huh! she must be a funny one!" she said.

I waited.

"And what did you think of me yourself?" she demanded.

"You made me think of when I was a child, and got in bad."

She flashed a look at me—a soft look, instantly hidden, and I was astonished to hear her laugh softly. Just one note. "That's not a bad way to put it," she said. Then immediately, in a tone of agony: "Oh, my God!"

I was very close to her then. I almost held my breath for fear of saying the wrong thing.

But the decision went against me. "No!" she cried with a violent shake of the black mane. Her face turned hard again. "What can Madame Storey do for me?" she demanded. "Can she get me out of here?"

I could make no answer to that.

Melanie went on in the old sneering, boastful vein: "Tell Madame Storey I thank you for her interest in me, but I can't use it in my biz. I'm a crook, and I'll herd with my own kind. I ask no favours of nobody. I stand on my own bottom, and take what comes as it comes. Nobody ever heard me whine for mercy!"

There was not so much hurt in it this time, and presently she broke off to ask me with eager curiosity. "What's she like, on the level. I suppose all that I read in the papers was just publicity stuff."

"We don't employ a press agent," I said.

"How old is she?"

"I don't know," I said frankly. "Young."

"Is she as good a looker as they make out?"

"You must have seen her photographs."

"Oh, I thought they were touched up."

"She's better looking than any of her photographs."

"And you're her private secretary!" said Melanie, with a wondering air. "Do you mean you're in on everything that happens in that office? All the big cases, and everything?"

"There is nobody so close to her as me."

"Aah!" said Melanie truculently, "you can't tell me that anybody like that, so rich and high up and famous, come 'close' to common people like you and me. Now I know you're lying."

This was just to lead me on, of course. I said: "She puts it all over what you call 'high-up' people, with a manner that is higher than their own. When we're alone together we're just like pals. We laugh and joke together. She treats me like her sister—I wish I could tell you better! She has the kindest heart in the world. She would be just the same to you."

As I struggled to convey my feelings about my mistress

the tears came into my eyes, and I swear, as she listened, Melanie's black eyes became filmy, too. Forgetting her pose, she said simply: "She has always fascinated me. I have read every word about her that I could get hold of. I felt in a way that she was like me, though of course she's made something of herself. She's on the right side of the fence and I'm on the wrong side."

"Why, that's funny," said I. "She said almost the same thing."

The girl looked at me with a burning curiosity.

"When I described the trial to her," I explained, "she said that had she been in the same circumstances, she would have acted the way you did."

"No! Did she say that?" breathed Melanie, great-eyed. "Think of that!"

I thought I had won her. "What message am I to take her from you?" I asked.

The question recalled her to herself with a painful start. "Message!" she said. "Don't give her any of that cheap line I handed you a while back. That's my regular line of tripe. I beat myself like an empty drum and that comes out. Tell her I— Tell her— What message can I send to a woman like that? Tell her if she feels friendly; if she wants to do something for me, she must drop me, see? There can be nothing between us. This is the straight goods, sister. I ask her as a favour to let me go. If she makes any other attempt to get in touch with me it will destroy us both!"

She went on in a lower voice—there could be no doubt of her earnestness: "Tell her—tell her we are just like ships that pass in the night. We make friendly signals to each other and keep on our way. I think she'll get that—"

"But I can't tell her just that without—" I began.

Melanie flew into a temper. Her eyes were full of tears. "Oh, for God's sake, are you dumb?" she cried. "Can't you understand English. I told you it was on the level. Do you think I'm telling you all this just for fun? You tell her just that, and nothing more."

"Can't you explain?" I begged her.

Her only answer was to throw back her head and loudly start singing a highly indecorous parody of a popular song. The ward-nurse came in, and angrily ordered her to be silent. Melanie answered her back pertly, and they embarked on a regular jawing-match, in which the nurse was unwise, for Melanie was far more adept at that sort of thing than she was. I went outside, sad at heart, for I felt that I had failed in my mission.

Shortly afterwards the regular night-nurse came on duty and I left.

When I came on in the morning, the patients told me that Melanie had been hitting up a racket all night. The head-nurse had complained to the authorities, and she had already been transferred back to her cell. This cut off any further chance of my seeing her.

But I had to go on working in that depressing place. I took care to make such breaks in the course of the day, that it seemed perfectly natural to patients and nurses when the head-nurse told me when I knocked off at night that I needn't come back again. I got back to New York at midnight.

Next morning I opened up the offices, which had been closed during my two days' absence, as Mme. Storey had no way of protecting herself from cranks and bores when

I was away. I made my report to my mistress in her room, just as I have set it down here, ending it by saying with a good deal of bitterness: "And so I have failed."

"Oh, I wouldn't say that," drawled Mme. Storey, teasingly. "You have planted a seed in the girl's mind. Let it sprout."

"But what further move can we make?"

She did not answer right away. Half turned around in her chair, she was gazing out of the window at the little green park. At last she said: "I believe that Melanie's friends are already planning to get her out of prison. That would be the bit of good news she received. It explains her miraculous recovery. Nearly everything she said to you suggests she had that thought in mind. As when she said: 'Can Madame Storey get me out of here?' And you were obliged to be silent.

"It explains her curious hesitancies and contradiction. She has thirteen years to serve, as she could hardly count on anything off for good conduct. Thirteen years in the life of a girl who loves life! it is everything. In her soul she may hate her former life and its associates, but sooner than face that thirteen years she chooses to stick to them. That is very natural. Now you see why she implores us to drop her. Any further move we made in her direction might queer her chance of escape. Well, let them get her out if they can. After that we'll see—"

5

A NEWSPAPER CLIPPING

A FEW DAYS after this Mme. Storey came in fresh and beaming from her morning's walk down to the office. There was a particular shine of amusement in her eye, "Bella, have you read the papers?" she asked.

"I only skimmed over the headlines," I said.

"This isn't front page stuff," she said, "but it has a special interest for us."

She laid a paper on my desk, folded in such a manner that my eyes immediately fell on the head:

EXTRAORDINARY ESCAPE FROM WOBURN
Girl Makes Getaway for the Second Time
Is Still at Large

"So you were right," I said solemnly. "You are always right."

With a laugh, she went into her room, leaving me to read the story. I kept the clipping, and I will reproduce it here; omitting only the part dealing with the girl's history, which you are already familiar with.

"Yesterday morning, when breakfast was carried to the prisoners in solitary confinement, the cell of Melanie

Soupert was discovered to be empty. She had sawed her way out during the night. On the theory, perhaps, that women are not so strong as men, the cell fronts at Woburn are not constructed of iron bars, but of an iron lattice work, with strips half an inch wide, and three-eighths of an inch thick. These are, of course, much easier to saw through than bars, and an enterprising prisoner occasionally succeeds in making her way out, but only to find herself in the well-guarded corridor, no nearer freedom than she was before.

"But there was no sign of the Soupert girl in the corridor. For awhile the manner of her escape was a complete mystery. At the end of the corridor there is a steel gate which is locked at nightfall, and cannot be opened for any purpose without setting off an alarm bell. This gate was found intact in the morning, and the apparatus for ringing the bell was in order. Even if she had got through this gate, which leads into the rotunda of the main cell-block, she had still to go through the main gate to the cell-block, where there are never less than four guards on duty, and others within call.

"The solitary prisoners are confined in a row of small cells on the lowest tier of the north-east wing. No prisoner in solitary confinement has ever before been successful in escaping, it is said. The corridor is lined with a row of windows over thirty feet high, which give light to all four tiers of cells. These windows have iron bars running up and down inside them. It was finally discovered that the bars at the top of one of the windows had been pressed apart sufficiently to permit of the passage of a human body.

"She had unerringly put her finger on the one weak spot of the prison defences; for the tops of the windows are rounded in order to conform to the architectural design of the prison, and the ends of the bars, therefore, are not sunk into the stone as is customary. The bars end an inch or two short of the stone window-frame.

"This leaves a row of free ends of varying lengths. The two middle ends being the longest, provided the most leverage. These she had pressed apart.

"Climbing to the top of the window had offered no special difficulty, because of the numerous cross-bars. Stuck between the bent bars they found the girl's lever, a stout piece of iron some three feet long. After having squeezed through, she had climbed down the outside of the bars, and slipped through a raised sash at the bottom of the window. The sill was only some ten or twelve feet above the ground. She was then in the prison yard, with a twenty-two foot wall between her and freedom.

"At this point the investigators were faced by a greater mystery than ever, for it was discovered that the strongest keeper in the prison was unable at the same time to balance himself up there, and press the bent bars back into place with the girl's lever. How, then, could a woman do it unaided? There were many other unexplained points; how had she procured that bulky lever, as well as the array of specially designed saw-blades, the package of lamp-black, and the oil-can that were found hidden in her cell amongst her meagre effects? Above all, how had she succeeded in getting over the wall?

"Later in the day, after the news had been telephoned to the surrounding villages, the mystery was partly cleared up by William Harper, a blacksmith of Wellandville, who said that he had sold such an iron bar to two men at eight o'clock the night before. Upon being brought to the prison, Harper unhesitatingly identified the bar. The two men drove up to his house, which adjoined his shop, in a Ford car with a semi-truck body, he said. The body was loaded with ladders, coils of wire, axes and other tools, and the men represented themselves as linemen, who had received an emergency call. They explained that they needed a short lever, and he let them have it, thinking no harm.

"In view of this statement, it is clear that Melanie Soupert was rescued by two men who went over the wall from the outside, climbed up the outside of the bars, and pressed them open to let the girl out. Then the three of them went back over the wall to the waiting car. Woburn prison stands in a somewhat out-of-the-way situation at the foot of the Windon Hills. The nearest village is a mile away, and, apart from the prison establishment, there are no buildings in the immediate vicinity.

"Yesterday afternoon word came from the city of Kingston, sixty miles from the prison, that the Ford car with all its paraphernalia had been found abandoned in the streets at daybreak yesterday morning. The licence tags had been removed.

"Many questions are raised by the escape. Melanie must have had a perfect understanding with her rescuers; how could this have been reached, when she was held *uncommunicado*, forbidden to receive visits or letters? It is true she spent one day in the Infirmary, but it is not thought she could have got anything there, since she could not have known beforehand that she would be sent there. It so happens that there was a probationary nurse working in the infirmary who has since been discharged. As a matter of precaution, a search is being made for this woman.

"People are asking how about the guards on the walls? There are eight little watch houses in the circuit of the walls, and in each an armed guard is supposed to be stationed at all times. It may be that the watch on the walls has become a perfunctory matter, since escapes in this bold manner from a woman's prison almost never occur. But the Warden claims that this is not so. He admits that one or more of the guards must have been extraordinarily careless—or worse.

"Apart from the blame attaching to the outside guards, it seems highly probable that the articles found in the girl's cell must have been passed to her by one of the prison employees. Six persons had regular access to her cell; four women keepers, and two head keepers, men. All six strenuously deny any complicity in the matter.

"A very unfortunate impression has been created by the affair, which is bound to revive the old gossip that in several of the state prisons there is a regular underground organisation for the purposes of assisting prisoners to escape—for a consideration. A rigid investigation is in progress."

I went into my mistress's room to talk the matter over.

"Well, Bella," she said teasingly. "I see they are looking for you."

But she could not frighten me that way. I knew I was safe under her protection. "What amazing boldness!" I said.

"Yes," she said with a half smile. "Imagine having a rendezvous with one's friends at the top of that tall window in the middle of the night! Imagine skimming over the prison wall, and hustling away through the night in one's trusty Ford! After solitary confinement, what an extraordinary joy in finding oneself free under the sky! It almost makes one wish one were a desperate crook!"

"I am quite content to forgo those pleasures," I said.

She laughed delightedly. She takes endless pleasure in drawing me out, as you have seen; but, bless her heart! I don't mind.

"Are you going to take any action, now?" I asked.

"Yes," she said. "Let us insert another personal in the *Sphere*. Take this down: 'X: Congratulations. Call us up some time. Y.'"

I wrote it down with, I suppose, a somewhat disapproving expression, for she laughed again.

"No," she said. "That's *too* immoral. We must uphold society. Cross it out, and try this: 'X. I am your friend. Call me up. Y.'"

It was so done.

6

THE OUTCOME

MEANWHILE THE PRESS of other business continued. Besides the ridiculous Van der Venter case which took up so much time, there was the affair of Lear Gaybourn, the gun-runner, which had international complications; and there was much routine business. Almost every day new cases were offered us which we had to turn down. Mme. Storey steadfastly refuses to form an organisation.

"It would enslave me," she says. "It would spoil all the fun. I will be a free lance until I die." Consequently she will accept nothing that she cannot give her personal attention to.

It was eleven o'clock in the morning, and I was trying to bring some order out of the conflicting affidavits in the Van der Venter case, and at the same time answer the telephone every few minutes, and receive numerous callers. I had, sitting in my office, a bank president, a police inspector, and two lesser lights, all patiently awaiting their turn to see my mistress. With her was a very great man indeed, who had come all the way from Washington to see her. I will designate him as Secretary X.

The telephone rang again, and I took down the receiver, swearing inwardly. But I instantly recognised the somewhat hoarse yet musical voice that came over the wire, and my heart began to beat with the most painful intensity.

"Is this Madame Storey's office?" Her voice was breathless, too, and that increased my excitement.

"Yes," I stammered. "This is Bella Brickley, her secretary. I know your voice."

"Can I speak to her?"

"Oh!" I said in a sort of despair. "She is so busy. Could you call again in a few minutes?"

"No," said the voice, sharp with disappointment. "I am watched. I don't know when I'll get another chance. But it doesn't matter—"

"Wait! Wait!" I said. "Hold the wire, and I will try to arrange it."

I tapped on the door of my mistress's room, and went in. She saw by my face that there was something in the wind. "That person whom we were expecting to call up is on the wire," I said.

There was no hesitation in her. "I am extremely sorry, Mr. Secretary," she said, "but this is a matter of the most urgent importance. I am forced to ask you to step outside for a moment, while I talk to this person."

The Secretary was a pompous man of great girth, whose shapelessness was emphasized by the formal clothes that government dignitaries affect. He was exceedingly affronted by Mme. Storey's simple request, and turned as red as a strawberry. But there was nothing for it but to obey.

As I followed him through the door, Mme. Storey said to me in a low tone: "Listen in."

Having seated my indignant Secretary, I flew to the telephone, and switching the call to Mme. Storey's desk, put the receiver to my ear.

"Hallo!"

"Is this Madame Storey?" asked the breathless voice.

Then my mistress's friendly, casual accents: "Yes. So this is you, my dear! I had to send a member of the Cabinet out of the room in order to talk to you."

"I never expected to be talking to you," faltered Melanie. "I don't know what to say now. Everything has gone out of my head."

"Well, the first thing to do is to arrange a meeting," said Mme. Storey. "Can't you come here?"

"No," said Melanie. "You don't understand. We can't meet. I'm watched every minute. They don't trust me."

"Who doesn't trust you?"

"I can't explain the whole thing. There isn't time. I tried to shake them—see?—and run my own show. That's why I was railroaded to Woburn. To make me feel their power. Thirteen years I was facing; I near went out of my mind. When they thought I had had my lesson they got me out again. They need me. But they're still leery of me. I'm not allowed out yet. When I do go out I suppose she'll go with me. It's just by a chance I could telephone. She had to go downstairs. When I hear her start up again, I'll have to hang up sudden."

"Where are you?" asked Mme. Storey.

"I won't tell you that," said Melanie despairingly.

"I understand," said my mistress with undiminished kindness. "Answer me this: If you could come to me, would you?"

"I want to," said Melanie very low, "but... but... maybe

you'd think you had to send me back to Woburn… It isn't as if I had any of the stuff put away," she added rather pitifully. "The woman got her pearls back. I haven't got a cent to my name."

"I promise you I'll never send you back," said Mme. Storey energetically. "I will take that responsibility."

"But you'd expect me to blow the whole game," said Melanie. "I don't know as I could do that. There's too many in it. Some are just plain unfortunate. It's all mixed up. I've got to decide what to do… Besides, if it all came out, I'd have to go back to Woburn anyhow."

"Hold on!" said Mme. Storey; "let's take up these questions separately. I want you to come to me for your own sake, primarily. There are no strings to my offer. We will make friends. If you feel like telling me the whole story, all right. But there shall be no constraint upon you. If you *do* tell me, I promise you that we will exact a pardon for you from the governor himself, before we tell another soul. Excepting Bella, of course."

"You are kind," said Melanie. "But you don't know what I'm up against. They would stop at nothing. They would shoot the governor himself sooner than have their game queered. If I came to you, they would croak us both."

"Nonsense!" said Mme. Storey crisply. "I have the means to protect you, and myself, too. I promise you full protection once you are inside my door. I will have twenty men for the purpose, should it be necessary. Not uniformed police, either, but my own men."

There was a pause, then Melanie's voice came firmly: "All right. I'll come."

"You can't say when, of course," said Mme. Storey.

"No. I must take my chance when I see it."

"At whatever time of day or night it may be, come to the office," said Mme. Storey. "I can best take care of you here. Even though I am not here myself, you will be expected; and you will find strong protectors waiting."

There was no answer from Melanie.

"Are you there?" asked Mme. Storey.

Her voice rang dead over the wire, and we realised that Melanie had been obliged to hang up in a hurry. But she must have received the gist of her instructions. I suppose we both offered up a little prayer that she might not have been surprised at the phone. It was painful to be left in such suspense.

I put up the receiver, and ushered the Secretary back into Mme. Storey's office. Not a muscle of my mistress's face had changed, but her expressive eyes sought mine gravely and questioningly. She was asking me with her eyes if she was leading me into more danger than I cared to face. I was afraid; nevertheless, I answered her with my eyes as courageously as I could. Meanwhile, the stuffed secretary had started a prosy, pompous speech. He thought he was everything in our lives.

When he had gone, Mme. Storey pressed the button under her desk that summons John Wagstaffe, our young janitor-engineer, from the basement. Mme. Storey employs a number of men, but naturally they do not hang around the office. There are only us two women there, and at my earnest solicitation this bell had been put in. It had come in very handy once or twice, when we wished to get rid of a nuisance.

John responded promptly. John is a host in himself. Like

Georges Carpentier, he combines brawn and charm in equal degrees. He looked a little disappointed upon finding that there was no one to throw out this time. He adores Mme. Storey, and only regrets that we have no occasion to call on him oftener.

"John," said Mme. Storey, "are there any vacancies in this building?"

"No vacancies, ma'am. But Mr. Spelman is trying to sublet. Parlour, bedroom and bath, second floor, rear."

"I'll take it," said Mme. Storey. "When can I get the key?"

"In just so long as it takes me to go downstairs and get it, ma'am," said John, grinning.

"There's a friend of mine, a young woman, who has dangerous enemies, John," Mme. Storey went on. "I have offered her a refuge here, and have told her that we will take her in any time of day or night. From this time on, I will keep two or three men here to protect her, and I'll count on you, too."

"Yes, ma'am!" said John enthusiastically.

"My men will sleep in the back room of my offices, and we'll save the suite upstairs for the girl. One of the men will be on duty down in the hall every night, after the building is closed, in order to admit her, should she come. She may come in the daytime. I will talk to the two hall-boys. Once she is in the building, you must all be especially careful about admitting strangers. No information of any sort must be given out. While she is here, all callers who ask for me must be seated in the hall while their names are sent up."

John fairly stammered in his eagerness. "Yes, ma'am; you can count on me, ma'am. The boys, too. No information about your matters is ever given out. I only hope they'll come, that's all. I hope they come!"

"That's all now," said Mme. Storey. "We'll talk about this again."

When he had gone, Mme. Storey gave me instructions to be transmitted to three of our men—Stephenson, Ketchell and Crider. Crider was one of the best men we had, and he could ill be spared from the work he was on; but he was such a sane, dependable fellow, it was a comfort to us to have him at hand.

"Are you scared, Bella?" Mme. Storey asked me, smiling. I denied it.

"The danger to us is not so great as the poor girl supposes," said Mme. Storey. "Once she gets inside our door, they will realise that the game is up, and run for cover. If they suspected her intention, of course they would stop at nothing in order to prevent her from carrying it out…" She paused, her face full of a grave concern. "Oh, well," she said, trying to shake it off, "she's a wise, wise kid. We can only hope for the best."

TEN DAYS PASSED without our hearing any further from Melanie. Of course, we had our work to do, and we could only give an occasional thought to the girl by day— thoughts that became ever heavier with anxiety as the days went by. Outside of office hours, the girl was continually in my mind. I tried in vain to picture her situation from the ominous hints she had given over the telephone; who were the dreadful "they" at whose mention the bold girl trembled? what sort of house was it where she was confined? who was this "she" who was her jailer? Mme. Storey and I discussed her very little. There was nothing to be said. If she did not come to us of her own free will, we could make no move to find her, for, as an escaped convict, she was as one of the living dead.

The three active, able men chafed very much at their enforced inaction. As the days passed and nothing happened, their situation began to appear ridiculous to them. Mme. Storey finally let two of them go in the daytime, with instructions to report frequently by phone. Crider, excellent fellow! remained with us, and all three still slept in the back room.

Then came the afternoon that I shall never forget.

A brilliant afternoon towards the end of May, and the little square outside our windows was gay with running children. In the office we were enjoying a blessed interlude of peace; and Mme. Storey and I—she at her desk, I at mine—were working busily to catch up with the arrears. Crider was in my room filing away the reports which had accumulated.

The telephone rang. Nowadays my heart always gave a little jump at the sound of the telephone bell, and this time the little jump was followed by a great one, when I heard the anxiously-awaited voice on the wire. There was a gay ring in it now. She did not ask for Mme. Storey, but delivered her message to me direct.

"Hello, sister! I'm on my way—that is, if it's all right."

"Surely, surely!" I said. "We've been looking for you."

"I know. I didn't dare chance the telephone again. Too near a thing that other time. I've been playing a deep part, kid. I've satisfied them now that I'm thoroughly broke, and to-day I was let out for the first on my own. I've been walking around to make sure I wasn't trailed. It's all right. Is *she* there?"

"Yes."

"I'll be there in fifteen minutes."

"Better take a taxi," I said. "It's safer."

"I haven't got the price, darling… Tooriloo…"

"Wait a minute!" I cried. I felt that Mme. Storey ought to be consulted.

But she had already hung up. I ran in to tell my mistress the news.

All pretence of further work was abandoned. Mme. Storey sent word down to the door that no one but Melanie was to be brought up. I stood in the big window in her room watching the sidewalk. This handsome, projecting window was put in when the old house was reconditioned. It fills the whole end of the room, with six casements overlooking the park, and a narrower one at each end through which we are able to look up and down the street. Mme. Storey and Crider were behind me. They had to depend on me to identify the approaching girl.

That ten minutes or so had all the effect of an hour. Finally I saw her turn the corner down at Fourth Avenue, which is about three hundred yards away. "Here she comes!" I said, and the other two pressed up close to look over my shoulder. Melanie walked with a fine, free stride. She had gotten herself up with the greatest care, and at that distance she looked as smart as a debutante. There were even flowers at her waist.

There we stood, the three of us, and saw all that happened, powerless to aid our friend. The street was almost empty. I remember there was a nondescript woman behind Melanie, and there were two well-dressed men, members of one of the clubs in our block, walking towards her. Around the corner came a black taxi-cab, which looked no different from any other taxi. Passing Melanie, it swerved suddenly into the curb, and stopped. Two men tumbled out. They faced Melanie. She half turned as if to run, but a hand was raised holding a short, thick weapon. It descended, and Melanie crumpled.

The sound of a scream reached our ears. Not from Melanie, but from the woman behind her. The two well-dressed men started running towards the trio, but one of the attackers turned, and pointed a gun at them. They fell back. The other thug dragged Melanie's limp body to the open door of the taxi. Getting in first, he pulled her after. His friend, still covering the club-men, backed into the cab, and pulled the door to. They were off.

All this happened in less time than it takes to read it. At the first sign of danger, our Crider had started for the door. Before he got out in the street, the taxi was gone. Mme. Storey had snatched open the drawer of her desk where she keeps a pistol. Her object was to shoot at the tyres of the taxi. But it did not pass our windows. Turning on two wheels up the west side of the little square, it turned again into Twenty-First Street, and was gone.

7

MME. STOREY LAYS HER PLANS

WHEN IT BECAME clear that we could do nothing to aid the girl, my strong and self-reliant mistress broke down. I had never before seen her so terribly moved. Her head hung down, and she gripped my wrist, as if for support.

"Oh, Bella! Bella! Bella!" she murmured heart-brokenly. "She put herself in my hands! She trusted in me. And I failed her!"

"No! No!" I cried. "It was not your fault. You could do nothing! The responsibility was hers until she got here!"

But Mme. Storey had already got her grip again. Her head was thrown up, and her dark eyes flashed. "By heaven, I'll make them pay!" she cried. "If it's my last act on earth they shall pay for this! Everything else shall be dropped. Government business or whatever it is. I will do nothing, I will think of nothing until I have avenged this poor girl— Quick! call Crider back!"

Crider was down at the front door, looking this way and that, uncertain which way the taxicab had gone. From the window I made him a signal to come up.

Mme. Storey was pacing up and down the room, pressing her knuckles to her temples. "Get Police Headquarters," she said. "Inspector Rumsey on the phone. Tell the

operator down there it is Miss Bessemer calling. Rumsey
will know that name."

Inspector Rumsey was her old and loyal friend, and
incidentally one of the best police officers in the country;
a man superior to political considerations.

While I was getting my call through, Crider came in.
Mme. Storey said: "They cannot know for sure whether
we expected the girl. It is essential to them to find that
out. Quick! Return downstairs, and tell the hall-boys that
anybody who asks for me is to be brought up. If they said,
'Madame Storey is not seeing anybody,' that in itself would
be suspicious. Warn the boys afresh to answer no questions.
Take them into our confidence. Tell them that our friend
was attacked on the way here, and the only chance of saving
her life lies in concealing the fact that we expected her."

Crider ran out. I got the inspector on the wire.

"Write out a description of the girl," Mme. Storey said
to me.

"My dear friend," she said to the inspector, "I am in the
greatest distress. I cannot be frank over the telephone, but
I will find a way to let you know the full particulars— No,
we cannot meet for the present, for I shall certainly be
watched— Listen! it is of the utmost importance that it
should not be known that this information came to you
from me, understand?

"The first thing to do is to send out a general alarm to
every patrolman on the force. Word it this way: At four
thirty-five this afternoon an unknown woman walking
east on Twentieth Street was overtaken by a taxi-cab at a
point a hundred feet or so east of Fourth Avenue. Two men
jumped out of the cab; one of them struck the girl with

a blackjack and dragged her into the cab, while the other with a pistol held off two men who ran to her assistance. The taxi then made off up the west side of Gramercy Park, and turned west in Twenty-First Street. We got the licence number." Mme. Storey read it to him.

"Here is the description of the girl," she went on, and read him from the pencilled memo. I handed her: "About twenty-six years old, but looks younger; taller than average, strong, graceful figure, and strikingly good-looking, in a bold dark style. Black hair, bobbed at her neck; large dark brown eyes. Was wearing a well-tailored blue suit, and small, black straw hat of the style known as *cloche*."

"As to the two men who attacked her," Mme. Storey went on, "I can only say that they were slender and active. They wore dark suits and tweed caps. There were several witnesses to the affair, and better descriptions of the men will, no doubt, reach you through the regular channels."

While Mme. Storey was talking, the buzzer sounded that announced the entrance of somebody into my room. She broke off, saying: "Send that out, and I'll call you up again in five minutes."

With quick nods she directed that Crider was to go in the back room, while I received our caller.

"Compose your face, Bella," she said sternly.

I put on my dark-rimmed glasses. They help me to look blank when I have need to do so. My heart was beating like a trip-hammer. In my room I found a slender, dark young man, who was apparently in the greatest excitement, but it was all put on, for his dark eyes were cool and hard. They bored me through like gimlets. Well, he got no change out of me.

"Is Mme. Storey in?" he cried, with seeming breathlessness.

"What do you want of her?" I asked.

"There's been a girl knocked on the head down the street and abducted in a car!" he cried.

I made haste to open the door, and he ran into my mistress's room. She was writing at her desk with admirable composure. She looked up in cool surprise. The young man repeated his announcement with added details.

"Good heavens! how terrible!" cried my mistress, springing up.

She turned to look out of the window, as was most natural, and I followed her. Quite a crowd had gathered on the spot where the outrage had taken place.

"Oh, they're gone," said the young man. "Made a clean getaway."

"Have the police been notified?" asked Mme. Storey.

"Sure, the cops arrived on the scene after everything was over."

"Why did you come to tell me?" asked Mme. Storey.

"Well, I heard somebody in the crowd say she was a friend of yours," he answered glibly.

I shall never forget the face of the speaker; sleek, sharp and insolent, with eyes as flat and expressionless as an animal's. He wasn't but eighteen or nineteen years old, but he looked *steeped* in evil.

"Good heavens!" cried Mme. Storey, opening her eyes very wide. "What sort of girl? Describe her?"

"I didn't see it myself," said the young man, "but I heard them talking." His description of the girl closely followed my own.

"That suggests nothing to me," said Mme. Storey, shaking her head. "I wasn't expecting anybody at this hour—You should notify police headquarters. Use my phone."

But the man, acting as if distracted, turned and ran out of the room. Mme. Storey and I exchanged a look. Crider came in from the back room.

"That was one of the two who seized Melanie," said my mistress bitterly. "He had changed his hat, that was all. It was hard to let him go. After they had gone a block or so, he dropped off the car and came back to see what was doing. It's an old trick."

"I can pick him up," said Crider eagerly. "Let me trail him."

Mme. Storey shook her head. "He would lead you nowhere. And the risk is too great—to her, I mean. There is one chance in ten that she is still alive. She is very useful to them. But if they suspected that I had any knowledge of their activities, it would seal her death warrant."

Crider turned away, keenly disappointed.

I got Inspector Rumsey on the phone again.

To him Mme. Storey said: "I shall be working myself on this matter, but it will be underground, and you won't hear from me till the result is known. I want you to put the regular machinery in motion, because nothing must be neglected, but I must beg of you to use the greatest caution. Unless you can take them by surprise, you will only find the girl's dead body at the end of the trail.

"It is about our usual closing time here," she went on, "and I mean to walk home in my customary leisurely manner. I shall no doubt be followed. I'll have Bella stop in at the Arts Club, on her way home, if you can meet her there in half an hour's time. She may be watched, too, but no one could get into the club who had not legitimate business there—

"You'll be there? Very good. Bella will go in at the Twentieth Street entrance, which is almost next door to our office. You enter from Nineteenth Street, and leave that way. You are not a member, are you? No. Well, ask for me, and they'll bring you to Bella. She will tell you the whole story. It's a very strange one, my friend. Better make no attempt to communicate with me through the usual channels. Good-bye."

To me she said: "You are to tell him the whole story of Melanie Soupert, so far as you know it. He's entitled to the facts. But warn him afresh to keep the real name of to-day's victim locked in his own breast. If it was published, it would be all up with her. Tell him that I promised to save the girl from serving out her two sentences, but if he gets hold of her, of course, he must be guided by his own conscience. At any rate, it would be better to have her back in Woburn than in her grave. And I guess you and I could get her out, Bella."

We still had some minutes before closing time, and she dictated letters to me for Secretary X., for Mrs. Van der Ventner and others, notifying them that she was obliged to drop all work on their respective cases for the present. She gave as her reason that her physician had ordered her to take a rest, and suggested that the work be given to an agency that she recommended.

"It's unfair and it's unprofessional," she said with a troubled brow, "but I can't help myself. At a moment like this all other considerations must give way."

She then dictated a notice to be given out to the press. "Madame Rosika Storey of Gramercy Park, is sailing on the *Baratoria* on Saturday at noon for her usual vacation in Paris. She will be away three months."

"To-morrow morning," she went on, "go to the Brevard Line, and secure the best available room on C deck."

"But you're not *really* going!" I said, opening my eyes very wide.

She smiled. "I shall appear to go. That is, unless Rumsey recovers the girl before Saturday. That's not likely. He's a first-rate man, but in this case he will soon come up against the political barriers: 'Thus far shalt thou go, and no farther!'"

Full of amazement, I digested this announcement.

"I see no way of getting my man but by slow, patient stalking," she went on.

"Your man?" I said; "there is a whole gang."

"There is certain to be one," she said, "from whom all the others receive their impetus. He is my mark."

"You are going into danger!" I said, with a sinking heart.

She shrugged. "You'll hear from me," she said. "Thank God! the telephone is above suspicion. They can't tap my wires."

"Let me share it," I begged. "How could I remain here day after day in suspense. Not able to reach you—not knowing what was happening..."

"My dear Bella!" she said, laying her hand on mine for an instant. "These are only sickly fancies. Surely, of all women, I ought to be able to take care of myself. I can't take you with me, my dear; it would double the risk, and besides, I must have some one here that I can call on in time of need." That silenced me, of course.

8

JESSIE SEIPP

NOTHING WAS OMITTED to create the illusion of Mme. Storey's departure for her usual three months in Paris. A brilliant group of her friends saw her off at the pier; including the Hon. Emmet Fogarty, Mrs. Cornelius Marquardt, Countess Montpellier, and others much in the public eye. All of which was commented on in the press. Mme. Storey herself gave out an interview, telling of her plans in detail, and she was photographed at least a dozen times on the sun deck of the *Baratoria*, for the rotogravure supplements.

A week later, her arrival in Paris was cabled back, and at intervals of two or three days thereafter, items appeared chronicling her appearance at Longchamps, at the Duchesse D'Uze's garden party, at a reception in the Elysée Palace, and so on. Even her costumes were described; all this was arranged for through an agent in Paris. For, of course, Mme. Storey never left New York.

With her departure, all activities at the office abruptly ceased, and my duties became merely perfunctory. I occupied myself chiefly with reading the newspapers and writing my stories. The newspapers never yielded a word that could be applied to our case. During the first few days I believe that I was followed wherever I went, but I was not sure, because Mme. Storey had warned me not to betray the least suspicion that I might be followed. At any rate, I had seen one or two men who seemed to ignore my existence rather self-consciously. One, a heavy, blond German with a pock-marked face and a lowering look, I had seen twice. But, after four days, nothing more of the sort had come under my notice, and I was beginning to hope that our efforts to convince the gang we had no interest in their doings had finally been successful.

On the fifth day Mme. Storey called me up. At the sound of the well-known, slow voice, with a little crinkle of amusement in it, a great gladness filled my breast. We conducted our conversation prudently, since there was a chance that we might be overheard, though it was a slight one. Mme. Storey's name was so much on all lips that the sound of it might have arrested the attention of even the busiest telephone operator.

"Hello, there!" she said.

"Hello yourself," I answered. "Are you all right?"

"Right as a trivet! What I want first is news; of course I've read the papers."

"There is no news, except what has been in the papers. Our friend has made no progress."

"Well, if no body has been found, that is something. Have they been interesting themselves in your movements?"

"I think so. You told me not to notice anything of the sort. Since yesterday, I think they've been called off."

"You'd better make sure of that now. Walk once or twice through one of the long, empty blocks in your neighbourhood, and look behind you. Seat yourself for awhile on a bench in the Park, from where you can see in every direction."

"I will. Have you made your plans?"

"Yes, but we'd better not go into details over the phone, I'm still looking for just the job I want. I must establish a background. I mean to be a laundry worker."

"A laundry worker; in July!" I exclaimed, thinking of her beautiful hands.

"It will only be a few days."

"But why a laundry?"

"The work is so hard, and the pay so poor, you can always get a job without any to do about references."

"I can't imagine you in a laundry," I said helplessly.

"I am much changed, my friend."

"Any instructions?" I asked.

"Yes. I want you to send a telegram to my well-known friend in Tuxedo. Do you get me?"

"You mean E.M.?" I asked. ("E.M." stood for Emily Marquardt—Mrs. Cornelius Marquardt.)

"Yes. I couldn't send it in my present make-up without exciting remark in the telegraph office. But you can. Send it from an office where you are known. Just say: 'Four o'clock, Saturday. If not convenient, name your own time.' And sign it: 'Louisa.'"

I repeated this over the wire.

"That's all now. I'll call you up at your boarding-house to-night."

I sent the telegram; and in two hours I got this answer, "I'll be there: Emily."

AT HOME THAT night, I was just finishing dinner when I was summoned to the phone. The instrument is in the hall, just outside the dining-room door; and as all the boarders pricked up their ears, it behooved me to be more careful than ever about my end of the conversation. The voice that came over the wire was strange to me; a slightly husky voice, speaking the clipped, derisive jargon of the streets.

"Hello, guy! Say, listen. T'ere's a band concert over in Tompkins Square t'night. Kalsomine yer neck and c'm on over."

I suppose I gasped audibly. A delighted laugh came winging over the wire, and I heard my mistress's natural voice.

"That's my new character, Bella. Hereafter, I must think in it, speak in it, walk in it, eat in it, and even dream in it!… Any news?"

Still a little dazed, I told her of the telegram I had received.

"That means you are to meet Mrs. Marquardt at the Arts Club at four to-morrow afternoon," she said. "In the morning's mail you will receive a letter which you are to hand to her. The answer, which will be simply yes or no, is to be conveyed to me through you. But tell her she had better consult her husband before she answers."

"I understand," I said.

Mme. Storey dropped into the vernacular again.

"Say, listen, guy, I got a job already. Pushin' a gas-iron over starched fronts. I put in half a day there. It's a fierce dump, but watcha gonna do? The bunch ain't so bad. And tough! my word! you gotta hand it to 'em!"

I had never seen (or heard) Mme. Storey in this rôle. It was marvellous. It scared me a little.

"Can we meet?" I faltered.

"Say, it would look funny if the like of youse was to be seen talkin' to the like of me. But we could give each other the once over, if you wanted. That was on the level about Tompkins Square. C'mon over. Know where it is?"

"No."

"You just hop an Eighth Street car bound east, and unload when you hear the band play. Walk up and down on the Avenue A side. If you see me, don't let anythin' on. I can't say posi*tive*ly I'll be there, but watch out for me. Bye-bye!"

When I left the telephone, old Mrs. Pruefrock looked in my face, and cackled. "Have you had bad news?"

I put on my plainest hat and boarded an Eighth Street car. I felt like one venturing into the unreal. Yet Avenue A was entirely matter-of-fact.

It is a quaint neighbourhood; the New York of sixty or seventy years ago, very little changed. The wide street is lined with plain, red brick tenements, only three stories high, decorated with rusty fire-escapes, and having little shops on the street level. Only the big, gaudily-painted electric cars that clang up and down are out of keeping; one calls up in one's mind the little horse-cars, with battered fronts and gleaming brass brake handles, that used to jog along to the accompaniment of a tinkling bell.

The people have changed more; for the ghetto is sweeping up from the South, fast obliterating the Irish-American element that first set the East Side's gallant derisive tone. The Jews have their qualities, but they are different. However, one still sees the Irish faces on the street corners, with their provoking eyes and wry mouths, uttering witticisms out of one corner.

It was a hot night, and the populace lay about on the grass of the little park undisturbed by the police, and listening to the music with the air of those who are consciously improving themselves. On the surrounding pavements promenaded the youths and maidens, these not giving a hang for the music, but probably enjoying it just as much. I joined the promenaders, keeping to the extreme outside of the walk, and making myself as inconspicuous as possible. I felt horribly out of place. Particularly my rainy day hat. I should have worn the gayest I had.

Walking towards me, arm-in-arm, came two girls, who were typical of the scene. One was tall, and had a great bush of crass blonde hair standing out from her head, and roving dark eyes. She wore a sports-dress of tub silk, which clung to her fine figure scantily. It had scarlet stripes three inches wide running up and down. Like all the other girls, she was outrageously painted; it almost robbed her face of humanity; nevertheless, there was something splendid and barbaric about her, that caused every youth who passed to cock an eye her way. Her companion was small and dark, and piquant; they made admirable foils to each other. They were closely followed by two young men, making humorous remarks which the girls made believe to ignore.

I walked to the end of the Park and turned around. When I came back I saw them again. They had stopped to listen to the music and I passed behind them. The young men had evidently been admitted to a footing of acquaintanceship; the two girls still clung together, arm-in-arm, but they now had a youth on each side. Obliged to keep in step with the slowly-moving crowd, I heard some snatches of their talk as I passed, but I could make nothing of it. It was just a lively noise.

One young man wore a straw hat with a very tall crown, and no brim to speak of. He said vaguely: "I'll tell the world—"

To which the tall girl replied: "There'll be no wash in Heaven."

And they shouted with laughter.

The other young man wore an alleged Panama hat, which was most unnaturally ironed into the shape of a Fedoro, with a little hollow in each side of the crown. With a killing side-glance at the little girl, he warbled: "Oh, Min! Oh, Min! Come down to your child!"

Whereat she replied with hauteur: "Somebody oughta give that buyd a wuym."

Then the tall girl announced once more: "There'll be no wash in Heaven."

And they redoubled their laughter.

The next time our paths crossed they were walking. It never occurred to me that one like myself could attract the attention of this giddy quartet, and I looked at them with frank curiosity as we passed. Imagine my feelings when the tall girl suddenly turned her head, and said close in my face in sepulchral tones:

"There'll be no wash in Heaven, kid!"

Her companions roared. As for me, I walked on a little dizzily, for in that flamboyant girl I had suddenly recognised my mistress. I recognised her, yet I couldn't believe in the evidence of my own senses. Mme. Storey, the elegant, the exquisite, the admired of New York and Paris, and that great, showy flower of the East Side! Yet they were one and the same! I don't know what I had expected to find; certainly not that. Arm in arm with a girl of Avenue A and flirting with two of its fellows! Was it any wonder that I felt as if I had flown apart, and was unable to collect the pieces?

But in due course my composure returned, and with it the deepest and richest feeling of amusement. What a marvellous piece of acting I was privileged to witness. Surely such acting had never been seen on any stage. What art, what humour, what humanity were in that impersonation; and it was all for me, so to speak; at least I was the only one in a position to appreciate it.

I turned back, eager to see all I could. The four had now seated themselves in a row on the grass, facing the sidewalk, and by taking fairly short turns to and fro, I was able to pass them frequently. They paid no further attention to me. It was chiefly that blonde bush of hair which had created such a change in my mistress's outward seeming. I saw that it was not a wig. She had bobbed her hair, and dyed it with peroxide to that peculiarly crass shade. She had frizzed it till it stood out perpendicularly from her head. The hair, and the heavy make-up, of course, entirely destroyed her usual expression.

But she did not depend on outward seeming. She had got under the very skin of her part. She portrayed a nature the exact opposite of her own. I could not sufficiently admire the subtle touches; the slightly thickened voice; the ungainly movements of her long body, which nevertheless expressed a natural grace; the crude gesticulation which suggested a powerful personality, but ignorant and unformed. It was a treat to see the way she made play with her hands in her fuzzy hair. She was studying her own effects, too, and enjoying them; one could tell it from the slightly withdrawn expression of her eyes. For conversation, that one phrase seemed to do her pretty well, on which she rang a hundred changes like a charming clown.

"There'll be no wash in Heaven!"

When the band put away its instruments, the crowd scattered, and I lost my quartet. I could not, in any case, have followed them. I went home, hugging the recollection of that rich, artistic treat, and dwelt on it half the night. There was an undercurrent of anxiety, too. To what dangerous end were these talents to be devoted?

The letter for Mrs. Cornelius Marquardt arrived next morning under cover for me. A bulky letter that I weighed thoughtfully in my hand. I a little resented that I had not so far been taken into the secret of the contents of this letter. Shortly before four, I carried it into the Arts Club. I had satisfied myself the previous day that my movements were no longer being watched.

Mrs. Cornelius Marquardt is, as everybody knows, a very great lady. She married the Marquardt millions under romantic circumstances; she entertains royalty; she possesses marvellous jewels, *et cetera*. She is a "friend" of Mme. Storey's, but I cannot say there is any great degree of intimacy between them. It may be simply that it suits these two great ladies, in such different spheres, to make an alliance.

Mrs. Marquardt came sailing into the club like a cup defender across the finish line. She greeted me with her well-known charm, which she turns on for the benefit of high and low alike, and immediately sat down to read her letter. This covered page after page with my mistress's characteristic, long-tailed handwriting, and it made me rather jealous to see it. Yet, as Mrs. Marquardt read, the natural woman began to crack the veneer of her charm, and I liked her better. Once or twice she giggled delightedly, and when she had finished reading, she looked both scared and delighted.

She said immediately: "The answer is 'yes.'"

I said: "My mistress suggested that you ought to consult Mr. Marquardt before you committed yourself."

"I will answer for him," she said. "I have already spoken to him in a general way about the matter." She tucked the letter in her bag. "Tell our friend," she said, "that as soon as I have committed the contents to memory, I will burn it."

Mme. Storey called me up at the same hour as on the night before. I conveyed Mrs. Marquardt's answer to her. I have been too well-trained to ask questions, but I suppose Mme. Storey must have heard in my voice that I felt my exclusion, for she said:

"Have patience until Tuesday morning, my Bella. It will all be in the papers."

She asked me if I thought she would pass muster in her new rôle; and I tried to tell her what I thought about it.

"That was only a preliminary study," she said, laughing. "It will have to be better than that to see me through to the end."

"The end of what?" I wondered—but did not ask.

"I shall probably not call you up again," she said. "Don't forget Tuesday. And, by the way, my name is Jessie Seipp. Good-bye."

"Ah... good-bye!" I said.

9

THE NINE DAYS' WONDER

I SPENT A wretchedly uneasy Sunday and Monday. Towards the end of Monday, especially, my restlessness became almost unbearable. "By this time," I thought, "the happening, whatever it may be, has already taken place." After supper, while I was vainly trying to occupy myself with a book, I was tormented by the knowledge that reporters, pressmen, and everybody connected with the newspapers must know everything by this time, while I, who was so deeply concerned in the matter, was still in the dark. I knew that morning papers came off the press at two or three o'clock; but I could not prowl around the streets at that hour.

After a few hours of broken sleep, I was out in the streets soon after sunrise. The news-stand at the corner was not open, of course, but the morning papers were lying on the sidewalk, tied up in bundles. This time there was no need of searching through the paper for what I wanted. It was displayed under a two column head on the right-hand side of the front page. I caught my breath when I read it.

MRS. CORNELIUS MARQUARDT
ATTACKED BY WOMAN THIEF

IN HER FIFTH AVE. MANSION

I pulled a paper from out the bundle, left three cents on top of the pile, and fled home, reading as I went.

I have the paper by me as I write; but to give you the whole account would encumber my story too much. It was a sensation of the very first class. Mrs. Cornelius Marquardt, the sacro-sanct, actually knocked about in her own home! The writers of the story seemed scarcely able to believe what they had seen and heard. The whole account seemed to be written with a gasp. With its introduction, summary, interviews, description of the Marquardt place, and history of the Marquardt family, it spread over column after column, so I will just give you the gist of it.

"Mr. and Mrs. Marquardt are spending the early summer at their place in the Pocanties Hills, before sailing for Europe on the 19th. Yesterday Mrs. Marquardt had occasion to spend the day in town, to attend to various matters. She motored in from the Westchester resort in her own car. Having finished her business, she had herself driven to the Marquardt town house, at number — Fifth Avenue, to obtain some personal articles that she had need of. It was then five o'clock.

"Owing to the extreme sultriness of the day, Mrs. Marquardt had already been impressed by the discomfort and suffering of those in the streets. As she crossed the pavement from her car to the door of her house, a girl who was passing swayed and staggered, and Mrs. Marquardt put out a hand to keep her from falling. The girl seemed to be about to swoon. Mrs. Marquardt looked around for her chauffeur, but he had already driven away to have his gasoline tank refilled.

"Mrs. Marquardt told the girl she would call a taxi to take her home, whereat the girl mumbled something to the effect that she had no home, and no place in the world to go to. Yielding to a natural impulse of sympathy, Mrs. Marquardt told her she could come into her house to rest until she felt better. The girl presented a respectable enough appearance, and no thought of the rashness of her act occurred to Mrs. Marquardt.

"Ordinarily, Mrs. Marquardt said, she would have rung the outside bell to summon one of the caretakers, but knowing that it would take him some time to reach the door from the basement, she opened the door with her own key, and led the girl in, meaning to give her a seat, and then call the servant. But the instant the door closed behind them, the girl straightened up, and crying out: 'Now I have you!' she attacked her benefactress.

"The girl had slipped a set of brass knuckles over her right hand unseen, and with these she viciously struck at Mrs. Marquardt's head, but that lady's hat and her plentiful hair protected her somewhat, and she was but partly stunned, She defended herself as well as she was able, meanwhile calling for help; but her cries must have been weak, for the two servants in the sub-basement heard nothing. The girl flung her in a chair, and yanking down a priceless antique Venetian embroidery from the wall, the vandal tore it into strips with which she bound and gagged Mrs. Marquardt. She then coolly proceeded to strip the unfortunate lady of her valuables; rings, ear-rings, and string of pearls. A pretty trifle of a beaded bag had fallen to the floor. It contained several hundred dollars.

"The girl, in her ignorance, thought that a house closed for the summer must be emptied of its servants, and with all the coolness in the world, she proceeded to saunter through the magnificent rooms, looking at everything, and picking up what small objects of value she was able to conceal on her person. Mrs. Marquardt watched her helplessly.

"When the girl disappeared up the grand stairway, Mrs. Marquardt struggled desperately to free herself, and succeeded in loosening her bonds sufficiently to permit her to crawl across the hall to the bell button, which she was obliged to press with her tongue. She kept her tongue upon it, until the two servants came running upstairs in alarm. These were William Beddowe, who has served the Marquardts for twenty years in the capacity of butler, and his wife, Sarah, whose position is that of second cook, when the family is in residence. The amazed servants quickly liberated their mistress.

"Hearing sounds upstairs that betokened the girl's approach, Mrs. Marquardt re-seated herself on the chair as if she were still bound, and the two servants concealed themselves close to the stairs. Thereupon, the unsuspecting thief almost walked into their arms as she came down. She had no opportunity to use her brass knuckles again. Such was the anger of the old servants at the outrage perpetrated on their mistress, that the girl was like to have fared badly at their hands, had not Mrs. Marquardt herself interfered to save her."

I was staggered by the thought of this situation. It must

have called upon considerable histrionic powers in Mrs. Marquardt to carry it off. I suspect that the whole elaborate plan was endangered at this moment.

"The girl was first taken to the East — Street police station, where she gave her name as Jessie Seipp; occupation, laundry-worker. She refused all further information. Her bearing was defiant. Apparently she had not known the identity of her victim; when she learned who it was, she was apparently pleased by the notoriety she had brought on herself. She said that the brass knuckles had been given to her by a 'fellow,' whose name she pretended not to know.

"In order to serve the convenience of Mrs. Marquardt, who was naturally much shaken by her experience, and wished to return to her country home, the Seipp girl was immediately rushed to the Woman's Court to be arraigned. Court had adjourned for the day, but Magistrate Mahan was summoned from his home, and the hearing was held. It was brief. Mrs. Marquardt and the two servants told their stories, and the girl was remanded to the Tombs to await trial. The magistrate thanked Mrs. Marquardt for the trouble she had taken to appear personally against so dangerous a malefactor. So far as could be seen in court, Mrs. Marquardt showed no marks of the attack.

"Brief as was the interval between the commission of the crime and the hearing, word of it had got about, and a great crowd thronged the magistrate's court in the expectation of getting a glimpse of the well-known society leader and the girl who had dared to attack her in her own house. On the stand, the prisoner, excited by the attention she was getting, dropped her reticence, and told her story in a theatrical way. She is a tall, finely-formed girl, with a bold manner; handsome in a common sort of way.

" 'Sure, I did it,' she said. 'I don't regret it. I'd do it again if I got the chance. You gents think it's hot in here, don't you, with your handkerchiefs stuffed inside your collars. You think it's hot out on the streets, don't you, with folks dropping on every corner, and being taken away in the ambulance. Well, have you ever been inside a hand laundry on a day like to-day? I guess not. That's where I worked.

"'I worked in the Nonpareil Laundry, on East Tenth. There was two girls fainted there to-day, and sent home. One came back later, though she couldn't hardly stand. But she needed the money. When three-thirty came—that's the hottest time of the day, though we don't have no ther-mometer where we can see it, I suddenly said out loud, 'I'm done! If this is life it ain't worth living.' And I takes my outside clothes, and I walks out, leaving the girls gaping.

" 'I walks up-town, where the rich folks live, I had the knucks in my pocket and didn't care what I did; robbery or murder. I been out of work, and I ain't got a cent. This town owed me a living, and I was going to take it, see? All them fine big houses so nice and cool inside, and full of rich things. And all shut up while rich folks was enjoying them-selves at their other big houses in the country somewheres, and me without so much as one cheap hall bedroom, where I could lay myself down. I was planning how I could break into one of them soon as it got dark.

" 'It was just by chance that I run up against this dame here. I didn't know who she was. Not that I care anyway. She walked across the sidewalk with her diamonds and her pearls and her emeralds, and I saw she was going into the closed-up house there. What a chance I says to myself. If I could get her inside there, I'd have her dead to rights. So I made out I was overcome with the heat, and she fell for it.

" 'They told you what happened after that. I thought the house was empty, being all boarded up. Well, I don't care, I had a good look at the inside of it anyway. Send me up, if you want. I don't care if I get the limit. It'll be cooler up there than the laundry.' "

I read this part again and again, picturing to myself the marvellous acting that had accompanied it. How I wished I could have been there to see it.

"The girl was taken to police headquarters last night and questioned with a view to discovering if she had any accomplices. None of the men at headquarters were able to identify her, and her picture was not found in the records. It is believed that this is her first offence.

"Owing to the fact that Mr. and Mrs. Marquardt have arranged to sail for France on July 19th, the case will be put at the head of the calendar. It will come up for trial within a few days."

In the foregoing I have given you only the essential points of the newspaper story. The rest was mainly gossip of the sort that is dear to the hearts of newspaper readers. In the news columns a decent impartiality had to be maintained, but there was also an editorial, in which the horror of the public at this unexampled outrage was expressed in strong terms.

The public *was* excited by the affair, if one could judge by that small section of it which resided in my boarding-house. At breakfast time, a storm of talk raged from table to table, and all the little feuds were forgotten. But I doubt if "horror" was the proper name for the feeling that was inspired. That was just the official view. Certainly Miss Pruefrock and her cronies moistened their lips in undisguised pleasure over the case.

During the days that followed, the newspapers continued to play up the affair. Between the hearing and the trial there was no real news forthcoming; but they ran a gossip story every day to whet the public appetite. The familiar talk of a crime wave was revived, and everybody abused the police, as usual. The head of the Commissioner was supposed to be due for the official axe; but nothing of that sort happened.

I realised that all this publicity must be included in Mme. Storey's design. Gradually her object became clear to me. She was advertising herself as a bold and reckless thief, with a grudge against society, in the hope of thus recommending herself to the gang we were after, as a worthy successor to Melanie Soupert. The plan was stamped with her individuality; but ah! how dangerous it was! I could not bear to think of it. Yet I knew I should have to live with this fear for many days to come.

She remained in the Tombs for a week only. I did not hear from her during this time, nor did I expect to. The weather remained very hot, and my thoughts were continually with her in her cell.

If only I could have sent her a basket of fruit, or something of that sort; but it would have been most imprudent. Jessie Seipp was supposed not to have a friend in the world. I read that a young lawyer named Baugh had been assigned to her as counsel. Presumably he did his best, but as it has no bearing on the outcome, it will not be necessary to mention him again.

I need hardly say how I burned to attend the trial. I tried to argue myself into the belief that it would be safe to do so. There would be a big crowd there; surely I could lose myself in it. And anyway trials were open to the public; why should not Bella Brickley attend as well as the next one? But all the time I knew I could not go. For suppose Mme. Storey was successful in drawing our quarry; they would have their scouts at the trial; and these might very well include the dark foxy youth, and the big pock-marked German, both of whom knew me well. I considered going in disguise, but this was not safe either, without Mme. Storey to pass on it in advance.

So I had to be content with the newspaper report. I need not go into detail. As trials go, it was not much of a one, because the girl had no defence. But her picturesque personality lent a zest to the proceedings. She evidently enjoyed the affair. She had no hesitation in airing her rude wit at the expense of the prosecutor, and even His Honour himself. She was outrageously defiant. You see, I write this as if this Jessie Seipp had been an actual person, and indeed the whole affair was so wonderfully carried out, there were moments when I was almost deceived myself.

At one time the judge seemed inclined to send her as a first offender to one of the reformatories. This endangered the whole careful plan. But for some reason most prisoners have an especial detestation for these institutions, and it was therefore perfectly in character for Jessie Seipp to launch out against it. According to the newspaper report, she said:

"Send me to prison, Judge. That's where I belong. I'm past the reforming stage. Anything by the name of reform makes me see red. I'd be like a devil unchained in that place. Give me straight punishment instead of moral uplift any day. When you're in a cell you know where you are. Your cell is your own anyhow. But in one of them reformatories they never leave you alone. It's worse than the German army. They drill your soul to do the goose-step!"

She was sentenced to Woburn for two years.

I READ IN the newspaper that they were taking a file of prisoners up to Woburn on the train that left Grand Central at noon on a certain Saturday. Surely Grand Central was one place where anybody could be seen without raising the question of why they were there, I told myself; and there could be no danger if I took care not to approach the prisoners. At any rate I went.

I got there a little early. Every part of the vast station was thronged with vacationers, and I felt safe from recognition in the crowd. But I wondered how I was going to get a glimpse of my mistress's face without pressing up close to her. I placed the train gate through which the prisoners must pass. It was towards the left hand side of the great central concourse, and I saw that I could command it from the low balcony that runs across below the gigantic window.

I went up there. The balustrade was lined with people waiting for friends, or simply interested in watching the animated scene below, and I was not conspicuous. It was a strange sight. All those thousands at my feet were weaving in and out like the pieces in a kaleidoscope, but there was no pattern. No doubt each individual was bent on a purpose highly important to himself; but the general effect was of utter confusion.

I presently made out that a motionless crowd was gathering outside the train gate that I was watching. Many others beside myself had read that item in the newspaper. A hot little spurt of anger rose within me; mere curiosity-seekers, I thought; have they nothing better to do! This was perfectly inconsistent, of course, My nerves were on edge. I had had too much time to think about that case, and not enough to do with it.

Finally I saw the tragic little procession appear from underneath the other end of the balcony on which I stood. It circled around the foot of the great stairway in the middle, and came back towards the train gate. Something less than a score of women walking two and two, with two guards going ahead to force a way through the crowd, and others on either side. Each pair was hand-cuffed together, and all were trying to conceal it by carrying wraps over their joined wrists. Hundreds came pushing to gape at them with that soulless curiosity, one of the ugliest of human expressions. To men prisoners the crowd would have been indifferent, but at the woman they cruelly grinned. I don't know why. Some of the prisoners kept their heads down; some grinned back cringingly at the crowd. All that I could see were pathetically young.

My mistress, conspicuous for her height, was one of the first two. She was the focus of interest. It was at her that the fingers were pointed, and one sensed the busy whispers: "There she is! There she is!" She had on a dark suit and a little black hat with that amazing blonde frizz of hair sticking out all around. She walked along, untroubled by the stares of the people, her own bright eyes busy. Completely protected by the personality of Jessie Seipp, she was enjoying the novel situation. She was going to prison happy, while I was free, and perfectly wretched on her account.

Her keen glance swept along the balustrade. I think she expected to find me there; she saw me, but gave no sign. Fixing her gaze at the end of the balcony, some thirty or forty feet from where I stood, her face lighted up, and she cried out:

"Bye-bye, ol' gal! There'll be no wash in Heaven!"

The crowd roared with laughter, and every neck was craned to discover whom she was speaking to. I was safe, of course. The train gate swallowed her up.

10

IN PRISON

THE SIXTEEN WOMEN, handcuffed two and two, occupied eight seats in a row in the day-coach, while their four
guards were distributed across the aisle. Since their brace-
leted wrists were invariably hidden, once they had taken
their seats there was nothing to distinguish them from
any other passengers, except that it was a little odd to see
so many women of such diverse types in a block together.
They were for the most part in excellent spirits, the train
journey being much better than what lay behind them, and
what was to come. On the train there was no attempt to
prevent them from talking to each other.

Having taken seats in the order of entering, Jessie Seipp
and her companion were in the rearmost of the eight seats,
where Jessie was able to watch the backs of all the other
heads in the party, and speculate on what was going on
inside them. Bobbed heads they were, nearly all of them,
and by preference a chemical auburn shade, chosen, no
doubt, to suggest the adventurous spirit of the wearer. The
oldest still lacked some years of forty; she was a professional shop-lifter, very fashionably dressed, and might
have been a rich woman on the way to her country house.
Beside her sat one who could have passed as her maid.

Nothing was known about the nature of her offence, for she kept her mouth tight shut. Two seats behind them sat an Italian girl with an infantile frightened face. She had been sent up for stabbing a man, and all the others regarded her with respect.

But Jessie's principal interest naturally was in the girl she was chained to. How extraordinary to be chained to an unknown! The backs of their hands lay together, touching. Ordinarily Jessie would have shivered a little at the enforced contact with strange flesh! but now—well, there was no help for it, and one simply did not think about it. This girl was *not* in good spirits. With her anaemic, rebellious face, and two-seasons-old blue suit, she looked like the young wife of a struggling clerk. Jessie felt a desire to make friends with her.

"Gee! I wish I had a cigarette!" she said cheerfully.

"You may as well make up your mind to cut 'em out now," the other said bitterly.

"Oh, I dunno," said Jessie. "Maybe I'll find a way."

"You're one of the ones that always gets what they want, eh?" said her companion with a sneer.

Jessie refused to be put out. "I gen'ally make out," she said.

"Well, you won't find what you're going to no bed of roses!"

"You been there before, I take it?"

The girl looked out of the window without replying.

"Let's be pals," said Jessie bluntly.

The girl turned her head. She had enormous blue eyes with a world of sullen pain in their depths. "Aah! you don't mean nottin' by that," she said with a sneer.

"What if I don't!" said Jessie with a shrug. "Let's be pals anyhow. My name's Jessie Seipp. What's yours?"

"Jean Hazard."

"Bet you made that up. Sounds literary."

In her turn Jean shrugged, without the vestige of a smile in her white face.

"What did they get you for?" asked Jessie. It was the customary way of starting an acquaintance.

But Jean looked out of the window again.

"Well, it's nottin' to me," said Jessie. "Me, I cracked Mrs. Cornelius Marquardt on the bean and frisked her em'ralds."

"Yes, I read about in it the paper," said Jean. "Was it your first job?"

"Yep."

"You were lucky," said Jean with a peculiar bitterness; "breaking into the news first-off like that. It'll attract the attention of the big fellows. You'll get a chance at the big money. I never had no luck. Everybody puts on me. Small jobs, and soaked the limit, that's my story."

"Maybe you ain't cut out for this work," said Jessie, in a tone that the hearer might regard as sympathetic or not, as she pleased.

"Too late to think about that," said Jean dejectedly. "I'm in it too deep."

"What you get?" asked Jessie.

"On'y a year this time," said Jean, hanging her head; "they wasn't but twenty-four dollars in the woman's bag. But this time—you see—" She choked, and tried to carry it off with a piteous swagger. "Aah, what the hell!"

"Oh, a year," said Jessie quickly. "With your time off— Look at me, with three years."

Jean's head went down alarmingly; it was partly turned from Jessie, but the latter saw tears fall in her lap. Big round tears from those big eyes.

"I got a little baby," whispered Jean; "a real little fella. I'm nutty about him—and this hot weather—"

Jessie's hand turned half-way in the handcuff, and Jean's came pitifully to meet it. They clasped. Jessie felt as if little knives were thrusting in her breast; her eyelids prickled; she almost came out of character.

"Aah, he'll come through all right!" she said jocosely. "Most of 'em does. Look at all the men there are clutterin' up the wuyld, the loafers! You and me will be out some day; we'll be pals on the level; we'll help each other out; if I have any luck, you'll be in on it—see?"

Jessie rattled on in this vein, and presently the heavy tears ceased to fall in Jean's lap. "Oh, well," she said with her piteous swagger. "I should worry! Ev'y day will be Sunday, by-and-by."

"Yes, and there'll be no wash in Heaven!" said Jessie.

Their hands continued to cling together.

"What d'ye mean, big fellows, that you was talking about just now?" asked Jessie.

"You know, the big operators; the top men. If they take an interest in you, you're fixed for life. Believe me, there's nothing in this independent stuff. You gotta have an organisation behind you."

"Well, I'm not interested for a coupla years anyhow," said Jessie with a laugh.

"They got their scouts in Woburn," said Jean. "They could get you out of there, if they liked your work."

"Did they ever approach you?" asked Jessie.

"Nah!" said Jean bitterly. "They wasn't interested in the likes of me. But I heard the talk."

"Just prison talk, I guess," said Jessie.

Jean shook her head. "There was a girl called Melanie Soupert—"

"Did you know her?" asked Jessie.

"Only by reputation. She wasn't there the same time I was. They got her out."

"I read about it," said Jessie. "But I thought that talk about the organisation for getting prisoners out was just newspaper talk; to fill up space like."

"It got her out," said Jean—"twice."

"Who are these big men?" asked Jessie carelessly.

"If I knew who they were, I wouldn't be here," said Jean.

"Will we see each other up there?" asked Jessie. "Will we be able to talk?"

"Maybe so; maybe not."

"What's the first thing they do to you?"

"Put you in solitary."

"Solitary!" said Jessie, surprised. "I thought that was just for the hardest cases."

"Oh, they don't call it solitary first-off," said Jean. "They call it detention or somepin. You see, it's this way; when the girls first come, after the trial and all, they're wild—see? They don't care what they do. So they chuck 'em in solitary for ten days or so to cool off. Then they're so glad to get out they obey any rule—see?"

"Gosh!" said Jessie. "And I thought the prisons was reformed!"

WHEN THE CELL door clanged behind her, Jessie Seipp's stout heart contracted painfully. There was a horrid finality in the sound. Up to this point, surrounded by her fellow prisoners, and by guards, keepers and officials with their amusing foibles, the whole adventure had been extraordinarily interesting, but alone within those narrow stone walls fronted by a steel lattice work, it began to take on a different aspect. She discovered primitive feelings in herself, whose existence she had never suspected.

The arrogant ego who sits enthroned in the centre of each one of us was filled with a sense of outrage. "Put *me* in a cell!" it seemed to cry; "How dare they!" To be sure, the other part of her, the sophisticated part which looks on from the outside, laughed, and answered: "Well, this is what you were after, isn't it?" But the primitive came up with unexpected strength—primitive rage and primitive fear. Of what avail was philosophy against the hard facts of stone and steel—against solitude, silence, and presently the dark?

A single glance around enabled the occupant to take complete stock of her cell. Eight by four in size, and perhaps eight feet high, the stone walls were smooth and unbroken. It contained nothing but a narrow shelf, on one side of which was the bed, a higher shelf on the other side for table, and some primitive water-works at the rear. When both shelves were down, you could not pass between without sitting down; but each was provided with hinges and a hook to fasten it back. On the bed was spread some coarse bedding; that was all. What light there was came from the windows in the corridor; there was no provision for artificial light. Jessie understood that she would be provided with a more comfortable cell later, but even ten days with no one to talk to, nothing to do, and nothing to read, loomed ahead like an eternity.

She wondered if she were in the same row as Melanie Soupert had been confined in solitary. It was a ground tier cell. The windows outside were just such windows as had been described at the time of Melanie's escape. At least thirty feet high, they gave light also to all the tiers of cells above Jessie's head. By turning her face sideways against the lattice, and squinting up, she could just catch a glimpse of the tops of the windows. They had round tops. Jessie saw that in each window an extra row of spikes had been sunk in the round top. These came down below the tops of the ordinary bars, so that the particular manner of Melanie's escape might never be repeated.

The arrival of Jessie's supper made a welcome break. The keepers on duty in the corridor were women, but there was generally a male head-keeper in the offing. Jessie exam-ined her keeper with a particular interest. What sort of woman could it be who would seek a job like this? This one was short and thick through, and might have been any age between thirty-five and fifty. Evidently her physical strength was her principal recommendation here. Her face was indifferent and brutalised. Jessie undertook to chaff her into some semblance of humanity.

"Hello!" she said. "What have we to-night? Patty de foy grass or Russian caviare?"

"Don't get fresh," growled the keeper, "or I'll bean yeh!"

"Good heavens!" thought Jessie; "and she could too, if she wanted to, with impunity. Who would believe me here?"

The supper was not much, as suppers go; merely a cup

of coffee, and two thick slices of white bread. But Jessie was not dependent on delicate feasting. It was honest food, and sufficient, and she did not feel at all ill-used on the score of its plainness. She only said to herself: "Just wait till I get out!"

Shortly after the dishes had been taken away, the prisoners were locked in for the night. This was accomplished by closing a steel gate at the end of each corridor. The lever which locked this gate also double-locked every cell in that corridor. All over the prison one could hear the bolts shooting like the rattle of musketry.

"Now for the hardest time," Jessie thought with a shiver. "It's hours too soon to sleep. What shall I do—lie down on my bed, and tell myself a story?"

But it transpired that the real life of the prison was just commencing. Jessie had no sooner thrown herself down on her hard couch than she became aware of a whispering creeping towards her like mice amongst leaves. At first it seemed as if it was in the cell. The disembodied voice was horribly disquieting. Jessie leaped from her bed, and clutching the door of her cell, pressed her body hard against it. Then she comprehended that it was not a single voice, but many whisperings up and down the corridor.

"Are they all mad?" she thought in horror. The impulse to shriek was strong in her throat, and her arms trembled with the desire to rattle the door.

Of one voice close to her—a hurrying, toneless voice, she was presently able to distinguish the words: "... Got him down. He was lying on his back with his neck twisted, and the blood running back into his curly hair. And him on'y a lad with his smooth skin and his red mouth. And they began kickin' him, the whole four of them, with their thick-soled shoes; kickin' his helpless body this way and that; kickin' his face with their dirty, cruel feet; and kickin' his head till he was all twisted up. I knew where the gun was. Would you blame me for snatching it up and firing it at them butchers? Would you blame me? Would you blame me? I'm only human. Yet they give me ten years!... Aah! poor people's got no right to be livin' anyhow.... Him? Yes, he got over it all right. And not a mark on him. Same sly grin. A woman can't stand out against it. And he's free to go about amongst them; that's what I'm thinking. And I'm here..."

Jessie wrapped her arms about her ears. It was too pitiful. Yet she had to listen. She understood by this time that the women were not talking to themselves but conversing from cell to cell. As the keepers presumably retired to the rotunda, and there was no danger of interruption, the voices became louder. Prisoners were not content with talking to their next door neighbours, but raised their voices to hail friends at a little distance. With dozens of conversations going on at once it was like a babel, yet with long practice each seemed able to pick out her particular voice and answer it.

Jessie presently distinguished a voice close to her, saying: "Hey, there! Hey, there! Hey, there! You girl in the next cell! Hey, you that was brought in this afternoon. Yella hair!"

Jessie realised that this had been going on for some moments. But the voice seemed to come out of the air; she could not localise it. "Do you mean me?" she asked astonished.

"Sure, I mean you. You're next to me, ain't you? You're

on my right, I'm on your left. Come over close to that side, and we kin talk easy."

Jessie sat on the end of her bed. Leaning her head against the stone, and putting her lips to the lattice work she was within a foot of her unseen neighbour.

"I don't suppose you got a cigarette," said the voice wistfully.

"Yes, I got a couple," said Jessie.

"No!" said the voice full of delight. "How did you get by with it?"

"Hid 'em in my hair."

"They made me take mine down."

"Mine's already down. It's bobbed. But it's bushy."

"Yes, I seen you when you went by. Have you got a match, too?"

"Yep. In the same place. But how can I pass it to you?"

"You're a first offender, eh? Take a hairpin and unbend it—"

"I don't wear hairpins."

"Well, stick your thumb and forefinger through, and throw it best way you can. It's on'y a few inches. I got three hairpins I can twist together. I'll make out to hook it in."

Here there was a long pause in the conversation, while the girl next door fished for her prizes. At last there was an exclamation of satisfaction, and the striking of a match; presently followed by a groan of content.

"Gee! I wanted that, kid! How many more you got?"

"Two more," said Jessie. "I'm smoking now."

"Got any money?"

"A few dollars."

"Smitty'll get you some, if you want to pay the price.

Smitty's the hard-boiled egg that brought your supper. She's a Shylock. God! I hate her! It's a dollar a pack."

"We'll have to have 'em," said Jessie.

"Say, I'm glad you're next to me, kid. I had a dope before you, and before her a murderess who got salvation."

Heads to the wall, and faces to the bars, they entered upon a long murmured talk. Prison had its alleviations after all. Looking sideways they could see each other's smoke drifting out. That made it wonderfully companionable. "What's your name? How old are you? What are you in for? What did you get?" such are the invariable openers. Jessie then listened to another tale of human frailty and misadventure which I shall not put down here, since it has nothing to do with this story. It made her heart swell with pity; it was not for her to judge.

The girl next door was Minnie Dickerson, and she was twenty-four years old. She had been in Woburn for over three years, and was looking forward to her release at Christmas. Her present predicament, "in solitary," was due to her having sassed the matron, but as the said matron was due to leave on September first, Minnie hoped that the offence would not count against her record.

Jessie took advantage of a lull to ask offhand: "Was it from this tier that Melanie Soupert escaped?"

"Sure!" said Minnie. "She had the fourth cell to the right from you. The window is the second one from the one in front of your cell. Funny you should ask about her. She was a pal of mine. When she was first sent up here over two years ago, we were cell-mates for a time. They all thought Melanie was a hard nut, but she wasn't hard to me. We meant a lot to each other. She was a bold and nervy girl; she attracted the attention of the big fellows—"

"What big fellows?" asked Jessie.

"Well, this one is called Jonathan Wild, but that's just a name they gave him. I think they got it out of a book. They say he's got an absolutely water-tight organisation. They say his influence extends right into the Governor's private office. He can do anything he wants. His particular graft is to help poor devils to break prison, and then set them to work for him, see? But as escaped convicts they belong to him body and soul, and I understand he's not one to let anything get by him. If they do anything to make him sore, he can have them back behind the bars within twenty-four hours, with added penalties. For that matter, he could have them knocked over the head, and stuck under ground if he wanted. Because in the eyes of the law they're as good as dead already. I say, you'd better be here."

"I say so, too," murmured Jessie.

"I was approached a little while back," Minnie went on, "but I made out I didn't get it. I on'y got six months more to serve; I'd be a fool to risk all the rest of my young days— This Jonathan Wild has a house somewheres in New York—I don't know where it is, where the cons are kept under cover. Pretty damned well under cover, as I understand, for they're never let out by day or by night except there's a job to be pulled off; a safe to be cracked; a mail truck held up; or the pearls plucked from some dame. Then they're shut up again after. All the regular business of the gang is carried on by the outside fellows who are not convicts. And they never come to the house, see? Oh, it's slick! It wasn't Melanie told me all this, I picked it up from the talk around the prison.

"And none of the poor birds in that cage are ever allowed to see the big boss. They feel his power without ever clapping eyes on him. He's a sort of a myth to them. His representative in the house is a woman. I've seen her. They say she has the entree to every prison in the State. Smooth as velvet she is. I wouldn't like her to get her hooks into me.

"But Melanie was a lively girl; you know, the hell-to-pay and don't-give-a-whoop kind. Always had to be doing something. So she fell for the proposition, and they got her out. This was over two years ago, and I suppose she's been working for them ever since. I never heard from her. Then she was sent back here, but we were both in solitary, and she was five cells away. We could holler to each other, but we couldn't have any intimate talk.

"But pretty soon I heard they were getting her out again. Of course everybody on the corridor knew about it; we could hear the rasp of her saw when all was quiet. Word was passed along to me from cell to cell what night it was going to be, so I waited up. As soon as she was out she come to my cell, and we saw each other again. She hadn't changed any, but she was better-looking. Her eyes were shining.

"She says: 'Hello, old kid! What's the good word?' And I says: 'Give my regards to Broadway.' She says: 'I can't stop; the boys are waiting for me. I just wanted to take a squint at your ol' mug.'

"She wanted to give me her saws, but they wouldn't have done me no good, as I had nobody on the outside to help me. It would only have got me in Dutch.

"I was half crying; all I could say was: 'Oh, Melanie!' And poke my fingers out through the slats at her. She says, making out to jolly like she always did: 'I been through hell, kid. And I'm going back—to the hottest part.' 'Don't do it! Don't do it!' I says. 'Thirteen years!' says she; 'I can't face it. I'd hang myself to the door of my cell with my stockings. Besides,' she said, 'I had a taste of heaven outside, too.' 'The real thing?' I says. She nodded. 'Like a book,' she says.

"She says: 'He was on the outside and I was on the inside, and the boss wouldn't let us be together. So we flew the coop. And got stepped on. The word went out that it was back to Woburn for me. In order to save my lad I made out to turn him down, see? Call him all names. He thought I meant it, and I never had no chance to explain. It's a near thing for me now. They're laying for me, and if I so much as cock my eyebrow crooked, it'll be Nearer My God to Thee.'

"She says: 'Promise me something, Min., you'll soon be out of here. If you ever come up with my lad, tell him I never changed. His name is George Mullen, and he's got an old mother keeps a little stationery store on Columbus Avenue. Her name is Harvest. Maybe you can reach him through her. If they keep me from him, or if they do me in, tell him I never changed, see? Tell him that one week was worth all the rest, and my last thought would be of that, see?'

"I was fair bawling by this time, and I couldn't say nothing, just nod my head. Melanie kissed me through the slats, and beat it. I watched her climb up the bars inside the window, and I saw them help her through at the top. I ain't heard nothing since, of course. I was half hoping they'd catch her. She'd be safer here."

11

THE VISITOR

THE LONG HOURS dragged by with deathly slowness. During the day a keeper sat at the end of the corridor, and any talking between cells would bring down a reprimand. For the most part the occupants of the solitary cells stood hour after hour pressing their bodies against the cell doors, all with heads turned to the left, in the hope of seeing somebody come along the corridor. But, except at meal times, there was rarely an occasion for anybody to come.

However, it was in the middle of the afternoon, when the heavy sullen figure of the keeper they called "Smitty" stumped down the corridor, followed as far as possible by every white face, and stopped at the door of Jessie Seipp's cell.

"You're ordered before the doctor," she grumbled.

"There's nothing the matter with me," said Jessie, surprised.

Smitty brought her face close to the lattice work. "Ah-h! what's the matter with you?" she whispered. "Are yeh so crazy about it in here? Don't you want a walk?"

"Why, sure," said Jessie.

The door was unlocked, and she stepped out. Though it was only the prison corridor, she felt like a released bird.

She tried her legs with delight, and discovered that they still performed their office. She had the merest glimpse of her friend, Minnie, as she passed, bits of a white face in the interstices of the lattice-work, with a suggestion of sunken brown eyes; fingers clutching the iron straps with nails bitten down to the quick. From other cells, cries, jocular and envious, greeted her.

"What yer doin' out of yer room?"

"Graft!"

"The Warden's got a crush on her!"

To all Jessie prudently answered: "Going to the doctor."

When they were near the end of the corridor, Smitty whispered out of the side of her mouth: "Don't let them see you out in the rotunda. Keep behind me, and when we get to the bottom of the stairs slide up. I'll follow you."

The chair, inside the gate, where the male keeper usually sat, was empty, and Jessie supposed that Smitty had an understanding with him to keep out of the way while they passed through. This was the gate which was locked at night. On the other side there was a little vaulted entry into which the stairs for that wing descended, and through the entry, the great rotunda of the cell block, where there were always people moving.

Jessie turned aside to the stairs, and Smitty, facing about, joined her. "You got a visitor," she said, leering with a horrible oiliness that was the natural complement to her usual brutality. "A real nice lady. I hadn't the heart to disappoint her, though it's as much as me job's worth. You wouldn't do me dirt, would you, when I'm tryin' to put somepin your way?"

It was revolting to have to play up to this creature, but

Jessie swallowed the dose. "Absolutely not, sister," she said. "I don't know what the dope is, but I'm ready for anything."

"A real nice lady!" said Smitty again. "She visits the prisoners just out of kindness. You can depend on what she says."

Jessie thought: "A recommendation from you ought to be enough to warn a one-year-old child."

They went up four flights of stairs. Inside the gate to each tier sat a male keeper, who glanced at them indifferently as they passed. They were no business of his. At the top they turned to the right, and came out on the topmost gallery encircling the rotunda. Since each wing had its own enclosed stair, these galleries were very little used. Half-way round the gallery, Smitty, with sly looks all around to make sure they were unobserved, suddenly pulled Jessie through a small door, which she made haste to close softly behind them. Inside, Jessie stumbled over some steps. Following Smitty up the steps, she bumped her head on a wooden trap-door in the floor overhead.

Smitty scratched on the trap in a peculiar way. There was the sound of a heavy weight being moved overhead, then the trap was lifted, and daylight came down. They mounted the remaining steps, and came out into a vast attic, or rather a series of attics, over the entire cell block, lighted by an occasional dormer window. Except for miscellaneous litter, the place was empty, and was apparently put to no use. The architectural design of the prison called for a pointed roof, that was all, and here it was. The centre of the space was closed in by the false dome of the rotunda, and the wings radiated out like the spokes of a wheel.

"What strange rites am I to participate in up here?" thought Jessie.

When she turned around she saw the person who had lifted the trap. She was surprised, because this woman suggested the most intense respectability. She looked like the mistress of a successful boarding-house; a woman with money, who considered every penny before she let go of it. Her face was a mask, but that was in character, too, for city boarding-house keepers have to learn to mask their features. It was rather a comely mask, with commanding gray eyes and a resolute mouth. She was over fifty, and what is called "well-preserved." Her hair was as black as coal. Her clothes were of excellent quality, but several seasons out of date—or of no particular date. These were her Sunday clothes, only put on for an occasion, and therefore expected to last for a long time.

Jessie could make nothing of her. She thought: "She'll have to give herself away when she begins to talk."

And indeed when Jessie's eyes had turned to her, the smile which overspread that respectable face was as false as hell; the watchful gray eyes had no part in it; nor had the dripping tones which issued out of it any connection with the tightly-controlled mouth.

She said: "You must think it's funny, deary, my seeing you up here. But it's all right. You're among friends."

Jessie had already adopted the part she was to play. She shrugged sullenly. "I can't afford to be particular," she said.

"How handsome you are, deary!" the woman went on unctuously; "even in the ugly prison dress. It's a shame to put a fine girl like you in solitary confinement. Prisons are wicked places anyway. It's the officials and the keepers that ought to be put behind the bars. I say—excusing your presence, Mrs. Smith."

"Oh, that's all right, Mother Simonds," returned Smitty, with a horrid grin. "I know you."

"What a precious pair of rogues!" thought Jessie. Yet she could very well understand how the despairing and rebellious girls from the cells would find this oily flattery a healing balm to the spirit.

"I can see, too, that you're a bold girl," she went on. "They can't break your spirit. When you get started, you don't care what you do. But I knew that already, having read of your arrest and trial in the newspapers. My! what nerve! Eh, Mrs. Smith?"

"It certainly was a nerve, Mother Simonds. When I read that in the paper, I says, 'I hope that girl gets away.' Although I am a prison keeper, I got my feelings."

"You're too good for the job, Mrs. Smith. I've said it often before, and I say it now."

"Well, sometimes I get a chance to do a bit of kindness to the poor girls," said Smitty modestly. Here it must have occurred to her that this was hardly in line with certain earlier incidents between her and Jessie, for she added: "But I got a lot to put up with. There's some of those half-wits down there would try the patience of a saint. And my temper do get a little hasty."

"That's only natural, only natural," said Mother Simonds heartily. She returned her attention to Jessie. "And I say when I read that, there's a girl I'd like to do something for. You know, I'm dead against prisons and everything they stand for, and sometimes, with the help of this good woman here, I get a chance to befriend a particular girl.

It's an awful risk, of course; I don't know what they'd do to me, if they ever found it out. But I can't help that. It's the way I get my pleasure. I don't make no boast about it. It's just the way I am."

"Liar!" thought Jessie; "your eyes are as cruel as gray seas!"

"On'y listen to her!" put in Smitty. "One would think that Mother Simonds wasn't the biggest-heartedest woman in the whole State!"

"You mustn't say that, Mrs. Smith," said the praised one rebukingly. "I'm a very ordinary woman. It's just that I've got a weakness for a bold and plucky girl. I'd do anything for her!" To Jessie, she went on: "I've brought you some candy in my bag, deary; for a girl's sweet tooth is cheated on prison-fare. Also some cigarettes, for I know you girls will smoke them. Let's sit down over there and have a good talk… Smith, you stay by the trap and listen." In those words the commanding nature peeped out for a moment.

They crossed the floor which was of wood, though the prison was supposed to be fireproof. Jobbery under the eaves, no doubt. The rambling, ill-lighted place seemed to extend to unimagined distances; with its unexpected angles and innumerable corners it had a mysterious furtive look. So far-reaching a place and so empty! Anything might have happened there; anything might have appeared around one of the distant corners. Under a dormer window, which had the yellow scum of years upon it, there was a long pine box which bore a suspicious resemblance to a coffin case—ordered for some occasion, perhaps, and not used. Mother Simonds sat down upon it, and patted the place beside her.

"My poor girl!" she said. "You don't have to tell me what you have been through. I know. I know. It must be terrible on one of your free nature. You will find Mother Simonds your true friend. You can tell her everything."

Jessie had resolved to say as little as possible. She must not appear to fall for "Mother Simonds" too quickly. A sullen savage dumbness would be the best assumption for her. "Give me the candy," she said.

It was expensive candy, and Jessie munched upon it with a very real satisfaction.

"Do you want me to take any messages out to your friends, deary?" asked Mother Simonds.

"Ain't got no friends," said Jessie.

"What, no friends!"

"None that matter. People are all right to jolly with, but that's all I want of them. Friends mean nottin' to me. A new lot ev'y time I change my job. That's me."

"I see," murmured Mother Simonds. "One of those strong, self-sufficient natures—Is there no fellow, though?"

"Fellas, huh!" said Jessie. "What do they care after the moment's past? I don't care neither."

"That's right, too. A girl ought to keep from getting tied up. But not many can. Not when they got your looks."

"Oh, I can handle the fellas all right," said Jessie. "Because I don't give a darn."

"How about your family?"

"Ain't got no family."

"How come that?"

"Well, my mot'er died when I was a baby. My fat'er, he gave me to his sister to mind, and he went away with anot'er woman. I don' know where he is. His sister got sore 'cause he sent nottin', and she treated me bad. I wouldn't stand for that, and I run away from her pretty near as soon as I could talk good. The Society took me up, but I made out I was simple, and couldn't tell nottin', so they sent me to a home for feeble-minded kids. By-and-by they found out I wasn't so simple, so they transferred me to a regular orphanage. I stayed there a good piece, then I ran away again. That time I made tracks for the country where there wasn't no Society. A farmer's wife took me in, and I gave her a song and dance. I made out to get a letter from my folks saying I could stop with her. She treated me pretty good. But after awhile I sickened for the city and I lit out again. Since then I allus been on my own. One job and anot'er; I took what come. I was allus big, and passed for older than I was."

Mother Simonds proceeded to put Jessie through a subtle and searching cross-examination. Believing that she had the girl going now, she unmasked those strange eyes, which were the colour of newly cast iron. While her tongue soothed and dripped with unction, she made the terrible lightnings of her eyes play about the head of her intended victim, seeking to charm her as a snake charms a bird. In this case she had more than an impressible bird to deal with. Behind the veiled eyes of the seemingly ignorant and sullen girl, lurked a power even more terrible. The cat, seeking to play with its victim, was being played with. I need not attempt to give you the whole of Jessie's answers, since they were all designed to carry out the effect already indicated.

"Do you find it pretty hard in solitary?" asked Mother Simonds.

"Hard!" cried Jessie. "Oh, my God! I could beat my head against those stones! I could rattle that gate, and screech the whole night through—but they'd only keep me there longer. All I can do is walk—three steps each way, and pull my hair! A few days more of it, and I'd go clean off my nut!"

"Yes," said Mother Simonds thoughtfully, "it's like that with your kind. They'll break you before you get out of here."

Jessie relapsed into sullenness. "Well, I won't break up quiet," she said. "I'll have a run for my money. I'll get me a knife one way or another, and stick it in a keeper."

"If you got a chance," said Mother Simonds softly, "have you got nerve enough to make a break for it?"

Jessie's eyes widened; she trembled violently, and clasped her hands. She appeared to be about to fall at the older woman's feet. "On'y try me!" she stammered. "On'y try me! Oh, my God! do you mean it? Don't say such a thing unless there's something in it!"

"Well, I been able to help one or two girls in the past," said Mother Simonds with a deprecating air. "I'm dead against prisons, I am. I'd do what I could to get a girl out, if I liked her."

"When? When?" cried Jessie imploringly.

"Oh, we got to wait our chance," said Mother Simonds. "Rome wasn't built in a day. The first thing is to get you out of solitary. You got to be a good patient girl, and obey all the rules. It won't be so hard, will it, if you got something to look forward to?"

"I'd do anything!" cried Jessie. "I'd risk my neck on the smallest chance!"

"Cut that!" said Mother Simonds, with an imperious

flash of the gray eyes. "You don't want to take any chances. You just do what you're told, see?"

"Oh, sure!" said Jessie, humbled immediately.

"You came from a laundry, didn't you?" said Mother Simonds, "maybe I can fix it to have you put to work in the prison laundry. I got influence in certain quarters—though the big officials don't suspect it. The laundry's in the outer yard. That would be fairly easy… I'll dope out a plan, and let you know through Smitty. She's safe as long as you don't get her in wrong with her bosses."

Little by little Mother Simonds was dropping the pretence of respectability, and by that Jessie knew she had made good.

"You understand it's up to you to get yourself out according to a plan furnished by me. Outside I'll have friends waiting for you with a car, and they'll bring you to my house, where you can lie low till they're tired looking for you. If anything goes wrong you got to keep your mouth shut about me."

"Torture wouldn't drag it out of me," murmured Jessie.

"Well, if you did let it out, you wouldn't get another chance later," said Mother Simonds coolly.

Jessie sought to give a convincing picture of the stubborn soul humbled at last. She fondled the older woman's plump and shapely hand. "What makes you so good to me?" she murmured. "I'm nottin' to you. What you doing it for?"

"Oh, I took a fancy to you," said Mother Simonds, scarcely troubling to hide the cynical leer now. "I like a girl of spirit… And I'm getting on. I want companionship. I keep a lodging house for men only, and I thought I'd like a girl around me. If you don't want to live with me as my daughter, you only got to say the word."

"It's more than I could a hoped for," said Jessie.

"Look at me!" said Mother Simonds in quite a different voice. Jessie raised her humble head, and the terrible gray eyes blazed on her. "Listen to me, girl! You're clever and game, and there's no height to which you may not rise—with the help of me and my friends. But you're also a passionate, ignorant fool, and without me you'd be back in your cell within a month. Girls like you are easy meat for the bulls. I stand for organisation and power, and safety. The whole world is yours if you want it. But remember: I am everything to you, and you are next to nothing to me, because there are thousands more like you. Work *with* me and I'll make you; work *against* me, and I'll leave you to break of yourself."

Jessie's head went down, and she spread out her hands. "Do what you want with me," she murmured.

Mother Simonds touched the bushy blonde head with two fingers, as it were to confer the accolade, and jumped up quite cheerfully.

"Very well, we understand each other then. You'd best beat it back to your cell, or they'll be blowing the sirens for you and Smitty."

"How will you get out?" asked Jessie solicitously.

Mother Simonds and Smitty both laughed with frank cynicism. "Don't you worry, deary," said the former, jocosely. "I got a magic wand. I can go straight through a two-foot stone wall. For me: 'Stone walls do not a prison make or iron bars a cage.'"

She lifted the heavy trap easily.

12

THE WARDEN'S GUESTS

THE LAUNDRY AT Woburn was housed in the basement of one of the industrial buildings in the outer prison yard. At midday in July it was, naturally, the hottest spot within the whole circuit of the walls. The greater part of the big rectangle was taken up by the steam laundry which washed the prisoners' clothes, but towards the front of the building where the stairs went up, there was a row of girls engaged on hand work for the household of the Warden, and other prison officials. Conspicuous among them was the tall figure of Jessie Seipp, with her great bush of blonde hair. Since make-up was frowned upon within the prison, she was unable to contrive the same brilliant appearance she had made at her trial; nevertheless, she had smuggled in certain articles of make-up, and she still bore but little resemblance to the self that Nature intended.

The girls had their dinner in the laundry, since it was easier to bring it to them than to march them back to the main prison under guard, and then back to work again. They appreciated the privilege while they ate and talked, even though there were several keepers present, they were able to feel like laundry workers outside. As usual, tall Jessie was the life of the party.

To have work to do, no matter how hard and how disagreeable, with fellow workers to talk to; to take part in the general life of the prison; and to have a cell that was like a stateroom de luxe by comparison with the first hole in the wall, this was a great improvement upon solitary. There was rich material, too, for the student of human nature, Nevertheless, Jessie could not be said to be easy in mind, in spite of her seeming high spirits. She was in the position of one who expects a decisive stroke of fate, but does not know when, nor from what direction. It is hard on the nerves. Jessie had had nothing from Mother Simonds except a single terse message via Smitty:

"Be ready to hop it whenever the word comes through."

One of the hand-workers, a dumpling of a girl called Doll Turner, had part of a newspaper. She said: "Gee! guyls, we're goin' t' have comp'ny. A bunch of them refawmers. Gawd, how I hate the breed!"

"Read it out," said another.

Said Doll in a sing-song: "The Patroon Club, the exclusive upper West Side organisation of women, has taken up the study of prison life in a serious way, and to-morrow (this is yestiddy's papeh) the members are going in a body to inspect Woburn prison, under guidance of Katherine Couteau Cloke—"

This name stirred recollections in Jessie Seipp of her other existence, which now seemed so remote. "Dear Katherine!" she thought, "what a shock it would be to her if she recognised me on the way through!" But it was dangerous even to think in this character, and Jessie made haste to say in the derisive drawl that the other girls associated with her:

"Ho-o-oly Mackerel!"

They laughed quietly, with glances askance at the nearest keeper.

Doll continued: "The party will number some forty persons. Two special parlour cars will be attached to the ten o'clock train from Grand Central. Upon arrival in Woburn a collation will be served at the local hotel, and the ladies will then motor to the prison. After an inspection of every department, they will be the guests of Warden Insull for tea, and will depart from Woburn on the return journey at 5.30."

"They'll be eatin' that collation right now," remarked Jessie pensively.

"What's a collation?" asked one.

"Suych me!" said Jessie. "Maybe it's a misprint for collection—collection of eats."

"Well, it'll be a collection of crows all right," said another wit.

After dinner an order was received for a general tidying up of the laundry, and, much against their will, the girls were forced to put on their blouses in the heat. They affected to scorn the coming visitors, but just the same their coming made a welcome break in the monotony. It would give them something to talk about for days to come.

It was about quarter to three when there was heard a bustle overhead, and the procession started to descend the stairs into the laundry, the portly Warden walking first with a very grand lady, who was perhaps the president of the organisation. The others followed after, two by two, quite a lengthy train. Miss Cloke, who was well known to all the girls, was in the second file with the next grandest lady, the vice-president, perhaps. As the handworkers were close to the foot of the stairs, they took them first in their tour.

There were six ironers, each with her board at right angles to the wall and the passage through. Thus while they were at work they could only talk to the backs of each other's necks. Jessie Seipp was the second in line. When Katherine Couteau Cloke passed by she stole a glance into the plain, harassed, and somewhat sad face of her friend. Evidently this "investigation" was an ordeal that the one genuine reformer was obliged to undergo for the sake of the publicity and the funds it brought to her work.

Tall Jessie and her hair attracted considerable attention, and one of the ladies asked audibly of a member of the prison staff who accompanied the party, who she was. He answered, whereupon the lady turned to a friend behind and gasped:

"My dear! That's Jessie Seipp. The girl who attacked poor Mrs. Marquardt!"

Thereafter, they passed it back from one to another as they went along: "That's Jessie Seipp. The one with the hair! Only fancy!"

Jessie attended closely to her ironing, with a sneer curling her lip; for she was thinking that the manners of the unfortunate inmates of Woburn compared very favourably with these ladies. She did not look up again until they had nearly all passed, when a something familiar in the words; "What! Jessie Seipp! You don't say!" caused her sharply to turn her head.

She received a surprise which tried all her self-command, for she found herself looking into the masked gray eyes of "Mother Simonds," who, for the moment, had adopted an expression of foolish benevolence. She had not made the slightest attempt to disguise herself. Her dowdy, well-to-do appearance was exactly in character with most of the other earnest ladies of the party.

Mother Simonds said to the lady beside her: "I will speak to the poor girl." Taking a step nearer Jessie, she said without batting an eye: "Are you well treated here, my girl?"

"Ain't got no complaint," muttered Jessie sullenly.

"Let me give you a trifle," she said, opening her pocket-book.

It was forbidden to give the prisoners money, but the harmless practice was generally winked at.

Mother Simonds pressed a half-dollar into Jessie's hand, and two other things went with it unseen; to wit, a scrap of paper, and a tiny key. Jessie, grinning, exhibited the coin to the girls and kept the other things concealed. Then it all went into her pocket. The procession passed on.

There could be no moment for examining the paper so favourable as the present, when all attention was upon the visitors; Jessie unfolded it in her pocket, and took it out concealed within her palm. In prison one becomes adept at that sort of thing. The scrap was covered with infinitesimal but perfectly clear handwriting. Jessie read:

> Wait for about forty-five minutes. Choose a moment when you are unobserved to carry some completed work to its proper basket. Pick up the basket, and carry it to the hoist. Tell the hoist-man the doctor has sent for his wash. Tell any one who may stop you the same thing. Cross the yard to the back door of the doctor's house, but turn aside on the path that leads to the Warden's. Give the basket to the cook. When her back is turned, slide up the back stairs. On the first bedroom floor the two rooms on the left as you face the front have been set aside for the lady visitors. In the front room you will find a small brown valise on the bed. It has initials: N. S. Open it with the key. Further instructions inside.

"Amazing woman!" thought Jessie. "Every detail of the laundry routine is familiar to her, and, presumably, all the other departments of the prison also!" Squeezing up the paper, Jessie put it in her mouth and chewed it to a pulp, then spat it out.

She considered what was before her. The manager of the laundry paid but little attention to the hand-workers, and the keepers probably would not interfere with the carrying out of so natural-seeming an errand. The one to look out for was Sarah Rekar, the head hand-worker, an old trusty, who was responsible for the others. Unfortunately, Sarah's ironing table was immediately behind Jessie. Somehow, she must be got out of the way for a moment.

There was a new girl on the hand work, a quiet little thing called Hannah, between whom and Jessie there existed one of those unexpressed bonds of sympathy. Jessie carried some completed work to the baskets, timing her act so that she would meet Hannah there. Out of the corner of her mouth she whispered to the girl:

"At half-past three keep old Sarah busy for a minute, will you?"

The girl gave her an eloquent look, but said nothing.

They had no clocks or watches, but such was the iron routine of the prison, that at any hour of the day the girls could have told you the time almost to a minute. Hannah's table was the last of the six. At half-past three she began to whimper and complain:

"I can't make these pleats lie down. The more I iron 'em the worse they get."

Jessie heard Sarah, behind her, put down her iron with a sigh. With a fast-beating heart, Jessie gave her a minute to get to Hannah's table and to apply herself to the pleats: then she quietly picked up what work she had completed and carried it to the baskets. Each girl did the work of one household at a time, and Jessie's at the moment was for the purchasing agent, but that didn't make any difference; she walked off with the basket, taking care not to look behind her. The hoist was beyond the stairs. She made the fateful corner without hearing any hail from behind her. The hoist-man looked at her grimly.

"Doctor sent for his wash," said Jessie.

"Aah," said the hoist-man, "ain't yer legs good? How about the stairs?"

Jessie smiled at him, and gave her blonde mop a toss. "It's hot," she said. "Be a sport and take me up. Don't cost you nottin'."

"Oh, well, you're a good-lookin' girl," he said. "Step in."

Jessie crossed the outer enclosure of the prison at a sober pace. There were plenty of people there on one errand or another, but the spectacle of a trusty carrying a basket of wash towards the official residences was an ordinary one. The blood was pounding in Jessie's ears. How much time could she count on? The girls would help her out some. When Sarah came back to her table and said: "Where's Jessie?" they would be ready with an excuse that would keep her quiet for a minute or two.

What would Sarah do when she did become suspicious? Sarah was crabbed, but at heart she wasn't a bad sort. Jessie knew she would have done all she could to keep one of the girls from making a break, but if she found her gone, maybe she'd give her a few minutes' chance. Or maybe Sarah was fixed. Jessie had gathered from her instructions that the cook at the Warden's was fixed.

In an open space behind the Warden's house a row of eight motor-cars was drawn up waiting to carry the ladies back to the station. "Shall I be in one of those when it drives out through the gates?" she asked herself.

She reached the doctor's back premises without being accosted. She was safer now, for the path between the doctor's house and the Warden's lay behind some ornamental shrubbery. But she was again exposed for a moment as she climbed the Warden's back steps. In order to save time, she ventured to open the kitchen door and walk in.

The cook was not surprised by her intrusion. She was another trusty, an Irishwoman of great girth. There was an all-comprehensive twinkle in her eye.

"Here's the wash," said Jessie.

"Sure, darlin'," said the other, taking the basket; and Jessie was well assured that its contents would never be found again. "We're havin' a big party," she went on. "Stop a minute, and I'll fetch you a little cake."

Before leaving the kitchen, she glanced expressively at a certain door. She scarcely needed to point it out, because this door had a step outside it, which signified clearly enough that the rest of the stairs would be found behind it. The cook went through a swing door into a pantry presumably, and Jessie slipped through the other door as softly as a snake and got it closed behind her.

On the first landing there was another door. Jessie listened behind it; then opened it a crack and listened; then peeped out. There was no one stirring on that floor. From below she heard the voices of the family on the porch. She flitted like a shadow along the hall and gained the first bedroom on the left. The light wraps and personal belongings of the ladies were strewn about the room, and there were more in the adjoining room. She found the brown valise on the bed, and carried it into the bathroom which was between the two rooms with a little sob of relief. The more dangerous part was over.

The valise contained a change of clothing, of course. The instructions which accompanied it were brief:

"Wrap up the prison dress in the paper, so if I have to open the valise the stuff won't give me away. Draw your hair down close with the hair net. Don't put on too much make-up. When you're ready, wait in the bedroom until we all get there. You can tell some story about having come back sooner. When we go downstairs, keep your mouth shut as much as possible, and watch how the others eat."

Jessie smiled to herself at the final instructions. She destroyed the paper.

Ten minutes later an elegant young lady issued out of the bathroom. What Jessie had to guard against was looking too elegant—for Mother Simonds. The dress was one of those straight silk slips which fit every woman, and are becoming to all—that is, all under a hundred and fifty. With it went a little crush sport hat, very smart, and the daintiest of shoes and stockings. The shoes were too big, but that would scarcely be noticed. For a final touch a pair of heavy rimmed glasses had been supplied to lend Jessie the earnest look characteristic of the ladies.

But she had no more than seated herself by the window to manicure her nails, when the door of the room opened and the Warden's wife entered. Swallowing a gasp, Jessie arose with her most charming smile.

"I hope you won't think I'm an intruder. It was so hot, I got a little faint. I left the others in the clothing-shop, and came back."

Now Jessie had command of the manner of a much greater lady than the Warden's wife, and that good soul was instantly impressed by it. "Why didn't you let me know?" she said solicitously.

Jessie remembered that the family porch was at the side of the house, and therefore conceivably out of sight of anybody entering the front door. "Oh, it was nothing," she said. "I didn't want to trouble anybody. We are giving you trouble enough—so many of us! The door was open, and I took the liberty of coming right in."

"That was right," said the Warden's wife. "How do you feel now?"

"Quite all right," said Jessie.

"Do come downstairs and wait with us. It's cooler on the porch."

They descended the stairs chatting amicably. Jessie complimented the Warden's wife upon her house, and the latter referred humorously to the drawbacks of living in a prison. At any rate there was no servant problem there.

On the porch they found the wives of other prison officials. Mrs. Insull hesitated. "I have forgotten your name," she murmured.

"Mrs. Boker," said Jessie.

She was introduced all around in due form.

"I met some Bokers at Upper Saranac," remarked the doctor's wife. "I think the initial was W. N."

"Distant cousins of my husband's," said Jessie carelessly. "We scarcely know them."

She was in great form; filled with a deep, inward amusement at the quaint situation.

The other ladies were not long in returning. They proceeded directly upstairs to titivate for tea. Only the Warden came around on the porch. Mother Simonds would have her moment of anxiety upstairs when she found no Jessie; but that couldn't be helped. Jessie had locked the brown valise as a precaution against possible snoopers.

To explain Jessie's presence, Mrs. Insull said to her husband: "The heat was too much for Mrs. Boker. She left you *en route.*"

The Warden was impressed by Mrs. Boker's good looks. "I missed you," he said gallantly,

Jessie swallowed a chuckle.

The Warden drew her a little aside from the others. "From what you did see, have you any suggestions to make?" he asked flatteringly.

"Good gracious!" said Jessie, making eyes at him; "it is not for a simple woman like me to make suggestions to *you!*"

They embarked on an innocent flirtation.

The other ladies streamed out on the porch, where tea was to be served. Mother Simonds' eyes fluttered over Jessie from head to foot, but gave nothing away. With *her* entrance on the scene, Jessie had to let a little awkwardness, a little self-consciousness appear. The complicated part that she was called on to play taxed all her powers. Fortunately, the Warden and his wife were now obliged to attend to their other guests, and they were aware of no change in "Mrs. Boker."

Tea was—well, like all such affairs. There was a tremendous gabble on the Warden's porch. In the middle of it the host was summoned into the house. He came back trying to hide a worried look under his smiles. Jessie manoeuvred herself so that she stood in front of Mrs. Insull when her husband joined her. She overheard their whispered conversation.

"What was it?"

"Another escape."

"Oh, my dear!"

"And all these damned women on the ground! It's too much! I ordered them not to blow the siren. There's been too much scandal about these escapes. Anything more would finish us here. I'm going to keep it quiet." Accompanied by the smiling Warden and the wives of the officials, the lady visitors, still talking vociferously, ambled across the grass to the waiting automobiles. Jessie found herself between a fat lady in cocoa brown and a thin one in American Beauty. Pleasantly excited by tea and talk, they included her in their conversation as if they had known her all their lives.

Warden Insull was not so worried but that he was able to single out the handsome Mrs. Boker for a word of farewell. "Come to see us again when it's not so hot."

"I shall," she sang back.

The great gates of the prison opened wide to permit of the egress of the Warden's guests; and the faces of all the guards wore a respectful expression that Jessie Seipp was not accustomed to see there. When the last car had passed through, she heard the gates clang, and her heart sang just as blithely as if she had been a bona fide prisoner. She looked around at the free fields and the wide sky, and found them good.

13

THE HOUSE ON VARICK STREET

UPON THEIR ARRIVAL in New York, Jessie and Mother Simonds had dinner at a modest hotel. The latter now signified that she was to be addressed as Mrs. Pullen. Beyond a brief commendation of the way Jessie had played her part, she was entirely uncommunicative. Evidently a hard taskmistress. But that was nothing to Jessie. Jessie made believe to be only anxious to accommodate herself to her mistress's every mood. Her task was easier now that she had only the part of Jessie Seipp to think of. By this time she felt thoroughly at home in Jessie's skin.

Between mouthfuls Mrs. Pullen—as she must henceforth be called—busied herself writing messages on a pad of the tiny sheets such as Jessie had received from her. Before the meal was over, a boy appeared on the scene to take the messages. He was a bright-eyed boy of sixteen with an attractive grin, who looked at the new member of the gang with strong curiosity. Jessie thought: "He's worth saving. I'll keep an eye on him."

Issuing from the hotel they entered a dingy, inconspicuous-looking car which was waiting nearby. No word passed between Mrs. Pullen and the driver. Inside the car was furnished with black cloth blinds all around, which Mrs.

Pullen coolly drew down. Jessie made no comment, but the other woman felt impelled to say:

"You understand, of course, that you'll be on probation for a while. You've got to satisfy us of two things; are you good enough to be of any use to us; can we depend on you to stick to the organisation. If we can't use you, it's back to Woburn for you."

You see, there was no longer any attempt to hide the nature of the business that Jessie was wanted for.

"Only try me," murmured Jessie humbly.

Mrs. Pullen only spoke once again during the drive. "Pull off the hair net and shake your hair out. There's no use letting them all see you can look so much like a lady."

Notwithstanding the drawn curtains, Jessie, by the exercise of those faculties which had made her famous in her other sphere of life, was able to follow the course they took. They drove west on Forty-Second Street. She got the Fifth Avenue crossing from the sound of the bell in the traffic tower, and Sixth from the rumble of the elevated road; the hubbub of Times Square was unmistakable. At Times Square they turned to the left, that is down town, and the street must have been Seventh Avenue, for they bowled along, unhindered by traffic. She marked in turn: Thirty-Fourth Street; Twenty-Third and Fourteenth by the bump of the car over the cross-town rails. The next slight bump meant the Eight Street line; as they had made no turn, they must be continuing on towards Varick Street. Presently they turned west for a short distance, south for a block, east again, and drew up at the kerb—the north side of a cross-town street, Jessie noted.

Mrs. Pullen took a peep through the door. "You must let me blindfold you," she said peremptorily.

Jessie submitted, as a matter of course. While Mrs. Pullen was tying the handkerchief, she used her ears to good effect. The elevated road could be heard a short distance behind them, and beyond that, but not very far away, the whistles of the ferry-boats in the North river. From just ahead of them came the sound of motor traffic moving at a considerable speed.

"Lower Greenwich Village," said Jessie to herself. "That's Varick Street just ahead. This is one of the little side streets off Varick, such as King, Charlton or Vandam."

Jessie was hustled across the sidewalk, and on over a worn brick pavement. By lurching a little, she made out that they were in a narrow passage; it must have been open to the air at each end. They then crossed some ancient, cracked flagstones, and Mrs. Pullen (who had Jessie by the elbow) unlocked a door.

"We are entering a tenement in the rear of one of the old dwellings of the village," Jessie said to herself.

The house they entered had that empty sound, unmistakable to sharp ears. So far they had been moving straight ahead; now they turned to the right, and Mrs. Pullen stopped again, letting Jessie stand alone. There were certain sounds Jessie could not identify, then a creak and a thud that suggested a sliding door.

"Some sort of secret entrance," she thought.

They then passed straight through another little house which had the same sound of emptiness, and out across another flagged yard. "We are approaching the rear of a house which fronts on Varick Street," Jessie said to herself.

"Four steps down. Watch yourself," said Mrs. Pullen.

They passed through an open door into a room which contained several people. Somebody freed Jessie's eyes.

It was an old-fashioned basement-kitchen with a cook-stove built into the chimney, and the built-in wooden cupboards, characteristic of old New York, which always exhale a strong smell of mice and croton bugs. There was an old gas-stove, too, which added its quota to the smell. The place was furnished with the usual kitchen parapher-nalia, and it was lighted by a single gas jet, most depress-ing in effect.

There were four men in the room. Jessie got them by degrees. With one exception they all wore a hang-dog look, which suggested to her keen eyes that the morale of the house was low. It was curious that nobody spoke at their entrance. They all looked at Jessie with a strong curiosity that was not without the suspicion of a leer. Then they looked uneasily at Mrs. Pullen, waiting for her to speak.

The exception that I spoke of was the youngest man of the quartet. He was a youth of middle height, unnatu-rally thin, with sandy hair and an expression of unpleasant sharpness. Clearly he fancied himself; and something about him made Jessie's bristles rise. Before ever he addressed a word to her, she was conscious of the desire to slap his face. Him Mrs. Pullen addressed.

"Anything to report, Sam?"

"Quiet as the grave all day," he said. "The telephone only rang once. That was Lippett to ask what time you'd be back."

Mrs. Pullen turned to Jessie. "These are your partners," she said with a contemptuous air; "get acquainted." How

different this was from the insinuating tone of her first
overtures to Jessie. "For the present," she went on, "you are
to confine yourself to this room, the room overhead, which
is the general sitting-room, and your own room on the
second floor, that I'll show you later. You are not to enter
any other room in the house until I give you leave. The boys
will tell you the other rules of the house. There's only one
thing I want to impress on you. All rules are the same, see?
and there's only one penalty. I tell you this for your own
good. You're a clever girl, and you ought to make a valuable
member of the organisation. But there must be absolute
obedience in all things great and small, or back you go."
She beckoned to Sam, and they left the room together.

The other three men followed them out with significant glances, and Jessie was aware of a certain relief in the
atmosphere when the door closed. But for the present the
men were guarded in their talk before Jessie. The leering
quality in their glances made the woman in her shudder.
She braced herself.

"They are not dangerous to me unless I think they are,"
she told herself. "There's only one way for me to act towards
them, and that is with frank and matter-of-fact camarade-
rie, as if I were a man like themselves."

One of them was an old man, the worst type of jailbird.
His years in prison seemed to have rotted him; his skin
was of a corpselike pallor; many of his teeth were missing,
and his unreverend white hair was coming out in patches.
The others called him Pap, and it appeared that he was the
cook. He said in a flip way:

"Have a pleasant journey, kid?"

"Tip-top," said Jessie. "In a parlour-car and all."

"Glad to get here, I guess, eh?"

"I'll tell you later," said Jessie dryly. "You three don't appear to be enjoying it much."

They all laughed, but it had a bitter sound. Pap said, with twisted lips:

"You get us wrong, kid. We're always merry and bright."

"Any cigarettes in the joint?" asked Jessie.

The second man got up. He was a fine specimen of physical youth; taller than the average, with a torso so deep it made his shoulders look narrow, well carried on slender, muscular legs. His skin was pink, and he had bright brown curly hair; asleep, he must have been uncommonly handsome, but when his eyes were open, no one on earth would have trusted him. He came closer to Jessie than was necessary, and sought to charm her with his masculinity; his voice purred.

"Here's cigarettes, kid. I'll keep you supplied. And anything else you want. I'm Cliff Hutchins."

The third man growled with a surprising suddenness: "Back up, Hutch! You cut that out!" The deep husky voice was full of suppressed fury.

The young man whipped around. "What's biting *you*, Combs? Can't I be civil to the girl?"

"Civil nothing!" growled the other. "D'ye think we're blind? d'ye think Pap and me is goin' to stand for yer lalligaggin' before our eyes?"

"Oh, excuse *me*, Bill," said the young man with heavy sarcasm. "I didn't know as you had any ambitions in that direction. Far be it from me to—"

After his surprising outburst, Bill relapsed into stolidity. "It's a waste of time to talk to you," he said. "I'll say no more. But I got this to speak for me!" And he showed a clenched fist as crude and massive as a bull-dog's head.

"Well, I'll talk to him!" Pap put in stridently (but all three were careful not to raise their voices). "I'm with you, Bill, on this. Does the —— —— fool think *we're* goin' to be bound by the rules if he chucks them?"

"Listen to Pap, now," sneered Cliff. "Durned if he don't want to lalligag, too, as Bill puts it so elegant. Say, Pap, if you was to go in for it, with your looks, I wouldn't be one, two, three."

Pap cursed him with a horrid fluency. His eyes rolled wildly. He looked around for a weapon.

Jessie took the floor. "Hey, cut it out!" she said with strong scorn. "Have you all gone bugs suddenly. Anyhow, I guess this rests with me!"

At this simple and indisputable statement, all three men fell silent. Pap turned to the gas-stove, muttering in a senile way. Jessie looked at this Bill Combs, full of curiosity. He was much the most impressive of the three, a huge man in his forties, with shoulders like a bull, and a heavy, brutalised face. But Jessie's keen eyes perceived something human and wistful there.

"I can make a friend of this one," she told herself; "he'll stand by me in this stew!"

To relieve the tension, she asked at large: "What are the rules she was talking about?"

Pap turned around with his fleering laugh: "The first one is, no sparking. There ain't been no occasion for it lately."

"What else?" asked Jessie.

"No fighting."

"That doesn't interest me. What else?"

"You mustn't show yourself at the front windows. Don't matter about the back, 'cause there's no windows overlooking ourn."

"Anything more?"

"When the missus is out, you got to take your orders from Skinny Sam, see? Sam has the power of life and death over yeh." This was accompanied by a horrid sneer.

"Oh, to hell with rules!" Cliff burst out. "The rules is whatever the old —— happens to feel like."

"And are you men content to let a woman run you?" asked Jessie.

"Easy, sister," said Big Bill softly. "You'd best stop, look and listen awhile, before you make up your mind about this house. It ain't no kindergarten."

"I'm only asking for info," said Jessie. "I want to know what I'm up against. All she told me was she kept a lodging-house for men, and she wanted me for company."

Bill and Pap laughed mirthlessly. Young Cliff was glooming. "And did you fall for that?" asked Bill.

"No," said Jessie frankly. "I didn't want to ask no questions. I wanted to get out."

"Well, I'll tell you this much," said Bill, "since you've got to know it anyhow; the dame upstairs is only a deputy here for the big boss."

"What's *his* name?" asked Jessie, making her eyes big.

"Anything you like," said Bill dryly. "Boss is enough name for me."

"Where is he?"

"For us," said Bill, "he is only a voice on the telephone."

There was a silence in the kitchen.

After a while Bill went on, holding up his cupped hand

in a primitive forceful gesture: "A voice," he repeated, "but he *has* us; like that."

Cliff got up with a muttered curse, and went to the window.

"Oh, well," said Pap presently, with a silly-sounding laugh; "what's the use o' grousin'? We're well fed here, and the bulls can't touch us."

Cliff whirled around. "Well fed?" he cried. "With *your* cooking! Oh, my God!— It's all right for you to talk. Your day is over. This place is Paradise alongside anything else you could expect. But look at me! look at me!"

"I don't see much," muttered Pap.

"I been tied up in this damn stable for a month with nothin' to do," cried Cliff, "and I'm fed up with it! Just a little bit more, and I'll squeeze that old ——'s windpipe under my thumbs upstairs."

"Oh no, you won't," said Bill stolidly, "you'll just take it out in talk when she can't hear you."

"Why don't you walk out?" asked Jessie, pointing to the open door. "It's only skinning over a few fences."

"Because I got nine years unexpired time at Sing-Sing," said Cliff sullenly. "The boss would have me back there before to-morrow night."

"Can't you hide?"

"Not from him!"

And Big Bill nodded his head.

Cliff came towards Jessie with glittering eyes. "But it's somepin to have you here," he said. "You and me is young, we could make it up to each other. We wouldn't—mind where we was then, eh?" He pressed close to her. "Oh, my God! but you look good to me, kid!"

"Cut it out, Hutch," said Bill, this time without any heat. "You ac' like a child. You know you gotta cut it out. Why can't you face it?"

"You mean you'd split on me, you damned informer," cried Cliff.

"I do," said Bill coldly. "Ain't I got the feelings of a man myself?"

Cliff lashed out against him. Bill sat stolidly filling his pipe, refusing to be drawn. The febrile Pap could not keep out of it, and the two became involved in a wordy altercation during which they forgot all prudence.

Suddenly the door opened, and Mrs. Pullen walked in, with Skinny Sam at her heels, grinning with a devilish malice. A chilling silence fell on the room. It was like the unexpected entrance of teacher, but there was a danger in the air infinitely more dreadful than a threat of the strap. And Mrs. Pullen never said a word; merely looked them up and down with her basilisk eyes.

She turned to Jessie saying: "You can go to your room."

"Yes, ma'am," said Jessie.

They turned out of the room. Jessie never saw Cliff again.

Mrs. Pullen and Jessie ascended the usual narrow, enclosed stairway to the main hall of the house. Jessie could have found her way around that house blindfold, it conformed so exactly to type. There was no light in the hall, and through the fanlight over the front door came a faint glow from the street lights. There were some old numerals painted on the fanlight, and Jessie read them backwards: 723.

"Seven hundred and twenty-three Varick Street," she

said to herself; "I can send my address out to my friends if I want."

Mrs. Pullen opened the door of the rear room on the second floor, and stood beside it with a key in her hand just like a jailer. When Jessie passed in, she closed the door without a word, and, locking it, descended the stairs.

Even the philosophic Jessie was moved to anger. "Inhuman wretch!" she thought. "She deserves to have her windpipe squeezed!"

Before lighting the gas, she went to the window to reconnoitre. "This is not much better than Woburn," she thought. The sky was obscured by low-hanging clouds which reflected the lights of the city in a faint pinkish glow. All Jessie could see from the window was a sort of darkish huddle. The rear tenement was distinguishable; also the tenement it abutted on, the one they had reached from the side street. There were about three houses facing the side street; and beyond them was a big dim yard, such as might be used for the storage of building materials. The block was closed in by the backs of the buildings on the next North and South Street, some hundreds of feet away.

Jessie then lighted up and looked around her. It was just such a room as might have been found in scores of the second-rate lodging houses of that run-down neighbourhood. It had no character; it contained not a single object upon which the imagination could seize. But Jessie was relieved on the whole; it was well enough; the bed was clean. At least, she did not appear to be expected to share her room, and that was a blessed privilege.

She lay on the bed with her hands under her head, staring at the ceiling. What a day, what a day it had been! And what a dangerous haven she had come to anchor in! She went over and over that scene in the kitchen. Life in the raw, assuredly. Her thoughts revolved principally about the figure of Big Bill Combs—the other two were negligible. Bill looked like a brute, and no doubt he was a brute; nevertheless, every word he uttered was charged with a certain massive dignity. Such as he was, he was the most nearly human thing in that terrible household, and she must make friends with him if she could.

Jessie had a stout heart, but she also had clear sight, and she could not disguise from herself the imminence of the danger in which she stood. She was aghast at it. In that house all the ordinary decencies of life that one took for granted were cast aside; and all the safeguards of an ordered life. One could not expect justice any more than kindness or mercy. Only unbridled savagery. She experienced what it meant to be an outlaw; to have every hand raised against her. She was absolutely at the mercy of this inhuman woman who was accountable to nobody except the powerful unseen one behind her. Jessie was appalled at the ingenuity of this pair who made a business of stealing the victims of the law in order to obtain slaves who had no recourse on earth from their tyranny.

While she lay there suddenly, out of absolute quiet came the sound of a scuffle below. It was only a slight scuffle, and soon over. It was followed by that most dreadful of sounds, a man's voice broken and gasping with terror, whining, moaning, imploring for mercy. She heard only the one voice, as if the poor wretch was faced by dumb enemies. The voice was silenced by a single, dull blow, and not another sound was to be heard.

14

THE OUTLAWS

NEXT MORNING CLIFF HUTCHINS was gone, but there was presently a new-comer. The household was at breakfast in the dreary sitting-room over the kitchen. Mrs. Pullen was at the table, consequently everybody looked glum, excepting Skinny Sam, who was exercising his wit, much to his own satisfaction. Occasionally Mrs. Pullen gave him a fond look. Pap carried the dishes in and out, and between whiles sat down to eat with the others. Jessie kept her face averted from him, for his table manners were not pretty.

A little bell sounded through the house. By now Jessie was familiar with the door bell and the telephone, and this was neither. It had a disconcerting effect on the gang; they stopped eating, and listened in suspense. Mrs. Pullen went swiftly to one of the windows looking to the rear.

The bell continued to ring. "Something's wrong," she said curtly. "Sam, look into the street and see if the front is watched. If it is, all make for the roof."

Sam ran out, and the others pushed out into the hall uncertainly. Then the bell stopped, and a breath of relief escaped from all. They drifted back into the sitting-room. Mrs. Pullen was still at the window.

Presently she said coolly: "It's Abell," and returned to her chair. The meal was resumed.

There were steps on the stairs, and a man came into the room carrying a small satchel. He was different from the others. With his keen, shrewd face and careful dress, he looked like a prosperous young attorney. But at present his face was as white as paper, and he had a reckless, apathetic look, either from fatigue, or from some powerful emotion. He dropped the satchel on the table near to Mrs. Pullen's hand, and came around to a seat on the other side, next to Jessie. Sunk deep within himself, he scarcely seemed to see her. There was something in his clean, thin profile touchingly young.

"Another one!" thought Jessie. "Poor soul!"

"What did you hold the sliding door open for?" demanded Mrs. Pullen harshly.

"It slipped its trolley," was the indifferent reply. "It ought to be fixed."

"You attend to that, Sam," said Mrs. Pullen.

Food was pushed towards the new-comer, but nobody paid any particular attention to him. He seemed little disposed to eat.

"Where you been since twelve o'clock last night?" said Mrs. Pullen.

"On the streets. I was chased. I couldn't lead them here, could I?"

"That's a lie," said Mrs. Pullen. "You forget I've read the papers. There was no discovery until two hours later."

"What do I care what's in the papers," said Abell, shrugging. "When they haven't got the facts they'll make up anything at all."

"But if you had been seen, they'd have that fact, wouldn't they?"

"Well, I thought I was chased," said Abell.

"You been to see your family," said Mrs. Pullen accusingly.

The young fellow raised his white face sharply and met her gaze. "Yeh, likely, ain't it," he said with bitterly curling lip, "that I'd go to them straight from a robbery with the stuff in my hands. They're making out in a sort of way without me. Do you think I'm going to drag them down to my level?… It's a fact I thought I was followed, and I wouldn't come back for that reason. It's a fact, too, that I went up there where they lived, and I walked past the house and looked at the windows. That's as near as I'm likely to get."

"How much is in here?" asked Mrs. Pullen, indicating the satchel.

"I didn't count it."

Mrs. Pullen opened the satchel, and took out packages of bills, and rolls of coins in paper. She counted it in a glance almost, and compared the total with the newspaper she had. From her grunt one might have thought she was disappointed to find that Abell was not trying to hold out on her. Abell sneered.

Presently Mrs. Pullen got up, taking the satchel, and made to leave the room. Abell jumped up, too, his white face working painfully.

"Kate," he stammered, "will you let me talk to him this morning?"

"Tell me what it is," she said with a disagreeable smile, "and I'll talk for you."

"Ask him," he said, forgetting everybody else in the

room, "ask him if he'll let me go now. In six months I've brought in seventy-six thousand dollars. Isn't that the price of a man's freedom? Two tricks a week on an average is too much to ask of a man; my nerves are shot to pieces. And anyhow I couldn't keep it up. Every theatre in town is laying for me now. In the next night or two I'll get a bullet through my head!"

Jessie thought: "So this is the nervy thief who has been sticking up the theatrical box-offices."

Mrs. Pullen said: "That sort of talk don't go with him."

"Well, then, ask him if he won't give me assistance," cried Abell desperately. "A scout, just to watch that I don't get plugged from behind."

"That doubles the risk for the organisation," remarked Mrs. Pullen.

"Ah! you don't care what *my* risk is!"

"Oh, I'll ask him," said Mrs Pullen indifferently, and went out.

Jessie supposed from this talk that she had gone to tele-phone the boss. Mrs. Pullen's room adjoined hers in the front, and the telephone was in there. But Jessie had already learned that the telephone was in a closet, only the bell outside, that it might be heard through the house. When Mrs. Pullen retired into the closet, and shut the door, not a sound could be heard in Jessie's room, or in the hall outside.

"Don't you wisht you could hear the number?" Sam asked Abell with a sneer.

"That wouldn't do him no good," remarked Pap. "He always waits in a pay station for her to call him up, and every couple of days he changes to another."

"Well, I'll use my influence for you, Abie," said Sam derisively.

"Sam," said Abell with a deadly quietness, "when they push me too far, and I go bugs, the first thing I'm going to do is to kill you. I won't put a bullet through you neither. That's too clean. I'll slit you."

Sam's shallow eyes bolted, and he showed his teeth.

"And I hope I'll be there to see it," said Bill Combs in his bass growl.

"Me, too!" added Pap shrilly.

Sam shot poisonous sidelong glances at them, but held his tongue.

When Mrs. Pullen returned to the room, Abell asked eagerly: "What did he say?"

"He didn't say nothing," Mrs. Pullen said coolly. "He don't listen to that stuff."

Abell's chin dropped on his breast.

WHATEVER HER PRIVATE feelings towards her might be, it was absolutely necessary for Jessie to insinuate herself into Mrs. Pullen's good graces. Unless she could induce them to trust her, to give her a little more rope, she, Jessie, was helpless. She therefore lost no opportunity of propitiating "Black Kate" (as they called her behind her back) but was always met with a contemptuous rebuff. As when, Mrs. Pullen getting up to leave the room again, Jessie said:

"Is there any work I can do around the house to help out?"

To which Mrs. Pullen replied with a hard stare: "You'll get your work when I'm ready to give it to you."

She called Sam, and they went out. Pap had retired to the kitchen, and as Abell was sunk within himself, Jessie and Bill Combs were, to all intents and purposes, alone in the room.

"What makes her so sore at me?" Jessie asked of Bill: "What have I done?"

"She ain't got nothin' against you particular," said Bill in his heavy way; "she hates women—that is women as is younger than herself. And she's just takin' it out on you. She wouldn't have you here at all, on'y she got orders from above."

"Wasn't there ever a girl in the house before?" asked Jessie.

"Oh, yes, they was a girl here before," said Bill evasively.

"What become of her?"

"Don't ask me questions, sis," growled Bill. "It's onhealthy. You just keep your eyes and your ears open around here, and you'll learn plenty to make you wise."

"But she told you to tell me things."

"Not all things," said Bill.

"There's one question I gotta ask," persisted Jessie. "I heard something last night. Where's Cliff Hutchins?"

"Back in the hoose-gow."

"Oh," said Jessie, relieved; "I thought they had croaked him. I couldn't sleep of it."

"Oh no," said Bill carelessly. "After a spell in the cooler, he'll be back on the job. They's on'y one thing they puts you out for."

"What's that?" asked Jessie, though she knew.

"They calls it treason," said Bill dryly.

A heavy anxiety settled on Jessie's breast. Was this the answer to that other question which Bill had refused to answer?

"How could they get Cliff Hutchins back to Sing Sing so quick?" she asked.

"Just hand him over to the police."

"Is there an understanding between the boss here and the police?"

"So it seems,"

"O-oh!" said Jessie.

"Now looka here, sis," said Bill, taking his pipe out of his mouth; "you said one question, and you ast me four already. Cut it out or you'll get us both in Dutch."

JESSIE WAS TIDYING up her room, when the door opened and Skinny Sam walked in without so much as by your leave. By the leer on his face he fancied himself irresistible.

"You get out of here quick!" cried Jessie, scowling.

" 'S'all right, kid," he said perkily, "the old un's gone to market."

"Whether she's in or out, you get out of my room!" cried Jessie.

"Say, you talk like the young Miss in her father's mansion; Act 2," he said, sneering. "It's wasted, kid. You ain't got no audience. Be yourself."

Jessie's arms itched to chastise the unpleasant little wretch, but she bethought herself she must avoid a fracas if she could. Physically, he was not very dangerous. She went on making the bed. Sam straddled a chair, and leaned his arms on the back in what he thought was a killing attitude.

"In this house we're down to rock bottom," he went on. "We can afford to be natural. We can let ourselves go. You'd be a fool not to take what fun there was going."

"Maybe it wouldn't be fun for me," remarked Jessie.

"Say, you're quite a jollier, ain't yuh? Well, it suits me. Gee! you got a peach of a shape. Makes my mouth water!"

A great anger surged up in Jessie, but she crushed it down. She merely looked at Sam.

He hadn't sense enough to get the significance of the look. "You're safe with me," he went on. "I got the old woman locoed; I'm her white-headed boy, and I can make her do what I want. I don't let my hand show, but it's really me runs this house through her, see? So whenever she's out of the way, you and I…"

"I don't follow you, kid," said Jessie dryly. "If I'm free to do what I want, being down to rock bottom as you say, I'm free to choose the man I'll take, ain't I?"

"Sure! and here he sits!"

"No," said Jessie, looking him over speculatively; "no, I can't say as I'd choose you. You don't impress me."

Sam got up. "You're quick with the come-back, ain't yeh, kid?" he said. "Me and you'll make a good pair. You don't know me yet."

"Nor I don't want to," said Jessie.

He came close to her. "Oh, that's what they all say at first," leering into her face; "but they changes their tune."

Jessie stepped back. "You want it straight?" she said grimly. "All right. I don't like you. If you was the last man on earth I'd choose to live single."

"Oh, is that it?" he snarled. "Well, you got to take me anyhow, cause I'm the master here, I can put you back in Woburn within a week. You ain't made none too good an impression here."

Jessie laughed.

"You can't afford to quarrel with me," he went on. "Wat t'hell, kid! We're wastin' time... Turn around!"

He came up behind her, and slid an arm around her waist. This left Jessie's arms free. She *did* turn half around, leaning back, and, with a full swing of her right arm, boxed his ear.

"There!" she said, "I wanted to do that since I first laid eyes on your ugly face!"

Sam staggered back, dazed and blinking, a comical sight. Then his face became convulsed with rage, and he made for her. She was ready for him. It was the first time in her life that she had been called upon to exert her strength against another, and to her joy she found herself strong and able. The weedy youth was like a rag doll in her arms. She hustled him around the bed, and held him against the wall while she got the door open. Then she flung him outside with such force that he collapsed on the floor. She slammed the door.

"If you ever come in here again," she cried through it, "I'll break a chair over your head."

No sound from Sam. She walked away from the door, full of a savage exultation. "I can take care of myself," she thought. But her feeling of triumph soon wore off, and she sat on the bed, scowling in perplexity.

She saw that this would only make her position more difficult. Her woman's instinct told her that it would be useless to complain of Sam to Black Kate. Sam had her ear, and Sam would not be slow to distil poison within it. In Kate, he would find a willing listener. Sam's boast of sending Jessie back to Woburn was not altogether an idle one. What a mess! She sighed. How tragic if, after all she had dared, her work should come to nothing now.

It occurred to her that it would be a good stroke of policy to tell Big Bill what had happened, and she immediately went downstairs. Abell had gone to get his sleep, and Bill was alone in the dining-room, laboriously reading the newspaper. Sam, who had been peeping from some corner, came creeping after her into the dining-room to see what she was going to do. Beaten and cringing, he was a loathsome sight; with his viperish glances he was trying to intimidate her.

"What was the racket upstairs?" asked Bill.

"Sam came into my room when I was cleaning up," said Jessie clearly.

"And what did you do?" asked Bill, putting down the paper.

"I threw him out."

Bill was slow in all his movements. There was an alarming rumble from somewhere within his big body, then an appalling explosion—of laughter. He flung back his head, and slapped his thighs helplessly.

"And you could do it, too!" he gasped, when he was able to speak.

Sam sneaked out of the room again.

"I thought I better tell you," said Jessie, picking at the soiled red tablecloth. "He'll try to make trouble for me with her."

"It's a nasty mess," agreed Bill, "but it's not hopeless. Be sure the boss got you here for some purpose, and he's not going to give it up too easy. Whatever they may tell you, a girl like you is not easy to get. Then I heard what happened, see? Don't run ahead to meet trouble, sis. Wait till it comes. I'll stand by you."

"Thank you," said Jessie.

There was a silence. Big Bill was looking at Jessie in a peculiar way, but she did not immediately become aware of it.

Finally Bill said: "Sam is a measly little swine. He's not worth a woman's notice."

"Sure he isn't," said Jessie.

"There's other men in the world," said Bill meaningly.

Jessie looked at him in horror. He hoisted his great bulk slowly out of the chair and, going to the door, closed it. He came back to her, his gross features working with emotion. At all times Bill had the wistful look of the Beast in the old story, who knew that he was repulsive to Beauty. It was intensified now; simple, piteous and absurd.

"How about me, Jess?" he said gently.

"Oh, my God!" she thought; "another one!"

"I know I'm no cake-eater," he went on; "but at least I'm a man, not a flash-in-the-pan; not a flea-bitten whippet like that one. Oh, Jess, I could love you well; I could stand by you through thick and thin. I ain't had much that was nice in my life. I'd be so damn grateful to you, my girl. I'm not young, but I'm not old neither. A man is different from a boy; he's had sense knocked into his head."

"Oh, Bill, don't!" she murmured in distress. "Oh, Bill, not *you!*"

"What's the matter?" he said confused. "Didn't you come to me natural just now? Don't that mean nothing?"

"Oh, Bill, I wanted you for a friend. I counted on you.

How can we live a life like ours without one friend? And where will I look for a friend if you fail me?"

"Fail you?" he echoed, spreading out his hands. "Ain't I offerin' you all I have?"

"Not that, Bill! I couldn't!" in desperation she blurted out: "There's somebody else—outside. I may never see him again, but I got to stick to him!"

"Oh," he said in quite a different tone, and stood looking at her for a long time without speaking. An ugly look began to appear in his slow, pained eyes.

"They're all alike!" thought Jessie hopelessly.

He suddenly put out his hand, and seized her wrist in a terrible grasp. "Damn you!" he said thickly—but there was as much pain as rage in his voice, "then what did you look at me so kind for?"

Jessie stood perfectly quiet. "Because I liked you," she said.

"Liked me! Yah!" he snarled. "What's that to a man? What's friendship mean? It's like handin' a starvin' man a hunk o' chalk to eat! What you want to tantalise me for? Women is cruel to men, and a man's prepared for it. But you let on you were different. Now you got me going, how can I stop?"

The skilled psychologist called upon all her knowledge of the human soul. "I am not afraid of you," she said steadily. "I saw from the first that you were not like the others. You could not hurt me, because I like you."

He flung her arm violently from him, and walked away. "Don't look at me like that!" he cried. "Don't look at me!"

Jessie considered whether it were wiser to leave the room

or to stay. To go might have the look of flight, and would instantly rouse the savage in him to pursue; so she stayed.

Bill flung himself into the chair he had first occupied, and gripped his head between his hands. "I want to do the right thing by you," he groaned. "You're as dear to me as a child of my own. But—but you don't know what a man's got to fight—his hunger—and his madness! There's a devil in me; after so much he puts me down, and then I don't know what I'm doing."

"Oh, Bill, I know," she cried warmly. "Bill, you're a dandy! I'm proud to know you! We *will* be friends."

"To hell with your friendship!" he cried, with a savage thrust of his arm. "Get out of here! I can't bear to look at you."

Since he told her to go, she hesitated no longer, but walked slowly out of the room, and upstairs to her own room. After all, she was only a woman, and how thankful she would have been to possess the key to her door!

She sat down on the edge of the bed, discouraged. To be sure, she had won for the moment. But this sort of fight is won only to be always more savagely renewed. "Oh, why wasn't I a man!" she groaned to herself. "Or why didn't I make myself up with a hump on my back, and a patch over one eye. How can I go on here?"

15

THAT EVENING

DURING THE MORNING Mrs. Pullen called Sam up to tell him she would be kept out all day by important business. Jessie heard this piece of information from Pap at lunch time. Except for Pap shuffling in and out of the room, Jessie ate her lunch alone. Both Sam and Bill were keeping out of her way for reasons of their own, and Abell had not come down from his sleeping room up on the top floor.

After lunch Jessie returned to her room. She kept the back of a chair propped under the handle of her door for what protection it would afford, but there was no attempt to disturb her again. She was sitting by her window for coolness when she saw Sam cross the yard below with tools in his hand. Evidently he was on his way to fix the sliding door. It occurred to Jessie that this would be a good opportunity to send a message outside. She knew that Pap and Bill were in the kitchen, two floors below. To be sure, Abell might come out of his room overhead, but he was so sore against the outfit, she was inclined to chance his betraying her. Her wandering about the house might easily be ascribed to a girl's natural curiosity anyhow.

The door of Mrs. Pullen's room was not locked. Jessie smiled at the picture that met her eyes, it was so different from what one might have expected. It appeared that, within her own sanctum, Black Kate was a bit of a sybarite. There was a deep-piled rug on the floor; there was a divan heaped with cushions in silken covers, each with a voluminous frill. The imposing brass bed had a lace spread and "pillow-shams," the pictures on the walls were of the melting school of Bougoureau; there was an immense bureau with an opulent display of silver toilet articles.

A hasty glance around assured Jessie that there was no written evidence that might be useful to her; the astute Mrs. Pullen would not be so foolish, of course. Her next move was to glance out of the window without disturbing the lace curtains. She saw that it was indeed Varick Street below. That thoroughfare is unmistakable owing to its recent widening, which has left all the ancient houses on one side of the street, with odd-shaped vacant lots, and crude new structures on the other. Jessie then went into the closet to telephone, leaving both doors open behind her to guard against surprise.

She called up your humble servant, Bella Brickley, and this brings me into the story again. I need not say how overjoyed I was to hear her dear voice again. I did not even know that she was out of prison, since the news of her escape had been kept out of the papers. It bowled me right over, and I blubbered into the telephone like a child.

It was all very brief. She gave me the main facts of the situation so phrased that nobody but myself could have understood it. She did not dwell upon her own danger, but I perceived it clearly enough, and then I was ready to weep with terror. Her instructions were that if I did not hear from her again within a week, I was to carry the infor-

mation to Inspector Rumsey of the police, for him to act
upon as he saw fit. But I was to make no move until the
week was up.

"Should I not arrange to have some one listen in on their
conversations?" I asked.

"No," said my mistress quickly. "They are too clever to
give themselves away over the phone. Besides, a sharp ear
can detect when the wire is open. If they suspected they
were watched it would frustrate my whole scheme. I want
them to have all the rope there is."

I bade her good-bye with a heavy heart.

JESSIE'S DISCOURAGEMENT WAS but momentary. The
greater the difficulties, the greater the demands upon her.
She found herself able to rise to them. Her course of action
was clear; apart from the detestable business of sex, she
must make these men *like* her. Impossible as it might seem,
they must meet on another plane than sex. She planned to
unite them with herself by means of their common resentment against their inhuman taskmasters.

All the men came to the supper table, and in addition
there appeared a new member of the gang, a big loutish
fellow, whom they called Fingy Silo. He, with his thick lips
and little swimming eyes, was the most frankly sensual of
the lot. A sweep of dark hair obscured his low forehead,
and his mouth generally hung open. He seemed to have
scarcely more intelligence than an ape, and he had in addition that quality of brutality which is purely man's, and
man's worst quality. Throughout the meal he stared at Jessie
unabashed. Jessie, blandly ignoring it, treated him with the
same offhand friendliness the others, but he only goggled

at her stupidly. She was at a disadvantage in dealing with such a one; her methods were too fine for him.

It was a curious assortment that faced her, and she the only woman amongst them. Bill Combs had recovered his usual stolidity and his face gave nothing away. Skinny Sam was quieter than his wont, and glinted at Jessie through his lashes with evil eyes. Then there was the decayed Pap with his senile giggle; little white-faced Abell, who scarcely ever looked up from his plate; and finally this big lout, Fingy Silo. Jessie gallantly applied herself to the unpromising material.

"Gee! this is as cheerful as a funeral!" she cried. "Cheer up, boys! There'll be no wash in Heaven! Don't yeh never have a word to say wit' yer meals? I should think yer food would choke yeh. Me, I gotta talk or die. Pass the lobscouce, Pap."

Only Pap responded at first. "You're feelin' pretty good to-night, eh?" said he with his disagreeable smile. He did not intend it to be disagreeable, but he was a little warped.

"Feel good!" cried Jessie. "I'm desperate. I gotta holler and act the fool to keep my spirits up."

This struck an answering chord in Abell, who lifted his head with a faint smile on his white face. It was almost the first notice he had taken of Jessie. "Like a kid, when he walks by the cemetery," he said.

"Sure," said Jessie, waving her hand about the table. "Look at them corpses."

There was something between her and Abell that the others did not share in; the knowledge of a better way of living.

"Speaking of corpses," she went on, "did you ever hear

the story of Crematory Johnson who riz and walked?" She told the droll negro tale with all the delicious mimicry for which she was famous in another sphere. Fun is fun just the same in any walk of life; Big Bill rumbled with laughter in his diaphragm, and Pap fairly squealed.

"Gee! Fuzzy-Wuz can tell a story all right," he said delightedly.

The name stuck.

Jessie capped it with another and another. Even Sam, seeing how the current was running, made haste to swim with it, and he, at least, made believe to laugh as heartily as the rest. The new-comer, Fingy Silo, continued to stare at Jessie like an animal.

Whatever a man's private griefs or passions, he can rarely resist an invitation to sociability. It worked a marvel around that gloomy board. Loud, cheerful talk became general, and all—excepting Fingy—beamed on each other in the most friendly fashion. No one could have supposed that a shadow lay on any of them. Both Abell, in his quiet way, and Bill Combs, in his stolid way, proved to have a talent for story-telling, and they added their contributions. Jessie was aware every minute that the ugly passions were only slumbering, and that a single wrong word would provoke an explosion. She ran the show.

In the middle of it, Abell said thoughtlessly: "This is just like old times!"

"What old times?" asked Jessie.

All the men turned silent and uncomfortable. Jessie thought: "They mean when Melanie was here!" She made haste to tell another story.

Some word brought up Woburn, and Jessie was induced

to tell the story of her escape. The incident of the Warden's tea-party made the most successful story of all, because that was real, and it came close home to all of them.

After supper there was a general move downstairs to the kitchen to smoke. "So far, so good," thought Jessie. "It doesn't mean much, but it's a beginning. Should I go to my room now? No, it would risk what I have gained. I must see it through to the end."

On the way downstairs she happened to be next to Abell. He slipped his hand under her arm, and whispered with a touching burst of confidence: "You know, I got a fine boy twelve years old. You wouldn't think it, would you? I was married when I was nineteen. He's most ready for High School already. That boy's going to make something of himself!"

"Isn't that bully!" Jessie whispered back, greatly moved. To herself she whispered exultantly: "I am making progress!"

In the kitchen Pap piled all the dishes in the sink, "until morning." Somebody suggested a game of Bridge. Bridge in a thieves' kitchen! This struck Jessie as comic. There were six of them, and only four could play; a dispute arose as to who should be included. The situation was too hazardous for Jessie to think of keeping her mind on cards, and she said: "Count me out. I ain't got no card sense."

Whereupon the dispute was reversed. Neither Bill, Sam, nor Fingy wanted to play then. Finally the game was given up in disgust. At this moment Sam, unluckily, happened to finger the bump on the back of his head tenderly. This induced Bill to tell the story of Sam's discomfiture that day. Sam retired from the room white with rage. The evening appeared to be spoiled. Jessie couldn't whoop up sociability again, for to be successful that sort of thing must appear to come about naturally. So she made believe to be bored.

"Can't anybody raise a song?" she said.

It transpired that Abell possessed a ukelele. He was sent to fetch it.

Totally unregardful of his listeners, Abell sat slumped down in a kitchen chair, his head brooding over his instrument, his eyes half closed. He sang coon songs in a droning, nasal voice, but with charm. He made no effort to please; he had temperament, as they call it; he gave himself up to his singing, and they all listened with pleasure.

It was a queer enough scene under the single gas-get. Every now and then air came through the gas-pipe, and the jet hissed and flared. The walls and ceiling of the room had been painted a ghastly blue, which was now much discoloured by greasy kitchen smoke. The edges of the cupboard doors were black with finger-marks, and most of the doors were hanging by a single hinge. Bill, Pap, and Fingy were sitting roughly in a row with their backs to the outside door and window, all three balancing on the hind legs of their chairs. The first-named was smoking an ancient pipe, much charred around the edge of the bowl; the other two lit one cigarette from the butt of the last. Abell sat across the room from the two stoves, his heels on the edge of a dresser. Jessie sat alone facing the three, with two doors at her back. One of these doors led to a pantry, the other to the basement hall.

Without appearing to, Jessie, while she smoked her cigarette, was studying Fingy Silo, who presented a new problem to her. He was still young, but a man of that coarse type loses the attractiveness of youth before he is out of boyhood—if, indeed, he had ever had it. He was immensely powerful without being well-shapen; his neck looked thicker than the head it bore. Jessie had scarcely heard him open his mouth; but her intuition told her that as a result of his long, brutal stare, he would presently act. How could one handle a man so impervious? You couldn't reach him from the outside. He was moved regardless, by slow, dim forces within.

Between songs, while Abell was tuning his instrument, Fingy arose, and coolly picking up his chair, carried it across the room and placed it beside Jessie's. This act had all the effect of a direct challenge to Bill, but Jessie saw that Fingy did not intend it as such. With perfect egotism, it never occurred to him that any other man might prefer a claim to the girl. Bill said nothing at the moment, but his pained eyes began to burn dangerously, and the air of the room became charged as with thunder.

Abell, with no thought apart from his instrument, began another song. Fingy behind his hand, with absurd obviousness, whispered to Jessie:

"Fuzzy-Wuz, you're a damn good-lookin' girl."

"Cut it out," said Jessie indifferently. "I'm not interested."

It did not penetrate.

From across the room came Bill's voice. The big man was still keeping a hold on himself. "If you got anything to say, Fingy, speak out."

Fingy looked at him with a surprised, black scowl. Then he looked at Jessie. It took him some moments to figure the situation out. Meanwhile Abell went on with his song.

Once more Fingy put up his hand. "Come on out in the yard," he whispered. "You can hear just as good out there."

"I told you to cut it out," said Jessie, giving him her full glance. "You may as well get it through your head. There's nothing doing."

But his little eyes gloated on her without giving a sign of having heard.

"Hold up a minute, Abie," said Bill, putting up his palm. The musician looked up in surprise.

"I got a word to say to Fingy," Bill went on. "We all know that this sort of business is against the rules. Well, none of us cares so damn much about the rules as that. But we can't all break this rule, and nachelly the rest of us isn't goin' to stand by and see one get away with it."

"That's just talk," said Fingy. "You mean you want the girl yourself."

"All right," said Bill sticking out his jaw. "What about it?"

"You'll have to fight me for her," said Fingy. There was something impressive about such simplicity.

"Any time," said Bill.

Jessie picked up her chair, and planted it with its back to the gas-stove, exactly between the two parties. "You can fight if you want," she said indifferently, "but it will do you no good. I don't want either of you. The winner means no more to me than the loser. I mean to keep myself to myself. Go on with your song, Abie."

The ukelele set up its whining again, but after a moment or two Fingy said to Bill in the same tone as before: "Well, are you man enough to fight for her?"

Bill said nothing at all, but got up with a surprising alacrity, an eager glitter in his eyes. Jessie was enraged by their attitude towards women. Obviously, her feelings meant nothing to either of them. But she had wit enough to see that the situation had passed out of her influence, and she kept her mouth shut. Abell got up with an air that said it was none of his concern, and went out through the hall. Jessie heard him mount the stairs with a sinking heart. The most nearly civilised one in the house!

She considered whether she should go to her room. But, no! One of them would only follow her there later, and she had no means of keeping him out. She must see the thing through on the spot.

Neither Bill nor Fingy had worn a coat in the kitchen. They now unlaced their shoes and kicked them off, eyeing each other. Pap was in great excitement. He took up his stand in the doorway leading to the hall, where he could see all that went on, yet keep an ear open for the possible return of Mrs. Pullen. Jessie leaned against a table, affecting to look out of the window. But she was not as superhumanly indifferent to the scene as she appeared. By keeping a little to one side of the window, she could see all that happened reflected in the glass.

She gathered that these affairs were conducted according to a code of their own. All contestants were in honour bound to make as little noise as possible; hence the stocking feet. There was no punching; that made too much noise; they wrestled; and, apparently, any foul grip and dirty trick was permissible, if you could get away with it.

The two men circled the floor, watching each other for an opening with dehumanised fighting faces. They were well enough matched; Bill was the more powerful, but Fingy was perhaps fifteen years younger. Their sagging clothes rendered their bodies hideous; their ugly flat feet seemed to adhere to the floor. There promised to be nothing glorious about this fight. Jessie shivered—not with fear, but with repulsion.

Pap, biting his fingers in the doorway, could not stand the suspense. "Aah! Mix it! Mix it!" he quavered.

Suddenly they came together. Bill had his mighty arms locked around the other's body, while Fingy, pushing with all his strength against Bill's chest, sought to raise his knee high enough between them to break Bill's hold. One forgot their cumbering clothes then; they were rather magnificent. Jessie was reminded of a pair of figures in a Grecian frieze that she had seen. That same pose had been caught twenty-five hundred years ago.

And Fingy succeeded; Bill's arms were burst asunder. Before he could recover, Fingy, making a half turn, hooked his throat within his left elbow, and catching the elbow with his right hand, dragged Bill's head back gagging, until Jessie thought his neck must break. He had his knee in the middle of Bill's back for a fulcrum. Back, and still back, Bill struggling in vain to turn within that strangling grip, his great chest bursting. Bill got an arm over Fingy's head, and his hand groped for Fingy's face; he found it; his flexed fingers found Fingy's eyes, and Jessie closed her eyes in horror. The pain forced Fingy to let go. Once more they circled for an opening. Jessie expected to see two bloody holes in Fingy's face, but apparently his eyes were uninjured. Bill was sobbing for breath. That was where his age told against him. Fingy, snatching for a hold, missed, and tore Bill's shirt half off his back. The vast back was too fat.

And so it went. Bill had plenty of strength, but he was

slow of movement, and his wind was not over good. Still, in a rough and tumble like that, mere bulk was an advantage. Fingy could not throw him. He fell on Fingy once, knocking the wind out of him, and savagely banged his head against the floor, until Jessie turned sick with disgust, but bit her lips to keep from crying out. She was not going to betray the least interest in the outcome, though they tore each other's flesh to ribbons. However, Fingy succeeded in wriggling free, before he was beaten into unconsciousness.

Bill was absolutely indifferent to punishment; planted like a great tree or a hill, he took Fingy from whichsoever quarter he came. On the other hand, Fingy had a wholesome respect for those terrible arms. Neither man had much science; Bill's ceaseless effort was to crush Fingy to his breast, and bear him down, while Fingy sought to hook him from the side, or from behind. Fingy played safe, aiming to let Bill tire himself out, and he bade fair to succeed too; for the big man's eyes became glazed with fatigue. It was not clean wrestling; many a blow was exchanged. Blood trickled down Bill's back, and running from Fingy's nose, got itself spread all over his face. Pap grinned, and held up his clenched fists at the sight. What was left of their shirts clung saturated with sweat to their flesh.

The big man proved to have a bit of strategy in his thick skull after all. He changed his tactics, and half presented his back to Fingy, as if inviting that hook which had almost finished him in the beginning. Fingy, suspecting a trick, refused, until Bill, with a vicious, foul blow, angered him beyond all prudence. Fingy hooked Bill savagely around the neck from behind; whereupon Bill dropped to a crouching position, and half-turning, got an arm under Fingy. Straightening up, he heaved the younger man clean over his head, Fingy's heels rapping against the plaster ceiling, and flung him with a crash on the floor. Fingy lay still. It seemed to Jessie that every bone in his body must be broken.

Bill stood back, looking down at him indifferently. As well as he could for panting, he said: "I guess that'll hold you."

Pap bustled in, and making haste to draw water in a dipper, flung it in Fingy's face. Fingy twisted his head from side to side, and presently raised himself, leaning against one quivering arm. Jessie was greatly relieved; she had no desire to assist at a murder. Fingy looked sick and shaken; all the vice was out of him.

"Can you get up?" Pap asked anxiously. "Try to get to your bed before Kate comes home."

Pap and Bill raised him between them, and Pap led him out through the door. There was a coat hanging on the back of the door, which Bill put on to hide his blood and his nakedness. He looked at Jessie in a proprietary way.

"Come on outside," he said with a nod.

"I won't," said Jessie.

He came towards her. She stood her ground, looking at him steadily. He thrust his hideous face close to hers. "D'ye think I'm going to listen to your nonsense now?" he said. "If you won't walk I'll drag you."

Jessie considered all her chances in a flash. Pap would presently return. But Pap was of no use to her. She would have a better chance of handling the man without witnesses. So she walked to the yard door, keeping her head up, and climbed the four steps with Bill at her heels. The night air was sweet in her nostrils. No lighted window looked down into that dark hold between the front building and the rear. This moment was to put her guiding maxim in life to the supreme test. She believed that a brave soul could not be humbled.

Standing in the very centre of the little flagged yard, she waited for Bill.

"Well, ain't you got nothin' for me?" he grumbled.

"No," she said. "I told you that before."

"I won you fair, didn't I?"

"You haven't won me until I give myself to you."

"It had to be either him or me."

"That's just a man's nonsense. *I* am the one to say who shall have me!"

"Hell, girl!" he said violently, "do you think you can live here amongst a lot of rough men without protection? And do you think you're going to get protection for nothing? Do you expect me to spend my strength fighting for you, and be satisfied with a 'thankee kindly?'"

"I didn't ask you to fight for me."

"Then he would a took you."

"I would say the same to him as to you."

"Aah! what's all the talk about?" said Bill violently. "I fought for yeh, and I won yeh; that's according to Nature."

"It's according to animal nature. Am I no more to you than an animal?"

"I'm done talkin'!" cried Bill. He flung his arms around her. "Oh, you beauty!"

Jessie stood perfectly still, leaning far back, and keeping

her hands up between them. "You are strong enough to take me," she said steadily. "But you can't do it."

"Why can't I?" he demanded with an oath.

"I'm done talking too," she said. "Look at me. *You know why!*"

It was light enough for them to see each other's eyes. "Don't look at me like that," he cried in a voice of rage and pain. "Don't look at me like that, or I'll do you a hurt!"

"Is it worth it, Bill?" she asked softly.

He flung her from him. "Get away from me!" he said thickly. "Get back in the house!"

She walked to the steps. Behind her she heard him cursing under his breath. The strangled sounds suggested a breast racked with pain. "Well—he's a man!" she thought. Entering the kitchen, he was hard on her heels. Pap had returned, but Bill paid no attention to him.

"Lookee," he said to Jessie. "This house ain't big enough for you and me. I won't be responsible. You better go back where you come from. You make too much trouble around here." His pain escaped him in a final low, bitter cry: "By God! if Kate don't send you back to Woburn, *I will!*"

A moment later Black Kate herself entered the kitchen from the other side. Her eyelids were down, and she was curiously white about the lips. Jessie saw that another storm portended from this quarter. Skinny Sam came in soon after her, looking smug and self-conscious. It appeared that the combination against her was perfect, and Jessie awaited the event like a good loser, with a shrug. Oh well, she had done her best!

It was a foible of Mrs. Pullen's that, when she was angriest, she made believe to be calm. Nobody was deceived by it. She did not speak at once, but poked around the kitchen, closing a cupboard door here, moving a chair there. Finally she said, apropos of nothing:

"So you've been having trouble with Bill, too."

Jessie saw that anything she could say would only make matters worse, so she kept still. Neither did Bill volunteer any information. The big man was still in the grip of the feelings he did not understand. His forehead was knotty with veins, and the hand with which he emptied his pipe, and started to refill it, trembled slightly.

"You cost me a good man last night," Mrs. Pullen went on; "and you've been making trouble in the house all day—Where's Fingy?" she demanded of the room at large.

"Gone to bed," said Pap.

"Him and Bill was fighting," said Sam.

"What, Fingy too?" said Mrs. Pullen, turning again to Jessie. "How many men do you want? All there are, I suppose— Well, you've done for yourself here. You can't say I didn't warn you. Before another day is out, you'll be back where there are no men."

Jessie looked at Bill, but he avoided her glance. Evidently he agreed with Black Kate.

"Have you got the gag and the handcuffs?" she demanded of Sam. "I don't mean to have any more uproar here."

Sain handed her the desired articles.

"Do you mean *now?*" asked Jessie, astonished into speech.

"This very minute!" said Black Kate viciously. "I know where to find one of Warden Insull's men. It'll mean promotion to him to carry the famous Jessie Seipp back to Woburn—Sara, go telephone Charlie to bring his car to the back entrance as quick as he can."

Sam left the room.

The steel bracelets jangled in the older woman's hands. "Put out your hands, girl!"

Jessie put her hands behind her and backed against a dresser. She had no thought of putting up a fight. She merely wanted to gain time.

"Hold her, Bill!" said Black Kate furiously.

Bill got up willingly enough. Jessie knew that to make an appeal to him would only be to call forth an angry retort. After that, manlike, he would have to stand by his spoken words. So she said nothing, but kept her eyes fixed on him steadily. She had only the time that it would take him to make five steps to win him. At about the third step he lost his air of willingness. At one pace from Jessie he stopped dead, and looked at the floor. Jessie was willing him to look at her. "Are you going to stand for this?" her eyes were asking.

He darted a furtive look into her face, then, just as if she had spoken, he cried with a violent gesture: "No! I'm damned if I'll stand for it!"

"What's the matter with you?" cried Kate furiously.

"The truth has got to be told," said Bill doggedly. "Did you think you'd get the truth about this—or anything else, from Sam?"

"You leave Sam out of this!"

"I was sittin' in the dining-room after breakfast," said Bill coolly; "and I heard Sam go into her room. And I heard her tell him to get out. And in a minute I heard her throw him out."

"That's a lie!" cried Black Kate.

"All right," said Bill. "Feel the back of your darlin's head, and you'll find the bump where he struck."

"Out she goes to-night!" cried Kate.

"All right," said Bill. "Remember, I'm as old a member of this organisation as you are, and I know how to reach the boss's ear without using *you* for my mouthpiece. If Jess goes back to Woburn, Sam goes back to Sing Sing."

It is terrible for one of these all-commanding persons to find himself or herself in an *impasse*. Jessie could almost have felt sorry for the woman. Black Kate changed colour and bit her lip. Finally she said, with a great air of carelessness:

"Oh well, I'll think it over for to-night."

A long breath of relief escaped silently between Jessie's lips.

Bill would not spare his adversary. "You'd damn well better think it over," he said. "To-morrow, too."

"That will do," said Kate peremptorily.

"I'm finished," said Bill, thus depriving her of even the poor satisfaction of the last word.

By this time Sam had returned to the room. He was despatched to the rear entrance to send "Charley" back when he came with the car.

"Go to bed," said Kate to Jessie.

The latter was very willing to obey. To have attempted to thank Bill then would only have caused more trouble; so she contented herself with giving him an eloquent glance as she passed.

Now Pap was so much excited by all that had happened, he scarcely knew what he was doing. Even as she left the room, out of the tail of her eye Jessie saw him cutting great hunks of bread off a loaf, and putting them on a plate. Her curiosity was instantly on the *qui vive*. "Who can that be for," she asked herself; "at this time of night?"

Jessie went to her room, and somewhat ostentatiously closing the door, listened just within. She heard Mrs. Pullen come up and go into her room. She heard Bill's heavy step pass her door, and go on up to the top floor. Then she heard Pap coming. When Pap had passed her door, she opened it a crack. He was carrying the plate of bread, and in his other hand he had a small pitcher, presumably containing water. "Pretty slim fare!" thought Jessie. When Pap had passed out of sight up the last flight, Jessie came out into the hall the better to hear.

Pap put a key into the door at the head of the stairs. At this moment the bell sounded that announced the return of Sam through the secret door. But it would take him a minute or two to cross the yard and mount the two flights, and Jessie waited. She heard Pap open the door above, and from within the room she heard a sound that caused her to catch her breath in astonishment; the jingle of a chain.

Pap said: "Here," and a whispered voice answered him: "Wait a minute, Pap. God! I'll go out of my mind if I never hear a human voice!" To which Pap answered in a whisper: "Nothin' doin'. She's waitin' for the key."

Jessie went back into her room with a fast-beating heart. A *woman's* voice! Surely it could be no other than the woman she sought! And so near! so near! An overpowering excitement filled her. However dreadful the actual situation might be, while there was life there was hope. All along Jessie had been tormented by the fear that after all

she might be too late. More than a fear, it had been practically a certainty. And now to be given assurance that she
was *not* too late! Ah! what a barren satisfaction in *avenging*
Melanie, as compared to the joy of *saving* her!

16

THE MEETING

IT WAS FIRST necessary for Jessie to make sure that the prisoner on the top floor was really Melanie Soupert. A dozen simple ways of accomplishing this suggested themselves to Jessie; the difficulty was to forestall the slightest chance of discovery.

Every move that Jessie made in this matter had to be successful, for there could be no second chances. The smallest slip-up would end everything; end Jessie, end Melanie. Indeed, Jessie was still wondering how, since they suspected Melanie's loyalty to the gang, they had allowed her to live so long. The worst of it was, that in a household of this sort all the members stuck close at home by day and went out at night; yet it was only by daylight that Jessie could *see* Melanie.

She waited and watched her chance. It was not easy to keep track of the whereabouts of all the members of so diverse a family, but she had to know at any given moment where they were. Black Kate had evidently made up her mind it would be wiser for her to remain at home that day; and she sent Sam out to do the shopping. She herself moved softly around the house, unexpectedly appearing in the kitchen and dining-room, and watching them all like a cat.

After the violent scenes of the day before it was quiet enough in the house. Jessie, of course, bore herself precisely as if nothing had happened. To a woman it comes naturally to do so; not to a man. Big Bill went about with a hangdog look. His eyes occasionally sought Jessie's face with a sullen look, but wistful too. There seemed to be something that he wanted to say to her. Jessie gave him every opportunity to say it, but it never came out. Fingy Silo's bold, stupid stare at Jessie was gone; when he looked at her now, it was with furtive eyes.

Sam had had a lesson too; he still glinted poisonously at Jessie through his lashes; but when Kate was anywhere about, he dared not look at her at all. The house was quiet enough, but appalling forces of meanness and hatred and brutishness lurked under the surface. Only Pap and little Abell were comparatively harmless, the one because he was old, the other because "he was in love with his wife," they said with scorn.

Jessie gathered from various whispered conferences that went on that Bill and Fingy were going "to turn a trick" that night. There was no animosity between the two where business was concerned. She also understood from a word or two that was dropped, that Abell would be out also, at least during the earlier part of the night. This would leave her alone in the house with Kate, Sam and Pap. She considered the chances. Pap slept in the room over hers, while Sam had the front hall room on the top floor to himself. However, she must first establish communications with the prisoner.

In the morning she carried a broom upstairs with which
to sweep her room; and afterwards left it in her room, as
if by accident. Pap did not miss it. Obtaining paper and
pencil was rather more difficult. Apparently nobody in that
house had any occasion to write. Finally, on a cupboard
shelf she picked up a sheaf of cigarette papers, which
would serve very well, but a pencil her sharp eyes could
discover nowhere either in dining-room or kitchen. It
would have been highly imprudent to ask for one. In the
end it occurred to her that if they played cards, they must
have a pencil to score with, so, hanging about the kitchen,
as if at a loose end, she said with a yawn:

"Gee! I gotta have something to do! Where are the cards
kept?"

Pap pointed to a drawer in the dresser, and there, among
odds and ends of all sorts, Jessie found several worn packs
of cards, and to her joy, a stubby pencil. Spreading the cards
on the kitchen table, she played solitaire, until Pap told her
ill-temperedly that she was in his way. Whereupon, Jessie
slung the cards back in the drawer—but kept the pencil.

After lunch the time seemed ripe to act. Bill, Fingy
and Abell had gone to their rooms to sleep, in order to be

fresh for the night's work. Kate was in her room, too, and also sleeping, Jessie hoped. Sam had been sent out on an errand. Pap was in the kitchen. She was not likely to get a better opportunity.

The bathroom of the house was next to Jessie's room, and therefore immediately under the room where the prisoner was confined. Jessie carried broom, paper and pencil into the bathroom, and hooked the door behind her. Drawing down the top sash of the window, she stood on the sill, and leaning backwards over the sash, thrust her broom up as far as she could reach, and waved the brush to and fro in front of the window above.

There was no response, and Jessie was finally obliged to let the broom softly brush against the sill of the window overhead. The risk was sickening, because Fingy was in the room next to the girl's; his window was open, of course, and he might not be asleep. Finally, through the window above, came faintly the rattle of a chain, and an astonished head stuck out. With a great uprush of joy, Jessie saw that it was indeed Melanie Soupert.

Jessie had never seen Melanie closer than five hundred feet, but the girl had often been described to her, and there could be no possibility of mistaking that bobbed black hair, those big dark eyes, and the resolute, beautiful mouth. Melanie showed with tragic clearness what she had been through; her face was gaunt, her hair unkempt, her eyes red-rimmed. She looked at Jessie in the purest amazement, for Melanie had no clue to her.

Jessie instantly laid a finger on her lips, and pointed to the window of the room adjoining Melanie's. Melanie closed her eyes and silently signified a person snoring.

Jessie, reassured, showed her the pencil and paper, and retired inside the window to write her note.

"I am your friend. I will help you. Have you got a couple of sheets? If you'll knot them and let them down when I give you a signal, I'll come to you to-night."

Jessie inserted the paper between the splints of the broom, and pushed it up towards Melanie. Melanie read it, and her dulled eyes began to shine again. She nodded eagerly. The paper she instinctively put in her mouth.

Jessie wrote her a second note. "My room is next to the bathroom. I am locked in at night. I can get across to the bathroom window all right. The rope needn't be but about eight feet long. It ought to have a knot every eighteen inches. See that the end is firmly secured to the frame of your bed. Let it drop over when you hear me scratch on my sill."

Melanie read this with more eager nods, and Jessie went back to her own room, well satisfied with the start she had made. She subsequently returned the broom to its corner in the kitchen, and the pencil to its drawer.

During the rest of the day Jessie mooned about those parts of the house that were free to her; the kitchen, the dining-room and her own room, apparently bored to extinction, but with her mind functioning in a high state of activity. Her prime object, of course, was to rescue Melanie, but it was of no less importance to get the big boss of them all. How to work the two things together; that was her problem. She could not allow Melanie to remain there indefinitely in danger; but on the other hand, if she got Melanie out, that would certainly blow the whole game. As yet Jessie had no direct lead to the man she wanted.

Black Kate joined the others at supper that night, and Jessie had a different part to play. It was useless, now, to think of winning Kate's good-will, and to seek to win the others while Kate was present, would be an unforgivable offence in the woman's eyes. So Jessie contented herself with marking time, letting it be seen, though, that she had nothing on her mind, and that she was perfectly willing to laugh and joke with anybody who gave her an opening.

But it was a sullen meal; an ordeal for a sensitive person to have to sit through it. Apart from Jessie, though, there were no sensitive persons present, with the possible exception of little Abell, whose thin face was bitter. The others seemed to find the atmosphere of hate and suspicion quite natural.

When the company around the table broke up, Bill Combs, with mysterious becks and winks, let it be still more clearly seen that he had a communication to make to Jessie. It seemed to Jessie that it was worth risking something to receive it; and with a meaning look at Bill, she went up to her room, and waited in the doorway. He presently came to her.

Bill was like a great mastiff trying to be friendly.

"You don't need to be afraid of me no more," he whispered huskily.

"I am not afraid of you, Bill," she said simply.

"Here," he said, "I wanted you to have this while I was out to-night. Maybe I won't be back."

"Won't be back!" she echoed in dismay.

He was rather pathetically pleased by her concern. "Would you care?" he said.

"You know you're the only friend I've got!"

"Oh, well, it's nothing special," he said. "But there's always a risk when you've got a trick to turn."

"And it's us that takes it," said Jessie.

"Oh, sure," he said philosophically; "whatever happens to us, the organisation goes on."

Meanwhile, Bill was pressing a cold, object of significant shape into Jessie's hand. It was a small automatic.

" 'Tain't loaded," he said, "I don't want no shooting here. But just to show it would protect you."

"Thanks, Bill," said Jessie. "But what have I got to be afraid of to-night? Not of Pap nor of Sam, surely."

"I wasn't thinkin' about them," said Bill, "but of Black Kate. She's got a nasty streak of cruelty in her nature. And when I was out she might try to take it out on you."

"I understand," said Jessie. "Thanks again, Bill."

"Don't mention it," said Bill seriously.

Jessie chuckled inwardly at the big fellow's new-found manners.

He went on up to his room, which he shared with Abell. Jessie went down to the kitchen. Always trying to make good with the gang, she volunteered to help Pap with the dishes. Before they were finished Big Bill and Fingy Silo set off through the back door upon the night's lousiness. Neatly dressed and freshly shaven. Jessie found herself inwardly smiling at their virtuous expressions. "How strange life is!" she thought.

Afterwards she and Pap sat down to a game of pinochle. In the kitchen they were pretty safe from Black Kate's presence, for the mistress of the house considered it beneath her dignity to sit down there. Neither Kate nor Sam troubled them during the evening. At ten o'clock Abell went out carrying his little black satchell. He gave Jessie a twisted smile; friendly enough, and inexpressibly painful.

And then, to Jessie's satisfaction, Pap began to yawn. "I wish I could give you a sleeping-draught, old man," she thought. The game petered out, and Jessie went upstairs.

Listening within her room, she heard Pap come up. He stopped at Kate's door for the key, handed in Melanie's meagre rations to her, and returned the key to Kate. Finally Jessie heard him enter his own room above her. In a few minutes Kate came along the hall and locked the door of Jessie's room.

Jessie paced up and down. She must give Pap plenty of time to settle down. A horrible indecision attacked her. She was seriously disturbed by Bill's suggestion concerning Black Kate. Suppose Kate came to her room while she was out of it? Better put it off until another night perhaps. On the other hand, the danger of Kate's coming would be the same every night. And that poor girl upstairs would be waiting the livelong night through for the signal. No! this night as well as another.

She jammed the back of the chair firmly under the handle of her door. That ought to hold it long enough for her to get back. It was only a matter of swinging down on the rope. But if Kate found her fully-dressed? She decided to go in her night-clothes. She hung the little pistol around her neck on a string. She tumbled the bed clothes.

When she was ready, she went to the window. All was dark outside. Whether Pap snored or not, she did not know. No sound reached her. She stuck her head out, and looked up. Over the sill above, and to the right, stuck another head, shadowy against the night sky. How long had Melanie been waiting there?

With her hand Melanie made a gesture of negation, Jessie was not to come yet. So they waited. At intervals Melanie left the window, no doubt to listen with her ear against the partition between the two rooms. A long time passed. Finally Melanie beckoned, and Jessie climbed out on the window sill.

The knotted sheet fell in front of her, and Jessie reached for it. It would be easier to go than it would be to come back, but Jessie had no doubt of her ability to make it. She grasped the rope, and swung over. Hand over hand she pulled herself up by the knots. Melanie helped her over the sill.

Jessie felt for the girl's hand in the dark, and squeezed it. There was no answering pressure, and things went swiftly through Jessie's mind. "Melanie has been thinking things over, and has become suspicious!" she thought. "It is natural enough. She thinks I may have been planted by Black Kate just to betray her." In an instant Jessie had changed her whole plan of action. She determined not to tell Melanie who she was. That story would sound too incredible, and might very well confirm the girl in her suspicions.

"Who are you?" Melanie breathed in her ear.

"Jessie Seipp," she answered. "Listen, and I'll tell you."

The two sat side by side on the bed. Always lip pressed to ear they spoke. Jessie apprehended that Melanie was dragging the chain from one wrist. Jessie kept Melanie's hand between both of hers, feeling that she must be assured in the end by the beat of her pulses that she Jessie, was her true friend.

"I was sent up to Woburn for robbin' Mrs. Cornelius Marquardt," Jessie whispered. "Up there I was put in the next cell to a girl called Minnie Dickerson. We used to talk nights. She told me all about you, and how you escaped from Woburn. She told me a lot about this gang too; I mean only what an outsider might know. She said they'd come after me, and they did. The woman of the house here, Mrs. Pullen, or Black Kate, as they call her. She came to see me at Woburn. And afterwards she got me out, and she brought me here.

"I been here two days now," Jessie went on, "and I picked up a word here, and a word there, and I finally pieced it out that you was locked up here. I seen Pap bring you your supper. Then I made a signal to you wit' t' broom, and here I am. It's a dirty rotten shame. I'm goin' to stand by you and be your friend."

"You can't do nothin' for me," whispered Melanie apathetically.

"I'm goin' to get you out and get myself out, too. Minnie was right when she said it was worse than suicide, goin' in with this gang. I on'y been here two days, but I seen how things are."

"There's no place we could go where *he* couldn't get us."

"I got friends who'll keep us close."

"What you want to do all this for? I'm nottin' to you."

"Well, I promised Minnie I'd be friends if I ever come up with you. We got to help each other out, ain't we?"

Still there was no response, and for a moment Jessie was at a loss. It would be fatal to try to force the girl's confidence. Finally mother wit whispered what to do. "Well,

I better go now," she breathed in Melanie's ear. "It's too risky, staying."

It worked. Melanie's hand instantly clung to hers. That slightly trembling hand was terribly eloquent. It spoke both of Melanie's longing to make a friend, and her fear of betrayal.

"Ain't you got nothin' to ask me?" she whispered to Jessie.

"No," Jessie whispered back. "You suspicion me already. If I tried to get anything out of you, then you'd be sure I was workin' for Black Kate."

"Will you come again?" Melanie whispered tremulously.

"No," said Jessie. "It's too risky. I won't come again until I got a plan all doped out. That may take time."

This simple speech turned the scale. For, of course, if Jessie was in right with Black Kate, she could come at any time. Melanie broke down. Half turning on the bed, she flung an arm around Jessie, and buried her face in her shoulder. It was the terrible and complete break-down of an ordinarily strong and self-sufficient nature. Melanie's whole body was shaken as by a violent ague of sobbing, though she made no sound.

Jessie held her close. "There! It's all right now," she whispered. "You and me'll see each other through."

"You—you don't know what I been through!" whispered Melanie, suffocated by her sobs.

"Sh!" breathed Jessie. "Don't try to talk, or you'll bust out. Just let it come easy. Do you good. I know how it is. I can guess what you been through, too. That woman is a fiend out of hell!"

"She—she—" whispered Melanie.

Jessie put a hand over her mouth. "Don't try to tell me now," she whispered swiftly. "Time enough later."

Gradually Melanie quieted down. "Ah, it's good to have you here," she whispered, clinging hard to Jessie. "If you mean to do me a dirty trick, God forgive you! 'Tain't worth your while. For I'm done! They've broke me!"

"You'll see whether I'm on the square or not," whispered Jessie.

After a while Jessie said: "I'm not going to ask you no questions. If there's anything you want to tell me go ahead. But it's nothin' to me."

"Ain't nothin' to tell," whispered Melanie. "You see how it is."

"There's one thing puzzles me," said Jessie. "I'm supposing they think that you've betrayed the organisation in some way."

"Yes, but they got no proof of it," said Melanie.

"Yes, but if they think so. They all tell me that a suspicion of treason, as they call it, is enough. I understand that there's a nice dirt cellar under this house that's waitin' for traitors."

"That's right," whispered Melanie, "and they mean to stick me under it when I've served their turn. They're tryin' to get another through me, see? There's a fellow has slipped out of the hands of the big boss. They're hoping that this fellow'll hear that I'm locked up here, and that he'll try to see me, or get me out, see? Then they'll nab him, and stick us both under the dirt together."

Melanie began to shake again. "That's what drives me wild," she whispered. "I don't care about myself. But he— he's had nothin' but trouble and hurt through me. We were crazy about each other. If I knew he was safe, I wouldn't care!"

"That's George Mullen," whispered Jessie.

"Where 'd you hear that name?" demanded Melanie, clutching her.

"Minnie Dickerson told me."

"Aah, Min talks too much."

"Maybe we can get word to him," whispered Jessie.

"That's just what I don't want," answered Melanie. "That would bring him. I'm scared now that he'll hear from somebody, who's heard it from somebody else, who's heard it from one of the men in the house, that I'm locked up here—at the mercy of Black Kate."

"But if we got the right kind of a message to him."

Melanie still shook her head. "I wouldn't tell you how to reach him. I think now that you're my friend. But that's something I couldn't tell to anybody on earth."

"I already know how to reach him," said Jessie. "Through his mother."

Melanie took her arm from about Jessie, and buried her face in her hands. "Oh, God! if any further harm comes to him through me—" she murmured.

Jessie put her lips to the girl's ear. "Sh!" she whispered warningly.

"Oh," said Melanie, "if Pap's awake, he's often heard me talkin' to myself. He won't listen."

However, she put her lips to Jessie's ear again. "Listen," she whispered imploringly, "if you're on the square, for God's sake don't try to send any kind of a message to him. I hope and pray that he's cleared out; that he's far enough away never to hear of me again!"

Jessie held her close. She whispered: "Well, the first thing we got to do is to dope out some way—"

The sentence never got itself finished, for a sound came from the floor below, that caused them to spring apart; the thrust of key in a lock.

"Black Kate," gasped Melanie; "at your door!"

In a flash Jessie was at the window. She tossed the knotted rope out, and climbed over the sill. A moment later, she was hanging in front of the bathroom window. Still clinging to the rope, she managed to pull herself over to her own sill by means of the shutters. She let herself down to a sitting position, with her feet inside, and let go the rope. It was instantly jerked up out of sight.

Black Kate had not yet got into the room. She was viciously pounding on the door. "Let me in!" she cried. It was the first time she had spoken. Jessie gave her heart a moment to quiet down.

"Let me in!" cried Kate again.

"Oh, it's you!" answered Jessie from the direction of the bed. "One moment."

She lit the gas, and took the little pistol in her hand. Then she pulled the chair from under the handle of the door.

Kate was still fully dressed; Sam was behind her. The violent oath on her lips was checked at the sight of the gun. She looked very queer. "Where'd you get that?" she demanded.

Nothing like the truth, thought Jessie. "Bill gave it to me," she said.

"Hand it over," said Kate peremptorily.

Jessie retreated one step, and slowly shook her head. "It's Bill's," she said. "I'll only give it to him."

Kate's face was hideous with rage. However, she decided not to force the issue. "Why didn't you let me in right away?" she demanded.

"I was asleep," said Jessie, with innocent eyes. "At first I thought it was one of the men."

"You don't need to fear any of the men when I'm in the next room."

"But if you found one of them here, you'd blame me," said Jessie.

Black Kate lost countenance again.

"What did you want of me?" asked Jessie, innocent still.

"Er—I thought I heard a noise in here," said Black Kate, looking around the room.

"I don't know—I was asleep," said Jessie demurely. She looked around, too.

In order to save her face Black Kate flew into a fresh passion. "You gotta understand that I make my rounds any time of day or night, as I see fit," she said.

"Oh, certainly," said Jessie humbly.

Black Kate slammed the door, and turned the key in it. Jessie looked down at the diminutive black object in her hand.

"Little friend, you did me a good turn," she murmured.

17

JESSIE'S TEACHER

IN THE KITCHEN next morning, Jessie and Pap were washing dishes, while Bill sat by the window, filling his first after-breakfast pipe, Evidently the expedition of the night before had been crowned with success, for Bill was in a high good humour.

"Like to take a walk?" he said to Jessie.

"Sure," said Jessie facetiously. "Were'll it be? Up and down the hall or out in the yard?"

"How about lunch at a Broadway hotel?" said Bill. "I'll blow."

"Don't make me laugh," said Jessie. "Me lip's cracked."

"On the level," said Bill, "orders has come through that you're to be taught the ropes, now, and I'm to be your teacher." He lowered his voice prudently. "You can't fool the big boss. Black Kate spoiled one good girl on him, and he ain't goin' to give her another. Say, maybe Kate didn't give me a sweet look when she told me the news. Oh no, not at all. But orders is orders. The boss has got his check on her, as well as the rest of us. So you can go out now, as long as I escort you."

Jessie could scarcely believe her ears. Her heart beat high. "Don't I need a disguise?" she asked.

"What for?"

"Against the police."

"The police ain't lookin' for you, sis. That's where you're in luck. No alarm for you was ever sent out. Warden's afraid of the publicity, I guess. He prob'ly has a man or two of his own lookin' for you around town, but they'll never find you, unless the big boss wants you to be found. If it wasn't for that, you'd have to stay indoors for many a day yet."

With a bounding heart, Jessie ran upstairs to fetch her hat. This had come sooner than she expected. Surely, with this greater freedom of action, she could soon accomplish both her aims. It would be too much to say that all looked clear ahead, but she could see light now.

Before returning downstairs, she ran into the bathroom for a moment, and sticking her head out of the window, scratched on the sill. Instantly a cautious head stuck out over the sill above. Melanie looked relieved at the sight of Jessie's joyous face. Jessie pointed to her hat, and signified in dumb play that she was going out. Melanie looked both pleased and dubious. Evidently Jessie's unexpected good luck brought back some of her suspicions. But if she thought about it at all she must realise that Jessie would never have run to tell her about it, if she were not on the square.

When Jessie got back to the kitchen, Bill said: "Orders is you are to go out by the front door. Kate uses the front door when she goes in and out by day, also Sam and Abie. Only me and Fingy has to go out the back way, 'cos we looks like shady characters. You walk up-town, and I'll overtake you by Sheridan Square."

The front door was always kept locked on the inside, and

Kate carried the key. She hove in view from somewhere to let Jessie out, and stood back with a pinched and bitter face. Jessie, making believe to be unaware of it, smiled at her as she passed, and ran down the steps with light heels. She will never forget the bliss of that moment. Varick Street is far from being beautiful, but to Jessie it looked like the New Jerusalem. Such a blue sky, such golden sunshine, such pleasant people.

Very soon Bill Combs came lumbering up behind her. He took her arm, and drew her to a stand at the curb. "Let's take a taxi," said he, "I'm flush."

"Where we going?" asked Jessie.

"Oh, nowheres in particular to-day. We's just havin' a taste of libetty to-day."

"Well, it's sweet," said Jessie.

When they had seated themselves in the cab, Bill inserted thumb and forefinger in his waistcoat pocket, and drew out a short string of pearls; not large pearls, but beautifully matched and lustrous.

"For you," he mumbled like a great clumsy schoolboy.

For a moment Jessie's breath was taken away.

"Part of last night's stuff?" Bill went on. "I gets little enough out of it, and I holds out on them when I can. These I picked up for you special."

Jessie trembled with inward laughter. What a funny compliment for a woman to receive. "Oh, Bill, I couldn't," she said.

"Why not?" he demanded, absurdly chapfallen.

"It wouldn't be square."

"Not square to who?"

"To *you*. The first time you got mad at me you'd say; 'What did you take them pearls for?'"

She had him there. "Aah!" he grumbled looking away, "you got too fine sentiment!" But he dropped the pearls in his pocket again.

"When do my lessons begin?" asked Jessie.

"Right now," said Bill. "I understand the boss aims to make you a first-class house-breaker," he went on coolly—and once more Jessie felt that queer start of inward laughter. "The last girl we had used to hire out as a servant in rich houses, and then lift the mistress's sparklers. A safe and sure stunt. But, of course, you're too rough for that kind of work."

This time Jessie giggled openly.

"No offence meant," said Bill, with an uneasy look; "you're a damn sight better lookin' gal in my eyes than she was. I just mean you ain't got the soapy look a servant has."

"No offence taken," said Jessie. "I get you."

"The boss believes that women ought to make the best house-breakers," Bill went on, "being as they're naturally handier, quicker and quieter. That's the modern idea; women are hornin' in everywhere nowadays. The trouble with them is, they don't gen'ally have the nerve. But the boss is satisfied you got plenty nerve, and I'll say you have too."

"Much obliged," said Jessie.

"Of course, I couldn't learn you everything you ought to know right off the bat," said Bill. "It'd take a year alone to show you all the different kinds of locks and how to pick them. But things ain't what they was when I went into the business. They ain't no more all-round men. This is the age of specialisation. I'll say it's easier than it used to be on account of organisation. Take our organisation. The outside men they picks the jobs, and dopes out a line of approach and all. All you got to do is follow instructions."

"Well, if I had a choice, I'd take the old way," said Jessie. "If I got to take the risk, I want to run the show."

"There's somepin in that," agreed Bill, "but I will say our organisation's got brainy men on the outside to plan things out good."

"Looks like to me they just use us like monkeys to pull their chestnuts out of the fire," said Jessie.

"That's so, in a way of speaking," said Bill. "But them's modern conditions. What ya goin' to do?"

"Do you know the boss?" asked Jessie.

"I seen him in my time," said Bill guardedly.

"What like man is he?"

Bill wagged his raised palm from side to side.

"Can't you tell me what he looks like?" persisted Jessie. "How old a man? Is he married? Does he lead a respectable life and all. Has he got some regular business for a stall? Is he well known around town?"

To all such questions Bill obdurately wagged his hand. "You hadn't ought to ast me them kind of questions," he said. "Maybe I could answer them, and maybe I couldn't. I don't want to know nothin' about the boss, as a man. It's dangerous. To you and me he's just an idea, sis. He's power—see? You and me is only a part of a part of the organisation. It reaches everywhere. The different parts don't even know each other. But from each part a line runs direct to the boss. He holds all the lines in his hand. He does what he wants. He's as high above you and me as God!"

"This is a free country, ain't it?" said Jessie, just to draw him out.

"I guess that slogan was invented before everything was organised," said Bill dryly. "Nowadays the individual man is nothing. All he can do is to join a good strong organisation. Then he can lie back, and let the organisation take care of him, and do his thinking."

"But they don't take care of us," said Jessie. "They let us take all the risk. They let us go to jail."

"But they get us out again, don't they?"

"Do you think the boss will let me see him?" asked Jessie.

"Why should he?" said Bill coolly. "You're on'y the youngest member."

"But he will, though!" Jessie vowed to herself.

They dismissed their taxi at Thirty-Fourth Street, and strolled up the Avenue. How good the well-remembered street looked to Jessie's eyes. She eagerly searched amongst the throng for old acquaintances. It was not the season for fashionable people to be in town, but she saw Mrs. Grantham, the wife of the famous aviator; the new Mrs. Norbert Starr, and Doctor Strailock. None looked at her, of course. Big Bill in himself was a disguise.

"The first thing I got to teach you," said Bill, "is to know the stuff when you see it."

"Solid silver's always got 'sterling' on it," said Jessie innocently.

"No!" said Bill jocosely. "Ain't you the knowin' one!... You needn't bother about silver, sis. Cash, of course, whenever it can be picked up, but precious stones is the main stuff. Always a steady market."

"You mean diamonds and pearls," said Jessie.

"Yeh. Them's the leaders. Sapphires and emeralds is just as good. Rubies too, but you don't see them much nowadays."

He brought her to a stand before the window of a famous jeweller. "This is what I wanted you to see," he whispered in her ear. "You see it's mostly diamonds. The world has gone mad over diamonds. It makes rich pickin's for us... Well, you don't need much instruction to tell a diamond. It's got life in it. Almost in the dark you can tell it. Consequently they're not much imitated no more; it don't pay. Those green stones are emeralds, and the blue ones sapphires. They're worth more than diamonds if they got no cracks. After you look at them a bit, you can't be mistaken in them neither. They got a high-toned look like a fine lady."

He led her on to another show-window, where many strings of pearls were displayed. "What do you think about them?" he demanded.

Jessie had to conceal her knowledge of pearls, of course. "Ain't they pretty!" she said rapturously.

"All phoney," said Bill. "Made on the premises here. Look well at them, so you won't make no mistake again. They're *too* pretty, in a way of speaking. Too smooth and round and shiny. That shine is on'y pasted on the outside. Now come." He proceeded to a window where real pearls were displayed.

"See, the difference?" he whispered, with the enthusiasm of an expert. "Real pearls don't shine—they glow. The shine seems to come from the inside—see? And they ain't machine-ground. They got little hollows like a woman's cheek."

From jeweller's window to jeweller's window, the lesson proceeded.

"There's another thing you want to learn," said Bill, when they finally turned down-town again, in search of lunch— "and that's this here psychology, as they call it."

Jessie smiled inwardly. This was teaching a cat to lap cream, indeed. "What's that?" she asked innocently.

"Well, it used to be called studyin' human nature," said Bill. "But now it's called psychology. It's knowin' people. Take that old dude ahead of us. What can you tell me about him?"

"He's got corns," said Jessie.

"Sure. But that ain't psychology. What's goin' through his mind?"

"He wants the world to think he's a regular devil, but it's on'y window-dressin'."

"Very like; but what I want you to notice particular is, he ain't the real thing. He ain't worth the pickin'. His clothes is all right, but that's all he's got."

"How do you know that?"

"By his anxious eye. A man with plenty money always has a calm eye. Take this guy comin' towards us—him with the roast-beef complexion and the thick-soled shoes. What's he?"

"I dunno."

"A bull."

"How do you know that? By his shoes?"

"No, that's just as it happens. I know it by his watchful eye. There's different kinds of watchfulness, of course. The old dude who passed us before—he looks at everybody to see if they're looking at him. But there's on'y two kinds of men has that hard watchfulness on the street—one's our kind; and one's them that's lookin' for our kind. And the difference between 'em is, a bull looks kinda pious because he's got the law on his side."

"Not so bad!" thought Jessie.

"The principal thing you got to learn in psychology," Bill went on, "is, how a man's goin' to ac' when you stick him up. There's mostly three kinds; there's the nervous man who hollers and crumples up; there's the ordinary, sensible man who puts his hands up when you got the draw on him; and there's the man with a hot eye who's bound to put up a fight whatever the odds."

"How about women?" asked Jessie.

"I don't know so much about women. They mostly always hollers."

The temptation to show off a little was too much for Jessie. "Let me see what I kin do with this now, psychology," she said. "Look at this woman comin' out of the store. The one with the little handbag. What can you tell about her?"

"I told you I ain't wise to women." said Bill.

"Well, let me see what I can tell you," said Jessie, studying the woman. "She lives in Roselle—that's over in Jersey, ain't it? She don't get to town very often. The part where she lives isn't all built up yet, and she has to walk to the station. She's a hard-workin' woman with a whole raft of children, but just the same, somebody's going to blow her to lunch to-day at a swell-joint."

"Aah! you're just guessin'," said Bill.

"No, I seen the whole thing when she came out of the store and turned around beside me. There was a little card sticking out of the flap of her handbag, and on the top of it was: 'Trains to and from Roselle.' She don't got to town often, or she wouldn't need no time table. There was good country mud on her shoes. I had a sight of her shopping list, as she put it away, and the first item was: 'Bloomers for Alice.' Well, she must have a lot of kids, or she wouldn't have to put down which one the bloomers was for."

"How about the bid to lunch at a swell joint?"

"Why, you boob, didn't you see her look at Tiffany's clock when she come out of the store, and put away her shopping list, and take out a pair of white kid gloves that hadn't been wore before?"

"Aah! you just made that up,"

"Let's follow her."

At Thirty-Fourth Street the woman turned into the Waldorf-Astorias.

Bill refused to concede Jessie's psychology. "Aah! it was just a lucky guess!" he said.

Bill's idea of a "Broadway Hotel" was scarcely Jessie's. Bill chose White's, an old-fashioned restaurant near Twenty-Eighth Street. There was a double row of long tables disappearing in an endless vista, each table with its end against the wall. The aspect of the place was somewhat dingy, but a savoury smell greeted their nostrils as they went in. This promised to be better than Pap's cooking. No doubt in a tonier place they would have been too conspicuous.

Bill did the honours gallantly. "Sit yeh down," he said, indicating a seat next the wall on one side, while he took a chair opposite. "What say to a nice dish of corn beef and cabbage?"

"Hey, give me that!" said Jessie, snatching the card out of his hand.

"A person would think we was married the way you boss me," said Bill, grinning.

"Well, I'm not lookin' for no corn beef and cabbage man," said Jessie.

"Anythin' you want!" said Bill largely.

During the next quarter of an hour there was silence.

"We must do this again," said Bill, picking his teeth.

"Suits me," said Jessie.

Unfortunately, repletion had the effect of making Bill tender.

"Ain't had such a good time in God knows when," he said, leaning over the table. "It's so damn pleasant walking around the streets with a good-lookin' gal. I ain't had much of that. Say, I know I got off to a bad start with you, Jess. I mistook you, and that's a fact. But I'm man enough to own my mistake; that's somepin, ain't it? You ain't always goin' to hold it against me, are yeh? You and me was made for each other, girl. Look how well we get along. If you and me took each other for keeps, life would be a reg'lar picnic!"

"Now, Bill!" said Jessie. "If we're goin' to have any more good times, you know you gotta cut that out. You know there's nothin' doin'."

"Oh, my God! but you're an aggravatin' woman!" groaned Bill.

As they were about to leave the restaurant, they met a friend of Bill's, an odd little gentleman with hair and moustaches dyed fiercely black; checked suit, red necktie and pearl-gray Fedora. Bill and he conversed in undertones, and Jessie, seeing that she was not to be introduced, sauntered through the door to wait on the sidewalk.

Now Jessie had great need to send a message outside the ring that hemmed her round. She had marked the cigar store next door to the restaurant; it had telephone booths. Bill lingered. At any rate the cigar store would be safer than risking the telephone in the Varick Street house again. Even if Bill cut up rough, she ought to be able to handle him.

Jessie moved unostentatiously out of range of Bill's vision, then whipped inside the cigar store, and inside one of the booths. Once inside the booth, she was invisible from the street.

About three minutes later she emerged to find a baffled and furious Bill standing on the sidewalk, looking up and down. When he caught sight of her, he could have struck her down, had he dared.

"What the hell—!" he muttered.

"I just been to telephone," she said.

She winced in the grip of his hand on her arm. "Who to?" he demanded in his furious whisper. "And what about? Damn you, are you tryin' to double-cross me? Was it to a man?"

"No," said Jessie. "It was to a girl."

"You lie!"

"It was to my pal, Canada Annie. She's all right. She's in the same business as us. I was tryin' to make a date with her. She's the best friend I got. I thought maybe if you and me went out again, you'd let me see her, if you was along."

"You won't get out again in a hurry, my girl," said Bill.

Nevertheless, Jessie perceived that he was partly mollified by her explanation.

"Why didn't you ast me if you could telephone?" he demanded in an aggrieved tone. "It would a been all right if I could hear all you said."

"I was afraid you wouldn't let me."

"Aah!" growled Bill. "C'mon home."

Of that telephone message that Jessie sent, more anon. First I must tell you what happened to Jessie and Bill on the way home.

18

THE MAN WHO WAITED

BILL WAS SULLEN now, and in no humour to spend his money on taxicabs. They walked over to Seventh Avenue, and took the plebeian electric car. They got off at the turn at Eleventh Street, and walked on down. Jessie was making no attempt to charm away Bill's ill-temper; better to let it wear off of itself, she thought. She perceived that she had succeeded in deceiving him; in his heart he believed the story she had told of her telephone call; and that was all that was necessary. She was well assured he would not tell Black Kate anything about it.

A block or two beyond Sheridan Square, there was a small temporary structure built on one of the cater-cornered vacant lots left by the street widening. It housed a store for selling soft drinks and candy. As Bill and Jessie passed this place they heard a low hail:

"Hey, Bill Combs!"

It had a peremptory quality that caused them to turn very quickly. Jessie beheld a blond young man of slender figure, but notably lithe and muscular. His thin and intensely masculine face had a look of reckless passion that is rare among tamed city-dwellers, and consequently attractive. At this moment his face was as white as paper, and his eyes fairly blazing with excitement. That look in itself created a breathless situation. Jessie stole a look in Bill's face. His heavy features showed no change; but from the narrowing of his pupils Jessie perceived that this meeting powerfully excited him also.

"Why, hello, George," Bill said coolly.

Jessie's heart gave a great leap in her breast. Could this be George Mullen?

Bill put forth his hand to the young man with an open look that Jessie, who knew the big fellow pretty well by now, saw was treacherous. Evidently the young man suspected it; for he said: "Never mind your hand. If you try on any dirty work, I'll hail the cop who stands yonder. There's no unexpired time waiting for me, remember."

"Why, George," said Bill reproachfully, "I always been your friend."

"Beware of the man who says that to you!" Jessie thought.

The young man *was* wary. "We'll see," he said. Coming still closer to Bill, he whispered tensely: "Where's Melanie?"

By that Jessie knew that this was George Mullen.

Bill looked at Jessie in a quandary. It was highly imprudent to allow her to hear this conversation, but on the other hand his instructions were not to let her out of his sight. He evidently decided that George was the more important, for he said: "You run along home, my girl, and let me talk to this man."

Jessie had no intention of obeying. She slipped her arm through Bill's, saying: "I don't want to leave you; he's dangerous."

Bill was highly gratified. Meanwhile, George had

repeated his demand for information. Bill's wits were not nimble enough to run two ways at once. He answered George, and let Jessie remain.

"She's safe," said Bill.

"Where?"

"In the house."

"I believe you're lying," said George with a tormented look. "I been watching the house, and I seen nothing of her."

"She's got to lie low," said Bill. "She's wanted."

He then recollected Jessie again. "Run along home, my girl," he said.

George saved Jessie the necessity of refusing. "Wait a minute," he said harshly. "Who is this girl?"

"What the hell!" said Bill, affronted. "She's a friend of mine."

"Is she in the house, too?"

"Sure," said Jessie, for herself, before Bill could speak.

"Then you can tell me if Melanie Soupert is there," said George.

Bill bent a look on her, threatening terrible things if she did not bear out his story.

"Sure, she's there," said Jessie.

"Is she treated good?"

"She's treated as good as any of us."

Bill looked relieved.

"If you know her, describe her to me," demanded George.

"Here, that's enough of this," said Bill, in order to save her the necessity of answering.

But Jessie spoke up: "She's a tall girl. About as tall as me.

Got bobbed black hair, and big brown eyes. She's the kind that don't give a darn."

Pure amazement made Bill look witless for a moment.

George was only half satisfied. "How do I know but what you're lying, too," he muttered wretchedly.

Bill's principal anxiety being relieved, cunning began to work in his deep-set eyes again. "Here, we can't discuss our private business out on the sidewalk," he said. "Let's go into this little joint, and sit down to a table."

There being no further occasion for sending Jessie home, she was included. The three of them went into the soft drink place, and sat around one of the flimsy tables on bent metal legs. Their heads came close together, and they talked in whispers.

"Now tell me straight, George," said Bill in seeming friendly tones; "what's bitin' you?"

"Aah!" said the young man, his features writhen with pain; "Melanie's been out of Woburn a month, and I ain't heard from her."

"But I understood it was all off between you two," said Bill.

"All off, nothing!" said George violently. "I'm her husband. It'll never be all off while I'm living."

"But she's got somepin to say to that too, ain't she?"

"I'll believe it when I hear her say it."

"I'm not on the inside," said Bill. "I on'y know what I hear. This is the way I understand it; if I'm wrong, put me right. As you was on the outside, and Melanie was on the inside, the Boss said you couldn't come together, the two crowds of us being forbidden to mix. So you and Melanie run away together anyhow, and got married, forgetting the first rule of the organisation, which is, that nobody can ever leave it for any reason whatsoever."

"We on'y asked to be let alone," said George sullenly.

"I know, I know," said Bill. "I don't say as I blame you. But the say-so of the boss always goes. That's what keeps the organisation together. And so you had to be disciplined. At least Melanie was; she was sent up to Woburn, but you got clean away. But before Melanie was sent up, as I understand it, she said she'd be a good girl, and she wrote you a letter sayin' she was done with you."

"She had to write it," muttered George.

"Maybe so," said Bill. "But she must have made fresh promises to be good, or they wouldn't have got her out of Woburn."

"If Melanie's in good standing with the organisation, what they want another girl for?" George demanded, looking at Jessie.

"Oh, hell, the business is always growin'!" said Bill.

"There's something wrong! There's something wrong!" said George, beating the little table softly with his clenched fists. "Melanie would know that I wouldn't take that letter she wrote on its face. She's always been on the square with me. Suppose she means to stick to the organisation. All right. But she wouldn't let me go on eating my heart out all these weeks. She'd find some way of sending me word—unless she was chained up."

This shot in the dark made both Bill and Jessie—for different reasons—exquisitely uneasy. Bill showed it in his face, but George, apparently, was not much of a physiognomist.

"Maybe she don't know how to reach you," suggested Bill.

"She has a way of reaching me."

"Maybe she forgot the address."

"Huh! Likely!" said George.

"George, I'd do any thin' I could to help you, short of gettin' in Dutch myself," said Bill. "Yours is an onusual case, George. We all feel sorry for you. It was the real thing between you and Melanie; you couldn't help yourselves. In a manner of speaking, you had the right to come together. But on the other hand you run up against a stone wall in the rules of the organisation. It certainly was a shame all around."

George had his suspicions of Bill, but the tortured heart could not stand out against this pretended sympathy. He partly broke down.

"Thanks, Bill," he muttered, hanging his head. "You always was the decentest of the lot. You don't know what I been through. Nobody knows. It's driven me clean out of my mind!... If I knew Melanie was all right I could bear it. It's not knowing. It's suspecting that they're torturing her somehow on my account. She's had nothing but trouble through me— Oh, God! if I don't get some relief I'll take an axe and smash down the door of that damned house, and see for myself. What do I care what happens to me?"

Jessie was deeply enraged to see the unfortunate young fellow's honest feelings thus made a mock of, and her friendly feelings towards Bill dried up for the time being. However, George was getting true sympathy from her.

"Maybe I could bring you to a meeting with her some-how," said Bill, with a crafty sidelong look at George.

The young fellow looked at him with a wild hope in his eyes.

Jessie was seized with panic. Oh, God! if he falls for this, how can I save them? how can I save them? she asked herself.

"Of course we can't do nothin' with Black Kate, that's certain," Bill went on smoothly, "and when she's out of the house the key of the front door is held by that little ——, Skinny Sam. You couldn't trust him neither. But Pap or Fingy, or Abie, would never interfere. Nor Jess here."

"You bet I wouldn't!" said Jessie.

If George had ever looked down he would have seen Jessie feverishly tracing with a finger on the knee that was invisible to Bill:

Keep away! Keep away! Keep away!

But George's strained eyes were fixed on Bill's face. Jessie ventured to touch his knee, and he glanced down abstractedly, but instantly returned his gaze to Bill's face. She dared not do it again.

"The thing to do," Bill went on, "is, sometime when Kate is out, to get Sam interested in doin' somepin, and then lift the key off him for a short while. We'll have Melanie waitin' for you, just inside the front door…"

"Yes—yes!" said George breathlessly.

"I'll egg Sam on to a game of pinochle with Pap, by putting up a wager, see? You may not know it, but I started life as pickpocket. Ain't had much practice lately, but my fingers are still souple enough for that. He carries the key in his back pant pockets. I seen it often. I'll prig it when the game starts, and Jess'll post as a scout in the lower hall, to watch that he don't miss it."

"Now we gotta arrange some signal to you when the coast's clear," Bill went on. "Lookee, Kate's got a couple of new statooettes on the mantel in the parlour. Little bronze guys with battle-axes, *you* know. I'll stand one of them in the window, see? when it's all right to come. That is, if it's day. And if it's night, I'll light the gas out in the hall. That jet is never lighted when Kate's home. Don't forget; the statooette in the window by day, or the light in the hall by night When you get the signal you tap on the door light, and I'll be right there with Melanie. She won't be sorry to see you, I guess. Oh no! Don't ring the bell, of course."

If he had thought for a moment, if he had been capable of thinking, George must have seen through this clumsy lure. But the madness to see Melanie had him in its grip. He could think of nothing else. Jessie felt half sick with apprehension. She could save George, of course, at any moment, by speaking out. But in that case she could never return to the house herself. Then how about poor Melanie, left chained and defenceless? Was there ever such a cursed coil of circumstances?

George was so completely mesmerised by his wild hope, that Bill ventured to go a step further. "Lookee," he said, "I gotta idea Kate is out this afternoon. There's no time like the present. You just give Jess and me fifteen or twenty minutes to get home, and get things fixed up, then you stroll down past the house, and maybe I'll have the signal for you already."

"All right!" said George breathlessly. "I'll wait here."

"That's understood then," said Bill. "C'mon, Jess."

He got up. With the idea of gaining time; of getting a chance, perhaps, to give George a signal, Jessie said:

"Can I have a box of candy?"

Bill was in high good humour again. "Sure!" he said, "the best in the shop!"

But while they were at the counter, George never looked around. And when the purchase was completed, Bill stood back to let Jessie pass out of the store ahead of him; so she could not even give George a backward warning look. They left him sitting at the little table.

When they had passed out of the range of George's vision, Bill exclaimed gleefully: "By God! that was a lucky chance! That fellow, George Mullen, is the only man who ever defied the boss and got away with it. If I can land him, the boss will give me anything I ask for! He'll put me ahead of Kate in the house! I'm a made man— You don't think he'll get cold feet, do you, and not come?" he broke off to ask anxiously.

"I think he'll come," said Jessie.

"Sure, he'll come!" said Bill confidently. "He's out of his senses to see that girl."

It was only too true. Jessie felt desperate. A dozen plans for saving Melanie and George had occurred to her, but none of them feasible. And she had no time! She had no time!

"Say," said Bill suddenly, "how the hell did you get off Melanie's description so pat?"

"I saw her," said Jessie shortly. Bill's conversation robbed her of what moments for thinking she still had.

"Saw her?" he echoed, astonished.

"I knew some one was locked in that room, from seeing Pap carry food up. So when I was in the bathroom, I stuck a broom out of the window to attract her attention."

Bill turned a face of angry concern on her. "Good God! if Kate knew that, it would be all up with you!" he cried. "Can't I never teach you to let things alone that don't concern you!"

"Well, it's lucky I did see her," said Jessie.

"Oh, as it happens, it is," said Bill. "I'm telling you for the future."

The little candy store was three short blocks from 723. As they crossed the last street before coming to the house, Jessie played her only card:

"We oughtn't to walk up to the door together," she said.

"Sure, that's right," agreed Bill. "The neighbours might get to guessing who your big beau was."

"You walk on," said Jessie. "I'll hang back till you turn the corner."

"No, I'll turn down Charlton to Hudson, and come back on Vandam," said Bill. "That's my usual beat."

Jessie breathed a little more freely. He turned down the side street. Jessie walked on a few steps, then waited, leaning against the railings of one of the old houses, pressing a hand against her heart to still it. She gave him a minute, then peeped around the corner. He was trudging down the block unconcernedly. She walked back across the street at a sober gait, so that if he glanced around his eye would not be caught by a running figure. When she passed the corner house, she gathered up all her forces, and ran like a deer back to the little candy store.

George was still sitting as they had left him. Jessie leaned on the table. "Listen!" she whispered urgently. "For God's sake, don't go to that house. It's a plot to get you and Melanie both. She's there—locked in an upper room. They're only keeping her alive as a decoy to bring you there. Keep away, and I'll save her for you. Keep away, and I promise to have a letter from her put into your hands within a day or two."

George stared at her wildly. It is doubtful if he got the full sense of her breathless words, but he was impressed by them. It only needed the spoken word to bring him to the sense of his danger. Jessie dared not wait to make sure of the effect. She ran out of the store, and back down the street at the top of her speed.

Sam let her in the house with a spiteful look. As he did not address her, she was not obliged to speak. With a great effort of the will, she concealed from him how she was panting for breath. She went directly to her own room and, closing the door, sat down on the bed to let her breast quiet down. She had been there a minute or two before the bell sounded which announced Bill's entrance through the sliding door. A great thankfulness filled her.

She went downstairs with a serene face. A growing excitement filled the house at Bill's story. They were all home, including Black Kate, and all of them were united for once by their common detestation of George Mullen. Human loyalty takes curious forms sometimes. The bronze statuette was placed in the window, and everybody waited, biting their fingers in their impatience.

While everybody's attention was concentrated on the ground floor, Jessie had a good opportunity to communicate with Melanie from the bathroom. She sent up a little note on the broom:

I must see you to-night. Drop me the rope when I give you the signal.

Melanie nodded.

Back in her own room, Jessie carefully folded the wrapping-paper from the candy-box, to serve Melanie as paper on which to write the letter to George.

There is no need to detail the various stages in the emotions of that household as they waited for the man who never came. From a savage anticipation they passed to a still more savage disappointment. When it became clear that he was not coming, they began to quarrel among themselves, as usual. Black Kate expressed a contemptuous disbelief in Bill's whole story, and Bill forced Jessie to corroborate it. Jessie did so, careful not to take sides.

When the others were not around, Bill continued to air his grievance to Jessie, spiced with strings of oaths, until she was fair tired of it. Human patience has its limits.

"You showed your hand too plain," she said.

"Yah! that's right! Rub it in!" snarled Bill "Maybe you're glad he didn't come."

"Well, since you ask me, I am glad," she said coolly. "I don't hanker to assist at a murder."

" 'Taint murder!" cried Bill. "It's justice! What right has the like of him to defy the organisation?"

However, after that he shut up about it.

19

BELLA IS DRAWN IN AGAIN

THE MESSAGE THAT the so-called Jessie Seipp sent over
the telephone, when she slipped away from Bill Combs,
was to me, Bella Brickley, as you have, no doubt, already
guessed. This is what my mistress said to me:

"Quick! Notebook and pencil, Bella. Take down all I say,
so you can't forget. I am pushed for time.

"I have reached a point in my work where I must have
outside assistance; a woman that I can associate with in
the character of Jessie Seipp. I must have some one who is
absolutely A-1; everything depends on it. The best woman
operative we ever employed is Madge Caswell. You have
her address. Get in touch with her at once. I know she's
available, because she called me up just before I disappeared, and said she'd be in town all summer, and wanted
work. Engage her exclusive services at her own terms until
further notice.

"She is to play the part of Canada Annie Watkin, Jessie
Seipp's pal. She hasn't got time to bone up a tough New
York accent; that's why I have her hail from Canada. Let
her talk in her own natural voice, and they won't know
the difference. Let her portray a keen, long-headed little
thief, without any sex allure, who works and thinks like a

man. She should dress primly, and keep a close mouth. Let her story be that after she had made a successful haul in Montreal, a year ago, the Canadian city became too hot for her, and she's been living under cover in New York since. She and Jessie turned a trick together last spring. I'll supply the details of that.

"Let her take a room in a second-rate rooming-house—not a regular thieves' hang-out, because Canada Annie has never established relations with the gentry in New York, but the sort of house where they wouldn't be too particular whom they took in. The house must have a telephone. When she is ready, let her advertise her address and telephone number by means of a 'personal' in the *Sphere*. Let her advertise a street five blocks north of the actual street, the number of the house, five numbers more than the actual number, and the telephone number five numbers more than the actual number.

"I can't say just how long it may be before she hears from me. Of course, she can't stay waiting in her room all the time, but tell her to be here at twelve o'clock noon every day, so that there will be one moment when I will know that I can find her.

"Got all that, old girl? Can't stop to explain now. I have a guardian angel with me. Be good to yourself. Everything's going fine. *Melanie Soupert is alive!* I have seen her and talked with her. Bye-bye."

I will not dwell at length on my feelings upon receiving this. I was relieved, and at the same time I was filled with fresh terrors on behalf of my dear mistress. Though she had treated things lightly, as she always does, I understood well enough from her crisp, rapid sentences, that the affair had reached a stage of the most critical importance. It was agonising to be told so little.

This was not business which could be discussed over the telephone, so I put on my hat and went directly to the address of Madge Caswell, whom I remembered as an attractive young woman, who hid under a jocular manner a very real talent for our sort of work. It was a relief to have the errand to do.

Miss Caswell lived in a boarding-house on East Thirty-Sixth Street. I was filled with dismay upon being told at the door that she was sick in bed. But as I mounted the stairs I consoled myself with the reflection that every one gets sick and gets well again, and the great majority of sicknesses are forgotten next day. I was still further reassured when I saw her sitting up in bed, the picture of cheerfulness, in a mauve boudoir cap.

But at the sight of me her face fell. "You've come to offer me work!" she said. "If that isn't just my luck!"

"You can't take it?" I said with a sinking heart.

She shook her head. "Doctor's just been here. Ordered me to the hospital for an op. to-morrow."

I sat suddenly on a chair. "Good heavens! what will I do?" I murmured. "My mistress can communicate with me, but I have no way of sending *her* word. *Her orders have got to be carried out!*"

"Important case?" asked Miss Caswell, full of concern.

"It's more than that!" I said. "Madame Storey's own safety depends on it!"

"Oh, what rotten luck!" she murmured, digging her knuckles into her cheeks. "And my appendix won't wait another day."

"Can you suggest anybody?" I asked helplessly. "It must be somebody on whom we can depend absolutely." I asked it helplessly, because, among operatives, the young woman who was sufficiently cool, resourceful and clever, scarcely existed. Madge Caswell was one in a thousand.

"How about a woman of forty?" she asked.

I shook my head.

"Haven't you anybody on your lists?"

"Nobody I would dare trust with this."

"What is wanted?"

I told her.

"Why don't you do it yourself?" she asked off-hand.

Now the same thought was lurking deep within me, and it threw me into confusion when she dragged it forth into the light. "Oh, I couldn't! I couldn't!" I cried in a panic.

"Why not?"

"I couldn't! Mme. Storey says I have no talent for impersonation."

"But you have brains. And the necessity of the case would spur you on to make up for your lack of talent!"

"I wouldn't dare take the responsibility!" I said, walking up and down the room in my agitation. "The least slip would be fatal to all of us."

"Now look here," she said sensibly. "If you took this job, you couldn't fail Mme. Storey, could you?"

"Of course I couldn't!" I cried.

"Well, there you are!" she said, smiling. "It means everything to you, whereas to an ordinary operative it means fifty or seventy-five a week."

I suddenly saw that there *was* no problem facing me, because there was only one course possible for me to take, and in that moment my panic subsided. "You're right," I said. "Such as I am, I'd be better than some one we didn't know."

"Good work!" said Madge heartily. "Now listen; you get your stuff together to-morrow, and I'll go have my appendix lifted. On the following day you come to me at the Good Samaritan Hospital in character, see? and I'll criticise your make-up. You come to me every day until Mme. Storey is ready to use you, and I'll coach you. It'll be better than flowers or candy for me."

What an admirable girl she was!

THREE DAYS LATER I was established as Canada Annie Watkin in a meagrely furnished bedroom on Twenty-Fourth Street, west of Eighth Avenue. Technically speaking, it was a respectable house, but the landlady had a tolerant eye, and all sorts of odd fish came and went. My appearance was so subtly changed, that had I met my dearest friend on the street, she would have said: "Why, doesn't that look like Bella Brickley!" without a thought of identifying me with myself. Like Mme. Storey herself, Madge Caswell believed that in the matter of disguising yourself, character was much more important than make-up. I had gone back to the unbecoming style of hairdressing that I had used when I first went to Mme. Storey—1900 style with a small bun; and in second-hands shop I had got me a suit and hat which made me look like a person whose only object in dress was to make herself inconspicuous. My new character was my continual study. I presented myself as a cagey little woman of uncertain age, with a close mouth and a wise eye. I cultivated the trick of looking down my nose, and sucking in one cheek. I used just a little make-up to give myself a pallid look.

Well, I had advertised my address according to instructions, and there I was waiting, scarcely ever daring to leave my room, for fear the call might come when I was out. I had left Crider in charge of the office, and I kept in telephonic communication with him. It was frightfully wearing on the nerves, because, you see, I didn't know of what nature the call would be; I couldn't prefigure the situation that I would presently be obliged to meet.

It came with great suddenness—and not by telephone, as I expected. Somebody knocked on my door, and when I opened it, I beheld my dear mistress, *alias* Jessie Seipp, standing there, with her outrageous bush of blonde hair, and her flashy, becoming costume. Behind her was a huge man, whose shoulders seemed to stoop under the weight of their brawn and muscle. He looked like a thug, neatly dressed. I turned a little giddy.

I leave you to guess what her feelings must have been at the sight of *me*. Nothing of it showed, of course. Without the pause of a fraction of a second, she caught me by my two elbows, and gave me an affectionate little shake.

"Hello, Annie!" she cried. "Gosh! it's good to see your ugly mug again! How are yeh, Annie? I telephoned old woman Schwimmer the other day, to get your address."

"Steady! Steady!" I whispered to myself. "Yes, she told me you called up," I replied in the colourless voice I was cultivating. "I was hoping you'd call."

"Well, here I am, large as life, and twicet as natural. This is my friend, Bill Combs. C'mon in, Bill, you boob, and close the door after yeh."

"Please to meet you," said the big man sheepishly. He looked me over with a comic expression of distrust.

"Cheer up, Bill, she won't bite yeh!" sang Jessie: adding to me: "His brain can't accommodate any but the simplest ideas, and he's surprised to find that you ain't another fly kid like me."

"Aah!" growled the big man, not at all displeased by her raillery. I saw in a glance that he was head over heels in love with her. That great coarse Hercules! Oh, my Lord! this added another perilous element to the situation.

There was but the one chair in the little room, which Bill took, Jessie and I sat side by side on the bed. She took my hand in hers, and flung her other around my shoulders. "No, Annie ain't a bit like me," she rattled on. "That's what I like about her. Takes all kinds to make a world. Annie's one of the cool and steady kind. She ain't got nobody, and I ain't got nobody, and so we 'dopted each other, like. Gee! it's good to see you, old girl!"

We smiled point-blank at each other, but exchanged no meaning glance. How strange! how strange it was to be playing a part with her. How I burned to know if she was satisfied with me, I could read nothing in her eyes but a bright, impersonal excitement; the excitement of an artiste in full activity. I was careful to keep my eyes empty.

I realised that I must not play too passive a part, and at the first pause in Jessie's headlong rattle, I said: "I was worried about you, kid. I read in the paper that you were sent up to Woburn for trying to rob Mrs. Cornelius Marquardt. That was a bright trick."

"Sure," said Jessie, "what they call a foxy pass, eh? I was sufferin' from the heat."

"How did you get out?" I asked.

"Oh, I just saw an opening, and I took it," said she. "It was just a lucky chance."

I realised that questions were indiscreet, yet I thought Canada Annie would ask a few. "Where are you now?"

"With friends," said Jessie demurely. "We ain't settled in yet, so I can't give you my address."

"Oh, excuse me," I said.

"Nothin' to excuse, Bill and me kin come to see you sometimes—can't we, Bill?—Bill's my chaperon."

"If we don't get too busy," growled the big man.

"And what are you doin' with yourself?" said Jessie; "livin' on your income, as usual, I suppose— This girl's lucky," she added to Bill; "she cleaned up all Montreal two years ago, and don't have to work no more."

"Well, not quite that," I said modestly.

"Where did you two first meet?" asked Bill. I could see that he was not at all disposed to be friendly towards me; not that he suspected I was other than I seemed; he was simply jealous of the fuss that Jessie made over me.

"I'll tell you," said Jessie quickly, "and you can see if I haven't got cause to stick to her— One day, last spring, I was fired out of my job as usual, and I was broke as usual. I wanted to go to a ball that night, and I hadn't no silk stockings to wear. I just made up my mind I'd help myself to a pair offen the counter. I went into a big department store, and there they were ready to my hand, piled deep in a long tray; special sale; women crowdin' round three deep. It looked too easy. I was just slippin' out a coupla pair, when a voice whispered in my ear: 'Drop them! The store-detective is watchin' you!' It was Annie beside me.

"Well, I dropped them, you bet, and walked away careless. She followed, and when we got to a different part of the store, we talked. 'You big fool!' she said, 'don't you know they always have a detective watching them counters?' 'How was I to know that?' I says. She says: 'Well, if you're goin' into the business, you ought to learn the rudiments first. Makes me sore to see a girl *asking* to be put away.'"

"She give me the rough side of her tongue, but I took to her just the same, and we walked out together. We sat down in Bryant Square and talked some more. She give me a line just like the Tombs Angel: for God's sake to give up that sort of stuff, it wasn't worth it, and get me some honest work to do. It was wasted on me; I told her I was off honest work for the rest of me life. Honest work had never done nottin' for me. I pricked up my ears when she said she'd been through it all, and it didn't pay. And I pestered her until she said at last, 'Oh well, if I was determined, she'd give me a little proper instruction.'

"Well, it turned out she had a little job all planned out, and she would be glad of a bit of help with it. It was a hotel job, She had spotted a certain couple who were stopping at the Richland, and by a simple trick she'd got an impression of their key under the clerk's nose, and had a duplicate made. Now she wanted somebody to stand watch for her, while she entered their room. She herself had taken a room at the Richland.

"We loafed around across the road from the Richland, and she pointed out the couple to me when they came out. They didn't look like real swell folks, and I wondered why she'd picked on that partic'lar couple, but I didn't say nottin'. Well, ten minutes later it was all over. She went into their room, while I waited around in front of the elevators with a glass in my hand. If either of the couple came up, I was to drop the glass on the marble floor, see? Annie said that would give her plenty time to get out of their room, and around the corner of the corridor at the back.

"But they didn't come back, and she worked undisturbed. She didn't get much, for it seemed they carried their money and valuables on them. Some real pretty studs and cuff-links, which I gave to my fella; a small diamond pin; a handsome cape with a fur collar, and oh Gee! Half a dozen pairs of silk stockings. She handed over the lot to me.

"Then the story came out. She told me she was Canada Annie, and she'd made a big clean-up in Montreal a year ago, and this guy was a lieutenant of police, or whatever they call it, who had come down to New York to look for her. So she entered his room, picked what was worth carryin' away, and left her card on the bureau. 'Compliments of Canada Annie.' That's her!"

You will observe how cunningly my mistress helped me out by the telling of this story. It established my character better than I could have done it. Bill Combs looked at me with respect, if not with liking.

"Real neat work," he said.

I perceived that some comment was looked for from me, so I said in the dry manner that I affected: "Oh, that was nothing. He was such a conceited fool he made me tired. I wanted to take him down a peg."

After that the conversation became general. Big Bill Combs became almost friendly. My mistress was a tower of strength to me. She played up to me so cleverly; she was always right there to help me out, and I lost my fear of not making good. I believe I did quite well. All the time I was anxiously wondering what was the real object of this visit. What was required of me?

Finally Bill said: "We gotta go, Jess."

And still it had not transpired.

The so-called Jessie went to the mirror of my bureau, as a woman does, and fluffed up her hair. "I look a sight," she remarked. She pulled open the top drawer in the most natural way in the world, and rummaged in it. "I suppose you haven't got any mascara," she said.

"No," said I.

She shut the drawer with a bang. "Oh, you don't care how you look!" she said.

"Well, looks is not my strong point," I said, looking down my nose.

"Bill, will you lend me the money to get some make-up going home?" she asked.

"Sure," he growled.

Suddenly, I got it. Mme. Storey's hands had been hidden for a moment in the drawer. She had left something there for me!

They left with good-byes, and promises to come again. As soon as I heard the front door close behind them, I ran to the bureau drawer, and there, sure enough, under my things, I found a folded square of white paper. Opened up, it proved to be a letter written on a single large sheet of shiny white paper, wrapping-paper, from the look of it. It was written in pencil in a laborious, unformed hand.

I shall not reproduce it here. Indeed, I had no business to read it myself, but how could I help it, since it bore neither address, salutation, nor signature. From the context, it was certainly from a woman to a man, but what woman or what man I had no means of knowing. In its simplicity, in its very crudity inspired with deep, deep feeling, it was the most touching letter I ever read. It made my breast ache.

The explanation came next day by telephone.

"Did you find the letter?"

My mistress's soft, distinct tones instantly told me that she was telephoning from within that house.

"Yes."

"Seal it in an envelope, and deliver it to Mrs. Henry Harvest, who keeps a stationery store at —— Columbus Avenue. It is for her son. Did you get that?"

"Yes."

"You did splendidly yesterday. Ta-ta."

"Wait, let me explain," I said.

"It doesn't matter, my dear. I'm satisfied." And the circuit closed.

I lost no time in starting for Mrs. Harvest's. Every older inhabitant of New York knows the little "stationery" stores of upper Manhattan, now almost driven out by more modern business methods. Rather pathetic little stores, specialising in the trifling and unprofitable wares that appeal to school-children, and ekeing out a bare existence by the sale of newspapers. Mrs. Harvest's was one of the survivals. Nothing in her store had been changed in twenty-five years, I am sure.

Mrs. Harvest herself was a plump and comely woman, who ought to have beamed with good nature, but looked harassed and subdued. There were children in the shop when I entered, and though she insisted on serving me first, I insisted with even more firmness that she serve them. When they were out of the place; I produced my letter, now in an envelope.

"For your son," I said.

What a searching look she gave me! She took the letter from me with a painful eagerness—yet she hated it. One could tell that by the way she handled it, and by the look of resentment that twisted her face.

"He ain't here," she said. "But maybe I can get hold of him. Will you come back in an hour for the answer."

"Well—I'm not sure that I can get an answer through," I said.

"Well, come back anyhow, on the chance."

When I entered the shop the second time, I saw that Mrs. Harvest had been weeping. And indeed, at the sight of me, the tears began to run afresh. She pressed my hand, and murmured not very coherently:

"Oh, I'm real glad you brought it! I hate that girl! I can't help it. I'm his mother. But it's done him good, it has. He's like his old self again."

She led me into a little homely sitting-room back of the shop. A young man, who was writing at the table, jumped up as we entered. He was blond and slender, and uncommonly good-looking. He had the wary look of those who live in danger. That look on a man's face is thrilling to a woman.

"This is not the girl," he said in surprise.

"That's the one as brought the letter," said his mother.

"Where did you get it?" he demanded suspiciously.

"It was passed to me by a friend of mine, Jessie Seipp," I said.

His face relaxed. "Yes, that's the one, Jessie," he said. "She promised it to me. Can you get an answer back?"

"I can't say for certain," I said. "I'll try."

He folded his letter, and was for slipping it in an envelope, but I said: "You'd better leave it open, if you don't mind. So if it was found on me, I could claim it as mine."

"You're right," he said, handing it over.

"You didn't name her, did you?" I asked. "Or yourself? Or say anything that could give others a lead if they read it?"

"No," he said. "Read it. There's nothing in it but what a friend might read."

I shook my head with a smile and put it away in my pocket-book.

He suddenly seized my hand. "You're a good sort!" he said, deeply moved. "You have put new life in me. Isn't there something I could do for you?"

"Not a thing in the world," I said. "I am repaid already." This was not exactly in character, but I couldn't help myself. The young man touched my heart. Any woman would have been glad to help his affair along.

"I'll find a way," he said. "What's your name?"

"Annie Watkin, I'm mostly called Canada Annie."

"I shan't forget you."

Two days later I got another telephone call.

"I hope to drop in on you this afternoon. I understand Bill and I are going out. I want you to get me a heavy wire-cutting tool. It must be strong enough to cut chain of the same size that is used for tyre chains. Get that?"

"Yes. How will I slip it to you?"

"Listen. Go down to a candy store, at the foot of Seventh Avenue where it turns into Varick Street. It's in a little temporary shack on the right-hand side going down. Buy a two-pound box of their best chocolates. When you get home, empty out the chocolates, and pack the wire-cutters in the box with paper to keep them from jolting around. Then wrap the box up again in the same paper and string. Don't matter if it doesn't look exactly the same as when it left the shop, for the box is supposed to have been opened once."

"I understand," I said. "I have an answer to that letter."

"Splendid! Put the letter in the box with the wire-cutters. And listen! Put the box in the middle of your top bureau drawer."

"I understand."

When Jessie entered my room that afternoon (with Bill at her heels, as before) she carried under her arm an exact replica of the box which was then resting in my top bureau drawer. She immediately opened her box and passed it round.

"Bill's present," said she. "Ain't he the generous guy!"

We sat about, munching the chocolates amidst more or less facetious conversation, which I need not attempt to report, since it had little bearing on the real situation. Bill seemed to enjoy the chocolates as much as the women did.

To-day I felt more assurance in my rôle; and I laid myself out to win Bill's favour by taking his part against Jessie; by appearing to recommend him to her. I was immediately successful; Bill turned the somewhat terrifying sunshine of his smile on me; and I am sure he was prepared to swear then that I was a fine little woman. It was a happy thought of mine; for it relieved the general situation very much, without committing my mistress to anything. Moreover, it had an important bearing on the final outcome, though, of course, I couldn't foresee that.

Well! when it came time for them to go, Jessie wrapped up her box of candy again in its string and paper. She laid it on the edge of the bureau when she went to "fix-up"; and pulled open the top drawer to search for a make-up rag. (Even Canada Annie had to have a make-up rag!) With the rag in her hand, she bent over the open drawer to bring her face closer to the mirror while she repaired her complexion. In straightening up, she caught her elbow on the edge of the box, and knocked it into the drawer. She instantly pulled it out again; only it was not the same box but the other one! Then she dropped the rag in the drawer and closed it. I never saw anything more neatly done!

The next telephone message that I received was the last one. This was two days later.

"My number has come through."

"Your number?" I echoed in confusion.

"I have been given my first job, my dear."

"Oh, heavens!" I gasped.

"But this is what I have been working for. It is all turning out better than I could have hoped for. I am going to Tuxedo Park to-morrow morning, and I have permission to take you with me."

"Am I in it, too?" I stammered.

"Only the preliminaries," she said, with laughter in her voice. "Meet me at the Erie Station in Jersey City in time to get the 10.45 train. Another one of my new friends will be with me. Remember, you have not seen me lately, but I called you up to-day to make the appointment. Bring a suit-case with enough for three or four days' stay. You will learn the rest then. Ta-ta."

I was thankful that there was no one in the lower hall of my rooming-house when I got that message. When I hung up, I had to sit down on the lowest step of the stairs for a moment, in order to recover myself. I understood, of course, that this "job" must be a robbery which had been entrusted to my mistress. And this would be no fake robbery, but a bona fide crime. I was simply appalled by the hideous danger.

20

ON THE INSIDE

I MUST GO back a little way now, in order to make clear to you what was happening in the house on Varick Street, in the intervals of the telephone conversations between Jessie Seipp and Canada Annie. I did not witness these incidents, of course; they were reported to me by my mistress when we met.

Her principal anxiety was on Melanie's account. She feared that, in their disappointment over the failure of Bill's ruse to draw George Mullen to the house, the gang might be led to do Melanie some hurt. Night and day she watched and listened for any move that might be made towards Melanie's room. But more prudent counsels prevailed; it was argued that as long as George had the least suspicion that Melanie was alive, and in that house, he must come sooner or later to find out. So they waited for him. In case he might be watching the house, they did not leave the bronze statuette exposed in the window continually, but carried it back and forth at intervals. However, as we know, George had an excellent reason for not coming.

No change had been made in the conditions of Melanie's imprisonment. Jessie mitigated it as much as she could by passing up candy and what other little delicacies she could procure, on the broom. After the second occasion, Jessie made no further attempts to visit Melanie. The risk was too great. It had been agreed that no attempt could be made to get Melanie out of the house until Jessie was ready to go too. Now that they had the wire-cutters, Melanie could be freed at any moment. Suspecting that her room might be ransacked when she was out of the house, Jessie ripped a little hole in her mattress, and hid the wire-cutters there, afterwards sewing up the hole in a way to defy detection.

The two girls exchanged frequent messages by aid of the broom. My mistress said, when she passed up George's letter to Melanie, the poor girl appeared to recover her lost youth. Her hollowed cheeks flushed, and seemed to fill out with happiness, and those great, agonised eyes were filled with a serene relief. She sent down a scribbled message:

"I can stand anything now."

To which Jessie replied: "Be careful not to let any change show in your face, or Black Kate will become suspicious. If they try to torment you again, make a racket, and I'll come. They wouldn't want me to see."

Melanie wrote: "They have not tried to hurt me since you came."

In respect to the other members of that curious household, no matter how intractable the material, Jessie never lost sight of her aim to win as many of them as she could. Black Kate was impossible; the middle-aged woman was filled with a hateful jealousy of the girl; and the fact that Jessie had been put under Bill's tutelage by a higher power, only increased her bitterness. Jessie kept out of her way as much as possible, and strove to give her no handle to use against her. Likewise, Jessie could do nothing with Kate's pitiful creature, Skinny Sam. There appeared to be no good in Sam's nature that she could get hold of. No matter how she tried to hide it, Sam's instinct told him that Jessie despised him as a man, and he was tormented with the spiteful malice of a small nature.

In other directions Jessie was more successful than might have been thought possible. In the case of Big Bill Combs, of course, she was not obliged to exert herself. I have already told you enough to show how rapidly Bill was succumbing to her influence. He still quarrelled with her violently and sometimes cursed her, but she had him with a crook of her little finger. She led her supposed guide and teacher around by the nose.

There had always been an unacknowledged bond between Jessie and little Abell. They were the most nearly civilised beings in that house. Jessie neglected no opportunity to strengthen the bond. Whenever they were alone together she encouraged Abell to talk to her about his wife and son, whom he loved in so piteous a fashion, and from whom he regarded himself as cut off for ever. It was Abell who used to return from his nocturnal errands with good things to eat for Jessie—most of which found their way to Melanie in her prison.

Then there was Pap. Jessie had no difficulty in winning him. Her good-humour, her kindness, her humanity, enslaved the old man. Unfortunately, Pap was but a weak and broken creature, and Jessie saw clearly enough, that if a crisis ever arose, Pap would be bound to line up with the strongest party. She worked to make her party the strongest, so they could count on Pap, too.

It was with Fingy Silo, that great, dull-witted brute, that Jessie had her greatest success. In view of her first encounter with him, Fingy might well have been regarded as hopeless material, but such was not the case. The situation, as regards him, can best be conveyed in his own words. He came up to Jessie in the dining-room one day, when the other men were not by, and said hoarsely:

"Say, listen, Fuzzy-Wuz, I got somepin t' say to yeh."

In spite of herself, Jessie looked wary. Fingy saw it and was aggrieved.

"Hell! I ain't goin' to hurt yeh," he complained. "Ain't I got decent feelin's same as anybody else?"

"Why, sure, Fingy?" she said quickly.

"Say, listen," he began again. "I want to tell you I got some new ideas about women from knowin' you. When you first come here, I thought as you'd pick out the best man amongst us, which is every woman's right, and so I fought with Bill for you, and he licked me. I thought as you'd be his woman after that, and I was just agoin' to bide my time till I could play Bill a dirty trick, and win you away from him.

"And then I seen that you wasn't Bill's woman, and I couldn't make nottin' of that. You treated us all just the same. You was just as friendly to me as to Bill. Well, I want to say I appreciate that, Fuzzy-Wuz. I guess I kin respect a woman who's absolutely on the level, as well as any man. And I want to tell you as long as you don't mean to play no favourites in the house, you can count on me, see? And say, Fuzzy-Wuz, at that, this house is a damn sight comfitabler place to live since you come here."

Jessie was genuinely moved. "You're all right, Fingy!" she cried heartily. "Put it there!"

They gravely shook hands.

Along about this time the household received a new addition in the person of Tim Helder. Tim was an elderly little rogue; alert, bright-eyed, and bearded like a hayseed. He had all the mannerisms that were popular in his youth; that is to say, he tipped his chair back, and stuck his thumbs in the armholes of his vest; he cocked his cigar up, and his hat down; when he had no cigar he chewed a straw. He loved to whittle a stick, and at other times he occupied himself by the hour with what he called "cork-work," a kind of tubular knitting, done on a spool with a hole in the middle.

Jessie immediately realised that the coming of Tim had the highest significance for her. He had a great reputation as a confidence man, and all the others looked up to him. Jessie saw that she must win Tim or lose them all. And Tim was a professed scorner of women. With perfect effrontery, he told her so to her face, and cocked his hat still more defiantly over his eye whenever she came into the room.

"Well, so much the better," said Jessie to herself, "he'll have to meet me on some other plane beside that of sex."

She understood that Tim had been on a job out of town,

which had been brilliantly successful. The details were not discussed in her presence. He was now going to "lie doggo" for awhile, he said. Jessie had this much to go on; he felt he had been done out of a fair share of the proceeds of his job, and was filled with a smouldering resentment. Moreover, he despised Black Kate.

She had an uphill fight. Tim loved his affectations, chief of which was summed up in the oft-repeated boast that, "No woman had ever come anything over him." He was angered by the attention which Jessie commanded at the dining-table, where he formerly had reigned supreme. No matter how demure a part Jessie played, the other men would turn to her for her opinion.

In the end Black Kate played right into Jessie's hands.

This was the evening following Jessie's second visit to me at the house on Twentieth Street. It was after supper, and the men were all sitting around the kitchen in their shirt-sleeves, smoking and talking, when Jessie entered the room. Tim Helder said in tones of audible disgust:

"Oh, Lor'!"

Jessie coolly lit a cigarette. "What you got against me, Mr. Helder?" she asked good-naturedly.

"I like men, and I like man-talk," the little old cock said with asperity. "When a woman comes around it spoils everything."

"Go ahead with your man-talk," said Jessie. "My ears ain't too tender."

"Yah!" he snarled, "you're one of the kind that wants to make out they're just like men! Monstrosities, I call them!"

"You're hard to please," said Jessie, smiling.

"Let her alone, Tim," growled Big Bill Combs. "She's got as much right here as any of us."

"Cut it out, Bill," said Jessie quickly. "Mr. Helder's got a right to express his opinion. I can respect a man who says what he thinks."

"Yen, that's right, turn on me now," said Bill, sore immediately.

"I ain't turnin' on nobody," said Jessie. "I was goin' to say that Mr. Helder's opinion of women was no worse to me than the line of stuff I get from most men. I on'y ast him to forget I'm a woman, and treat me like a human being the same as himself."

"Yah!" snarled Mr. Helder. "You ain't the first woman as asked me to treat her the same as a man. Them's the most insidious kind."

Jessie ignored this. "I came down to hear the rest of the story about the guy who floated a loan of fifty thou. from a national bank and got away with it. Go ahead, Mr. Helder."

"Aah!" he said crossly.

"You just got to the place where the guy switched the envelope containing; the good securities for the other one, and then Sam broke in on you, and I didn't hear the rest."

"Well, fellas, it was this way," old Tim began, pointedly ignoring Jessie, but beginning the story, nevertheless.

It was not destined to be finished that night, for Black Kate made one of her periodical descents on the kitchen, with Sam at her heels. She was in a grinding temper, and looked around spitefully for something to vent it on.

"Huh! hanging around the men as usual," she said to Jessie.

Whereat little Tim rose in her defence, as pugnacious as a terrier. That was the way he was.

"Aah! she's got as much right here as anybody!" he said.

Jessie smiled to herself, and silently thanked Kate for aiding her thus.

Kate ignored Tim. She would remember that speech later and pay him off. "Where you and Bill been to-day?" she demanded.

Bill informed her with more force than politeness that it was none of her business.

"We'll see about that!" snarled Kate. "You've been told to teach the girl what she ought to know, but I'm still the head of this house, and you're both subject to my orders, see? We'll see whether it's any of my business or not!"

"Ain't nothin' to conceal," said Jessie mildly. "Me and Bill just walked around."

"Walked around!" sneered Kate. "And what does he teach you, walkin' around?"

"All about the different kinds of people," said Jessie, "and how to tell what they'll do, and how to handle them and all. He shows me all the different ways of effecting an entrance into houses and stores."

"Does he teach you loyalty to the organisation?" demanded Kate.

"Disloyalty" was Kate's bugbear. With her unbridled bad temper and tyrannous ways she made everybody in the house hate her, and then made believe to ascribe their black looks to "disloyalty."

"Why, sure," said Jessie. "That goes without saying."

"Oh, does it?" said Kate. "Not with me! Let me tell you, I'm far from satisfied with you, my girl. There's a look in your eyes that tells me you're a whole lot too big for your shoes. You've got to be taught your place before you'll be any good to us. You've got to learn that the organisation is everything, and you are nothing— Come with me!"

Jessie followed her out of the kitchen, wondering greatly what was in the wind now. Sam went with them, and Bill Combs brought up the rear, to make sure that no harm was intended Jessie. Up three flights to the top of the house they went without exchanging a word. Kate stopped in front of the door facing the top of the last flight, and producing a key, opened the door, and struck a match.

In the sordid little room Melanie sat on the edge of her bed, elbows on knees, and head gripped between her hands. She did not look up at her visitors. Upon her right wrist was a heavy steel bracelet, from which a chain ran across the room to be fastened to a staple driven deep into the frame of the door. An ugly sore showed where the fetter had chafed her wrist. Her dress was unkempt, her hair tousled. It was a terrible picture, and doubly terrible in the uncertain light of the match, which only made a little pool of brightness in the obscurity of the room.

It was not really so terrible as it seemed, for three hours before, Jessie had seen Melanie's head sticking out of the window, full of hope and courage. Jessie commended the girl's powers of acting. For her part, Jessie made believe to be as powerfully affected by the sight as Kate designed her to be.

"Oh!" she breathed, full of horror. "Who is she?"

"Never mind her name," said Kate, with a hateful smile. "She won't have no further use of a name."

"What did she do?"

"She tried to betray the organisation."

The match went out, and Kate closed the door and locked it. In the darkness of the landing she said to Jessie in a terrible voice "That's what we do to traitors. That's just the beginning of her punishment. So mark well, my girl, and watch your step."

Jessie made believe to be tremendously impressed. "You won't have no trouble with me," she murmured, making her voice tremble. "The organisation means everything to me. I'll serve it well."

There was a light on the next landing, and as they descended the stairs, Bill looked at Jessie, full of uneasiness. He did not know how far she was putting this on, and manlike, he thought: "If she can put it over Kate like this, why not over me?"

When they re-entered the kitchen, the four other men were still sitting around sullenly. Kate had thrown sand into the machinery of a pleasant evening. Kate's bad temper was not yet glutted. Tun was seated as usual, tipped back in his chair, with his thumbs forked into the armholes of his vest, and his hat cocked over one eye.

"Take your hat off when a lady comes into the room," said Kate.

"I will, like hell," said Tim. "That ain't no way to speak to a man."

"Then knock it off for him, Sam," shouted Kate.

Which Sam did with a sweep of his arm, grinning.

Tim was over sixty years old, and incapable of putting up a fight against a youth like Sam, however poor a specimen. He sat there, his limbs trembling, and his face working with the helpless rage of the aged.

Jessie saw a golden opportunity. Matters were already so bad between her and Kate, there was nothing to be lost there. "Shame!" she cried.

Kate's face turned livid with rage. "So!" she cried. "You ain't learned your lesson yet, eh? Well, I'll teach you now, my girl. Sam!"

But Big Bill coolly stepped in front of Jessie. "Go slow," he said in his heavy way. "I got somepin to say to this."

"Me, too!" growled Fingy most unexpectedly from his corner.

"And me!" said Abell, standing up.

Black Kate faced them, balked and furious. "All right! All right!" she cried stridently. "You're all traitors! The boss shall know of this!"

"Well, be sure to tell him the whole story," said Bill.

Kate flung out of the room. Sam, with an indescribably sly expression, seated himself in the dark corner by the pantry, prepared to listen.

"Get the hell out of here!" said Bill.

"I got as much right as—" began Sam.

"Get out, before you're kicked out, you damn spy!"

Sam beat a hasty retreat through the hall door, and Bill closed it. "She knows better than to telephone the boss," he said coolly. "She's supposed to run this house without runnin' to him with complaints."

"That woman makes our life here a hell," said Jessie, in a low voice. "How long are we going to stand for it, boys?"

Deep growls answered her from this side and that. She judged that the time was almost ripe.

"What's the matter with her anyhow?" asked Tim querulously. "Her temper was always oncertain, but now she's like a crazy woman."

"Jealous of the girl," said Bill laconically. "Jess has been put under my charge."

Meanwhile Jessie had picked up Tim's Fedora, and brushing it with her sleeve, she put it back on his head. "Here, Mr. Helder. Say, it done my heart good to hear you speak up to her. Anybody could see you're not afraid of her."

Tim mumbled something a little sheepishly. From that moment he was Jessie's!

"If she's supposed to run this house without any trouble," Jessie went on softly to the crowd in general, "all we got to do is to make trouble for her—plenty trouble, to get her fired."

Nobody answered her. All the men looked uneasy.

"All we got to do is stick together," Jessie went on, feeling her way with them. "This whole show is organised to keep us under. Well, what we got to do is to organise to protect ourselves."

"You cut out that kind of talk, kid," said Bill roughly. "You're only giving her a handle to use against you."

"Oh, it's not up to me," said Jessie cunningly; "I'm only a new-comer here. Now, if a man like Mr. Helder was to take the lead—a clever man, and an important man in the organisation, we could do something."

"Sure! Sure!" said Tim cynically. "Much obliged to you for mentioning my name. How long d'ya suppose it would take the boss to step on me?"

"We wouldn't push you forward as our leader," said Jessie eagerly. "We'd show him a united front. All standing together. He couldn't step on us all, could he? Men as useful to him as Mr. Helder, and Bill, and Fingy and Abell? No! He's a business man. You all tell me that. Well, what does a good business man do when he finds himself up against an unbreakable combination. He gives ground as far as he has to; that's what he does."

"That's all right," said Tim bitterly; "but our boss has got a handle to use against us, different from ordinary bosses. With him it's behind the bars for yours!"

"Suppose he returned us all behind the bars," said Jessie, "That 'ud be switchin' off the juice that makes the wheels go round, wouldn't it? He'd hesitate before doin' that. We're the headliners of this here show; we bring in the coin. And suppose we were behind the bars, would we be so much worser off? I say no! We make him rich, and what do we get out of it? He takes every penny off us, and keeps us locked up until he wants us. Galley slaves, that's what we are! Are you goin' to stand for it? It's up to you. Me, I'd sooner be a prisoner than a crawling slave!"

"Whisht, girl, whisht!" said Bill scowling. "This ain't no sort of talk from you."

But she had him half convinced. She had won the attention of all the men. They listened to her, biting their fingers, their eyes full of a sombre resentment.

"Why is it we're like a pack of slaves, jumpin' at the crack of the whip?" Jessie went on. "If you look into these here rules we hear so much about, you can see that the whole idea of them is to break us up and keep us apart, so he can handle us one at a time. He treats us like dogs now, because he thinks he can. Well, we're no better than dogs if we're goin' to stand for it!"

"She's right!" Abell suddenly broke in, in a low, tense

voice. "And I'm with her, for one. These people are hounding me to my death just as surely as if I was bound for the chair. Well, I might as well have a run for my money. I'm in on this!"

"How about you, Mr. Helder?" asked Jessie. "You got the best head in the crowd. We can't do anything without you."

"Aah! this is just young people's talk," snarled Tim. "I heard it all before. Ain't nothin' in it at all!"

"Are you satisfied with what you get out of it?" asked Jessie.

"Satisfied!" he cried, jumping out of his chair in his agitation; "They robbed me of my rightful share. I ain't got a penny, not a penny! And I'm sixty-three year old. Pretty soon I'll be past this work. What then? Sent back to rot behind the bars, I suppose."

"Well then," said Jessie, "stand out with us for a fair division, and decent treatment."

"Maybe I would if I thought you'd stick," he grumbled. "But you can't depend on the young."

"We'll satisfy you as to that," said Jessie. "How about you, Bill?"

Bill was chiefly concerned about Jessie's danger. "Where you get all such ideas?" he demanded. "An ignorant girl like you."

"Anybody can fight for their rights," said Jessie.

"God! if they heard what you said!" Bill said with a fearful glance towards the hall door. "God! they'd snuff you out so quick! That girl upstairs, what she did was nothin' to this!"

Said Jessie: "They couldn't touch me, Bill, if you and the

others stood behind me. If we made our slogan: 'One for all; and all for one!' they'd have to listen to us."

"I couldn't let 'em hurt you," said Bill, whom emotion made sullen, "whatever the rights of the case was. If you got to go against the boss, I got to go too, though I believe he'll pulverise us all."

Fingy did not wait to be asked. "Me, too," he said, coming forward. "I already told you I'd stand by you, Fuzzy-Wuz, not thinking anything like this. But it goes, see? One for all, and all for one, I says."

"How about you, Pap?" asked Jessie.

"Oh, leave me out! leave me out!" cried Pap, wild with agitation. "I'm on'y the cook. It don't matter about me!"

"You matter just the same as any other," said Jessie. "For look; if you lined up with Kate and Sam, that would make it five to three, see? It looks almost like an even break. But if you came with us it would be six to two. Or three times as many."

The other men glanced at each other; their look said: "That girl has a head on her!"

"I'm not the man I was!" wailed Pap. "I couldn't go through with a thing like this. I on'y want to be left alone."

"You ain't got nothin' to do," said Jessie, "except stand with us."

"Well, I suppose I got to!" groaned Pap, wringing his hands. "You're a terrible girl!"

"I'm not the leader," said the cunning Jessie. "I just brought the matter up. Mr. Helder will tell us all what to do."

"If we're goin' to act, let's act quick!" muttered Abell.

"But not too quick," said Jessie, who having dropped

her seed, now wished to give it time to sprout. "We'll talk about this again. We got to be sure the time is ripe before we act. A handclasp, boys, to seal the bargain."

In the middle of the kitchen, they made a wheel, their clasped hands forming the hub.

"Now, all together," whispered Jessie.

In low tones they repeated in unison: "One for all, and all for one!" And separated with slightly exalted breasts.

Presently Bill said, harking back to what had happened earlier: "It wouldn't surprise me if the orders was on the way for the kid to do a job. That's why they wanted to throw a scare into her this evening."

"So much the better!" said Jessie quickly. "If it's an important job, and I pull it off in good style, look how it will strengthen our organisation. For then I'll be a person to reckon with, see? They need a woman operative, and need her bad."

Once more the men looked at each other, as much as to say: "What a girl she is!" Or they might just as well have said: "What a fellow!" For Jessie had at last succeeded in forcing them to accept her on a basis which had nothing to do with her sex.

21

A COUNTRY EXCURSION

AS SOON AS I saw Jessie Seipp's companion in the Erie Station, I guessed that it must be the mistress of the house on Varick Street. I didn't then know her name; a handsome dark woman of fifty, very well preserved; dressed in a rich, respectable, slightly old-fashioned style.

After Jessie and I greeted each other as friends who had not met for some time, Jessie introduced the woman to me. "Meet my friend, Mrs. Simonds," said she, "or Mother Simonds, as we gen'ally calls her— This is my pal, Canada Annie Watkin, Mother."

I could see that my mistress's tongue was in her cheek, but the other woman could not. This "Mother Simonds" set out to be very agreeable to me—too much so; her tongue dripped treacle.

"Pleased to meet you, dearie. It's real nice you can go with Jessie for a few days. Be a pleasant outing for you. All your expenses paid, and three dollars a day for yourself."

I murmured my gratification. I dared not look at my mistress, for I was certain there was a twinkle concealed in her eye at the humour of the situation. That three dollars a day was the crowning touch!

"What are my duties?" I asked.

"There ain't any," said Mother Simonds. Lowering her voice to a confidential whisper, she went on: "You see, dearie, I run a little detective agency, very private and exclusive, see? and Jessie's got a bit of work to do for me in Tuxedo. Well, she can get away with it better if she has a companion, see? two decent, respectable working girls taking a bit of a vacation in the country, see? All you got to do is be her companion."

We made our way to the train gates, and Mother Simonds handed us our tickets. Her unchanging smile looked as if it was painted on her face.

"Well, good-bye, girls," she said. "Be good, and you'll be happy"—this with a roguish wag of her forefinger. "When you get back, Annie, make Jessie bring you round to see me some time. Me and you ought to be better acquainted." So we left her, looking after us.

Walking down the platform together, Jessie said: "You wouldn't think, would you, that at home she was an unchained she-devil, and that the greatest satisfaction she could get in life would be in sticking a knife between my ribs."

"Good heavens, why?" I asked.

"It's a long story," she said. "I'll have a chance to tell you now. Think of it! three or four days together in the country! And with the full permission of my masters! Isn't it wonderful?"

"Isn't it going to be dangerous?" I asked anxiously.

"Not until later."

When we found seats in the train, Jessie told me how the situation had come about.

"Yesterday," she said, "orders came through for Jessie

Seipp to go to Tuxedo Park and stop at a certain modest hotel, in the character of a respectable working girl taking her vacation. In the evenings I was told to attend a certain little country dance hall frequented by the servants of the rich people in the neighbourhood. Here I am to scrape acquaintance with one Alfred Booker, who is valet to Mr. Walbridge Sterry, the multi-millionaire. I am supposed to fascinate Booker—who is a great lady-killer in his own circle—to gain his confidence, and to learn from him the prospective movements of his employers during the coming week."

"Then what?" I asked.

"That I have not been told," she said. "These orders came to me through that woman you just saw—Black Kate, we call her, much against her will, for she would rather put me back behind the bars in Woburn than give me a job. As soon as I heard what I was to do I asked if I could have a companion.

" 'No,' she said.

" 'But it says I must be a respectable working girl,' I objected, 'and they always travel in couples. That's how they advertise their respectability. A girl stopping alone in a country hotel would be fair game for all men. How could I keep the others off while I waited for the one I am sent after?'

"Black Kate shut me up. 'All you got to do is follow your instructions,' she said. She wants to see me fall down on my first job, of course. I took the matter to Bill. He managed somehow to get word through to headquarters, and in the afternoon word came back that I was to be provided with a companion. Naturally, that didn't make Black Kate feel any better towards me. So there's the situation, my dear. We will advise together as to the proper way of fascinating a valet."

During the rest of that railway journey Jessie related to me the incidents of her imprisonment, her escape, and the subsequent days in the house on Varick Street—part of it, that is, for it took many an hour for her to tell the whole. All of this I have already set down in its proper place chronologically. She talked in a whisper, and we were careful to preserve the outward appearance of the parts we were playing; for it was quite possible the gang might be having Jessie watched on first being sent out alone.

We found the village of Tuxedo Park a very undistinguished collection of houses. The fashionable life of the place centred around the little lake in the hills, which was invisible from the railway. We never did see it. The hotel we were sent to was a run-down place of a special character; that is to say, it catered to extra servants, servants in search of a job, and to all the queer hangers-on of the rich who were not desired, or for whom there was no room under the roofs of the big houses around the lake. Two working girls seeking a country vacation were quite in character there.

"This is seeing Tuxedo from below-stairs," Jessie whispered to me. Within half an hour of our arrival, she could have had her pick of the half-dozen fellows hanging about the place—young men with an unwholesome, house-broken look; but we kept ourselves very much to ourselves, as befitted respectable girls.

After supper we walked up and down the single long street of the place, arm in arm, like many another couple of girls out prospecting. We had plenty of offers of company, too; at least, Jessie had. All the offers were turned down with expressions of the most rigorous virtue. We had a good deal of time to kill before it would be time to go to a dance. Finally we went into a candy store, and as we purchased chewing-gum, Jessie said to the clerk.

"We're just up from the city, me and my friend. Any excitement in this burg evenings?"

"Well, there's Foley's dance hall," he said.

"Where's that?"

"On the Ramapo road. You walk out of town in that direction, and when the road forks, keep to the right. You can't miss it."

"Much obliged," said Jessie. "We'll look it over."

"I'll see you there later," he called after us.

"Not if I see you first," said Jessie to me.

While we were still a quarter of a mile away from the place we could hear the moan of the saxophone. It was a hastily erected pavilion in a little grove beside the road. The sides were open to the evening breezes, and a deal of cheap bunting had been used to give it a festive look, now sadly washed and tattered by the summer rains and winds. It was crowded with perspiring couples doing all the most eccentric varieties of fox-trot. There were about as many styles of dancing as there were couples. We found a little table adjoining the dancing floor, and ordered two sarsaparillas. Jessie surveyed the scene like a conqueror.

"Have you got a description of the man we want?" I asked.

She shook her head. "Only that he comes here regularly, and that he's a devil for the girls. That will be enough."

"How on earth can you pick him out in this crowd?"

"You'll see," she said, with half a smile.

When the music started for the next dance, we took to the floor, and Jessie guided me around in a masterful fashion. To have seen her, you would have thought she had been frequenting cheap dance halls for years. She had, to the life, the haughty, touch-me-not manner of the girl who guides another girl, disdainful of men. I just let myself go within the firm compass of her guiding arm, without exactly knowing what my feet were doing. We seemed to get along all right. We were frequently hailed by the youths along the side lines, and pairs of them even tried to separate us, only to be haughtily pushed aside by the flat of Jessie's hand, as we sailed on.

In our slow gyrations, swinging up to one couple, and sheering off from another, Jessie, her bold, dark eyes roving about, missing nothing, kept up a curious line of conversation, presumably for my benefit, which ran something like this:

"She told me his name was Alfred Booker—" A pause to give time for one couple to go, and another to approach— "Of all the fellows there they said the best dancer was Alfred Booker—" pause—"She was crazy about a fellow called Alfred Booker—Alfred Booker—Alfred Booker—" and so on. And so on.

When we returned to our table, more fellows came up, but Jessie remained obdurate. Her reply, delivered in the haughtiest manner, was always the same:

"We're waitin' for friends."

We danced again.

During the intermission that followed, there came to our table a young fellow who had more style than most of the swains present. With his wavy blond hair and incipient side-whiskers, his bold nose and predatory mouth, he would have been quite good-looking, had it not been for the pasty complexion, and the smirk of the house-servant off duty. His extremely fashionable clothes, which were yet somehow not quite the thing, stamped him for what he was; a gentleman's gentleman. The type does not change, though fashions do.

"Good-evening," he said, with all the assurance of one who is not accustomed to being turned down.

"Excuse *me*," said Jessie haughtily. "I don't remember your face."

"You know *me*," he said, not in the least abashed. "'Cos a friend of mine heard you talkin' about me on the floor."

"And who may you be?" queried Jessie coldly.

"Alfred Booker."

"O-oh!" said Jessie, expressing volumes in a side glance, and bridling a little. "Is that who you are."

He slid into the seat beside her. I was sitting across the table.

"What was it you was sayin' about me?" he asked with intense curiosity.

"You ought to know if your friend heard it."

"She only heard you mention my name. Go on, tell me."

"I rally don't remember," said Jessie, hiding an imaginary yawn.

I watched and listened with delight. That marvellous actress opposite me had, as you can see, subtly changed her rôle. The downright outspokenness of the East Side girl was now sophisticated by the airs and graces of the

servant's hall. The young man understood her perfectly—
he thought.

After much pressing she coyly confessed that she had
heard a girl in the dressing-room say that Alfred Booker
was the best dancer on the floor, and she supposed she must
have mentioned it to her friend.

"Well, come and try me out," he said, as the music started
again.

It was a treat to watch them dance.

When they returned to the table she had him going
fast. She said:

"Meet my friend, Miss Ruby de Simmer… Mr. Booker."

He gave me half a nod. "You ain't told me your name
yet."

"Miss Miriam la Count," she said languidly.

"Gee!" said the young man. "Any relation to Queen
Mary?"

During the rest of the evening, he never left Jessie's side.
Other girls walking or dancing past our table made eyes
at him in vain. Decidedly, Alfred Booker was the catch of
Foley's. He addressed a good deal of his conversation to
Jessie's ear in tones so low I was unable to catch it; but I
judged from her curt refusals that it had to do with various methods of getting rid of me. While they danced I sat
alone. I was thankful, though, that nobody came to ask
me, for I would never have been able to play up to those
self-assured young village sports.

When Jessie said it was time to go, Mr. Booker steered
her affectionately along the village road with a hand under
her elbow, whispering into her ear, while I tagged along

on the other side. We halted outside the hotel, and Mr.
Booker, eyeing me, said pointedly:

"Don't let us keep you up, Ruby."

Jessie instantly slipped her hand through my arm, and
turned on him. "Say, who do you think you are, speaking
to my friend like that?" she demanded haughtily. "If you
want to know it, I prefer her company to yours!"

I thought this was pretty strong, but she knew her man.
He cringed under it. "Aw, I didn't mean no harm," he
muttered. "It was just a joke."

"Then beg her pardon."

"Say—I'm sorry," he mumbled.

"Oh, that's all right," I said quickly.

Jessie relented. "Well, good-night, Alfred," she said
sweetly. "Thanks for a pleasant evening."

"See you to-morrow, two-thirty," he said.

Jessie explained to me that as he was free the following
afternoon, he proposed to borrow a friend's car, and carry
us over to Greenwood Lake.

"A summer vacation place exactly after his own style,"
said Jessie. He had promised to bring along a fellow for me.

Well, he turned up more resplendently dressed than ever,
and driving a fine car, which I suspected had come out of
the Walbridge Sterry garage. With Jessie beside him on
the front seat, the effect when he drove fast was not so *very*
different from that created by his master and mistress. The
fellow he brought for me was not much; I should not have
rated him above a fourth or fifth line fellow; nevertheless
he had the cheek to look disappointed when he saw me,
and scarcely opened his mouth the whole way to Greenwood Lake. As soon as we parked the car there, he disap-

peared, and was not seen again. Alfred was very sore, for this threw me on him and Jessie again. I felt rather foolish.

We rowed on the lake in a clumsy, flat-bottomed boat, and had refreshments on the porch of a cheap summer hotel, filled with the most awful specimens of clownish and dishevelled vacationers. Afterwards we drove over the hills at a furious rate; for, it appeared, Alfred had to be back at six-thirty—to dress his master for dinner, I suppose. Jessie and I had to walk into the village rather ingloriously. Alfred made a date to meet her at Foley's later.

I tried to beg off from Foley's that night—"I am only in the way," I said; but Jessie would not hear of it.

"You've got an important part in this comedy," she said. "As they understand the game, as long as I keep you by me, it signifies 'nothing doing,' see? And when I let you go, it means the bars are down."

That night was largely a repetition of the previous one, with this exception; that Alfred was much more deeply enamoured. She played him with a rare skill; she knew exactly when to advance and when to retreat. "These experienced lady-killers are the easiest game of all to bring down," she whispered to me. She was not very successful though, in getting him to talk about his employers. Alfred wished to pose before Jessie as a king of men, and he was chary, naturally, of bringing up anything that suggested his menial state.

It was on our third night at Foley's that the vital piece of information slipped out. "You're only goin' to be here a week," said Alfred, "and just by bad luck I gotta be away two days! Ain't it rotten?"

"How's that?" said Jessie.

"The folks—thus Alfred always referred to his employers—are goin' to motor down to New York on Friday
morning. Friday night they're goin' to some big jamborree
out at Glen Cove, Long Island, and they'll dine and dress
in the New York house, and go back there to sleep after
the garden fête, or whatever it is. We won't get back here
till late Saturday."

"Too bad!" said Jessie, with cruel indifference. "I'll have
to get me another fella for them two days."

"Aah!" said Alfred, scowling.

Nothing more was said about it.

Next morning Jessie and I went for a country walk. From
the next village she telephoned the important information
down to New York, and we waited around awhile for her
further instructions to come through. She issued out of the
telephone booth with rather a peculiar expression.

"Well?" I asked eagerly.

"I am to get Alfred to invite me to visit him in the
Walbridge Sterry's town house," she said.

"Oh heavens!" I said. "Must you go through with it!"

"Oh, Alfred's a cinch!" she said carelessly. "Suppose I had
a real man to deal with."

That night, our fourth and last at Foley's, Alfred was full
of gloom. He evidently believed that by the time he had
returned to Tuxedo, he would for ever have lost his chance
with the desirable Miriam la Count. And Jessie lost no
opportunity of subtly promoting that idea. The conceited
young fellow suffered cruelly. Finally he blurted out:

"Look ahere! If I pay your fare down and back, will you
meet me in New York to-morrow evening? I got to go
down with the folks in the car."

"Ruby, too?" asked Jessie wickedly.

"Aah!" said Alfred, twisting his shoulders.

"But I'm on my vacation," said Jessie.

"What of it?" he said eagerly. "Look at the fun we could have in New York. Not like this burg. I'll be off for the whole night. We'll go down to Coney Island. I'll blow to the whole works. Will yeh? Will yeh?"

"I can go to Coney Island any time," said Jessie.

"Well, what else would you like to do? There's everything in New York. You only got to name it."

Jessie, however, wished to make him name it.

"A roof garden? The Follies? One of the big dance halls?"

To each of these Jessie shook her head.

"How would you like to see our town house?" he asked as a last resort.

Jessie suddenly raised her eyes in a glance that intoxicated the infatuated youth. "I'd like that," she murmured.

"Well, that's easy fixed," he said. "Nina Trudeau, she goes down with the *madame,* and she'll have her fellow to see her to-morrow night. We'll make a little party of four. There won't be nobody else in the house but the cook and the second butler. I'll square them. I'll show you the whole house."

"Oh, will yeh?" murmured Jessie ecstatically.

"But you couldn't bring Ruby," he said.

"Oh, I wouldn't expect that," she said, demurely letting her eyes fall.

The young man was beside himself with delight. "Good work!" he cried. "I'll be free as soon as I get the folks out of the house. That'll be eight-thirty or nine. Where'll I meet you?"

"Where is the house?" asked Jessie.

"—— East Sixty-Third."

"I'll wait for you at the Park entrance," said Jessie. "Just behind the Sherman statue."

"I'll be there with bells on!"

During the rest of the evening Jessie's manner towards Alfred was much warmer than heretofore, and the young man scarcely knew which end he was standing on. When we parted for the night, Jessie said:

"Shall I see you before you go?"

"No, worse luck!" he said. "We'll be busy all morning getting ready, and right after lunch we start."

"Why do you start so early?"

"The *madame's* got to get to town in time to get her jewels out of the safety deposit. This is going to be a big affair."

At the mention of "jewels," my heart rose slowly into my throat.

After lunch next day, Jessie and I were hanging about the snuffy parlour of the little hotel, waiting to see the Walbridge Sterry outfit drive past. We intended to take the first train after they had gone. While we waited, we amused ourselves by reading the local newspaper, copies of which were lying on the table. Suddenly my attention was arrested by a sharp exclamation from my companion.

"Read this!" she said, pointing to an item. "It has been clipped from a New York paper, and is therefore, several days old."

I read:

"It has lately become known that Walbridge Sterry, of New York and Tuxedo, is the purchaser of the marvellous Pavloff tiara, once the property of the late Czarina of Russia, which was brought to America to be sold by His Highness Prince Yevrienev. This is said to be one of the most valuable pieces of jewellery in existence, and it is known that the price paid by Mr. Sterry runs high into six figures. He presented it to his wife on her birthday. Certainly no other American woman possesses an ornament to match it.

"Those who have been privileged to view it, describe it as a marvel of the combined arts of lapidary and goldsmith, in the florid Russian manner. Diamonds, rubies and emeralds are the leading motives, combined with a row of priceless black pearls. The centre of the design is formed by the famous Pavloff emerald, which was presented to the Emperor Paul of Russia by a Tartar chief—a square-cut stone, one of the largest emeralds in existence.

"Mrs. Walbridge Sterry is taking a prominent part in the grand Oriental fête to be given at Idlewild, the famous B. B. Hagland estate near Glen Cove, next Friday night, in aid of several charities. In the pageant of All Nations which opens the affair, Mrs. Sterry has chosen to appear as Catherine the Great of Russia, and it is an open secret that she will wear the Pavloff tiara as part of her costume. All society is on the tiptoe of expectation."

"So that is the milk in the cocoanut," said Jessie softly.

I was half beside myself with terror. "Must you? Must you?" I cried helplessly. "This is too terrible! How can you hope to—singlehanded—I never thought of anything like this!"

"What, Bella!" she said firmly, "just because the loot runs into six figures instead of five! Mrs. Sterry isn't going to lose her bauble. This is playing directly into my hands. Unless I have made an error in my calculations, before to-morrow morning comes our work will be done, my dear."

The Walbridge Sterry cortège went by in two fine cars. From the second one, the infatuated Alfred cast a side-long look of yearning towards the hotel. As soon as they were out of sight we got our suit-cases, and walked to the railway station.

22

A LITTLE PARTY BELOW STAIRS

AS SOON AS Jessie and I reached town, we had to separate, because, naturally, I was not supposed to know anything about the Varick Street address. Jessie proceeded there, while I went to my room on Twenty-Fourth Street, where I waited all afternoon within hearing of the telephone, half sick with anxiety and suspense.

Jessie had already telephoned ahead the substance of Alfred's invitation for the evening, and she found further instructions awaiting her, through Black Kate. Black Kate, impressed by the magnitude of the task which had been allotted to Jessie, was obliged for the moment to conceal her real feelings towards the girl. She had Jessie up in her own room, where they could talk without any other member of the gang being present.

"So you made a mash on the valet," sneered Black Kate.

Jessie shrugged.

"Have you got him just where you want him?"

"Pretty much."

"Well, your instructions are to get him to let you stay in the house all night."

Jessie expected something of this sort, and she was not at all put about. She judged it prudent, though, to make believe to protest a little. "Do you mean that I am supposed to…"

"A girl in your position can't afford to be too particular," said Black Kate.

"Oh, well," said Jessie shrugging. "I can handle him."

"In a house as big as that, with so few people in it, he can easy conceal you," said Black Kate.

"Sure," said Jessie. "What else?"

"In the early part of the evening," said Black Kate, "you must familiarise yourself with the interior of the house, so you can find your way about later."

"Alfred promised to show me around," said Jessie.

"Oh, he did, did he? Nice of Alfred. When Mr. and Mrs. Sterry come home, the jewels will be locked in a safe in their private sitting-room on the second floor. Another operative has secured the combination of that safe, which will be given you. Do you know how to work the combination of a safe?"

"No."

"Well, I'll give you a lesson on our safe here, before you leave. Inside the safe there's a locked steel drawer, and you'll be provided with a duplicate key to that, also. Do you know what a tiara is?"

"A sort of crown."

"That's near enough. You bring the entire contents of that drawer, just to be on the safe side… When you go in to-night you want to satisfy yourself how the door is fastened at night, so you can get out when you're ready. And get your Alfred to show you where the switch is that turns the burglar alarm on and off, so you can throw it off before you go out."

"I get you," said Jessie.

"Well, that's about all, then. After the master and the missus get home, give them an hour or so to settle themselves, and then go get the stuff. The sitting-room, where the safe is, in the middle room of their private suite; and on either side of it are their bedrooms. Then make your way out of the house. There's a private watchman in that block you want to look out for. You can locate him from the vestibule of the house before you show yourself."

"Suppose, when I'm ready to get to work, Alfred gives me trouble," said Jessie coolly.

"I was coming to that," said Black Kate. "There'll be drinking during the evening. I'll give you some drops to put in Alfred's glass, when you're alone with him. It'll put him to sleep."

"Nice little plan!" thought Jessie. "I can make a better one at half the risk."

"Can I go out this afternoon?" she asked Black Kate.

"No."

"But I've been on my own for the past four days."

"I don't care anything about that. Orders is orders."

"Can I go with Bill, then?"

"No. What do you want to go for?"

"I need a few things."

"I'll supply you with everything you need... You'd better sleep till supper-time."

Jessie went away to her own room—but not to sleep. There was much to be thought out. Later she heard Kate leave her room, but she went no farther than the dining-room below, and Jessie dared not risk the telephone. On the other hand, it was absolutely necessary for her to communicate with Melanie, and she might not get another chance. She wrote a short note, and getting the wire-cutters from out their hiding-place, carried them into the bathroom with the broom.

A scratch on the window-sill brought Melanie's eager head out of the window above. The girls nodded and smiled at each other. They dared not exchange a word, for the windows of the dining-room below were open. Jessie tied the tool to the brush of the broom and sent it up to Melanie, together with the note. Her note said:

"To-night I am sent out on my first job. I expect to be back before morning. But in case anything should happen, you must have the wire-cutters. If I don't come back, take the first chance to make a break for it, and go to his mother."

Melanie nodded to show that she understood. Her lips shaped the words: "Good luck!" She put the note in her mouth. Jessie went back to her room.

It occurred to her that it would be just as well to avoid seeing Bill Combs alone, if she could, and she determined to stay in her room until the crowd gathered for supper. But Bill, suspecting her intention, perhaps, came upstairs, and tapped respectfully at her door. She had to open it.

"How about to-night?" he asked anxiously.

"Everything's fixed."

"What's the dope?"

Jessie was in a quandary; whether she told him, or whether she refused to tell him, it would put him in a rage. "Ask Black Kate," she said.

"Aah!" said Bill. "Is that your all for one, and one for all!"

"Shh!" warned Jessie. "She's in her room… Don't you

see I got to carry out instructions to-night, in order to put myself in a position where I can say somepin to them. This is a big job, Bill. It's the Russian Crown jewels."

"Yeh, I know that," said Bill. "But I want to know if they're taking care of you right."

"I can take care of myself," said Jessie.

"That's no answer," said Bill in a furious whisper. "How you goin' to get in that house? That valet fellow is taking you in, ain't he? For a price. By God! do you think I'm goin' to stand for that? What are the Russian Crown jewels to me? I kept a hold on myself; I been on the square with yeh. What for? On'y to let the first—"

"Easy, Bill, easy!" she implored. "You'll spoil everything. To-night I'm goin' to set you all free. Listen! do you think I'm a fool? Do you think I'd do *that* for the organisation? It's true, those were the orders that came through..."

Bill clenched his great fist, and lurid, whispered curses issued between his teeth. "I'm through! I'm through!" he muttered. "I don't care what they do to me..."

"Listen!" said Jessie. "I know a trick worth two of that. I got a plan of my own."

She whispered in Bill's ear. The dark flush died out of his face, and a slow grin spread there.

"By God! you got a head on you," he whispered. "You ought to be the boss of this organisation yourself!"

At eight o'clock, Jessie prepared to leave the house. To her chagrin, Black Kate announced her intention of accompanying her. Jessie had been under espionage every moment since getting back, and had had no opportunity to make her most vital arrangements. There was no help for it. Kate remained at her side until they came within sight of the Sherman statue, and then watched from across the street, until she saw Jessie picked up by Alfred.

Fortunately for Jessie, Alfred was like putty in her hands. The gentleman's gentleman was fairly trembling with eagerness, confident that his reward was in sight at last. Jessie said to him:

"Before we go into your house I want to telephone to Ruby."

He frowned. "Aah! where is she?"

"Here in town. She wouldn't stay up in Tuxedo without me. I'll just string her along, and then I'll be with you."

They walked along Fifty-Ninth Street, until they came to a drug-store where there were telephone booths. Black Kate was not in sight. Jessie was well aware that she might still be watching, but it hardly mattered now. Things were started, and nothing could stop them until the end.

Thus, at a few minutes before nine, after waiting on tenterhooks since three in the afternoon, I got my summons to the telephone.

"Paper and pencil, Bella. Put everything down in order to avoid any possibility of mistake: Hire a car by the hour, so you can get around quickly. First: in case of a slip-up to-night, I have left the means of escape in our friend's hands, and have told her to go to Mrs. H. You must go to Mrs. H. and warn her that the girl may turn up, and that she must take care of her. Arrange through Crider, so that they can call on our organisation for any help they may need. This is a remote contingency, I hope.

"Second: Go to Inspector Rumsey, and tell him the situation. Say that I hope to deliver the master crook into his hands before morning. Let him post half a dozen men secretly about the house that you know of. Explain to him about the secret entrance. Let him have the telephone wire from that house tapped to-night. The number is — Spring. If all goes well they will telephone from the house for our man to come there. When he hears that, let Rumsey take his measures accordingly. Warn Rumsey not to interfere with the man on his way to the house, or he'll leave me up in the air. Let the man enter unmolested. When he comes out again, he must be taken into custody. When he has his man fast, let Rumsey gather his men together, and apply at the front door of the house. If it is not immediately opened to him, let him break it down. But while he is doing this—this is most important, he must leave the side entrance absolutely free. I have loyal friends and helpers in that house, and I am in honour bound to let them escape.

"Third: When you have settled everything with Rumsey, drive out to the Hagland estate at Glen Cove, to see what you can of the Oriental fête. It's a public affair, and you can get in for five or ten dollars, or whatever it may be. Keep Mrs. Walbridge Sterry in sight as well as you can. Follow them back to New York when they leave. What I want you to do is to establish the time when they get home. Then dismiss your car.

"One hour and forty-five minutes after the Sterry's have got home, I want you to walk through Sixty-Third Street from Madison Avenue to Fifth. You are to look for the private watchman in that block. You may recognise him by his gray uniform. When you meet him, make believe to be taken suddenly ill. Heart attack. Get him to assist you to the all-night drug store on Madison Avenue, just below Fifty-Ninth. Detain him with you as long as you are able.

When I come into the store you may appear to get better. We will not recognise each other. Should I not come within half an hour, go right back to your room."

I repeated all this to my mistress, and we bade each other good-bye.

Of my part, during that terrible night, I need only say that I was able to carry out all her instructions to the letter. I saw the two private detectives that the Walbridge Sterry's brought back from Glen Cove with them, and saw them taken into the house. I was driven nearly frantic with anxiety, for I had no way of warning my mistress, who was then inside.

To go on with the adventures of Jessie:

The Walbridge Sterry house, which was one of the show-places of New York, was hidden away in the middle of the block of a mere side street.

"For the sake of the quietness," explained Alfred, who was jealous of the family's prestige. It was a new building in a severely handsome style of architecture—the sort of house that promises gorgeousness within. It occupied several frontage lots, and was quite shallow, so that it had good light from the rear, something that even the richest people in New York were not assured of, Alfred pointed out.

Alfred and Jessie entered through a steel gate at one corner of the façade. Jessie made Alfred go first, "to show the way," and as she pulled the gate to, after her, she contrived to catch her dress in it. This gave her an opportunity to turn around and examine the lock. It was an ordinary spring-lock, protected by a steel plate with curved edges from any possibility of being opened from the outside. A short distance within the gate, there was a door. This also had a spring-lock, also a bolt, which was presumably shot at night. Jessie photographed the position of the locks on her brain, so that if she came that way later in a hurry, she would know just where to put her hands.

Inside the door there was a landing, with a door at the right. Jessie greatly desired to know what was behind that door, but judged that it was a little too soon to ask questions. Alfred led the way down a narrow stair into a corridor running back to the servant's dining-room, a pleasant room facing the rear, and well furnished. Evidently the Sterry's were not niggardly below stairs.

There were three people in the room, whom Alfred introduced as: Mr. Spinney (evidently the butler); Miss Trudeau (Americanised French maid); and Mr. Simpson (an admirer of Miss Trudeau's). They greeted Jessie with no great cordiality, and it was clear to her that Alfred had not brought his girl into the house without considerable opposition on the part of the other servants. Jessie applied herself to charming it away. She foresaw that a crisis must arise the moment she and the amorous Alfred were left alone together, and she therefore desired to keep the party together as long as possible.

Mr. Spinney, being only a second butler, was not quite the majestic creature that usually presides over such a servant's hall. However, he was the principal person present, and Jessie devoted herself first to him.

"It was real nice of you to let me join your little party," she said in the confidential tones that no man over forty can resist in a woman. "I did so want to see the inside of such a fine house."

"Hum! Ha! Yes!" said Mr. Spinney.

"Maybe you'll show me a little bit of it later."

"Ha! Yes, yes," said Mr. Spinney. "Of course, it's an old story to me."

"Have you been long with the family?" asked Jessie.

"Seven years, miss. I started as cellar-man, and rose."

"Of course you would," said Jessie.

Mr. Spinney began to think she was a most unusual girl.

Jessie turned to the ladies' maid. "It must be heavenly to work in a house like this," she said. "So much space and all; no crowd."

Trudeau, a black, raw-boned creature, with little of the traditional charm of the French woman, but capable, said with a snap of her black eyes: "Oh, a grand house isn't everything." She wished to let Jessie understand she couldn't come over her as easy as she could a man.

"Wouldn't you like to see the house, too?" Jessie asked Mr. Simpson, a big, slow fellow, who looked like a returned doughboy, and would never look like anything else.

"Well, I'd hardly like to presume…" he said, glancing sheepishly at Miss Trudeau.

"Oh, you can if you want," she said indifferently.

Thus Jessie made sure that the house would be viewed in a body.

From the kitchen, next door, they were presently joined by Mrs. Pitt, the cook, a comfortable body, whom Jessie had no difficulty in impressing favourably. Jessie begged permission to peep into her kitchen, a marvellous place, where every known culinary appliance was installed.

Alfred was not a very perspicacious person, and it never occurred to him to inquire why the haughty Jessie should suddenly choose to reveal herself in such an amiable light. Manlike, he took it all to himself. It delighted him to see his girl make good "with the bunch," and he became more and more infatuated with every passing moment.

"Say, Mr. Spinney, ain't you got some ginger ale on the ice? If you have I got somepin to put in it that'll make the girls feel good!"

"Oh, Mr. Booker, ain't you terrible!" said Mrs. Pitt. "How about some nice crackers and cheese with it?"

Ten minutes later all six of them were seated happily about the table with their refreshments before them. Even the suspicious Nina Trudeau partly unbent. Jessie unlimbered her story-telling faculty—just a little; for she did not want to start Alfred thinking; nor did she wish the others to ask themselves how so clever a girl could have fallen for the foppish and empty-headed Alfred. She gave them just enough to start the others.

Mrs. Pitt was an innocent old party, who added greatly to the hilarity of the company by her incapacity to see the point of any joke. It was Alfred's great stunt to ask her conundrums with perfectly meaningless answers.

"Mrs. Pitt, what is the difference between a cock-eyed rooster and a man with one leg?"

"Well, what is the difference, Mr. Booker?"

"The higher, the fewer."

"Why, of course!"

"Mrs. Pitt, why is a mouse when it spins?"

"I don't quite get that, Mr. Booker."

"Why is a mouse when it spins?"

"Well, why is it, Mr. Booker. I give up."

"Just because."

"Oh, how comical!"

It presently appeared that Mr. Spinney played the bones. Mr. Simpson produced a mouth organ from his breast pocket, as big as a cake of chocolate. So they had music. It was all as cosy and friendly as possible.

"Can it be that I am going to rob this house to-night?" Jessie asked herself, with a feeling of curious unreality.

"Take your hat off, dearie; it's more comfortable," suggested Mrs. Pitt.

But Jessie knew she would have need of that hat later. "It's hardly worth while," she said. "I'll have to be going soon."

Alfred began to get uneasy at the duration of the party. "Well, if we're going to take a look around upstairs…" he said.

There was a general move. Mrs. Pitt said she would remain behind to clean up.

Outside the servants' dining-room there was a sort of central hall with many doors. One of these doors opened to a service stairway which they started to ascend.

"This stair runs all the way to the roof," Mr. Spinney remarked.

They issued out into the central hall of the house at the street level. It was a wide foyer, floored and lined with marble, magnificent in its stark bareness, with a sweeping stairway of marble and wrought iron at the back. At the rear of this floor was the dining-room, a noble apartment forty feet long. At the sight of it Jessie exclaimed in wonder.

"But you should see it when all the plate is displayed!" said Mr. Spinney.

He was then for leading the way up the grand stairway,

but Jessie had a particular reason for wishing to see the front. "What's over here?" she asked, striking off.

In front of the great foyer there was a square vestibule, with the front door on one side, and a small room on either hand as you entered. The front door was a massive affair of wrought iron and plate glass. Jessie, as if in idleness of mind, turned the knob, and found that it swung open easily. The door had only the usual spring-lock upon it, which worked automatically. She peeped into each of the small rooms.

"These small rooms are intended for cloak-rooms, when the family is entertaining," Mr. Spinney explained. "At other times they are used by the footmen, and for persons to wait in, who are not exactly friends of the family."

"In the room on your left as you entered, there was a door on the far side. Where does that go to?" asked Jessie. "I thought that was the side of the house."

"That leads to the landing just inside the service entrance," said Mr. Spinney.

Jessie remembered having seen that door from the other side.

"With a house full of rich things like this, I should think you'd be afraid of burglars every night," remarked Jessie.

"No," said Mr. Spinney, "when we retire for the night, the burglar alarm is always turned on."

"What's that?" asked Jessie innocently.

"It's an electrical appliance connected with all the doors and windows. After it is turned on, if anything was opened, it would ring a gong in the house, and also sound an alarm in the office of the protective agency, who would have their men here in a moment or two."

"Do show it to me," begged Jessie.

It appeared that the switch was in the same small room to the left of the front door. Mr. Spinney good-naturedly opened a little cupboard in the wall, and showed her the switch.

"When the handle is up, it's on," he said; "and when it's down it's off."

"Think of that!" said Jessie.

They then ascended the great stairway, padded with a red carpet as soft as grass, to the palatial rooms above. These were the entertaining rooms; a beautiful salon, stretching across the front of the house; a great central hall; library and music room at the rear. It was all very wonderful; and Jessie looked, admired and asked questions without stint. But her real interest lay in what was above. Unfortunately, it appeared that the tour was to end here.

"Well, that's all," said Mr. Spinney.

"What's on the next floor?" asked Jessie.

"That's the private suite of the master and mistress," said Mr. Spinney. "Sitting-room, bedrooms, boudoir, and all. I don't feel as how we ought to walk through their private rooms."

"Just a peep inside the sitting-room door," begged Jessie.

"Oh, well. Just the sitting-room."

They went up another flight. The sitting-room was in the middle of the front of the house. Like every other room in the house, it was full of rare and costly things, but it had an inviting and livable look. It bore the marks of use. Jessie spotted such homely objects as a work-box of Mrs. Sterry's and a row of the master's briar pipes.

Mr. Spinney explained that the master's bedroom was

on one side, and the mistress's on the other. Back of the
bedrooms were dressing-rooms, wardrobes, bathrooms, etc.
At the rear of this floor, Mrs. Sterry's boudoir was on one
side, and Mr. Sterry's den on the other.

"I didn't know there was so many different kinds of
rooms," remarked Jessie.

In the sitting-room, she had no difficulty in picking
out the safe, though it did not advertise its nature, being
contained in a handsome walnut cabinet between the two
windows. She also chose her hiding-place behind a Span-
ish screen of decorated leather in the corner.

They started down the service stairway, Mr. Spinney
in advance; then Nina Trudeau and her friend; Jessie and
Alfred bringing up the rear. At the next landing, Alfred
laid a hand on Jessie's arm, and whispered:

"Let them go on."

They waited in the dark until they heard the others pass
out on the basement floor; then Alfred softly drew Jessie
through a door. They were on the main floor of the house,
among the great rooms.

"I want to show you something," said Alfred.

"What will they think?" protested Jessie.

"Oh, they'll just think we stopped to spoon on the stairs."

Without lighting any lights he led Jessie through the
music-room, and through a French window on to a little
balcony which overlooked a sunken garden in the rear of
the house. It was very pretty, but that was not what Alfred
had come for. He slipped his arm around Jessie's waist, and
his lips sought hers greedily.

Jessie, instantly on the alert, slipped sideways out of his
embrace, and faced him. "Hey! cut that out!"

"Aw," said Alfred, reaching for her again.

"Cut it out, I say," said Jessie evading him.

"Aw, you said…"

"I said nothing."

"Well, you gave me to understand…"

"I can't help it if your understanding's defective."

"Aw!…"

Jessie felt a moment's compunction on Alfred's account. There was justice in his protests. He was getting a raw deal in this affair. However, in a game of such magnitude, one could not regard the feelings of so insignificant a pawn.

Alfred began to grow sore. "You shouldn't have come here if you didn't mean nothing by it."

"I wanted to see the house."

"You gone too far now to turn me down. I won't take it from yeh."

He came at her in good earnest then. Jessie retreated through the French window. There was a short, sharp struggle inside, all in silence. Jessie was easily a match for him. Women are called the weaker sex, but I have noticed they can defend themselves very well against men when they have a mind to. Jessie tore herself free, and waited for him. When he rushed at her again, she presented a shoulder, and catching him full on the chest, sent him flying backwards, full length on the floor.

In a flash she was out of the room. The door was open. She pulled it to after her, to delay him, and went down the great stairway as if she were running on a hundred little feet. I have seen her do that. When she got to the bottom Alfred was at the door overhead. She sped across the entrance hall, and got the front door open. Then the heavy, thudding slam of it sounded through the house, an unmistakable sound.

But Jessie was not outside, of course. She dropped to the floor, and crept on all fours to the little room on the left.

Alfred reached the front door a second later. He opened it, but did not run out. Jessie could see the motionless shadow of him. No doubt it had occurred to him that if she was gone, she was gone, and he could not very well chase her bareheaded through the streets. At any rate, he broke into a low, thick cursing, and let the door close.

Jessie retreated softly through the door into the side corridor. She could not be sure which way he would go then. He might turn on lights. Listening at the crack of the door, she heard him come towards it, and flitted as quietly as a ghost down the stairs, and along the corridor to the rear. The door of the servant's dining-room stood open, and Nina and her young man were sitting on the sofa within. The voices of Mr. Spinney and Mrs. Pitt came from the kitchen. As the hall was dark, Jessie had no trouble in getting past the open door unseen. She opened the door leading to the service stairway, and waited on the bottom step listening.

Alfred came along the corridor, and entered the dining-room.

"Where's your girl?" asked Nina indifferently.

"I'm goin' to take her home now," said Alfred. "Came after my hat... She asked me to tell you good-night," he added as an afterthought.

"That's real kind," said Nina sarcastically. "Tell her the same from me."

Having presumably secured his hat, Alfred returned along the corridor.

Jessie went softly up the service stairway for three flights, and made her way to the sitting-room in front.

23

THE BURGLARY

IT WAS STILL something short of eleven o'clock when Jessie stole into the sitting-room, and the Sterrys did not return until half-past one. The time seemed interminable to the waiting Jessie. She left the door open to guard against surprise. She expected Nina to come for the purpose of laying out her mistress's night things, or Alfred to perform a like office for his master. But it must have been done earlier, for neither of them appeared. In the dense silence that filled the house, she heard the servants, one by one, go up the back stairs to bed.

The tedious wait proved to be very valuable to Jessie. She spent the whole of it stretched out on the floor in front of the safe, working the combination from the memorandum that she had. She soon memorised the figures; more than that; she worked at it until she found herself able to shut off her little pocket light, and open the safe merely by the feel of the lock, and by listening to the click of the tumblers as they fell into place.

It was with a little sob of relief that she at last heard the automobile drive up to the door, and the people enter below. She stole to the door of the room and closed it, since it was customarily kept closed, and went behind her screen.

She had previously satisfied herself that there was nothing behind the screen; therefore, no reason for anybody to come to that corner. The screen was purely for ornament.

Mr. and Mrs. Sterry entered the room, and closed the door behind them. They were in the middle of a conversation which was unintelligible to Jessie, since she had missed the key word. They were evidently fatigued, and the talk soon lapsed. They moved here and there about the room. Finally Mr. Sterry said:

"Hand me the gew-gaws."

He was evidently kneeling in front of the safe.

His wife presumably handed over the jewels. "Oh, I wish they were safe out of the house," she said nervously. "I shan't be able to sleep a wink for thinking of them."

"Well, my dear, that's the penalty for having such things," he said. "Uneasy lies the head, etc., etc.... I wonder if it's worth it."

"Are you sorry you bought it?" she asked quickly.

"I bought it for you, my dear. Are you satisfied?"

"Oh, yes! I had a veritable triumph to-night. There wasn't a woman present who wouldn't have given her eyes to be me."

"I dare say, I dare say," he said. "...It is beautiful," he went on dreamily—evidently he had the tiara in his hands, "quite beautiful enough to go to hell for—if one wasn't so civilised. These stones are like little living eyes peering at one—or it's as if each one had a soul imprisoned within it."

"Mercy!" she said. "Do put it out of sight, Walbridge. It makes me nervous when we're alone here."

Jessie heard, successively, the steel drawer flung in, the

safe door closed, the handle turned that locked it, and the knob of the combination spun around.

Mrs. Sterry then went into her own room, and Mr. Sterry into his. They left the doors open, and talked across the sitting-room; talk of no moment, mostly dealing with the events of the party that night. Finally, Mrs. Sterry said:

"You leave your door open, Walbridge, so you can hear anything, and I'll close mine."

"Why close yours?" he asked.

"Because I don't want to hear anything."

He laughed. "Don't you feel safe with our two brawny defenders downstairs?"

At these words the listening Jessie's heart seemed to miss a beat. Here was something outside of her calculations. Two brawny defenders! Who were they?

"No, I don't feel safe!" complained Mrs. Sterry. "I'm as much afraid of those two as I am of anything. Here they are right inside the house. What's to prevent them stealing upstairs and blackjacking us in our beds!"

"Oh, my dear! my dear!" laughed her husband. "There are some honest men in the world. These fellows are hired to protect us; men don't go back on their responsibilities like that. And suppose they were tempted; they're known men; they know they'd be caught within an hour."

"There's no provision for them to sleep anywhere," said Mrs. Sterry.

"They're not supposed to sleep. They're going to sit up until they're relieved at eight o'clock. They asked me for a pack of cards!"

"Where are they playing?"

"In the cloak-room to the left of the entrance, with the

door open. If you stuck your head out of this door and called, they'd be up here in three jumps."

Jessie's heart rose slowly in her throat, and seemed to stick there. The switch which controlled the burglar alarm was in the cloak-room to the left of the entrance. She could not get out of the house without throwing it off!

Mr. Sterry came out into the sitting-room, and switched off the lights. He offered to close the door of his wife's room, but she had changed her mind about that.

"It makes you seem too far away," she said.

Her husband went into his bedroom for the last time, leaving the door open behind him.

Jessie settled herself for a long wait. According to the schedule she had laid down for herself, they were to have half an hour to get into bed, and a whole hour to settle themselves to sleep, before she got busy. She hoped that they might both be snorers; it would be so reassuring. Mrs. Sterry's highly nervous state did not promise well for Jessie.

They occasionally spoke to each other back and forth across the sitting-room. Mr. Sterry's voice took on a sleepy quality. Finally he did indeed begin to snore. But his wife woke him up.

"Walbridge! Walbridge!"

"Hum! Ha!... What is it, my dear?"

"Please don't go to sleep until I do."

He gave a short, exasperated laugh. "Well, let me know as soon as you've gone, my dear."

Very soon he began to snore again. His wife did not wake him up, but Jessie could hear her tossing on her bed, and uttering little complaining noises. At length these sounds too, were stilled.

Jessie sat listening; listening. Through the open windows came the deep night hum of the city which is never stilled. Occasionally a particular sound separated itself from the hum, such as the rumble of an elevated train from Third Avenue, or the purr of a rapidly moving automobile. Then Jessie heard some one softly whistling in the street below. This would be the gray-clad watchman. The sound resolved itself out of nothing as he slowly approached the house, and faded into nothing again as he went on. Jessie could even distinguish the air; it was *Traumerei.* These musical souls turn up in the oddest places. "So much the better," she thought; "if he has a tender heart he will not be able to resist Bella."

Every now and then, Jessie cast the light of her tiny flash on the dial of her watch. And each time she thought her watch must have stopped. It was the longest hour of her life.

Meanwhile, she debated how to solve the problem of the two guards below. "Assuming that there are two men playing cards in the cloak-room, what must I do? I must make a noise somehow that will draw them out. I must manage to make a noise at a little distance from myself, so that when they run out of the room, I can slip in." She thought of Mrs. Sterry's work-box on the centre table. A spool of thread!

Quarter of an hour before the time she had appointed with me, Jessie decided to start. As she snaked her body across the floor of the sitting-room, her heart pressed up suffocatingly into her throat. "So this is what it feels like to be a thief," she thought. "Hereafter, I will always remember it, when I catch one."

How thankful she was then, for her long practice with the combination of the safe! When her fingers met the knob, they knew by instinct what to do. She turned it forward, then back, listening for the slight sounds from inside that she had learned to know. Through the open door on her right came the comfortable sounds of Mr. Sterry's snoring; through the door on the left—nothing. Was Mrs. Sterry lying there with wide open eyes, listening? The mental picture caused Jessie's hand to tremble.

At last the tumblers of the combination fell into place, and Jessie grasped the handle of the lock. She turned it with the most exquisite care, the grate of steel on steel makes so significant a sound. Just as she was about to pull the door of the safe to her, Mrs. Sterry spoke.

Jessie's heart seemed to turn over in her breast. She clamped down the screws of self-control. For she had to turn that handle back to its normal position with equal care, before she dared leave it. One of them might come out and switch on the lights. Jessie slipped back to her hiding-place behind the screen, where she sat, sternly forcing her trembling body under control.

She heard Mrs. Sterry's voice again, and realised from the quality of it that the woman was asleep. In the sudden reaction that followed upon her relief, she trembled more violently than ever, and was forced to stretch herself out on the floor, clenching her teeth, before she could regain command of herself. Yet, throughout her terrors, Jessie, true to her nature, was watching herself from the outside with a sort of amusement. "Well," she thought, "for pure excitement, there is nothing like committing a robbery. But I can do with less."

She returned to the safe, and pulling open the door, inserted her little key in the drawer, and pulled that out with infinite care. The tiara was contained in a little bag, drawn tight with a tape. Through the sleazy material, Jessie could feel the sharp points. There were also one or two flat cases in the drawer, presumably containing other jewels; but Jessie, notwithstanding Black Kate's behest, let them be. The tiara would serve her purpose sufficiently.

Keeping her hands under iron control, Jessie closed the drawer and locked it; closed the door of the safe, and turned the handle. Finally she gave the knob of the combination a twirl to set it. There only remained to search Mrs. Sterry's workbox on the table. Jessie chose the coarsest thread, judging from the size of the spool, and made for the door. She took whole minutes to turn the handle of that door—a door handle is treacherous! and to release it when she was outside. When her hand dropped from it she breathed a sigh of relief. That much was over.

She went softly down the first flight of stairs, and half-way down the second. There she sat down to consider her further moves. She still had ten or fifteen minutes before it was time to leave the house. From where she sat she could see across the wide foyer the light streaming out through the open door of the cloakroom; and occasionally a murmured word in a man's voice reached her, as one of the players scored in the game.

Her first thought had been to conceal herself in the other cloak-room, but the door was closed, and it would be too risky to attempt opening it, immediately opposite the door of the room where the men were. They were trained thief-takers, she supposed, with eyes and ears on the alert.

So she looked around for some other hiding-place in the foyer, but there was none in that empty place. If any alarm was raised, the first act of the men, naturally, would be to flood it with light. Jessie determined to act from the service corridor behind the cloak-room.

She had first to dispose of the tiara. There was but one possible place for that; shoved down inside the top of her stocking, the curve of the ornament to her leg. The folded-up bag went with it.

Jessie then retraced her steps to the main floor of the house, where she unscrewed a bulb from one of the sidelights about the walls. One bulb was not heavy enough for her purpose, so she collected three, and tied them together with thread. She hung this cluster on a tread over the top of the door that led to the service stairway, making sure that there was space enough for the thread to pass freely back and forth when the door was closed. She then descended the stairway, paying out the thread from the spool as she went. There was a little well in the middle of the stairway, down through which the thread might pass without having to turn any corners.

Across the little central hall in the basement, and back through the narrow corridor towards the service entrance, she went, paying out her thread, and continually pausing to make sure that it was still running freely. Her principal anxiety was lest she might not have thread enough; but she remembered with satisfaction that most spools are marked "50 yards," and this was a full spool. She arrived outside the door to the cloak-room, with plenty to spare.

Wrapping the end of the thread around her forefinger, she cast a light upon her watch. It was then three-fifteen, that is to say, the exact moment that she had told me to get busy in the street outside. She gave me five minutes, seven minutes, to do my job. Meanwhile, with her ear to the crack of the door, she listened to the slap of the cards on the table, and the murmurs of the two men as they scored their points.

When the proper moment arrived, she gave the thread a tug, and it broke. Instantly she had the satisfaction of hearing a sound like an explosion within the depths of the house. The two men in the cloak-room leaped up, knocking their chairs over backwards, and ran out. Jessie instantly opened the door. The little wall cupboard was almost within reach of her hand. She pulled open the door, and jerked down the handle of the switch that controlled the burglar alarm. A second later she was back in the service corridor with the door closed behind her.

She reached for the street door. This was the door by which she and Alfred had entered the house, you remember. Bolt and spring-lock, she had it all fixed in her mind. Between the door and the iron gate she paused for a second, peering between the bars for the watchman. But I had done my part, and he was not there. She ventured out with a horrible sinking feeling. Suppose Mr. or Mrs. Sterry stuck a head out of the window. She would have to trust to her heels then. However, no alarm was raised. She walked sedately to Madison Avenue. As she turned the corner she looked back. Still no alarm. The furious beating of her heart quieted down.

24

THE MUTINY

YOU CAN IMAGINE the little comedy when Jessie came into the drug store. There was I, sitting on a chair in a state of semi-collapse, with the druggist offering me something in a glass, and the gray-coated watchman looking on solicitously. I drank what was offered me—I suppose I was taking a considerable chance; and immediately said I felt better. The watchman, suddenly recollecting his job, expressed a hasty wish for my recovery, and beat it out of the shop. The druggist offered to send for an ambulance, but I insisted I was quite well again.

He then went to wait on Jessie, who asked for headache tablets, a very natural request at that time of night. Jessie expressed her sympathy for me, and we all got into talk. The druggist asked me where I lived. I gave an address nearby, and Jessie volunteered to see me to my door. So we walked out of the shop together. How simple!

Jessie whispered: "Is it all right about Rumsey?"

"He's on the job," said I.

"Good! Then I can go ahead."

"Have you got the tiara," I asked trembling.

"In my stocking," she said dryly.

"Anything more for me to do?" I asked.

"No," she said. "We'll take the Broadway subway down, and you can drop off at Twenty-Third."

As we turned the corner into Fifty-Ninth Street, we came face to face with Black Kate, who was evidently waiting there for us. She gave me a poisonous glance. Here was a pretty how-de-do!

"What's she doing here?" she demanded.

Now my mistress, faced by a sudden and unexpected situation, will always tell the truth. "She's been helping me," she said coolly. "If she hadn't taken the watchman out of the way, I wouldn't be here myself."

"Why didn't you ask me for assistance," said Black Kate.

"I've heard others ask you," said Jessie coolly.

Black Kate was in a fix. Devoured by rage, she was afraid to exhibit it before a stranger. She didn't know how much I knew. "What does she expect to get out of it?" she snarled.

"That's between me and her," said Jessie.

"Well, come on home," said Black Kate.

In the dark part of the block, under the wall of the Savoy Hotel, a dingy, inconspicuous car was waiting by the curb. Black Kate opened the door. "Get in," she said to Jessie.

Jessie hesitated. As she explained to me afterwards, she didn't know Charley, the chauffeur; she had no influence over him. She suspected they might stop the car some place, and the two of them take the tiara from her forcibly, and thus destroy all her work.

"Get in," Jessie said to me.

"She can't come with us," said Black Kate blustering.

"Unless she comes, I don't," said Jessie.

There was a brief pause. Then Black Kate changed her tune. I suppose it suddenly occurred to her that this was the best way out of her difficulty, after all. "Get in! Get in! Both of you," she said with a hideous smile, which suggested to me that if she had her way, I would never get out of that house, once I got in. I knew far too much to suit Black Kate.

So we all got in, and the car started.

"Let me see the tiara," said Black Kate.

"I will, when we get home," said Jessie.

"You give it to me now!"

Jessie made no answer to that. Black Kate started to curse her, then threw me a sidelong look, and fell silent. Finally she asked in a strangled voice:

"What's the big idea?"

"They say that bit of jewellery's worth near half a million," said Jessie coolly. "I ain't agoin' to hand it over till I'm satisfied what I get out of it."

Black Kate started to laugh. It had a truly horrible sound. "All right, all right," she said. "We'll settle all that when we get home."

I need not say how terrified I was by this unexpected turn of events. My whole body was damp with a cold sweat. But it was not so bad though, as one of those terrible situations where you have to make up your mind what to do. I had my orders, and there was no choice but to obey.

Nothing more was said. We rolled rapidly through the streets, and in about ten minutes pulled up at the curb in a dark block of old-fashioned houses. The house before which we stopped was vacant, and advertised for sale. At one side was a narrow, arched opening, leading through to the rear, and of course I recognised the place as the masked entrance of the house on Varick Street.

We three women got out, and entered the narrow passage. I heard the car drive on. We crossed the narrow court behind the front dwelling, and paused, while Black Kate opened the door of the rear tenement with a key.

I whispered to my mistress: "I am not much disguised. Remember, two of the men of the gang know me."

"They were outside men," she answered. "They do not come to the house."

There were two rooms in this little tenement. Black Kate forced us to wait in the first, while she manipulated the secret door within. But her carelessness in revealing the entrance from the street was additional evidence of her determination never to allow me to leave the house again. I shivered. I had confidence in my mistress, but just the same it is staggering even to learn that somebody desires your death.

She held the door or panel, or whatever it was, back, for us to pass through. It was too dark for me to see how it was contrived. I heard it slide shut behind us. We passed through the second little house, across the flagged yard, and down four steps into a dark room, that I knew must be the kitchen where so much had happened. As we entered, some one lit a flaring gas-jet and I beheld a meagre, ill-favoured youth with sandy hair, who could be no other than Skinny Sam.

His eyes opened wide at the sight of me. Black Kate whispered something to him, and he quickly lowered his eyes. Black Kate led the way out of the kitchen; Jessie followed; I was behind Jessie; and Sam last. The narrow hall outside the kitchen was dark. I was half aware of a door being opened beside me, then I was seized and violently thrust through it. An instinct, quicker than a lightning flash, warned me that there were stairs on the other side of that door. I made a wild pass for the stair rail, and just succeeded in saving myself. Heavens! what a narrow escape! It turned me a little sick. The door was slammed shut, and a bolt shot.

My impulse was to fling myself against the door and shout, but I restrained it, for fear of spoiling my mistress's game. She knew where I was, and she would take her own measures. It was a hideous moment. Listening with my ear pressed to the crack of the door, I heard a scuffle outside. I heard Black Kate's voice, low and excited:

"Hold her arms! Hold her arms! It's in her stocking!"

Then I heard my mistress's voice raised high:

"Bill! Bill!"

That gave me my cue. I added my shouts to hers.

I had the unspeakable relief of hearing a heavy body come half tumbling down through the house. As it rounded the stairs a growling voice demanded:

"What the hell's the matter here?"

"Canada Annie," replied my mistress, panting. "They threw her down cellar."

"That woman is a spy!" said Black Kate stridently. "She knows all about our affairs. It's a matter of life and death to us!"

"She's no more a spy than I am!" said my mistress indignantly. "She helped me to-night. You wouldn't protect me."

"You had no business to ring in an outsider!" cried Kate.

Bill said to Sam, I suppose: "Get out of the way!" The bolt was shot back and the door opened.

"You'll pay dear for this, you fool!" cried Kate to Bill, half beside herself.

"Well, anyhow," he growled, "she don't go down cellar till there's been a proper inquiry."

We all went upstairs in a confused manner. Bill had Jessie by the arm, and I pressed close behind them. We went into the room over the kitchen, and somebody lit the gas. A cheerless untidy room, with a dining-table covered with a hideously dirty red cloth. The light revealed Bill enveloped in a voluminous bathrobe, his hair standing on end, a figure at once comic and terrible. Black Kate's face was livid with rage. Other men came running downstairs in various states of undress. I recognised them all from my mistress's descriptions; the big lout, Fingy Silo; Pap, the decayed ex-convict; the neat little Abell; and finally the terrier-like figure of Tim Helder.

All wanted to know what was the matter.

"Matter enough!" cried Black Kate. "Jessie has let this stranger in on the secrets of the organisation. What am I goin' to do with her? Let her go so she can tell what she knows? I leave it to you, men."

Old habit was strong with them. The thought of the "organisation" had entered into their very souls. All scowled at me and muttered—even Bill.

Jessie saw that her influence over them was slipping. "You all know me," she cried. "I will answer for this girl as for myself!"

But Tim Helder shook his head. "You took too much on yourself, my girl," he said.

"I say—to the cellar with her," said Black Kate. "We can't afford to take any chances."

"You're right!" cried Sam loudly.

The others seemed half inclined to agree. If I had been a man, I expect I would have received short shrift at their hands. But in the eyes of all of them, except Sam, I could perceive a certain reluctance to hurt a woman.

"Who's goin' to do it?" muttered Fingy Silo.

"I will," said Black Kate, with a gloating look at me that made my blood run cold.

Fingy turned away with an indifferent shrug.

My mistress was not at all dismayed. "She helped me bring in half a million to-night," she said coolly. "Is that nothing? I say, test her out, and if she makes good, take her in with us."

"That's not for you to say!" cried Black Kate furiously.

"No harm in givin' her a show," growled Bill.

"No!" cried Tim Helder. "The more women, the more trouble!"

"You all know the orders," cried Black Kate. "Strike instantly at anything that threatens the organisation. That's how it's always been preserved."

"Put it up to the boss," said Jessie.

Black Kate's expression changed. Staring hard at Jessie, she pulled down the corners of her mouth in a derisive and hateful smile. "I've no objection to doing that," she said. "I'll call him up first thing in the morning."

"You ain't helpin' your friend none by that," said Bill uneasily to Jessie. "The boss, he picks his people wherever he has a mind to. He ain't goin' to stand to have one shoved down his throat."

"I'll take my chance of that," said Jessie, boldly bluffing.

"When he hears who she is and what she's done, he'll be glad to get her."

Several of the men smiled rather pityingly at Jessie.

"Get back to your beds," said Black Kate.

There was no great haste to obey her.

"Whadya mean, brought in half a million?" Bill Combs asked of Jessie with strong curiosity.

By way of answer, Jessie retired into a corner of the room, and turned her back on them.

"Get out!" cried Black Kate furiously, trying to shepherd them with her arms. "You all know you got no concern with each other's jobs."

But Jessie already had it out. She whipped around, holding the tiara aloft in her two hands. "Look, boys, look! The Russian Crown jewels!"

Black Kate made a vicious snatch at it, but Jessie coolly held it out of her reach. Kate collided with Bill, who thrust her indifferently to one side. "No harm to take a look," he growled.

Meanwhile Jessie was crying: "Look! Look! Look," and exhibiting the treasure all around.

The glittering bauble in Jessie's hands cast a spell on everybody in the room. All else was forgotten. Even I forgot my perilous situation when I looked at it. How can I describe it? It was as if dozens of particoloured little suns were rising out of Jessie's hands. The thing had a truly infernal beauty. But it was not its beauty which cast the spell. The hearts of these rough men were hard to beauty. It was the spell of immeasurable riches which lighted the shine of cupidity in their eyes, and caused their lips to part, and their breath to come quickly. Gleaming black pearls as big as sparrows' eggs; flashing diamonds; rubies like drag-on's eyes, and the cold fire of enormous emeralds, greener than the sea. Broken, awestruck exclamations came from their lips.

"My God! look at that!"

"I never seen the like of that before."

"Nor will you ever see its like again!"

"God, Jess, you're a wizard!"

"Put it in your hair, Jess! Nobody's got a better right!"

Jessie put it in her hair, and turned herself about, smiling at them gaily. From across the room Black Kate and Sam watched the scene with bitter faces.

Jessie cunningly sought to work up the men's cupidity. "The paper said it was worth half a million," she said. "And they said Walbridge Sterry got it at a bargain, because there wasn't half a dozen men in the world with the money to put into such a thing. Taken down and sold separately it would bring half as much again. That in the middle's the biggest emerald in the world."

"Let me have it in my hand for once, Fuzzy-Wuz," begged Fingy.

"And me... And me!" from the others.

"Sure," said Jessie, "I regard every one of us as having a share in it."

It was passed around from hand to hand.

"When you're ready to hand it over..." said Black Kate, from between tight lips.

Jessie took it back into her own hands. "Half a million, at the least," she said to the men. "And I brought it in, with the help of Annie there. It's my job. And I guess it's a big job, even for this big organisation."

"You're dead right!" somebody said.

"Well," said Jessie meaningly. "Are we going to divide or stick? It's up to you, boys? Shall I hand it over to her on her say-so?"

"No!" cried Abell and Fingy simultaneously. And "No!... No!" Bill and Tim came in with a moment later. Pap said nothing, but at least he ranged himself on their side of the room.

"What does this mean?" demanded Kate, white to the lips.

"It means we're going to stick together hereafter," said Jessie.

"Are you going to hand over that stuff, or ain't yeh?"

"I'm willing to hand it over on certain conditions."

"Yes, just a few reasonable conditions," said Tim Helder.

"A conspiracy, eh?" cried Kate. "I said this girl was dangerous. You, Bill, this is where your craze for her peroxide hair has landed you. Anybody could see you're dippy about her. You're too old for love, Bill, your wits is softened."

"That may be," said Bill undisturbed. "But I'm on'y one."

"She's got you all locoed!" cried Kate furiously. "All of you's ready to let her twist you round her pinky. My God! what a set of fools you are, standin' there! You, Tim, and you, Bill, at least you are old enough in the organisation to know what will happen. What's this emerald crown to the boss? Less than nothing at all. But the organisation is everything. It's not the first time you have seen some fool operative try to make trouble amongst the others. What happens, eh? What happens?"

"Same old line of talk!" interrupted Jessie. "And all designed to split us up."

Black Kate essayed to laugh. "Suppose there are a half dozen of you in this! What do you count against the whole power of the organisation?"

"We count this much," said Jessie. "All these dozens of other operatives are just scouts and runners-up for us. We're the principals of the show. And if the boss steps on us, his business stops, see? If it breaks, it will be his doing, not ours. We're strong for the organisation. We on'y ask to be treated like human beings."

All the men signified their approval.

As the discussion went on, Black Kate cooled off. From the first day she had hated Jessie with all the power of her soul, and up to this time Jessie had always succeeded in putting her in the wrong. Now Black Kate felt that her feeling was justified; Jessie was giving her a handle to use against her, and the older woman had a sweet foretaste of triumph.

"Well, what are your conditions?" asked Kate.

"A fair division of the stuff," said Jessie. "So much to the one that brings it in, and so much to a general fund for all of us."

"How you going to secure those conditions?" asked Black Kate, with a sneer.

"This is a business organisation, isn't it?" said Jessie. "You're always telling me so. It ought to be run on business principles then. We want a contract with the organisation."

Black Kate laughed outright; nevertheless, Jessie's word was cunningly chosen. "Contract," was a slogan, a rallying-cry. Every one of the men took it up.

"We want a contract. We want to know what we can expect!"

One by one Kate tried to detach them. "It's no use talkin' to you, Bill; you're cracked about the girl. But you, Tim, I never saw a skirt come around you before. For your own good, I ask you to keep out of this. Let them run their heads into a noose if they want."

"I want a contract," said Tim obstinately.

Kate turned to the next, who was Fingy. "You're a young man," she said, "with your future before you. What you want to queer it like this for? This girl's got nothing for you. When there's mutiny in the air like this, that's the time for a young fellow to get on, by sticking to the organisation."

"Nothin' doin'," said Fingy.

"You, Abell," she went on to the next; "the boss was talkin' to me about you a couple of days ago. 'Abell's done well,' says he; 'he's entitled to a vacation.'"

"You're lying!" said Abell contemptuously.

"And you, Pap," said Kate, with a curling lip; "what you want, a contract for cooking? You ain't entitled to any percentages nohow. There's nothing in this for you. You must have set your heart on dying behind the bars."

Pap, livid and sweating with terror, was incapable of answering her. However, he made no move to desert his associates. They gathered close around him to give him courage.

Kate shrugged. "Well, I done my best to keep you from committing suicide," she said. "You're bent on it. All right. I'll call up the boss. I guess this is important enough to wake him out of his sleep." She paused at the door of the room and turned. "If any one of you wants to save himself from the general clean-up, let him speak now... It's your last chance."

There was complete silence in the room.

With a laugh, Kate went on out.

Sam was still in the room, and the others gathered in a close group in the corner by one of the windows. The feelings of solidarity and defiance had roused all the men to a pleasant state of excitement. Jessie worked amongst them to stimulate it, and keep them up to the mark.

Kate returned to the room, smiling still. "He's coming right over," she said. "You ought to be flattered. He'll be here inside ten minutes."

A significant silence fell on Jessie's followers. She was aware of a shiver of apprehension passing through them. On the other hand, Kate and Sam were gleeful. It was nothing to Jessie. She had gained her point. A great satisfaction filled her.

25

THE BIG BOSS

THE ATMOSPHERE OF the dining-room in the house on
Varick Street was tense. The five were gone from the room
a few minutes to dress. Jessie had given them the tiara to
keep. When they returned, the two parties in the household waited and watched each other from opposite sides of
the room. I must say that the morale of the larger party, that
is, Jessie's party, suffered most under the strain of waiting.
Only two of the men, Bill Combs and Tim Helder, had
ever seen the Boss, and the others seemed to be filled with a
sort of superstitious terror at the thought of being brought
face to face with this mythical personage. This was of small
moment to Jessie; however, she kept up a decent pretence
of trying to hearten them. Observing that little Abell's
face was growing whiter, and his lips more tense, she said:

"After all, he's only a man like yourself."

"Sure," said Abell, with a boyish swagger. "I'm not afraid
of him!"—but it rang hollow.

The little whispering group in our corner became quieter
and quieter. Big Bill frequently wiped his face. Even that
human oak tree was nervous. It was clear though, that we
could have depended on this one to the death, had we need

of him. The glance that he bent on my mistress was slavish in its devotion.

Black Kate and Sam, who, you may be sure, missed not the slightest change of complexion in our party, grew correspondingly more sure of themselves. Yet Kate was a little worried too, by my mistress's unconcerned air. It was clear from her expression that she suspected Jessie might have a trick up her sleeve.

He did not come in ten minutes, nor in twenty. Very likely he purposely delayed his coming to heighten the effect.

Then we lost Pap. Suddenly the poor wretch, with a groan, went staggering over to Kate, spreading his hands out. He could not speak at first. A revolting figure of broken humanity. One turned one's head away from the sight. An animal-like growl of rage broke from Bill and Fingy.

Sam gave a loud brutal laugh. He could be very brave against poor Pap. "Get back!" he cried. "We don't want you, old general debility!"

Pap found his voice. "I ain't took no sides," he quavered. "I ain't said a word no way or the other. I don't want no trouble with nobody. I'm neutral."

"There's no neutrals in the organisation," said Black Kate.

Pap's voice scaled up. "I ain't said a word! not a word!"

"You didn't speak when you had the chance," said Kate. "Get back to your friends."

Pap turned around. All our men, of course, were scowling ferociously. The pitiful old wretch, with a face of despair, staggered towards the door. Fingy made a move in his direction, but Jessie laid a hand on his arm. We heard Pap stumble down the stairs.

Sam looked at Kate inquiringly.

"He can't get out," she said coolly. "He don't know the trick of the sliding door."

A general discussion arose as to what should be done with me. All the men on our side thought that I ought to be kept out of sight at least until the major question was decided. They thought I would confuse the issue. Black Kate affected to believe that there was no place where I could be safely confined, except down cellar. Jessie refused to allow me to be put down cellar. So I stayed where I was. On our side Jessie's word was law.

The suspense became unendurable. During the last few minutes nobody said a word. We were all concentrated on the business of controlling our shaking nerves. Only my wonderful mistress maintained her air of unconcern. She lighted a cigarette. That simple act administered a jolt to Black Kate's assurance.

When the front door bell sounded through the house, one could almost have sworn that one heard the beating of the eight hearts in that room. Black Kate was very pale when she went out. Nobody else changed his position. My mistress dropped her cigarette on the floor, and trod out the light.

Black Kate re-entered the room. Our eyes were fixed on the door in mingled curiosity and terror. There was nobody behind her. There was a pause long enough for our heart-strings to squeeze up in apprehension. Then a masked man entered the room.

The mask was no more than a narrow black strip across

the upper part of his face. A mere stage trick, but most infernally effective. It brought mystery into the room with him. I could hear the strong men in front of me catch their breaths in terror. Little Tim Helder took off his hat; a significant gesture in him. Something went out of the backbones of all those men. Had we been depending on them, we would have been lost. I stole a look at my mistress's face. Outwardly, it expressed a blank, but I could see that she was smiling inside. A woman of iron!

As for the rest, the man who came in was tall and heavily-built; a middle-aged man one would suppose from his girth, though his black hair was still unstreaked by gray. He wore his hat throughout, and kept turning a thick black cigar between his teeth. The lower part of his face expressed a coarse strength, but the mask dominated all. Apart from that mask, an ordinary gross figure, one of thousands in the streets of New York. But the mask dehumanised him, and rendered him a figure of terror. I was teased by something familiar in his aspect, but my wits were too confused to track it down.

He instantly spotted me. Two blue sparks shot out at me from the apertures in the mask. "Who is that woman?" he demanded.

His voice was extraordinary. It was completely divested of all human tone whatsoever. It was like a voice issuing out of a void. Another stage trick, perhaps, but it added enormously to the man's impressiveness. My knees shook under me. Yet I had a sense of having heard that voice before.

Black Kate answered him. The imperious woman was humble enough before him. "Her name is supposed to be Canada Annie Watkin," she said. "Jessie Seipp used her to-night without my knowledge as a sort of look-out on the Sterry job. As long as she'd been let into the secret, I thought I better bring her down here, and ask instructions."

He said nothing. He had the impassiveness of a Chinese idol. From one man to another, his glance turned, the blue sparks shooting through the holes in the mask. It was curious, though you could see his eyes were blue, and though the whole of his lower face was exposed, you could not figure to yourself what the man looked like. It is the area immediately surrounding the eyes that gives a face its character.

Black Kate asked humbly, "What must I do with Canada Annie?"

"Orders will be given you," said the impassive voice.

So much for me.

I saw the gray, decayed figure of Pap hanging about just outside the door. Curiosity was stronger than fear. He had to come back. An outcast from both factions, he awaited the outcome tremblingly.

The man turned the icy blue points of his eyes on my mistress's face. He met his match there. She adopted a dull, stupid look, and held his gaze unflinchingly. It was a sort of duel. I think he must have been surprised. The secret of his power was that he wasted no words. Any ordinary man would have made some blustering speech such as: "What's the matter here?" or "What do you want, girl?" He merely looked. He let the others talk. They all fidgeted. Black Kate could not keep her mouth shut.

"That's her!" she burst out. "She's the cause of all the trouble. From the moment she entered the house! Trying to vamp the men and all. Setting them fighting. And now this conspiracy. The Russian jewels have turned her head. Wants to make terms before she hands them over. She thinks she can tell us where to get off, the young fool!"

Bill Combs interrupted her. "You can't get the truth about a young girl from her, boss! You know her. She hates a woman who's younger and better-looking than herself. Let me tell you about this vamping business. A lot of us men cooped up here in this house, and a fresh and hand-some girl coming amongst us; of course it made trouble. That weren't *her* fault. It was the men made the trouble, not the girl. She's been on the square with all of us. Ask them! Ask them! What's biting Kate is, *her* man tried to—"

Here Black Kate began to shriek accusations in the effort to drown him out. Others joined in, and a furious wrangle resulted. It was a weird scene. All that noise, and the two principals, the only two who mattered, facing each other composed and silent. Finally the man held up his hand, and they all fell silent, as if the wind had suddenly been let out of them.

"I'm not interested," he said in his remote voice. "Only in the work." He addressed Jessie. "Did you carry out your orders to-night?"

"Yes,"

"Where's the stuff?"

One of the men had the tiara. Which one I did not know.

"Before I hand it over, I got something to say," said Jessie in the heavy, dogged style she had adopted.

Without changing his voice in the least, he said:

"I do not discuss terms with you. I issue orders. If the

orders are not obeyed..." He concluded with a forcible gesture.

"Just the same, I'm going to say my say," said Jessie doggedly. "We ask to be treated as human beings, that's all, and for a fair division of the profits."

He coolly ignored her. "Where's the stuff?" he repeated, turning to the men.

Fingy Silo's eyes bolted, betraying him as the possessor of the loot.

"Hand it over," said the masked man.

Fingy drew back in a horrid state of indecision.

"If you give it to him we're done," warned Jessie.

"Hand it over," repeated the masked man in his quiet, awful voice.

"What's the matter with you all?" cried Jessie. "Will you let him bluff you? Are you full-grown men, and taken in by a bit of hocus-pocus like this? There are four of you. Tear the mask off his face. You'll only find a man like yourselves behind it. A fat man, too soft to put up a good fight!"

A slow smile wreathed the lips of the masked man. He stood before them perfectly motionless, the two blue sparks shooting out of the holes in his mask. He gave them plenty of time to act on Jessie's suggestion. But the four cringed before him abjectly.

"Then I'll show you!" cried Jessie, making a move forward.

One could hear the gasp of horror that escaped them. Bill Combs flung his arms around Jessie.

"No, no, my girl!" he muttered aghast. "No, no!"

"Hand over the stuff!" the masked man said to Fingy. It was evident that he sneered.

And Fingy, hanging his head, placed the tiara in his hands. It had been returned to its little green baize bag. The masked man looked inside to make sure that the contents were intact, and pulled it shut again, without betraying the least concern.

"It's no use," Fingy muttered shamefacedly to Jessie. "You can't stand out against him."

Bill released Jessie. She tapped a fresh cigarette on the back of her hand, while the men looked at her, astonished at her effrontery. She was just as well pleased, of course, not to have the scene prolonged.

"It's nothing to me," she said, "if you enjoy being hocussed."

And so the great conspiracy petered out.

The masked man turned to leave the room without another word. It was extraordinary what a capacity he had for keeping his mouth shut.

"What am I to do now?" Kate cried helplessly.

He paused. "Go back to your beds," he said as if faintly surprised. "Nothing is changed. The orders will be issued as usual, and if they are not obeyed, the penalty is the same. If anybody still thinks he can buck the organisation, let him try, that's all."

"What will I do with the girl?" asked Black Kate.

He hesitated just for the twinkling of an eye. I suppose it occurred to him what a wonderful servant Jessie would make, if he could but bend her will to his.

Bill Combs spoke up. "Boss," he said, "I've learned my lesson. And I'm prepared to serve the organisation faithful if you'll let me. Boss, this girl, she didn't mean no harm.

She's new here. She didn't know what she was doing. She's learned her lesson now, if you'll overlook it."

In view of Jessie's open defiance this was rather ridiculous. But one couldn't help but feel for the big fellow, whose devotion blinded him to the truth.

"Boss, she's one in a thousand for our work," he stumbled on. "And… and…" he glanced around. "Aah! I don't care what you all think—I can't let any harm come to her. And if you're too many for me, if she goes, well, I got to go too."

My heart warmed towards that great brute of a man, whose heart was so deeply stirred.

The masked man said in his detached voice: "For the present, the girl is placed in the custody of Bill Combs. She is not to be allowed to leave the house."

"Thanks, boss, thanks," said Bill humbly. "I will answer for her."

Observe how cunningly the man evaded his dilemma. If he had pronounced Jessie's doom on the spot, Bill would certainly have run amok. There is not the least doubt but that he would have had Jessie removed from the house next day.

He left the room in an impressive silence. None of the men dared move. One could see through the meretricious means by which he held them subject. Nevertheless, I for one, was not strong enough to stand out against him. Kate, key in hand, hurried after to let him out. He did not linger in the hall for any whispered consultation with her. That would have destroyed the awful inscrutability with which he surrounded himself. We heard her let him out, close the door after him, and turn the key.

Waiting for the expected denouément, my heart beat with great slow thumps like a hammer in my breast.

Black Kate started back for the dining-room. Before she reached the door, we heard a scramble on the front steps of the house, a pounding on the door, and the boss's voice with all the inscrutability gone out of it, just a plain terrified voice: "Open! Open!" But immediately came the unmistakable sounds of his being dragged down the steps.

Kate, with a gasp, darted into the front room to look out of the window. She instantly came running back to us. Her face was blanched to the colour of ashes. In the dining-room door she stumbled and sank to her knees, clutching her breast, and sobbing horribly for breath. Bad heart.

"The police..." she gasped. "They've taken him!"

There was an instant's silence in the room, then utter confusion. Black Kate got to her feet, and leaned against the wall.

"It was her... it was her!" she gasped, pointing at my mistress.

My mistress seized my wrist and backed with me to the fireplace. From the bosom of her dress she whipped out the little gun that Bill had given her. I didn't know then if she had ever had the opportunity to load it. I know now that it was loaded.

It seemed to me as if they were all milling around the room like trapped rats. The only one I can remember clearly is Bill Combs. Bill turned a face on us black and terrible with rage, and raised his clenched fists above his head.

"By God, girl, I was on the square with you!" he cried hoarsely. "I was ready to go to my death with you. And this is what I get for it. You're nothing but a spy! You've sold us out! Well, God damn you, I'll kill you before they take me!"

"Easy, Bill!" said my mistress, keeping her eyes fixed unwaveringly on his. "It's true I had him taken, and I want her," pointing to Black Kate. "The rest of you are free. The back way is open. Beat it!"

It is doubtful if they got it the first time.

"Beat it!" she cried, raising her voice. "I am still your friend, I promised you that I would set you free to-night. And if in the future you need a friend, come to me. I will help you to a fair start!"

At this moment we heard a peremptory knocking on the front door. They turned and scuttled down the basement stairs.

"Sam! don't leave me!" cried Black Kate.

He turned snarling: "To hell with you, old woman!" and disappeared.

Still racked with pain, Kate attempted to follow. My mistress covered her with the gun.

"Not you," she said sternly. "A bullet if you move!"

Black Kate sank groaning on a chair.

Bill Combs still lingered, goggling with amazement. "Who are you?" he demanded hoarsely.

"Rosika Storey," said my mistress.

"Oh, my God!" stammered Bill. "And I thought... I thought... Now I see it!"

A strange cry broke from Black Kate.

"Beat it! Beat it!" said my mistress urgently to Bill. "I cannot save you after they are in."

He turned and ran down the stairs with remarkable celerity for his size.

I heard other steps on the stairs, and an uncouth figure appeared in the doorway. I recognised Melanie Soupert, gaunt, dishevelled, weak from her imprisonment. The steel bracelet still dangled on her sore wrist, but the chain had been cut off short. She looked like a figure risen from the grave. But her sunken eyes glowed with something of the old spirit.

"What is it?" she asked breathlessly. "I couldn't stay up there like a trapped rat."

"It's all right," said my mistress, holding out her hand to her. "Our friends are at the door!"

Melanie did not notice me at first. She half collapsed within my mistress's embrace. "Oh, Jess! Oh, Jess! Oh, Jess!" she murmured.

Black Kate looked on at this speechlessly. The woman was half out of her senses with pain. She looked like a wounded wild animal.

Meanwhile, the knocking on the door was redoubled. The door key still hung from Kate's nerveless hand. I took it, and ran out. I opened the front door, and Inspector Rumsey and four men came tumbling in. I pointed silently to the dining-room door. I followed them in.

For a second the inspector looked blankly at my mistress, then his face lighted up. "It's you!" he cried in great relief. "Is everything all right?"

"Right as rain!" she said smiling. She looked down affectionately at the dark head on her shoulder. "This is Melanie Soupert. I have her safe!"

The inspector snatched off his cap. "By God, Madame," he cried heartily, "you're the greatest woman of your time!"

Melanie quickly raised her head, and looking in my

mistress's face with something like alarm, tried to withdraw herself from her embrace. "Who are you?" she whispered.

I was just behind her. "Melanie, don't you remember me?" I asked.

She turned her head. Her big dark eyes widened.

"Bella!" she said in amazement. *"Bella Brickley!"* She looked back at my mistress with eyes bigger than ever. "Then you must be..." she stammered. "You must be..."

"Your friend," whispered my mistress.

"That is Madame Rosika Storey, the master-mind of us all!" cried Inspector Rumsey magniloquently.

Melanie tried in earnest then to detach herself from my mistress's supporting arm. "You mustn't... you mustn't!" she whispered, with hanging head. "Not the likes of me!"

Mme. Storey clung to her, smiling, and Melanie subsided.

"You did it all for me?" she whispered.

"Did you think I was going to let you go?" asked my mistress.

Melanie began to weep out of sheer weakness and relief and gratitude.

To the inspector Mme. Storey said, pointing to Black Kate, "That is your prisoner. She appears to be ill. You had better have medical assistance for her. But watch her well."

"Never fear, Madam," said the inspector grimly.

"You have the other one?"

"Safe outside, Madam. He's handcuffed."

"Did you search him?"

By way of answer, the inspector handed over the little green baize bag which had passed through so many hands that evening. My mistress made sure that its contents were intact.

"Bring him in for a moment," she said.

How different was the second entrance of that man. The super-boss, the man of mystery, had been brought low indeed. He had been unmasked, of course; one of his eyes was beginning to purple, and his lip was cut. Yet he still showed traces of his power. He kept his head up doggedly, and he preserved his remarkable faculty for keeping his mouth shut.

I recognised him now, and a great round "Oh!" of astonishment was forced from my breast. It was John McDaniels, the head of the famous detective agency, which had acquired such a name among the rich for the recovery of stolen valuables! Of course! Of course! Now I began to see it all. As the inner workings of the scheme revealed themselves to me, I was all agog with amazement. The detective agency was equally a part of the organisation, of course. One department of the business robbed the rich, and another department recovered their jewels—if the reward was sufficient. Furthermore, the outlawed part of the organisation aided convicts to break prison, while the reputable part instantly "ran them down," if their master was displeased with them. How simple, how ingenious, how efficient!

My mistress showed no surprise at the sight of him. I learned later that she had recognised him upon his first appearance.

"Madame Storey wants to have a look at you," said Inspector Rumsey, as he led him in.

He never batted an eye. Not a muscle of his face changed.

He met her gaze point-blank with complete effrontery. Oh, truly a remarkable man!

"I'm not going to indulge in any moral reflections, McDaniels," said my mistress; "it's not my line, only feel like saying, when I look at this poor girl, that I regard this as the best night's work of my whole life."

He kept his mouth shut, and continued to stare at her with the hardihood of a savage animal.

"Have you nothing to say for yourself?" cried the inspector roughly.

McDaniels cast a look of ineffable contempt upon him. There was old bad feeling between these two. "Not to you," he said.

"He does right to keep his mouth shut," said Mme. Storey. "What is there for him to say?... Take him out."

He was led away. Two men were told off to guard the house until daylight. Then the inspector turned to us.

"Well, ladies," said he; "I guess the night's work is finished."

"What say, Melanie," said my mistress, smiling, "shall we beat it out of here?"

"I ain't got no hat," murmured Melanie abashed.

We laughed.

"Well, it's past four," said Mme. Storey. "They'll think we've been on a party."

"Where you goin' to take me?" murmured Melanie.

"There's a little flat on Gramercy Park that's been waiting for you for weeks past. If you'll take in Bella and me until breakfast time, we'll all have a chance to tidy up."

Melanie smiled like an abashed schoolboy.

If I live to be ninety I will not forget the starry look that appeared in the eyes of the girl as she came out on the stoop of the house, and lifting her face to the sky, breathed deep of the delicious morning air; for it was growing light. It was worth all we had been through. Oh! a hundred times over!

26

CONCLUSION

AT HALF-PAST TEN next morning Mme. Storey was seated at her desk, and I at mine, and all the lurid events of the preceding days had taken on the semblance of a dream. We were reading the letters that had come in during my absence from the office. They were of no great importance, since my mistress was supposed to be in Europe. The door between the two rooms was open, and we were talking idly back and forth. Heavens! how sweet was the feeling of perfect relaxation after having been keyed up so long; how delightful was the free exercise of one's own personality, after having been forced to play an alien part. How I loved the calm and the coolness of our beautiful rooms! When I first came in, I had gone about like a fool, stroking everything.

Melanie was still asleep upstairs. As soon as we had put her to bed, Mme. Storey had carried me up to her own place, where she had put the services of her expert maid and masseuse at my disposal. In an hour I felt like a new woman. Neither of us had any desire to sleep; it was too good just to be; and we had issued forth in search of the most luxurious breakfast in New York. My mistress looked perfectly radiant. In honour of the occasion she had put on a sports dress of some rare eastern silk, with a gay all-over design of little dancing men. She had dyed Jessie Seipp's crass locks to darkest brown, the colour of her own hair, while waiting for it to grow out, and had subdued the frizzled bush with a net. She looked like a lady again—a lady! she looked like a Duchess!

We found our breakfast at Antoine's *recherché* little place on Park Avenue. Need I say how we enjoyed it? You must take a plunge into the underworld to appreciate to the full the delights of fine napery and silver, of delicate food. A table by a window with a rose or two upon it; an awning to mitigate the brightness of the morning sun; it was like heaven. And now we were back at Gramercy Park waiting for Melanie to wake up. Melanie and Mme. Storey were much of a size, and Grace, Mme. Storey's invaluable maid, had brought down an outfit from her mistress's wardrobe for Melanie.

The door from the hall opened, and a lady and gentleman came into my office. I closed the door into Mme. Storey's room. I was surprised, for, of course, we expected no visitors of importance; and these were people of importance, one could see in a glance from their clothes, and from their assured manner. The lady was a beauty, though no longer in her first youth. All their breeding and assurance could not conceal the fact that both were very much excited.

"Is Mme. Storey here?" the gentleman asked.

"May I ask the nature of your business?" I said politely.

"I cannot tell that to any one but her," he said. "I am Walbridge Sterry."

As soon as he spoke, I recognised them, for, of course,

their photographs have been published. "Mme. Storey will be glad to see you," I said.

Opening the door again, I announced them. I followed them in. Mme. Storey arose with a smile. We both supposed they had gone to the police and had been referred by them to us.

Mr. Sterry said with an air of great relief: "How fortunate we are to find you. We just came on a chance. Nobody is in town now."

Mme. Storey and I exchanged a glance. So they had not been to the police! They did not know that we had the tiara! What a piquant situation was developing.

"Well, as a matter of fact I am supposed to be in Paris," said Mme. Storey dryly.

"Indeed! I must have missed the announcement of your departure," Mr. Sterry said politely. "I shall not waste time in explanation," he went on. "I do not know if you happen to be aware of it—the newspapers have gossiped about it, but I purchased the Pavloff tiara from Prince Yevrienev."

"I have read it," said Mme. Storey.

"Well, it's been stolen!" he said, flinging down his hands.

"Stolen!" echoed his wife.

"Ah!" said Mme. Storey, who could not resist drawing them on just a little. "The recovery of stolen goods is hardly in my line."

"I know! I know!" cried Mr. Sterry; "but surely this is an exceptional case. They say that you can perform miracles. In the first place, I want a little disinterested and intelligent advice. I have not been to the police yet—you know the police! Should I go to them and have a great hue and cry raised in the press. Or should I keep our loss a secret, and conduct a private search?"

"We think it was stolen by a woman," Mrs. Sterry chimed in. "It appears that last night my husband's valet brought a strange girl into the house to sup with the other servants. He says she left early; but we found upon questioning him that he did not actually see her out of the door. The natural assumption is that she concealed herself in the house until later."

"She must have had confederates though," put in Mr. Sterry, "for she possessed the combination to the safe. A curious feature is that there were other jewels of value in the safe which she never touched."

"Only fancy!" said Mrs. Sterry with a shudder. "She must have been hidden in the room when we came in!"

With a peculiar smile, Mme. Storey pulled open the drawer of her desk. How she loves a dramatic moment like this! She took out the little green baize bag, and laid it on top. When Mr. and Mrs. Sterry saw it, their eyes almost leaped out of their heads. When Mme. Storey opened the bag, and took out the gleaming crown of little suns, soft cries of astonishment broke from them.

"Is this it?" asked my mistress with an offhand air.

"Yes! Yes!" they cried breathlessly.

"Oh, what a blessed relief!" sighed Mrs. Sterry, handling her precious tiara. "I have almost come to hate it! It is such a responsibility."

"I quite hate it!" said her husband bluntly. "But what are we going to do? We can't sell the thing…"

"This is a veritable miracle," he went on, with a wondering glance at my mistress. "How did it come into your hands?"

"It was recovered at four o'clock this morning from the person of John McDaniels, whom I was watching in respect to other matters."

Husband and wife exchanged an odd look. "McDaniels?" said the former, "you don't mean the well-known detective?"

"None other," said my mistress.

"Well," said Mr. Sterry, "this grows queerer and queerer. My wife and I have already been to McDaniels' office, and we found it closed."

"Yes," said Mme. Storey dryly. "It would be."

"He enjoyed a considerable reputation among people we know for his success in recovering stolen valuables," said Mr. Sterry.

"Naturally he could get them back, since it was he who had stolen them," said Mme. Storey dryly.

"Incredible!"

"What about the girl who entered our house?" asked Mrs. Sterry.

"I can't tell you anything about her," said my mistress coolly. "One of McDaniels' many tools, I suppose. I content myself with breaking up the traffic."

"And may we take it with us now?" asked Mrs. Sterry eagerly.

"Certainly. If you will give me a receipt to hand to the police."

The conversation became general then, and Mr. Sterry led the way around gracefully to the question of Mme. Storey's fee.

"Not a cent!" she said, when she saw what he would be after.

He insisted. He would not take no for an answer. "I could not rest easy under such an obligation," he said.

"Well," said Mme. Storey, in her large way. "What is it worth to you?"

"Say, twenty thousand?"

"Too much. Halve it, and send a cheque to my friend, Katherine Couteau Cloke for her work in the prisons. That's the worthiest cause I know."

"It shall be done," he said. "But it should come as from you."

"No," she said firmly. "You don't owe me a cent in this case, my dear sir."

As the Sterry's were leaving, Mme. Storey said casually. "By the way, have you discharged the valet?"

"Not yet," said Mr. Sterry, "but of course I shall."

"But consider," said Mme. Storey, "this woman, whoever she may have been, was evidently a high-class thief, and a past-mistress of the art of fascination. How can you blame a simple youth for yielding to the blandishments of such a one? If he is a satisfactory servant in other respects, I'd think it over. This will have taught him a lesson."

"Very well, I will think it over," said Mr. Sterry.

"That was the least I could do for poor Alfred," said my mistress, smiling, when the door closed.

Soon afterwards Melanie came downstairs. The girl looked lovely. To be sure, she was still thin and hollow-eyed as a result of her horrible imprisonment, but a touch of make-up in Grace's skilful hands had done wonders— that and happiness. Mme. Storey's pretty clothes became her wonderfully. As I have remarked before, Melanie had an instinct for nice things and knew how to wear them. She was still shy with us, and said very little, but her eyes were eloquent.

"We're going to have lunch up at my place," said Mme. Storey. "Let's go."

It had previously been agreed between my mistress and I that it would be impracticable to bring about a meeting between Melanie and George at the office, since George must know that that was Mme. Storey's address.

"I've got an errand uptown," I said. "I'll join you later."

Mme. Storey and Melanie went off in one taxicab and I in another. I had myself driven to the little stationery store on Columbus Avenue. I had a good deal of trouble identifying myself to the worthy Mrs. Harvest. She did not care much for the change in my appearance.

"Is George here?" I asked.

"No," she said, "but I think I can get hold of him. Come back in half an hour."

I think he was there all the time, and that this was just a regular formula she had adopted. However, I had myself driven around the Park, and returned later, as she requested. I found the handsome, blond George in the little rear sitting-room. He opened his eyes at the sight of me.

"What's the big idea?" he said.

"Well," said I, "I just got tired of looking like a frump, a has-been, a school-ma'am from the back counties. A friend of mine showed me how to fix myself up. How you like it?"

"It's all right," he said without enthusiasm. For George there was only one woman in the world. Well, my feelings were not hurt.

"What's the news?" he asked with a painful eagerness.

"Nothing special," I said. "I had a bit o' luck, and I want to blow a good-looking fellow to lunch, that's all."

"I ain't exactly advertising myself in public," he objected.

"That's all right," said I. "I know a quiet little place."

"Well, if you want it," he said. "I certainly owe it to you."

We drove down East Sixty-Second Street. There was nothing grand about the exterior of Mme. Storey's charming little house that would intimidate George, but he pointed out that this was obviously no restaurant. "I never said anything about a restaurant," I replied uncandidly. "This is my friend's house."

In the quaint and unusual interior, his instinct recognised something rare and fine. He scowled suspiciously, but manlike, hated to betray any reluctance before a woman. He followed me upstairs to the amusing 1850 living-room that looks toward the little garden in the rear. Mme. Storey was waiting there. Melanie had been spirited out of sight.

"Do you recognise your friend, Jessie Seipp?" asked my mistress, holding out her hand with a smile.

"No!" he said bluntly. "But… but… Yes, I do! What does it mean? What is the game?"

"The game is over. I am Rosika Storey, and this is Bella Brickley, my secretary."

A trapped look came into his face. His wary glance flashed around the room, calculating the chances of escape.

"We don't want you," said Mme. Storey. "John McDaniels and Kate Pullen were our marks. They are behind the bars."

"And Melanie? Melanie?" he cried, wild with anxiety.

"Look behind you," she said.

Melanie was in the doorway. I have already told you how beautiful the girl was when her ordinarily hard expression was softened. She looked now like another Rosalind, boyish and tender.

George looked at her as if he beheld her in a dream—a world of wistfulness in his eyes. He was afraid to put his dream to the test. "Melanie... Melanie," he whispered in a kind of terror.

She smiled enchantingly.

They approached each other slowly. He was hushed with emotion. "Melanie... is it really all right?" he whispered.

Mme. Storey and I could stand no more. We were already at the door. "Lunch is in the room underneath this," she called hack over her shoulder. "Come down when you like."

Black Kate died of heart disease while awaiting trial. I doubt if there was a soul on earth to lament her passing. We never did learn precisely what she had made Melanie suffer during her imprisonment. The very recollection of that time was a torment to the girl, and we avoided any reference to it.

In the cellar of that ugly little house on Varick Street, two human skeletons were discovered buried in the earth. These murders, for murders they certainly were, could not be proved against John McDaniels, but he was convicted on a score of counts, and received in the aggregate sentences far exceeding the years he can expect on earth. Nor is he ever likely to receive a pardon. "The blackest criminal ever tried in our courts!" the District-Attorney termed him, nor did anybody feel that the description was overdrawn.

The only thing I regretted was the escape of Skinny

Sam. When I voiced my regret, Mme. Storey said, smiling soberly:

"But, Bella, I couldn't single out Sam from amongst the other inmates just because he was a horrible little wretch, and I despised him. I was faced by a difficult moral problem, my dear. Strictly speaking, I ought to have handed them all over to the State, but I had appealed to their friendliness, and if, after that, I had betrayed them, I could never have looked myself in the face. The only possible distinction I could make was between slaves and slave-drivers. I caught the drivers, and gave the slaves a chance."

Poor old Pap was found wandering the streets in a half-crazed condition, a day or two after, and was returned to Sing Sing to serve out an old sentence. Mme. Storey subsequently exerted her influence to secure a pardon for him. She has supported him ever since in a suitable home.

We never saw Bill Combs again. I suspect he was too much of a man ever to come to a woman cap in hand. Nor did we ever hear of Fingy Silo or Tim Holder. Presumably, all three of them succeeded in keeping out of jail, or we should have known of it. Some time later Sam was arrested for robbing a woman under peculiarly atrocious circumstances—just what you might expect. It went hard with him, for he had an old sentence to serve in addition. We did not feel obliged to interfere in this case. He had had his chance.

Abell did come to see us—in fact, under another name, he is working for Mme. Storey at this moment. She has never had cause to regret giving him a chance. He is one of the best men we have. We were the means of bringing about a reunion between him and his beloved family, one of the most touching scenes I ever beheld. George Mullen is making a place as a master-electrician, and Melanie is raising a family.

As for myself, in regard to these three: Abell, George, and Melanie, I count them among my best friends. I would trust them further than anybody I know. They have been through the fire. They are honest from conviction, not from inertia. In all three of them I find an almost painful punctiliousness. They might be said to lean over backwards in their determination to be straight.

www.ingramcontent.com/pod-product-compliance
Lightning Source LLC
Chambersburg PA
CBHW030927020726
47498CB00001B/147